Coast is author David Carnegie Young's eighth book, his first novel – the latest in a body of work exploring landscape, loss and memory. After many years working as a journalist and editor he has freelanced as an environmental historian.

Among his publications are *Faces of the River, Woven by Water: histories from the Whanganui River* and *Our Islands, Our Selves: a history of conservation in New Zealand.* Currently, he is working on a book on sustainability in the Pacific.

COAST

I dedicate this book to my father, Philip and to all those who profess to the exacting art of fatherhood.

David Carnegie Young

COAST

Vanguard Press

A CIP catalogue record for this title is
available from the British Library.

ISBN 978 184386 685 5

Vanguard Press is an imprint of
Pegasus Elliot Mackenzie Publishers Ltd.
www.pegasuspublishers.com

First Published in 2011

Vanguard Press
Sheraton House Castle Park
Cambridge England

Printed & Bound in Great Britain

The inspiration for this work stems from the special coastal landscapes of Turakina-Koitiata, New Zealand and St Cyrus, Scotland. My father, Philip, was essential to the book's creation, both informally and consciously. Otherwise, this is entirely a work of fiction, albeit hooked on some real historical characters and events. I am grateful for the sustained and loving encouragement by my family – Miriama, Reuben and Aliscia, and particularly my wife, Scilla, who carefully read and made wise editorial comment on numerous drafts. My thanks to Tom Scott, Ken Ross and editor Anna Rogers, who read this novel at various stages and were most helpful in their comments, and to Bob Kerr, whose painting of Turakina beach graces the cover. A throw-away line from curator, Kate Martin, about Gaelic speaking ministers at Turakina, was more influential than she could know.

Alan 1

1958

It was a day of endless blue, a curve of summer from sky to sea. Most of the time the breakers rumbled and tumbled upon one another – unruly surf with foam skating in the wind right up the steep wet sand of the tide. But this was one of those rare days when, from early morning, the wind stood still; people awoke in the village, and nodding across geranium-lit fences to their neighbours pronounced with a rare anticipation, 'She's warm alright – have you seen the glass? It's really high. Gunna be a scorcher. One out of the box.'

We entered the blue sphere in a small rowing boat and pulled out through a whisper of surf – hardly a breath of it. There was the mildest chop upon the water, moving the boat like a hand on a cradle.

Once over the sandbar my father reached into his shirt and pulled his Park Drive from a leather pouch. He took the shreds and rubbed the tobacco between flat palms, before laying it in the crease of a Zig-Zag rice paper. He rolled the paper up to its edge, licked and joined it, before attaching it to his lower lip. Cupping his hands around the matchbox he struck a flame and put it to the durrie. There was a fine issue of smoke, almost ritual with its familiar, comforting smell – the smell of my father as the boat rocked gently in the sun, water slapping and slurping its hull. Then, after drawing deeply, he spoke: 'Keep rowing, son, there's a good spot, but it's good a mile offshore.' He flicked the match away and grinned. 'You'll have blisters by then.'

We rowed in silence. I got giddy as the line of baches up on the dunes slowly retreated behind a miasma of heat dancing on the shining black sand of the foreshore. 'Look at that,' he said, gazing out to sea. 'Horizon's as sharp as a knife – it'll be fine for a few days yet.'

Occasionally a long blue wave would peel off the top of the horizon, just a hump to begin with, moving toward us. By the time it reached us it was curved, but never enough to displace us. I tried to count and see whether it was true what they said, that every seventh wave was bigger. I'd never been out here with him before. I knew that we could swim if we had to. My only concern was if Dad put out the long line there were the hooks that trailed into the water. They might catch in your flesh and hold you somehow, drawing blood.

Each breaker slid in underneath, picked us up and then pushed on past the boat toward shore. If the wind did come up, even a little, there was still the possibility of more surf to contend with as we made our passage back to the beach. After half an hour we reached the place where he thought the choice spot was, a place where there was a bed of pipis. We let down the anchor on a chain which rattled noisily as it played out for about fifteen yards, sending up a tracery of bubbles before its splayed feet hit bottom grabbing at the sand. It was so clear I could see the anchor, set in the ripple patterns the sea's movement had made on the ocean floor.

My father didn't waste any time. I watched him, square shoulders under his blue checked shirt, an intense redhead, his blue eyes intent on the task in hand. He threw away his cigarette and snapped open a box, baiting his line with travally. 'The Whitakers were out here last week,' Dad said. 'They caught a dozen snapper, eight-pounders on the top of the tide. They must have hit a shoal of them. It's a grand day for fishing – we can't miss this time.' Jimmie had told Dad how to locate this pozzie. The idea was to line up your boat with the trig and a stand of cabbage trees near the shore.

I feathered and stowed the oars while he baited a line for a rod. The sun beat down out of the clear sky, and we pulled on hats, but there were few bites. The boat seemed small. It rocked gently, the only sound the slop of sleepy waves on the hull, the fitful creak of an oar. It was like going to sleep when you were small, almost relaxed, but still wondering what might lie under the bed. Although I'd come out through the waves in the kayak, I'd never been so far out to sea before and – no getting away from it – it was thrilling.

'Wouldn't it be great, just for once, to catch enough to give a few away? To be able to go round the neighbours with a few fillets?'

Then he said something, out of the blue, for he never spoke of him. 'You know, Hector, your granddad, used to love coming down to this beach.'

After an hour he rolled and lit another one. When that had gone he said, 'Nothing doing, maybe we're not in quite the right place.' He held up a finger to one eye.' It's hard to tell just how far out to come. Let's give it a try a bit further out.'

Just as we were about to take up the oars to row, a gull flew over the boat and we seemed to turn on the anchor, despite no discernible current. Suddenly there was a jerk and within half a minute we had a fight on the end of the line. Something big had taken the bait. The ratchet on the reel seethed in its closely milled teeth, the stainless steel revving and screaming as the rod curved into a great hoop, errrrrr-errr, errrrrr, errrr, and the big fish began to jerk in all directions, taking the boat with it. My father grabbed the rod from me, a new smoke pasted to his lower lip, his breaths coming close together. About two fathoms down I could pick out the dark swishing shape of the fish becoming visible deep in the ocean's white stomach. As it broached for the first time, I shouted in a hollow voice, 'It's a shark, a shark. Gee, Dad, let it go.'

To my father the idea of severing the line was never a possibility. He never threw anything away and he never gave up. That would have been quitting. He played the fish to the limits of the tackle, as much as his strength would allow, winding in the fighting animal, whipping the rod up sharply on whatever slack he could win and then whipping it down, to haul in a bit more nylon. Slowly, struggling all the way, as he shortened the line, he brought the fish in close. It was large enough – over six feet – but the boat was not more than ten feet long. As it came alongside, its shiny torpedo back menacing in its proximity, I took the rod and handed Dad the gaff, and he drew the barbs into its perfect side. 'We got him, we got him,' yelled my father. 'Ah, what a beauty. No wonder nothing else was biting with him around.'

In one massive heave that tilted the boat sideways he hauled it on board. 'Keep its nose to the bow and I'll just get a knife into its throat.' The animal writhed and slithered in protest, setting the boat rocking wildly again. Blood spurted from the gashes of the gaff. He bludgeoned it with a metal bar on the head as it fought and twisted in the gunwales. It lay there heaving and showing its teeth in a great grimace. Suddenly we were acutely conscious of our bare feet. Dad whacked the shark some more until it lay subdued but twitching and enormous, this sudden addition to our payload. Then he cut its throat.

It was beautiful, teal-coloured, a deeper shade of the sphere we had entered, and sleek – as though turned on a lathe – for speed. A vibrant, living being that I felt sadness for but elation too in the moment, almost awkward, a triumph over not the fish, but over the momentary closing of separation between myself and my father.

Long after I had grown to manhood I persisted with fishing, from boat and shore, never with much luck. I told myself that this was, if nothing else, a great way of getting to some special places. But there was something desultory about it that I didn't quite understand.

One day, fishing from a boat in the Sounds, there were pied shags on rocks drying their out-spread wings and then diving into the shimmering water. My son and I watched them, never knowing where or when they would resurface, and finally I hooked one trying to steal from the baited line. There was no alternative but to pull it in, heavy as sin, hold the bird and attempt to extricate the offending barb from its bill, with the shag flapping and fighting desperately to get

16

away. It was messy, a real dog's breakfast. I would need some expert intervention. I had to go and find help from the keeper of the lodge, but as I tried to set it free something inside me that I had long been reluctant to release spoke to me. I realised that I really didn't enjoy fishing one bit. That all these attempts at finding the prize in the ocean's blue had nothing to do with fish – all this time I had been fishing for my father.

Hector 1

1908

I should have known to pay more heed to those inner voices, because things could hardly have turned out worse that day. I can see it now – everything remains as vivid as though it were yesterday. I tied the horse to a buried log reaching out of the sand and made my way across the last rough fields before the beach, a light wind in my face. I realised I would need to take my boots off, so I tied the laces together and hung them from my neck. Then I rolled up my trousers. I waded through a slunk that was shallow but boggy. I'd not seen mud like this since the floods we'd had at home back in 1898 – it was an ooze. My white feet were almost glued into its pugginess.

Overhead a skylark was in full song, although the sky was still dark with cloud. I heard a bittern make its distinctive booming call. I pushed through huge flax plants, much bigger than a man, that clattered like wooden blinds. I came to duck shooters' bothies, makeshift from flotsam timbers and corrugated iron. These were lined up in a row on a small machair-covered dune. There were bunks inside and below was a flat-bottomed rowboat, moored by a piece of hemp to a log. I stepped into it and, standing, poled across the slunk, intending to wade the river, which from the distance, seemed wide. I had been warned that an early Anglican missionary had drowned somewhere around here when his horse was crossing the river. Quicksand, they said.

As I approached the bank the sound of rushing water was stronger. Coming across a line of low dunes I found the river, which last time was a footling thing, but now in full spate, about half a mile across. It was unbelievable – an altogether different animal. It brimmed along the line of dunes that were its banks and tore into them like a boar into a loaf of bread. As I watched, a whole cliff of sand – it must have been at least three coal-wagons full – got the runs above the bouncing water line and toppled into the river with a loud shush. Had I been standing there, I would have gone too.

The river was moving in such a spate it was menacing, a chocolate-coloured wild animal that could not be contained. Across the width of the river floated an assortment of driftwood, much of it living trees just a few hours earlier. In the main current a large tree trunk, complete with branches and leaves, hurtled down the roadstead like a runaway cart; willows bobbed everywhere, freshly-sawn timber and solid, squared bridge-stays strewed the surface. Some of this material was turning end over end in the flood. Batons, strainer posts and tangles of fence wire went shuddering past. Whole farms undone. Occasionally I saw, too, the dark shapes of cattle beasts, bloated bellies upwards, 'the bailiffs of bankruptcy', we called them at home.

Then, in the mid distance, I could see something out of the ordinary that had been snatched by the flood. It was bobbing and juddering towards me, with sharp outlines as it came around the far bend of the river. At first I couldn't make it out. It seemed rectangular, a farm bothy, maybe, rearing up above the lunging logs with their quivering branches. As it drew nearer it was quite plain: an intact Maori 'warri' coming down the flooded river. I recognised it for I had seen one or two – in fact, I had passed one earlier that day on the track out to this beach. The house bore carvings either side of the door, with an iron roof and floorboards still intact and it nodded down the river headed for the sea. It must have come from a riverbank site further upstream. I couldn't understand how it stayed upright, shaking, but almost regal. I came to a stop, dumb-struck, as I watched it sail out towards the ocean like some river craft from Egyptian times.

Beyond the beach was wild, the breakers all mixed up, the white foam churning at the black sand, and its 'top cream'

19

blowing along the beach. Gulls circled aimlessly in the grey sky. As I had on my first visit, I found this coastline's lack of definition somewhat alarming – it seemed to simply curve in sand for a hundred miles, maybe more. Where I came from there were dunes, but the shore was shaped too by cliffs, rocky outcrops, coves and big rocks that made up the coastline. But here there was nothing to break its sweep. And a wind that seemed to blow without end.

Then I heard a keening and a greeting such as I had not known since Scotland. I turned, and up on the river bank, not a hundred yards away, was a group of Maoris on horseback, their bright clothing pulled and flapping in the wind. I was still getting the measure of Maoris and I was startled by the suddenness of their arrival in this place of solitude. It was the first time I'd seen them up close. They were like us, yet not. Very dark, but brown, not black like Africans, with curly jet hair. Their eyes flashed in fear and excitement. They rode as though they need not apologise to anyone for who they were. As if they had a right to be here. It was something that I somehow hadn't expected from native people, yet somehow it made sense. After all, it was I who was the new arrival.

They cantered up along the bank towards me, horses blowing and shining with sweat. There were no greetings. The oldest of them wore a waistcoat, fob watch and old navy pinstriped trousers. He set it all off with a scarlet neckerchief. He was a fit-looking fellow. The woman was in a full-length purple frock under an Astrakan coat. The other two men wore grimy topcoats and bright silk scarves tied round their heads. One of them, a large man with longish hair, I noted, wore a red tartan shawl tied across his shoulders. They were all bare-footed, riding bareback and they were staring at the house in disbelief. They looked sick at heart. The two younger men, clasping flax for reins, heeled their mounts into the river, each holding a length of rope in readiness, like a cowboy.

It seemed they intended to hog-tie their dwelling. I watched anxiously. I wanted to tell them to take care. But I felt so much the intruder anyway that I daren't open my mouth. Besides, I was an irrelevance. The river was deep below the bank and they swam their horses out to intercept their bothy. The woman set up a distraught wailing. They got one rope around a bargeboard but, try as he might, the man with the pinstripe jacket and fob just couldn't get the second rope to hold. Everything was moving too fast. Suddenly, as the rider manoeuvred in the flooded river, his mount stumbled badly and he got in the way of the house as it turned in an eddy.

The next thing I knew the rider was unhorsed and pinned in the water beneath the house. It must have banged his head as he fell. I saw just a forearm come up and, momentarily, the man's face clenched in desperation, but he barely got his mouth to the air, he was gasping like a fish. Then he was gone. The other rider tried to get to his companion, but the house caught by the river seemed to go over the top of the drowning man. The horse clambered back on shore, wet and naked without its rider. All I could do was stand and gaze at the surface of the muddy water. There was nothing we could do.

There was nowhere to search in all that heaving water and logs and flow. The river had swallowed him and he was gone without trace. The woman on the bank seemed to dissolve into the mud. She rolled up in her shiny purple dress into a heap on the grey pug of the river bank, screaming. She squirmed into the mud, she collected it in her hands and plastered her face and hair with it. Then she picked up a sharp stick and cut herself about the cheeks until they bled. All the while she wailed, a hollow, shuddering cry in drawn out waves like a song. Among the few English words I picked up was a refrain, a name, *Robina Dunlop, Robina Dunlop,* but none of it made sense to me.

The others ran along the beach but there was nothing to see or do. I was distressed at my own helplessness. I couldn't swim, but even if I could, it'd be no use. It was a double tragedy for these people. They'd lost their house, which, as I later came to understand, they saw as an ancestor, and now as well they'd lost a son, and brother besides. The other horseman came ashore, looking cold and miserable. The woman tossed him an old blanket that he wrapped around him and they went off, weeping, to make a fire.

I noticed the old man had dismounted and lay helpless in the mud. He was not moving. I went over to him. His face was white, he seemed to have stopped breathing and his eyes had lost their light. When I approached he muttered at me something in Maori and then English, 'My son, my son.' Then it was the woman who spoke, in a fury: 'He chief – this man, son – all gone, all gone. Go away, go.'

I looked down the river towards the mouth. I could just make out the outline of the house in the sea mist. It danced in circles on the bar, as waves slapped and broke over it. It reminded me of a shipwreck I'd once seen on the bar at Montrose, except shipwrecks usually headed in to shore. This one was headed out on the flood-tide. I went along the banks, searching, hoping to catch sight of life. Somewhere there in the muddy water was the body of a man who just minutes before had been breathing. Now his horse pranced riderless and skittery along the riverbank, pulling back its head and whinnying. One moment there was life unsuspecting, the next, nothing. A civilian death, a brute act of nature. I'd never seen anyone drown before and I wished I hadn't. I was so new to all of this and the experience left me feeling edgy, wondering whether my parents' warnings had been correct about coming to this new land.

Then, gradually, I realised I was in shock – I was cold and not properly concentrating. I raced after the wild horse and eventually took hold of it and tried to settle it down. I struggled for composure. What a to-do for the Maoris this must be. How might they conduct their funeral without a body? This was something Scots fishers often had to contend with. And now I'd seen for myself with what violence this land treated the unwary.

Doug 1

1920s

I remember Jimmie Cameron's shrill whistle outside the Broadway shops in Marton, as he slowed in his van to gather parcels for his daily rural delivery run. It must have been 1923. That was before my father, Hector died, when I was six. Jimmie had one of those whistles that not all men can do, pulling their lips in really hard and whistling between his teeth on the in-breath.

The sound was so penetrating, the shopkeepers could hear it – too right they could. They'd bustle about and send their assistants running out onto Broadway to collect or dispatch Jimmie's delivery. His Royal Mail contract involved newspapers and bread and general daily requirements for cockies in the near and far country areas of his run. 'There you are then – good as gold,' and he'd give a grin, reaching out through the kerbside window. Then he'd gun the engine and pull out into the street again. If you were standing close by, his whistle was enough to make you want to cover your ears. It actually hurt.

Jimmie was strongly built, not tall, but erect, muscular and tireless. His body was a no-nonsense kind of body in a no-nonsense bloke. He and his wife Marge were more than good to me as a young sprog, keeping an eye out, with my father ill and mother at the end of her tether with me.

On this particular day he looked at me and grinned. 'How's your Daddie doing, Douglas? You tell him from me I want to get him down to the beach for some fishing, just as soon as he gets himself right. You be sure tell him, tell from me now, won't you?'

'Yes, Mr Cameron, I'll tell him.'

'Now you get away home, you're too young to be here on your own.'

It was through the Camerons that I had my first introduction to Koitiata Beach, a place my father had loved from his early days in this country, before the Great War. Even in the 1920s it was quite a journey. Once you got off the main highway the road was just a track in the sand, crossing streams with no bridges, everyone hanging off the running-boards to hold the back wheels down in the soft patches and pushing the Model-T up over dunes. It was a lot of fun. You'd give her the gun on the soft bits. There were a number of rumpty gates to open. We had the use of Bert Whitaker's bach – it had been knocked up from car cases – Ford and General Motors. It was covered from the weather with malthoid, a tarred heavy paper over the roof and the sides. Bert's place was right down on the edge of the lagoon – not much flasher than a maemae.

Later Jimmie bought a place well back from the beach. It was tidy, a well-built weatherboard house completely furnished, all necessary living equipment, for 300 pounds. This was luxurious compared with Whitaker's place. I spent many happy days with the Camerons as I grew up, fishing, swimming, playing cards and roaming up and down the river. Sometimes we went out to sea line fishing in Mr Whitaker's hardwood flat-bottomed boat.

Whitaker had planted whale ribs on either gate-post at the entrance to his bach. Welcome bones, you might say. He usually sported a pair of waders that came up to his crotch, secured by straps. I am sure he liked to think of them as 'sea boots'. Maybe he wanted people to believe that he was some kind of seaman. In fact he was a carpenter and one of those blokes – I was going to say 'lucky blokes' but that's not quite right – who was too young for the first war and too old for the second. His massive boat could have been a tender to a whaler. The thing was so heavy it took a heap of men to move it on land and four pairs of strong-arms to manoeuvre it at sea. Off that coast it had to be heavy. More often than not there was a wind blowing onshore, and the beach was usually choppy, with unreliable surf coming in. In making passage out through the waves it was not unusual to tip over on the bar where the waves suddenly got bigger. I well recall how on one occasion we were four or five hundred yards offshore when a rogue wave threw the boat, spilling us into the briny. It was always a bit dicey, that coast.

We had no life jackets; they were unheard of back in the Depression. Luckily, Jimmie was a good swimmer. But Bert Whitaker was the one who got into difficulties – and was he a scone-doer. 'I'm drowning, I'm drowning,' he yelled as he started to sink. We reached over, hauled him in, his sea boots bursting with water, onto the bottom of the upturned boat. Slowly we were carried back on the tide to shore, minus our snapper catch. Jimmie read my thoughts. 'Just hang on to the boat and we'll drift ashore, laddie,' he shouted as waves crashed over us. 'Everything comes ashore on this coast – given enough time. Whatever you do, though, don't let go.'

We gripped the boat as it tossed its way through the lines of breakers, and then, as our feet touched the bottom, we dug in and held tight to stop it moving back out as the waves ebbed. It was really hard work. We turned it and found something to scoop out the remaining water before we hauled the boat ashore, two-parts empty. We tipped it over to drain before carrying its dead weight across the sandpit to the river. Bert was feeling sorry for himself. We had to row across the river before dragging it on a trailer to get it back to the bach.

I suppose Whitaker could have drowned. But the upset was nothing to get the bowels in an uproar, it was just a nuisance to be tossed out and if anyone had been watching, it would have looked much worse than it was. At that time I had not long started to roll my own 'durries'. I had two ounces of Park Drive that had to be dried out on the rack above the blazing fire that Jimmie got going with driftwood so we could all warm up. The tobacco took on a distinctive salty flavour.

The beach was never short of driftwood because of the river's raids on the back country. After a flood the odd ex-crim and assorted characters who lived there used to head out to compete with each other for the choicest native timbers for the fire. There was an unwritten law. Once they had chosen a piece of wood, they stood it up and laid it on another log, to indicate it was theirs. The time of hauling it home was then a matter of their own choosing. Woe betide anyone who believed differently. These blokes could do their block – everyone knew that – it had to be seen to be believed. Only scraps over whitebait pozzies were more violent.

As always, when we got home Marge was a real sport. 'I do have some tins of salted herring in the cupboard. Would you like some of that?' and she would laugh. 'Jimmie, you can dig a few potatoes, would you mind? You pull some mint, and I'll make a salad.'

She was an interesting woman. Occasionally, Jimmie would say, 'I'm off. My wife is having a spooks' evening.' As a Rosicrucian, Marge felt the need to stay in touch with the afterlife, and a group of her friends would come over for an evening to join her for the odd séance. That was something I never took part in; it never appealed in the slightest. But she was so positive about life that these activities never fazed Jimmie. Just after the Depression, when I must have been about eighteen, she bought Dale Carnegie's *How to Win Friends and Influence People* for my mother.

She and my mother were also keen on unorthodox medicine. One night I went with Mother to a neighbour's where the lady of the household, a heavy woman, who suffered an attack of lumbago, was spread out on the couch. The young fry were ushered into the next room and Marge Cameron was called for. The door into the lounge was left partly open, allowing me a view of proceedings. Mrs Carter was partly disrobed. Mrs Cameron got to work on a manual generator driven by hand and attached to a glass bulb hand-niece. As she cranked the handle, she moved the glass just above Mrs Carter's exposed rear and legs. An eerie purple light was given off, accompanied by an audible crackle. This was ultra violet treatment, a sure cure for many ailments.

Jimmie lost the Royal Mail contract during the Depression. Being Jimmie, he immediately launched into road transport between Wanganui, Palmerston North and Marton. At some stage, the Government protected the railways' monopoly with a forty-mile limit for all road transport operators. Jimmie's response was to build a fleet of about six Chevrolet one-ton trucks. He and Marge did most of the work with the help of drivers and an office girl. They built up a flourishing transport business. This was terminated at the outbreak of World War Two as the government of the day impressed most suitable vehicles for use into the war effort. Jimmie was compensated for the loss, no doubt at some low figure. 'They took you for a mug, Jimmie,' I suggested.

Jimmie shrugged. 'Och, worse things happen to people every day. You canna fight the government.' He never mentioned it again. That was Jimmie; whenever he could he ducked what life threw at him and when he couldn't, he took the tackle, grinned and just got on with it. Nothing ever seemed to get him down. He was a man to aspire to.

Yet he never spoke of his past or his origins. My mother knew from Mrs Cameron that he and his sister were more or less abandoned by their mother at a very early age, leaving them to fend for themselves in a very poor part of Glasgow. So he was my father's friend, a bit younger, a Returned Man too – an ambulance driver. A great mate to have beside you if you got into any kind of scrap.

Alan 2

1950

In the 1950s the Sunday drive following the Sunday lunch was still in vogue. We'd pile into the Ford Prefect, my brother, me, and Mum and Dad, in our Sunday best, and visit other families and relatives for afternoon tea. A regular excursion involved us climbing the great tower erected to the Memory of the Fallen on the escarpment overlooking the river. Built from quarried shell rock, the tower was shaped a bit like an old-fashioned stemmed cocktail glass, from the bowl of which people could drink in the view.

The concrete staircase curved in an upward spiral around the edge of the tower, with a landing every thirty or forty steps. At the top we gazed west to locate our place, within an easily identified precinct built on low hills, sand dunes actually, formed since the last Ice Age. Running towards the sea, these hills were decked out in red roofing iron, tamarisks, flowering gums and the plane trees that were pollarded with such savagery, for most of the year without their leaves they looked like amputees. Roads of asphalt snaked along the ridge tops and branched off down the flats. We could easily pick out our school beside the steeple of the hill-top church, skirted in pohutukawa, and from there look for our home. Seeing the whole sleepy town spread out below offered a child a sense of belonging.

But when my dad dandled my young brother on the parapet at the top, his legs swinging over the rim, I came to know the drunkenness of vertigo. Everything started to swim and reel away from my vision. Hundreds of feet below, I could just make out, on the asphalt and grass, an upturned face. It was my mother's, and she was pleading, 'Doug, don't do that. Doug, put him down, put him down, for Pete's sake!'

In those days there was no hood of mesh across the viewing platform. People then didn't seem to engage in spectacular acts of public suicide. No matter how bad things got, good citizens put their heads down and quietly just kept on going. At least that's how it seems, looking back.

I was not born a child fearful of heights and had already begun to climb trees. I had started inside the spongy reassurance of huge mattress-like macrocarpa boundary hedges with their brush-like greenery fanning out from every horizontal branch. Once you got inside, falling was not an issue. There was always another branch to cushion you. Macrocarpas made great places for huts, a hideaway where no one had the faintest idea where you were – even at teatime As confidence grew I'd climb higher, making a platform for a hut where once we had lit a fire to roast potatoes in their jackets up in the crook of the branches. It was a gesture to cosy domesticity that almost burnt the hedge down and enraged my father with my stupidity.

But now, on the top of the stem tower, I felt terror for my brother, Barry. He was dressed in a Fair Isle jumper, I recall, worked by our mother in the pattern of a yellow cat. He didn't say anything but his expressive blue eyes were wide with fear as my father, a nuggetty bull-at-a-gate sort who would have protected his family to the death from anything, lifted him back inside the safety of the parapet. To this day the fear of the tower drags each step on my trudge up the 350 steps, locked in its steep spiral. At every landing, castle-like viewing ports with bars afford a glimpse of how far above the ground you are. It still takes a bit of self-control to contend with those old shadows.

But there was another shadow, darker than this new-found vertigo: I realised that something wasn't quite right – anxiety wasn't a good feeling to have about your father. I struggled to decide which was worse, my fears of my brother hurtling from the tower to his death or the discovery that my father was a risk-taker. Years later, when we were out on a walk together, Barry remembered the tower episode. 'Oh yes,' he said. 'I was terrified, too right. I've never been more scared. I couldn't even make a sound.'

I still cannot fathom what was in my father's mind. It was still only a few years after the end of World War Two with its uncountable dead, its maimed and damaged. There was a sense then that war was something men did to each other on a generational basis. But our Returned father was fit and active and alert. All around us were memories and stories of sacrifice, loss and of unattainable physical male bravery. They lurked in the galleries of our childhood.

A painting of a young British gunner in action in World War One hung in the school hall. He was only fourteen, we were taught, 'Just a few years older than yourselves.' His ship was under sustained attack from enemy warships and was going down. He stayed at his post, firing his guns when all about him was cannon-fire and death. You could see the flames flaring in the painting, like a vision of hell. That's where he died. What would it be, to die alone, under fire, on a burning ship, aged fourteen? You never forget those stories – you weren't allowed to. The principal, a Returned Man and a mustachioed ex-officer of severe bearing and shiny, kow-tow shoes that clicked as if he had just come right off the parade ground, reminded us of our debts in front of black stage curtains: 'Faith of our fathers, known of old, we will be true to thee till death'.

The local art museum often displayed a large painting of a local aircraftsman, another impossible war hero model. He was depicted aboard a shot-up Wellington bomber returning from a raid over Germany. He clambered out of the cockpit, the slipstream tearing at his jacket, onto the wing to extinguish a blazing engine. This spectacular act of courage, still over enemy territory, allowed the crew to make a safe journey home. I would return again and again to that heavily-framed picture, to contemplate his bravery and sacrifice.

Reliving his hazardous passage out onto the wing to the seat of the fire, I felt some of the terror for his predicament and awe at his courage. 'Yes,' my father would say in answer to my questions, 'it would be very windy out there. He actually broke the surface of the wing by stamping into it with his boots. That was to give himself handholds and footholds. Otherwise he would just have been blown away.' I stood before the depiction and marvelled at this act of sacrifice.

'Do you think he looked down, Dad? Wouldn't he have been scared? How cold was it? How could anyone do that?' It was beyond anything that a boy could imagine, to make the transition from where we stood to heroic manhood. How on earth did men become men? My mother knew the story and she gave me the clincher: 'He was a good friend of a friend I'd been at school with – a nice chap, softly spoken and always well dressed. It was so sad; he was killed on another bombing raid a few months later, just before the war came to an end.'

At primary school Anzac Day services I thought of him and the young gunner and dutifully of my two grandfathers as we sang Kipling's *Recessional*, with its dirge-like eloquence. It was incomprehensible, but its rhymes and rhythms were charged with the drumbeat of Imperial glory. My favourite verse was:

> The tumult and the shouting dies;
> The captains and the kings depart:
> Still stands Thine ancient sacrifice,
> A humble and a contrite heart.
> Lord God of Hosts, be with us yet,
> Lest we forget – lest we forget!

The late war still touched everything in the 1950s. Even on beaches the struggle remained a physical presence in the concrete defence bunkers, 'pillboxes' my father called them, that seemed to command every beachhead. Now toppling, overgrown boxthorn bushes displaced the barbed wire. Barry and I would crawl inside the bunkers and look out through the slit, our hands on a hot, jerking machine gun, as the Jap hordes disembarked from landing craft and advanced towards us.

Approaching Eastbourne, Wellington, for summer holidays, thousands of high wheelbase American trucks were parked in hundreds of rows on the reclamation. 'Army surplus' Dad called them, purchased for on-sale to contractors in a country desperately short of overseas funds. As kids we understood that we were part of something different, of a time 'after the war'. All men were either Returned Men or they were not, which told you whether they'd been in the war. Things were left unsaid if they weren't Returned Men, but you knew it wasn't good enough. Conchies, well, once you understood what they represented, they weren't much better than homos. In the suburbs, looking back now, the memory of war became an undeclared red line drawn across the ledger page – once it was fought to a standstill, everything that happened afterwards was in marked reference to it. War's end offered a new beginning, a fresh start to everything – new roads, houses, schools and churches, kindergartens, gardens and 'parks' for the blossoming families and communities of the post-war era.

Ours was a 1920s villa on one of the rising dune-ridges. In the early 1950s my father took up shovel, spirit-level and wheelbarrow to excavate the hillside at the front so as to build a garage from concrete blocks. It was not long before I, Doug's red-headed pocket edition, became engaged in operations as an excavator of great industry behind the house. Despite the gradually civilizing effects of suburbia with its slowly accumulating fences and gates, concrete paths and driveways (now there was a status symbol, especially if a man laid them himself), standard roses and fruit trees and lawns, there was still opportunity for young boys to inquire heartily of their backyards with shovels.

Barry and I went hard at it. During an early foray my father warned me, 'You'd better be careful, you'll undermine your mother's clothesline.' The clothesline in question was my mother's joy, a modern revolving design spinning on a concrete pillar around which arms, interlaced with hexagons of wire, moved in the ever-present wind. This new design replaced the old continuous wires rigged between two posts propped up high by a long fork-ended pole to dry the family wash.

But it was the word 'undermine' that had the power to inspire both wonder and terror. Sometimes I ponder on whether words such as this carried sufficient awe to inspire continuing and diligent action in a child in the face of personal discomfort and fatigue. My mother's response was that 'someone will break their blinking neck' – most likely herself as she struggled in a westerly, sheets cracking like sails, to peg the family washing to the line.

As we went in deeper, in search of 'undermine', I grew proud of the straight dark edges I carved from the sand with the bottle-green-handled spade, the surplus borne away in a noisy, rumbling wheelbarrow – the signature melody of men at work.

I was excited by the forms my spadework revealed; disappointed as the sand dried, changing colour from black to a grey with worrying trickles, runnels and sometimes minor collapses. Barry wasn't so driven as I was. He helped for a while before he cried off, 'This is dumb, I don't want to do this. I'm going to play with someone else.'

I couldn't understand why he didn't want to dig.

'Aw, come on, can't we do this together?'

'Nah, I don't want to.'

Alone I continued to strengthen the excavation with uprights and cross-trees and boards hammered together, blackening fingernails and blood-blistering fingers. In the manner of all risk-takers, be they gambler, racing-car driver or alpine climber, the game was not to cause 'undermine' but to visit its edge and taste its possibilities without actually causing collapse. Then, to top it all off, sheets of old corrugated iron, stacked for one of Dad's rainy days and commandeered for the task, were deployed as a cover and dressed with sand to convey the illusion of a cave, of unplumbed depths. This structure we entered mysteriously by way of a ladder descending into darkness.

Digging and underground forts became the new neighbourhood contagion, with other boys soon hard at it, throwing up piles of sand in backyards like an invasion of badgers. Every hour at school was devoted to thought and talk and planning; every spare moment of daylight boys shovelled and hefted and built.

I was unsure, however, whether my father really approved of what I was doing. At first he seemed to find it amusing. But he was given to sudden changes. One day, the central pole for the clothes' line, buried a couple of metres into the ground, became dangerously exposed. 'Time to call it a day, Alan,' he said, sternly. 'Someone's going to get hurt – fill it in. And do it now.'

Barry had no interest in cleaning up the project. 'Come on, you were part of this, give us a hand,' I tried to bully him into helping and got a telling off for that. To disobey was more than my life was worth. From somewhere, probably from his special suitcase, Dad had found a leather dog-collar. A few strokes across the back of the legs revealed it to be a far more painful instrument of punishment than anything previously meted out to us. But it seemed such a waste to undo all that work. I left it and hoped that Dad would forget.

'You just don't do as you're told. I've told you, time and again, but you take not the slightest bit of notice. No more warnings – that's the stone cold finish.' A blue vein pulsed in his temple.

'But, Dad, I haven't finished my work.'

'Don't answer back – that tongue of yours will get you into a heap of trouble.'

'Dad, Barry was supposed to help and he hasn't done anything – he just took off when there was all that work to do.'

'Don't answer back. He wasn't even involved. Don't answer back. Just do as you are told.'

'Dad –'

'Don't "Dad" me. I've heard enough. Fill it in and then go to your room. No tea tonight.'

'But Dad –'

'Take your punishment like a man and don't answer back, show a little respect. I'm telling you straight and you'd better listen. My God, no one likes a smart Alec – when you get out into the world you're going to find life out there tough, you cheeky little bugger.'

I capitulated to such anger – it was not just to the sanction, but to a terrible judgement, that put me beyond the pale. I was abandoned by him. Later, alone in my room without food, I would be visited by my mother, who would soften the stance and bring up a sticky dinner re-warmed in the oven. Peas especially never seemed to reheat well, they simply imploded. She spoke quietly. 'Here we are, son, you won't disobey your dad again will you? And for heaven's sake, just leave your brother alone.' Then she'd usually give me a hug.

'No, Mum, sorry.'

So she and I would work it out, but Dad and I didn't, and Barry would cop it again from me. So the cycle would continue. More hidings, more missed dinners and always the early-to-bed punishment, which meant missing the special radio programmes, like Jim Henderson's *Open Country*.

It all just seemed to happen; a small trickle would start and suddenly, without knowing it, there was a complete cascade in the relationship with my father and no way out, no way that I could see to escape, as the walls of my room closed in on me, from a kind of damnation. I would fixate on the red flowers in the wallpaper.

He was a hard worker, my father, and a way to garner a bit of approval was to go out on the section, and take the initiative to mow the lawns, cut hedges or trim weeds. But if we were asked to do it, or were in our rooms, reading, it might be: 'Well, I'll go to buggery, they're taking a break. Come on, you great lazy lummoxes, lounging 'round in the fart sack. Get out there and earn your keep. Uninvited guests, yes, uninvited guests, that's what you are.

'There's lawns to mow and hedges to be cut. The edges need doing. What's wrong with you? No motivation, you're enough to give a man the heeby-jeebies.' If I complained, it was, 'If it was good enough for me, it's good enough for you.'

Barry was always smart enough to stay quiet. I'd get into rows with my father at the drop of a hat. It wasn't what either of us wanted, but when I thought about it, strangely, there was a bit of me that almost liked it. Or was it more that baiting and harassment had developed a familiarity that provided its own kind of bleak comfort?

Watching him, trying to figure him out, my father seemed to me to be happiest at the edge of the family domestic circle. He found the salve of solitude, lone figure wandering a coast from which he could return to us.

Hector 2

Ploughman

Today brought a break from the wind – a fine, clear autumn morning, the ranges sharp on the horizon. Some years ago, back in the 1860s, the Hendersons were part of a large group of Scots immigrants. They had bought tracts of land in the Rangitikei that often didn't need a lot of clearing, in places where they tell me the Maoris were few and largely untroublesome. Compared with what they had contended with in the Taranaki, or even Wanganui, this was heaven. They'd done well with their farms – gotten into Parliament, the top ones ruling the roost. Some of them, like the Wilsons for whom I'd occasionally worked, had taken a real punt and borrowed in order to ride out some of the ups and downs. Now their grand homes, their extensive gardens and their coaches-and-fours put them back into the wealth and position some had been accustomed to in the old country. Old man Wilson, a patriarch with a Highlander's Berber nose, once told me after a lantern-slide lecture he had delivered on river erosion, 'Don't be a ploughman all your life, laddie, see if you can't get into a small business. Have a look around, find what takes your fancy. I might be able to give you a wee hand – I know people who can help.'

Alex Stuart, out from Perthshire, who has also settled in the district, at Runnymead, South Makirikiri, gave me a job on one of several prosperous farms he ran in the district. Alex was an early contractor who got started in metal pits and road construction. I was hired as a ploughman and general hand. 'Sure, we can give you a job, Roberts. It won't be much pay to start with, two pounds a week, but there'll be board and keep – as much as you can eat – all good wholesome food. After three months, when you've shown what you're worth, we'll speak about a proper rate of pay for you.'

I love the horses, a big Clydesdale plodding ahead of the furrow, steadfast as a Free Kirkman, tossing its head and flicking its tail all day long. There is contentment I had never known before – the days being so much warmer out here and for so many more months than back home in the Mearns. I never tire of improving my skill with the plough. I love the way it opens a seam in the dark, rich soil, curling back on itself, moving like the horses' wake. Many of the birds that come to feed on the freshly-turned earth are so familiar from the old country – blackbirds, starlings, finches, chaffinches and territorial gulls.

It is a solitary business, ploughing, and much of the land here is on rolling hills. I was born a Lowlander and I'll always be a Lowlander. That's why travelling so far across the seas to this new home was not difficult – it is familiar country, yet not. From high spots on a clear day you can see the blue sea to the west and the white cone of Mount Egmont rising clear from the ocean to the north-west. To the east is Ruapehu, another volcano. And in the gloaming, especially before storms, the sky fills with flocks of birds moving inland by the thousand, rising up and swirling back on themselves much the way waves break on the shore. I do not know the names of these birds, but to look at them fills me at times with a longing for the familiar shore.

Yet there is something in the roll of these rich hills coming gradually down over some miles towards the dune lines and the sea that is so familiar. Sometimes, after a few days of cloud and closs, you can wake up here and the sky is suddenly clear and the wet fields so bright and lit up silvery. Everything shines so much that you have to screw your eyes up so as to see properly. It's impossible to describe.

The big worry in my work is the roots and stumps of black pine forest that stood in places here before the Europeans came. They are the bane of a ploughman's life; their hardness damages the steel of the plough edge. But they tell us of a time when Maori came, when this was a place where forest grew everywhere. Sometimes, watching the flapping of the wood pigeon as it strikes out across the meadows, like a trained swimmer for his next resting point, there seems to me there is a sadness in this land. The bird is ungainly in setting flight and in landing, beautiful up close with its reds and greens and its white pinafore. The locals value its flesh as a great delicacy. But they tell me their numbers have fallen rapidly in the past twenty years ago.

Lately on the Stuart's the ploughing took me to the far end of a paddock. Here was a glen where the ravening fires had not reached. There were some big trees, very grand, crowned with shiny ferns and great tangles of vegetation. Beneath, tiny young trees were coming away in their thousands, with ferns and orchids and many little plants I did not know. It was cool in there and quite hushed, but difficult to pass through because of hoops of vines as thick as your thumb. As I stood in there I heard the call of a bird, as beautiful a sound as I had ever heard. It was as though the entire forest was stilled by its call, somewhere between a keening and a calling, but rich and full. It was eerie. I heard a flutter and looked up to see a dark bird like a crow moving among the tree tops.

I know that the work I am doing here is helping to feed mouths. But when you get to thinking about it, taking trees, it's like killing a sheep – there is no point in sentiment. We have to live.

At these times of wistfulness, I am visited by second sight, *An Da Shealladh,* the gift, as they say at home, of the seventh son. I see a beautiful enclosed garden in a place that I do not believe is familiar to me from direct experience, but it has the sense of early childhood. The garden and its well-kept lawns and flowerbeds are enclosed in a high wall of dry-stone, with a stout wooden gate at one end. There are children playing: two girls in layered white dresses turn a long skipping-rope, chanting a song about the days of the week while a third, a younger one in a straw hat, runs in and out of the rope. A boy in a sailor suit chases a whippet about and then shimmies up a tall tree, pretending to escape while the dog barks.

The tree stands in a corner of the garden. I do not recognise its type – it is tall and leafy and of beautiful proportions with its lower branches spreading like a skirt from a bustle, as a tulip tree does, out over the children in the garden. As I watch, the tree takes on a magnificent golden-orange glow as if from some radiant power within it. When the children see this they shriek in terror and run from the garden, leaving the gate open. I often dream, but seldom have I dreamt a dream that left me with such foreboding. I wake feeling disturbed, my mouth slavering. I have to get up and look at the unfamiliar stars rolling through the night sky to settle myself. I take comfort from the words of Addison's great hymn, drawn from the Psalms: 'The spacious firmament on high with all the blue ethereal sky; and spangled heavens a shining frame, their great original proclaim…'

For me there is no deeper satisfaction, at the end of a day, than in looking across three acres of turned dark earth, with not a weed, not a blade of grass in sight, a field laid out like a fresh tablecloth before the meal is served. I'm weary as I take the horses, strong Clydesdale and Shire crosses, from their harnesses. Such good-natured beasts they are, so stolid and reliable. They care for a gentle word as much as the next man; they love me to stroke their muzzles and foreheads. I sometimes sing to them as we head back to the yard for water, oats and a rub-down. I think they enjoy a Scottish air – certainly, of all God's creatures they are the ones who respond to a kind word with a dignity that few dogs have. Behind us the entire field is spread out naked beneath the sky, ready for seed, the furrows casting their shadows in the late afternoon sun. It's bonnie soil to work, no question, and a ploughman who has proved himself is never short of work here.

A great joy to me is that there is no dunging to be done. So much of our winters in the Mearns were given to dunging, in terrible weathers more often than not, the wind driving in from the North Sea, carrying sleet and snow. As ploughman, it was for me to do the drilling, but it was all the gathering and hauling and the making of the dunghill in its layers that took the effort.

You wouldn't believe it, there are Scotch thistles thriving here already. We have to take the good with the bad. If we have the Clydesdales, from home, why wouldn't we have Scotch thistles? Even in winter here in New Zealand the sun is so often sitting on your shoulder; we have many blessings to count.

There is this sharpness of the light here – I have to write of it again. After rain, when the wind stops, it is dazzling on a spring morning, the skyline you could pare cheese on, shadows bold as a bobcat. It is so different from those soft pastels of our Mearns. The light on the hills of South Makirikiri is so special a man from anywhere could still feel at home with it – especially at eventide when there are clouds over the Tasman stacked to the heavens in rolling stooks, cumulus and high cumulus. Sometimes it slants light down in the late afternoon like the hand of God in a children's picture book. It picks out a greenness that is bright in the blue landscape. But these great effects in the skies – it's partly to do with their expansiveness – they were all there in the Mearns. These lands, just a few hundred feet above the sea, with their slow and rolling decline down to the coast, their great fertility in brown, not red soils, and the way the weather rolls in from the coast – it could be looking down from St Cyrus to the sea. I have a need on some occasions to remind myself I wasn't toiling behind a couple of Clydesdales in the Mearns.

Of course, the summers back home were never like the blessed summers we have here, October to April. All this puts me in mind of how the man who ups and leaves his birth family grows to love the land he tends and the family he raises. But at times, when you least expect it, there's always a pang. So in some ways you can never leave a place. For myself, it's the things you took for granted and never considered before you left, little things really, like those village church bells calling, that you don't hear a lot around here.

I am often put in mind of the story my mother told me of a kirk, further down our coast, that over the centuries was gradually taken by the sea until it disappeared entirely. And of how for years after the spire disappeared you could still hear its chimes ringing out beneath the waves. It's quite silly when you think about it, but long after one might have thought the corrosion would have stopped the clapper, people still heard it. For me, whenever I walked on a beach, even a New Zealand one, I would find myself always half expecting to hear a church bell.

Some migrants cling to far more than that and much good it does them. When I think back, those that pin their plaid to the clan memorial at Culloden, those that spit words checked out in brass over Rob Roy's grave, *McGregor Despite Them* – all that can be deliberately and thankfully left behind, tossed into the churning wake of a ship departing from a homeland. But some never want to let go.

Doug 2

Early 1920s

Hector, my father, knew his horses. I can remember my parents were in a horse and trap outside the Marton Post Office when a brass-radiator Model T Ford back-fired and the horse, it shied and started to bolt. My mother was just stepping up to board the trap, with her foot on the step, one hand holding on to me, when father raises his hand, and in a firm voice said, 'Stay tight'. The horse settled.

It is my earliest memory of him; it must have been about 1922. The memory I kept returning to, long after his death. Thinking back, it represented stern love and certainty. Those things were not to last, which is why I remember. When I think about it, I have kept that picture by me through all my life until, to my astonishment, I am in my ninetieth year. I have this uncanny sense of looking back down the corridors of my life as if I am examining someone else's – except that I know more about that person than did the reckless man who was living his life at the time. How wise we are afterwards! But a man can't have regrets, they're for the feeble-minded and there is always more life to be lived.

I have one memory of a softer Hector (it's only now I feel I can refer to him by his Christian name) when occasionally he took down his fiddle from a battered case above the wardrobe. He was a slim man, of strong bearing – not so different from my own build, and probably average height for the times. His sandy hair was always neatly parted and his mouth was stern. Little did I know then that his face was set by pain.

He would scrape the bow with an orange cake of resin, translucent and sticky, before picking up the instrument and tucking it under his chin. When I think of it, that gesture reminds me of the way a mother holds hairclips pinched in her mouth while brushing her daughter's hair. It is the same kind of concentration.

Before he got sick, my mother would accompany him on the piano. They were both musical, and they loved to sing the tunes of the late 1890s. Sometimes, halfway through a song, they would begin a verse, each offering entirely different lyrics and my mother would burst into giggles. 'Oh, Hector,' she would sigh, pushing strands of her auburn hair back from her face as if she wanted that moment to go on, to somehow keep that special feeling by touching her face. They would pause, count the beat and start in again.

The house was pretty spare, and the lounge furnished simply. But we did have the piano and over the fire a portrait of his mother – whose dark eyes seemed to enter you, then follow you wherever you were in the room. There were a few pictures of horses. On the mantelpiece sat a small silver cup, engraved *Wee Donald*, for the victory of a shire horse that had won something in Scotland. When my parents played together the small sitting room was transformed – filled with life from another place they still called 'home'.

Marton in the Rangitikei is not much changed physically then from what it is today. But it was a bustling little market town on the Main Trunk Line – in the 1920s the place had far more zip and go. There were characters. I don't know – we don't seem to make those types any more. As life's got easier for people the characters have disappeared, along with all the good jokes.

Many of the men from that time I associate with horses. They were on horseback clopping up and down the street, in horse-drawn traps and they had horses at hitching rails outside hotels, horses drinking from the trough at the Post Office with their riders watching over them. Drunks and schoolboys often took a dunking in those troughs. In some ways Marton after the First World War was not so different from the towns of Merry England.

There were enough horses in the district to support at least three blacksmiths as well as a wheelwright and coach-maker. I often stopped to watch the smithy at the end of Broadway through his doorway, which was opened to the street on pulley rollers. He was stringy and strong-armed in an old woolly singlet. The flicker of light from his fire played on his shiny face as he warmed a piece of glowing iron and belted the daylights out of it until it took on the shape he wanted.

You could also see the odd drover, drunk as a lord, swaying in the saddle as he was carried home from a local by his horse. Beer was much stronger in those days. There were many in the churches opposed to the demon drink. They had my mother on my back to attend Temperance Union meetings. Soon after my father died she threw out the last of his Scotch, emptied the sherry down the sink and tied a blue ribbon over the stern matriarch gazing down from above the fireplace.

A few years later she turned to me: 'Doug, I want you to sign the pledge – for my sake you must do this, son. Look at that poor Carmody family, they all suffer because of that man's drunkenness. They don't have clothes, or proper food on the table, and he takes to poor Mrs Carmody. All Christians, son, must help get rid of this evil.'

At sundown, Dick Carmody, the lamplighter, would appear in our street, with a triangular ladder strapped to the crossbar of his bicycle. He wore a broad-brimmed hat and a tweed jacket in all weathers. He would stop at street corners, place his ladder under the light and climb up to turn on the gas, using a flint and striker. He'd then move on to the next corner. At sun-up he reversed the process, extinguishing the lights. There was something reassuring about his comings and goings, and he always had a 'gidday' for a curious young boy. Even as a lad I knew that he had a great capacity for liquor. He would patronize the Club Hotel at 10am and an hour later you'd see him carrying his Port Sammy, holding two square riggers of beer, which would keep him going through the afternoon. At 4pm he would pick his way back to the hotel where he would repeat the same performance, with a couple of recharged riggers to see him through the evening. No one knew what demons he was keeping at bay. But when speaking of him, my mother whispered the words 'Passchendaele' and 'few survivors'. I think the whole town understood that very few in his unit had survived. But you didn't hear that from Dick.

I trundled the wooden handcart down clattering streets to fetch snapper heads for our chooks from the fishmonger. As I was going off to sleep I would sometimes recite the names of those in each house down three or four blocks, and then back up the other side to our place again. It was somehow reassuring.

I could cut across the empty paddock next door to where the wood and coal man, Stan Winchcombe, released his big draught horses at night. They were always overjoyed to be let loose after a hard day between the dray shafts, their steel-shoed, shying hooves making sparks as they struck the big stones in the paddock. I'd go past Mrs Baden's, the old German widow. You could see her in the afternoons sitting in a rocking chair in her front room, bright covers on her head cushions. She had two daughters – Gertrude taught the piano, Clare the violin. I took piano lessons for a while but my heart was not really in it. I wanted to be on the loose with my mates, or down at the pool – though I did win the Johnson Cup at a Scout Concert playing *Heart's Ease*.

One day as an adult, on leave from the war in the Solomons, I joined Stan Winchcombe, now as bald as a badger, for a noggin at the Club Hotel. The pub had a long polished bar top with a chrome rail around it, to which the bar-flies clung all day, defending their territory.

'What kind of a day have you had, Stan?'

'Oh, exceptional, Doug, exceptional.' He took another draught – he was in great form, his cheeks bright, standing barely upright, hanging onto the bar rail for support. 'I went and cut the hedge at the Presbytery. O'Rourke, the priest, invited me in for a whisky. I helped him out by drinking half his bottle. I was badly shickered, you see, the day I got married. I thought I had given him two one-pound notes. When I sobered up next morning, I found to my horror I had given him two five-pound notes. Ten bloody quid to a priest! I wasn't even Catholic before I got married. It took the shine off my wedding, I can tell you. Ever since, I have been trying to reclaim the eight quid owing.'

Once my father became really ill, my tasks increased. I had the job of catching and killing the hens for eating. I dispatched them with the tomahawk or by wringing their necks. I was also taught how to pluck them. I was about five years old.

Work pretty much dominated my waking hours outside of school. House lighting was from coal-gas supplied from the local gas works. But I had to chop wood and bring it in with heaps of coal every morning. The ash compartment of the Shacklock had to be emptied every other day, and I kept it supplied with wood and coal. If the stove was not cleared of soot, the whole kitchen would fill with smoke. Hot water was drained from a brass tap on the side of the stove into a bucket for a bath. I did most of the fetching and carrying, even as a little fellow – it was my duty, without question. My mother recompensed me occasionally with a penny or occasionally thrupence.

It meant that I didn't have a lot of time for play. There was this lad down the road, Garth, who was as good as I was at getting into trouble. Garth was as straight as a die – you knew where you were with him. We became mates early on. His family were as poor as mine, so we did almost anything to make a buck.

In spite of all the difficulties that people went through at that time, it was surprising what a boy could do to improve his situation. I used to harvest cocks-foot seed from the grass verges of the roadside. I'd dry and wrap the seed-heads in sacks, then beat them with a solid piece of wood. That made seed collection easy and when I had sufficient, I'd go down to the merchant to cash them in for a few more shillings. Garth and I also took a penny each on the sale of empty beer and medicine bottles. Sometimes we stole the brown, hexagonal medicine bottles from the private hospital, Hazlehurst, to sell them back again to one of the Marton chemists.

A couple of 'dippers', Gospel Hall members who operated a cash and carry grocery store, paid my mate and I half a penny each for bottles when the going rate was one penny. The second time they tried it, Garth stood there and said, "My father says you're a pair of lousy psalm-singing knee benders! Stick your bottles up your jumper.' Their eyes popped out of their pudding faces. Those blokes did nothing for our appreciation of religion.

I delivered veges from the Chinese market gardeners; for a shilling I cleaned the brass plate set in the brick frontage of an accountant's office. I emptied the waste-paper baskets, which also yielded a supply of used stamps – great trading material. Periodically we would set up a stamp-soaking enterprise on the kitchen table, coaxing the stamps from their envelopes and setting them in the sun to dry. For the most exotic or valuable stamps we would use a special steaming technique to lift them without doing damage. Unfranked New Zealand stamps could be reused, making the exercise all the more worthwhile.

In those days starlings were a pest to farmers and by climbing trees – which we did anyway – a boy could earn a penny a shell for blown starlings' eggs, threaded on a string. We handed these in to a sallow figure hunched over a desk in a corner of the county office. He had lost his right arm in the war and we watched him laboriously enter the numbers into a register, then scrawl out a receipt. He'd always eye us up as he handed over a florin or a shilling and, without fail, say the same thing, in a voice like a rasp on pumice. 'Don't spend this all at once. Save the pennies and the pounds will take care of themselves.'

'You're telling me,' Garth muttered, and then, more quietly, 'Silly old git,' testing the old vet's hearing as we rushed out.

Alan 3

It was only after a swim at the beach – because there was no cigarette immediately after a swim – that you smelt him himself, his sweat. On a warm day, he smelt like the sea, his great love. He never entered it gradually, or tentatively, as most people do, but always in a headlong run down the sand, full tilt, hitting the first knee-high wave in a dive. Then he would strike out in a determined crawl, up and down in the turbulence, heading for deeper water. 'Come on, get into it! What are you waiting for? It won't get any warmer.'

As our confidence grew, this is how we boys learnt to hit the surf. Occasionally, the waves would be too big and on one occasion at least Barry, being smaller, had his face wiped in the grit at the bottom of a wave. 'I don't like this, I want to get out,' he'd wail, sand through his hair, trapped in his ears and the corners of his shut eyes. 'Get back in again, son, or you'll never do it,' Dad would tell him, a bit forcefully at times. 'You know Johnny Weissmuller – one of the great Tarzans – was an Olympic swimmer. Don't you want to be like him?' That sounded to me like a reason to keep swimming. I soon found the secret to enjoying the surf was to be able to stay under for a long while, waiting for a big wave to pass over.

When we finally emerged from the water, shivering, our father would grab his coarse khaki ex-service towels and rub us down, 'to bring back the circulation'. He did it with such vigour that I swear that the salt combined with the towelling action tore at our young skins. It was painful. But if we didn't squawk, at least we knew we weren't sissies. When we were dry Dad would light up.

Even when he was fixing something – a toy or a toaster – he had smoke rising from an ash-gathering fag, his breath drawing in gasps because his hands were too preoccupied to remove it from his mouth. Sometimes he'd fix the broken object, but other times not. And when he failed, a string of oaths issued forth: 'Bugger, dam and blast the bloody thing'. But when he swore, his anger seemed more theatrical than real, as if he couldn't trust himself to lose his temper and swear at the same time. Times like that, I'd keep well clear of him.

He wanted us to learn but impatience ruled his teaching. 'Control,' he would tell us, 'is everything. Self-control.' But things could go wrong for anyone at any time.

Reminders of this came early. There was a farmers' field day at Raetihi, a town perched at the top of the then notorious Parapara Road that slid through the papa country to the north. It is the faintest of oldest memories now, blotched with spurting blood. It begins in early morning, probably the day before: a squawking hen flaps around the yard as we chase it. Once it was caught, he holds its neck on the block raising the axe above the bird's protests, and then it falls, blood on white feathers, leaving a twitching corpse.

Plucked, stuffed and cooked, overnight the chook becomes a cold meat lunch at a picnic area en route to the field day. The bird is unwrapped from a red-checked linen tea towel. It is served with slices of white bread sawn from a barracouta loaf with Dad's tomatoes and lettuce and shelled, glistening, boiled eggs – a family favourite. A beloved great-aunt and -uncle are with us, their laughter and chatter part of the happiness of this day. They have brought along their red Thermette which is fired up with gathered twigs at the roadside to make tea.

The impression continues to build – a line of men in uniform black singlets, white trousers and polished boots, who clamber up onto their stations for a wood-cutting competition. On a signal they wield their axes with ferocity, arcing back and forth and, twisting their bodies, slanting across in a regular, apparently effortless pattern, the axe biting deeper with every blow into the shuddering block, chips exploding into the air; a few cross-strokes and a sprint at the end to be the first to knock the top off the block. The whole lot seem to finish within seconds of each other.

During the contest someone's axe slips. The memory of the chook is collaged into it – blood gouts and stains white trousers, a terrible injury. Axemen are tough men. It's good to be tough.

'No one likes the sound of grizzling kids,' Dad often said. 'It gives a man the hebbie-jebbies.' From an early age, if I hurt myself I was enjoined by my mother, 'Bite your lip and be a brave soldier.' From her, there'd be acceptance and maybe the comfort of a cuddle. My father's only comfort, though, was to tell me about the right-of-passage rituals for Indian braves. 'One of the things they had to do was to put their hands in boiling water and not make a sound. That was how you became a brave.' It was like telling a boy about the heroism of the gallant airman on the blazing wing of his aircraft. But this was Dad's upbringing and youth – and, see, it hadn't done him any harm, had it?

***

Koitiata beach, Turakina was a short distance by car from our home, a place you could take us kids to for a run and a breath of fresh air – a bit of a blow. Or you could buy a piece of lupin-covered sand and try to put down roots into its shifting sands, which is what our family did. It was a place that encouraged practicality and austerity – where ordinary people could build their modest beach house at a small cost. There were about twenty baches when we first came, built mainly from Fibro-light. With Jimmie Cameron's help on the difficult stages, Dad built the two-room construction for the cost of the cement, some corrugated iron for roofing and a truckload of cheap, saggy heart rimu for framing. This timber was so hard that Dad had to drill every nail hole by hand.

Items like nails, guttering and spouting just had to be purchased, of course, but most of the building was traded

52

or given. A gift always became a form of trade too because his code insisted that you never took anything for nothing. There could be no debts of any kind – even when people were happy to move things on, or simply be generous. This allowed a man to maintain his independence. 'We don't owe anyone anything,' was his proudest boast.

Our place became our second home. It was, everyone said, a great place for kids. Here clothes not quite ready yet for the ragman were given an entirely new lease of life. Koitiata was not the kind of beach where people in swimsuits took their towels and Coppertone sun-cream and lay for hours in the sand, as people did in magazines. People never said to their friends of Koitiata, as they did of Caroline Bay or the Mount, 'We're headed for the Mount this Christmas, we're taking the caravan.' Chances were if they made it down the gravel road to our beach there'd be mud everywhere from the last flood. The mud was so thick that until it dried it would melt between the toes and cling even to the soles of the feet. There were miles of driftwood and wind and there was the brown river to wade across. At Koitiata we learnt to put up with all weathers, including, in some seasons, its almost continuous westerlies, as maddening as a pack of hounds frenzied with a rabbit that tugged and pulled at everything in sight.

If it blew for a week the wind might be unbearable, but it was also energising. It bestowed on us a sense of being utterly alive. Windless places aren't like that. If you were down-wind from a dead cattle beast, washed downstream, you got another take on its airs – it was a great leveller. From its buffetings we developed our sense of the world based on how people behaved, rather than the way people dressed or what they drove, if anything. As Dad said, 'Everyone downstream of a dead cow has the same stink up their nostrils. People with tickets on themselves wouldn't last five minutes here.'

Koitiata fitted entirely with my father's intolerance of what he liked to call baloney and of people who gave themselves airs, women who 'boiled the dog' as my mother liked to say. 'So far up himself, he wouldn't know if it was night or day,' Dad'd say of someone who displayed the aplomb of the upper crust. 'Listen to the way he talks. Bloody poof. Wouldn't be surprised if he sat down to pee.'

Even when it wasn't, if he heard something that wasn't quite on the level, like me bringing home a hard-luck story, he would growl, 'What a lot of baloney.' And that was it, baloney – stone-cold finish.

If the beach retained its own bastions in wind and mud and sharp sticks in the sand, these conditions only served to make it a haven for birds. Koitiata lay on the Taranaki Bight, several hundred kilometres distant from one of New Zealand's great wildfowl sanctuaries at the top of the South Island and only about 100 kilometres north of another. Immediately conspicuous were the pied stilts, elegant browsers lining up in shallow estuarine water for food, or flash-legged, high-stepping the shiny tidal mudflats as if they were picky eaters. I remember the first time a friend, a Maori mate, showed me a dotterel's nest, a simple rearrangement of seashell fragments in grit, in a scrape. It was hidden behind a low dune for protection, with three brown-splodged eggs in it. Its delicate vulnerability spoke of the time before wild cats became a deadly part of the beach's ecology.

At ebb tide in autumn we watched the sandbars loaded up with fat terns, standing in rows facing symmetrically into the wind. Some of these birds flew in the face of winter, out-running its shadow, all the way back to the northern summer to the Soviet Union – home of the Sputnik, the only satellite in the sky, and Nikita Kruschev. That was a marvel. The ever-resident black oystercatchers heckled and jeckled along the shoreline, always keeping their distance. In nesting time they feigned a damaged wing to draw us away from a nest. Perhaps the ultimate bird that lived somewhere in the rushes by the river was the bittern. We knew even then that rarity of species gave a special value to them. On early whitebaiting mornings you might hear the bittern boom out its mating call.

Once we actually saw it, neck stretched, beak into the air, its speckled plumage and balletic stance contriving to make a beautiful but not entirely successful camouflage against the jointed rushes.

Twenty years after the Great Slump of my parents' day, this coast fitted the lingering Depression mentality like a worn soft-leather glove. A place where you could live on almost nothing. The few permanent inhabitants with suitable windbreaks could grow vegetables, working with compost and bore-water, coaxing sand into soil. They maintained small windmills to generate electricity because for years the village had no power. Everyone laid in sufficient firewood from off the beach to keep warm, or even cook with. And there was ever the prospect of fishing – often an illusion into which local men cast enormous effort and ingenuity.

Bert Whitaker set the scene in male territoriality. Tall and gaunt and tough, he was also miserable, living behind heaps of choice firewood, beyond his whalebone gate-posts. In the tail-end of storms we would come upon him stalking the wild beaches, seeking out the best fire material and the new whitebait pozzies as the river remade its path. As a retired builder he knew well the true burning timbers the region yielded up: matai, maire, totara and rata. Some arrived in the form of lost fence posts, wires attached. This kind of booty could cause wars on the beach. Once, a local wit quipped of him, 'Poor Mr W., he's down to his last forty cord.' As he got older, his threshold of tolerance for the community in which he lived declined markedly. Us kids usually steered well clear of him.

One New Year's Eve, though, we decided we'd had enough of grumpy Bert. We dragged one of his prize lots into a bonfire that blazed festively into the night and continued to smoulder and smoke for several days. The next day he went around making accusations, but we lied in our teeth. His wrath would have been too much to bear.

'You boys were seen on the beach last night.'

'Oh, we just went over to collect some bottles, Mr W. It wasn't us.'

'If ever I catch you doing this, I'll tan your hides, there'll be no beg-your-pardons.'

'Aw, Mr W., we wouldn't do anything like that.'

'Well, be sure you don't. And don't go calling me Mr W.'

While beachcombing we'd come across small jewels glittering in the sand – bits of worm-eaten timber no bigger than a hand, with verdigrised nails driven in. They shone with attachments of torn, sand-blasted copper, in shades of green and amber. It was actually Bert who told us its origins – Mum had asked him. 'Ah,' he said, without hesitation. 'That's from a ship, the *Robina Dunlop*. It was wrecked right on this beach here back in the 1870s. She was copper-bottomed, sheathed to protect it from sea-worms.'

My grandmother, my father's mother, occasionally inquired about the Koitiata. 'Have you seen the terns and oystercatchers – I used to love them on those strands in the outgoing tides. Such beautiful creatures.' Tall, stooped and bespectacled, she lived in a semi-detached brick State tenement of the sort erected by the Labour Government just after the war – the architecture of long-delayed State decency. Its neat concrete path, flanked by a guard of standard roses, led to high concrete steps and floors raised well above the damp for ventilation. It had one of those doorbells that not so much rang as crunched when you pressed it. She was always pleased to see us for a Sunday visit in our Sunday best, the long prayers of church still sticking like old dressings to our bended knees, bare on the wooden kneeler.

Pikelets were her forte, thickly buttered and spread with apricot jam. They were laid out with sponge-cake and baked ginger biscuits on plates with doilies, awaiting our arrival under beaded muslin. Seed-cake was her specialty. A mustard-coloured china teapot did the honours and orange cordial was a treat for the children. 'Alan, you get down those glasses, the ones with the red frosted glass on them, and you pour for Barry and yourself, that's a good boy.' It was mandatory that Barry and I would 'do the rounds' of this food. My grandmother would always laugh, in a pleasant way, to see us as we worked our way sampling the plates.

Nana expected good behaviour. We always thanked her for afternoon tea. When we started learning piano, she expected recitals, the piano's lips peeled back from its mouth of keys, ready and glittering in reproach for the unpractised. Barry was often keener than I to make an offering, and he charmed them all by singing along as well, something I could never do. When he was little his favourite was, 'Coming through the Rye', sung in a fine soprano.

'Well done, well done, Barry,' she'd say, always generous in her praise, clapping and laughing. Sometimes we were allowed to take down a piece of flat black stone from the top of the piano and hold it so that it wouldn't drop. 'That was given to us by a Maori, many years ago.'

I spent time with her on my own as a child. Once, and I remember it vividly for she had never before spoken of him in my presence, she told me a story about Hector going down to Koitiata and meeting Maori there, whom he befriended. 'Your grandfather loved it there,' she said, twisting a tea-towel tightly in her hands. 'He was always wanting to get down to the beach; he said it reminded him a little of his Scottish home.'

It was only in the laying of Florence finally to rest in late winter sunshine that I appreciated how long the life she had led had been spent alone. It probably explained why she had been so demanding of her son, my father. He was forever chopping wood, pruning trees and doing lawns for her, even in his sixties. 'She thinks you're still a boy, Doug,' my mother would say, knowing he felt he had to act on his mother's expectations. When she came to stay she always brought a small hunch-backed wooden clock. It had a loud tick that kept the time at her bedside – 'kept the time', as if seconds and hours were freshly sliced chunks that a 'timepiece' could hold behind glass like a sealed jar of preserves.

***

This coast had been a reasonable place for fishing, but after the naval survey ship *Lachlan* detonated its way right round the Taranaki Bight, bringing up fish by the ton with its bilious depth-charges, for many years they were a lot scarcer. Ever the optimist, my father's catches were so rare that none of us ever expected anything. He'd always come home much later than he'd said.

From the bach window at the end of the tide we could see his figure from away off, on the long walk home across the mudflats, carrying his split surfcasting rods, bait bag and – usually this was a much lesser burden – catch bag. 'Here he comes,' my mother would smile the knowing smile of the empty-handed fisher's wife, as she turned from the window, her fair hair catching the light. 'I'll put the frying pan on now. You never know, he'd be tickled pink if he caught something. But never mind if he doesn't.' She was almost merry as she threw together a salad and potatoes and some cold corned beef from the kerosene fridge. It was the *idea* of being able to feed the family at apparently no cost from the harvest of the sea – that was what was important to him. And, whatever the catch, we came to understand, he was happy just to have been out there on his own.

The greatest prize was whitebait. On those rare occasions when for some reason the cattle loosed along the mudflats in autumn hadn't trampled the entire spawning grounds, he'd come home with a feed. It was sheer delight. Delicately flavoured fresh whitebait fritters confected with just an egg, a couple of spoonfuls of flour, a dash of salt and a squeeze of lemon – lightly fried in sizzling butter – were the caviar of New Zealand.

'Come on, you boys,' my mother would call from her place at the stove, jiggling browning fritters in the hot

58

terrazzo pan with a fish-slice, 'I'm sure you've got room for another one, give us your plates.' Even with a full belly, you never wanted to stop.

Usually Dad heard about big runs of whitebait after the event. 'They say they were running yesterday,' he'd announce over dinner at home. 'Norm got three-quarters of a bucketful on Thursday. The O'Hagans took home so much, Mack had to take off his shirt and tie the sleeves so that he could lug it all back to his truck. Lucky he didn't catch any more. I'll try to get down there during the week – take a couple of hours off work – too many 'baiters there at the weekends.' But we never saw catches like that – not remotely.

The competition, the idea that others were making a catch when we weren't, was a painful matter to him. Bert was king, claiming a new spot before each season opened. He had been known to physically attack anyone who took his claim. When the whitebait were running, all the good pozzies were quickly snapped up, occupied at ungodly hours before dawn, and 'baiters would edge up in front of others' nets until they got so close, someone started shouting. The local gossips loved recounting the latest set-to amongst the 'baiters. Once territory had been agreed the whitebaiters would huddle in freezing, damp silence for hours, watching, waiting, smoking, until the moment when the bait arrived. Good catches or not, they were a grizzly lot.

Tiny, translucent fry, whitebait were caught mainly in wire-framed open-mouthed nets tucked in beside the bank, facing prayerfully towards the mouth. You could see the ripples of shoals moving up the river, a dark bundle, stippling the surface of the water with their pulse, a writhing swarm wriggling its way up against the current. Once netted, as you lifted them clear of the water they thrummed like a swarm of bees thudding their tiny tails against the sides of the fabric. To feel even a half cupful of 'bait in your net was to feel the thump of life, like a jerk from a fish on a line or the kick of a baby in the womb. Sometimes we used large cane-hooped nets bound to poles to reach out and scoop up shoals, usually from the river mouth itself or from the tiny edge-waves of a making tide, as they ran like a sewing machine needle through cloth, along the sandy bank.

It was those rare, telling, teeming moments that kept my dad there and kept bringing him back, through winter and early spring. More often than not the hours passed and the rewards remained negligible. There were plenty of them, these impatient men at Koitiata, trying out their patience and that of their neighbours. The idea of a catch, of something for nothing, especially if it was fresh fish, inspired them all, and even turned my father temporarily into a patient man.

When it came to dealing with adults, more than anything else childhood was about waiting, experienced through the gap between what children wanted and what adults insisted upon.

Waiting politely was thought to be good for a child's character. After spoiling your children, the worst thing that could ever be said of a kid was that they kicked up a fuss.

'Dad, is it lunchtime yet?'

'No, you'll have to wait another twenty minutes.'

'Dad, I'm hungry now.'

'Just wait.'

'I'm off, then, there's nothing here – I'm going back to the bach.'

'No, stay here, you need to put in the hours for 'bait, show some patience. Don't be a quitter.'

'Dad, I'm cold and hungry. Desperate. I have to go – bye.'

'You'll get nowhere in life if you give up that easily.'

Whether it was for the Springboks to begin their long-awaited tour, or Uncle John to arrive in his Chevrolet to take me to stay for the school holidays on his farm hacked out of the vertical papa country on the Kawhatau, a tributary of the Rangitikei, waiting was the game. If you had anything to do with adults they made you wait. Hanging round 'Like a wet week' or for 'A month of Sundays' was what kids did. Fishing was about waiting. Character-forming.

*　*　*

Haircuts were a ritual of dread between father and sons. As tonsures went in those days, no man worthy of the term ever showed anything other than newly-shaved stubble from his chin to a plimsol line about two inches above the ear. This was the infamous 'short back and sides'. Something like it had been in vogue throughout my father's life. Barry and I used to dread haircut day because they were home-delivery. Dad did the cutting, swinging us up on a makeshift platform on the old highchair. Dad's hand-shears were stainless steel and worked manually by squeezing the handles together. Alas, he had little finesse and little more patience. The shears would bite in, and at the end of the stroke they would grip and grab. We sensed his impatience. As he released the cutters he would pull out small chunks of hair from the side of the head. This need happen only a couple of times before I would send up a wail that was enough to set the quiet neighbourhood on edge.

As my distress mounted, above the sound of my cries I could hear on the sloping lawn a faint tripping sound like grasshoppers through the catch in the weave of buffalo grass. When I looked down, the insects were boiled sweets, brightly coloured and wrapped in clear twisted cellophane. On the property below us, under our presiding sand hill, lived a Scots couple, middle-aged, childless and wonderfully good-humoured. Their accents were Doric Scots, thick as Aberdeenshire porridge; they were always 'dinna carin' and 'dinna kennin'. 'How are ye, young skinamarinks, this mornin'?' they'd chuckle. It was they who tossed up the placatory sweeties. Dad said they were 'kindness itself'.

Their front room was graced by a clinker fire surround – brass-topped firing instruments gleaming spick and span in their rack on the hearth. On the quarter-hour sonorous

61

whirrings preceded the portentous chimes of the third member of the household, a grandfather clock. They had Toby jugs on the mantelpiece and one of those metallic nigger pageboys, as people called them, who held his hand out for a penny. They also kept a pink-tongued Scotch terrier, about as friendly as they were, who slept on a tartan rug in a wicker basket. 'Here's a sweetie, Alan, noo there's a good boy,' Jessie'd call up to me in my distress. Then more urgently, 'Stop your greetin' noo, Alan, stop your greetin'.' They couldn't bear to hear children cry, God bless them, and from that time I have not heard a Scot speak without being filled with good cheer.

Since any self-expression involving the use of hair was associated with unmanliness (except for an oily DA haircut that slowly came into vogue after the arrival of the highly suspect Elvis), home cutting was a regular ritual until I was eight. It was the same cut that our servicemen had to save them from infection in the malarial swamps of the Pacific, or whatever scorpions might lurk in the deserts of North Africa.

Indiscriminate, universal circumcision in the '40s and '50s in New Zealand was probably continued for the same reason. No boy remembers the pain of having his foreskin removed as an infant – although even to a small inquiring boy it is soon obvious that the unspoken scar is not God's handiwork – but the haircuts I do remember.

Once I had a bike I had the means to make it down to the barber's under my own steam. The bike was a full-sized adult one. My father got it second-hand for five quid. He extended the thickness of the pedals with wooden blocks so I could grow into it. Nothing ever seemed to fit. It didn't matter. Like most kids then, we were forever growing into things, or growing out of them.

The barber, in high-collared white coat, was a Salvationist who gloried in the name of Bill Cropp, which, given the hair styling he unfailingly dispensed to flocks of post-war boys, proved that God did indeed have a sense of humour.

Another Returned Man, he was peevish, thin and a heavy user of Brylcreem, a no-nonsense emulsion that made men's hair as lustrous and stiff as furniture lacquer. He stood all day at his large upholstered chair before a full-length mirror, using scissors and an electric razor. He wore a steward's short white buttoned over-jacket. Usually about a dozen boys were lounging around the room waiting for a haircut, quietly reading *Archie*, *Blondie* or *Donald Duck* comics, as well as a few well-thumbed *Classics*.

If anyone looked like playing up Mr Cropp would bring them into line with a few sharp cuts of his tongue. 'If there's any more of that behaviour you boys can just scoot out of here. Outski, vamoose, go, beat it! And don't come back.' His irritability was such that few crossed him. Many men were like that. You didn't want to be near them; they were niggly old buggers really.

When your turn finally came he'd make a parson's collar with a piece of toilet paper around your neck and throw a cape over you.

Occasionally he'd talk religion. 'Have you read the Bible?'

'Yes, bits of it, Mr Cropp.'

'Not the whole lot? I've read the Bible from cover to cover. Twice. There are some great stories in the Bible. The Bible is not just God's Word, it's the greatest work of literature in the English language.'

At the end of the cut, which would take about six minutes, the cape was ceremoniously whipped from your shoulders. Shorn locks, all one and a half inches of them, tumbled to the floor as you stole a glance into the mirror. Mirrors were about vanity and, as in all other things, you mustn't stare. If you did, someone'd catch you: 'Stare cat, stare cat, stare cat, stare.' Mr Cropp would then reach for his trusty bottle of Bay Rum, depress the plunger and rub this whisper of the Caribbean vigorously into the scalp. 'Fifteen men on a dead man's chest, yo ho ho and a bottle of Bay Rum.' His finale was a triumphal victory lap around his victim, showering him with the big two-handed spray bottle of cologne. I must have been all of thirteen when, due to a mild lapse in crew-cut maintenance, I came to realise that my red hair was naturally curly. But there was no question of having even moderately longer hair – that was unthinkable. The 1960s hadn't quite arrived.

Hector 3

The other day one of the men came into my hut and while reaching in his pocket a large clam-like shell fell from his dungarees and clattered to the floorboards. 'Ah,' he grunted as he reached for it, 'this is the fellow I picked up last weekend at the Douglas's. We were on a cliff-top near Ngaruawahia, a place some miles inland of here. You ought to get up into this area, Hector,' he told me. 'I have never seen anything like this country in all my travels. It is like a picture-postcard, truly quite remarkable.' I didn't know this fellow well but he showed a great deal of excitement. Picking up a lead pencil, he hurriedly drew on the back of a mail-order catalogue that I had lying about.

His sketch showed a series of great parallel-running terraces that dropped down into a long wide valley. At the heart of the valley was what must have been a curving river. But the river was so deeply cut down, there was no sign of water, just the banks of its meanders disappearing into deep trenches.

'What kind of soil is that?' I asked him. 'Is it good farmland?'

'Well, the flats where the forest was, is good farming country. But the land itself is really consolidated mud deposits; they seem to think the deposits were put down a long time ago, all laid under the sea. This is why you get all manner of shells and things.'

'Ah,' I interrupted, 'just like that legend the Maoris have about this island being hauled up from under the sea.'

'Be that as it may,' this laddie replied, 'it's very soft mud rock, and the river just keeps cutting it down. Terrible country to build roads in. It keeps falling away on them.' He then drew a great, high-stepping bridge across a gorge. 'This is where the Main Trunk rail goes through too. They have constructed a couple of mighty steel viaducts to span some difficult places. It's tough work – I'm told the workmen use a lot of pure alcohol on their joints there.

'The viaducts are as good as anything you'd see at home. But what they have to work in, it's all so unstable, this country. The farmers who live by the river at night often hear the sound of the cliffs breaking and falling down into the caverns of the rivers with a terrible crumbling sound.'

A few weeks later I had the chance to ride up the Rangitikei Valley as far as the first viaduct. Oh, what I wouldn't give for one of those farms – they are doing well, there is plenty of feed even in August, the stock are in great condition – I wish my father could see them – and their fences are fine, tight-wired affairs.

They have put up several new railway towns along the main trunk line as it runs through there, which now house the staff for the stations Their wooden water-tanks are prominent beside great mounds of coal, just like in the old country. At one of them there is a landslide. Underneath it a family of five was entombed, buried in their sleep. A shocking business. It's not the first time it's happened in those parts.

As I write this I am drawn to consider people leaving the snugness and familiar comfort of their own towns and villages in the old country for places like this. It takes a bit of gumption. I am always amazed, whenever I think of it, at how people can make the journey out here and then try to fasten themselves to this land. The wonder of it is how they carve out their farms and build their dwellings, setting up their familiar dinnerware on a sideboard, perhaps with a bit of family silver, and carrying on building a life here as if they had never left home. But this isn't 'home', it's somewhere else and a man cannot assume that this place, no matter how much he may try to make a go of it, is not without its surprises.

I went to sleep in my hut that night but awoke much later – I'd had a nightmare. In this dream I was in a place that I didn't recognise, and we were in battle with some denizen

66

and what woke me was the horror of men around me, who were lying dead in heaps before the creature's cave. It was horrible. I lay awake thinking about it, shaken, wondering what it might foretell. The night was still and cool and from some trees nearby I could hear a morepork calling its rather mournful cry.

Doug 3

My father built a chicken run before he became ill, and I helped him, learning with great pride how to blacken my thumbnail with a hammer. 'Och, silly laddie,' was all he said. Then we covered the woodwork in creosote. It was one of the last things we would do together. The sweet scent of creosote on a summer's day is one of those things that always brings a rush of happiness.

Before very long, it was me who had to prepare the mash morning and night, clean the perches with kero to keep the mites away, clear out the laying boxes and deliver the eggs. I took them to Lamerton's, the grocers', in a small wooden-wheeled handcart. There was no paving, and the roads were often uneven and with a deep ditch running down one side to take heavy rain. One day, bumble-footed, I tripped and smashed a load. What a mess a dozen eggs can make. My father was furious. 'If I was stronger, I'd tan your hide – you young wraitch,' he said in his thick Scottish accent. His face was tight and scary – I knew his gruffness, but this was a stranger. 'I should send to Scotland and get you a kilt – it'd make it easier to give you a good thrashing.'

As his illness worsened, he made several trips to the hot pools and spa treatment in Rotorua. Within two years he had moved from sticks to crutches to a Bath chair. He became an invalid with all the bad grace of a man who had been active. Once he started using the sticks he was grumpy – he must have been in a lot of pain.

I wanted him to be there to teach me rugby, football and cricket. But I, and I say this only with reluctance, because I do not want to sound like a whinger, was the one who pushed him about in his Disabled Servicemen's chair. They put in a ramp for wheelchair access to our house. The chair was a light one, sprung between three wheels. Two handles connected to cranks on the axles provided the motive power. The smaller wheel at the rear was steered by twisting a stirrup handle. Pushing him along rutted lanes and gravel roads, I found, was hard work and – I've never spoken of this before – I felt exposed, publicly humiliated, a second-class citizen.

His condition was, however, not at all uncommon. Just along the street was a Returned Man, Frank Turrell, who owned a turret top Chevrolet Tourer with buttoned canvas and celluloid sides. In one of my first rides in a car he and his sister took me across to Feilding. Silas had a gammy leg from the war that gave him the wobbly gait of a performing ape. The whole country was full of disabled veterans. In people's homes the front rooms were often cluttered with crutches and Bath chairs. There were veterans who were amputees, or blind, shell-shocked or suffering the effects of lungs laced by chlorine or mustard gas. Many were recluses behind drawn blinds. If you entered their homes they sat in the corner, silent, unaddressed figures, occasionally referred to with no thought of a reply – as if they weren't really in the room. There were smells associated with them, some medicinal, some very earthy. Their wives, if they had them, were saints. People then knew their duty; it was written in their faces. Kids knew they had to show respect. Death was much closer than it seems today and it affected everyone in small communities.

One day, when my father was away for treatment in Rotorua and mother was out cleaning the church, Garth and I, still Cubs, were practising on kettle and bass drums for a Scout concert. We were in the living room making a fair din. Two doors down another old soldier was dying. His big son, Gerard, came over and belted on the front door. We were too scared to open it. 'If you little brats don't stop that drumming right this minute,' he shouted through the latch, 'I'll belt you so hard, I'll send you right into the middle of next week.' We complied immediately. The poor fellow died a few days later.

Not long afterwards, paralysis set in on my father. Before they took him through to Wanganui Hospital I was summoned to his bedside. His last words to his small son were, 'Look after your mother, won't you?' He knew he was a goner, but there was one consolation that I came to, donkey's years later. He had seen comrades die terrible deaths in great numbers on the Western Front. We know now that many died without comfort, in quagmires, in their own blood, terrified, often alone or with men who were in no position to offer them anything. The worst deaths must have been in the cold and loneliness on the barbed wire in No Man's Land. But there were many kinds of terrible deaths. For some reason my father had been spared all of that to sire a healthy son with his beloved wife. While terribly premature and lingering, his was a death between crisp clean sheets in a warm hospital in a new land far, far away from all that. But it's a square-off, that kind of thinking – it doesn't bring your father back.

My mother, poor thing, was so grief-stricken, she was in no state to attend his funeral. It was only the neighbours persuaded her to go. I went to stay in the country with friends until she was ready to face life again. I was left feeling cheated, resentful – someone had dealt me a lousy hand in life and it took many years to shake off that sense of being singled out personally by fate for misfortune.

Those last words of his stayed with me for many years. People were very good to us. Marge and Jimmie Cameron became more and more like parents to me but I still had to help find the shekels to keep the family off the bread-line.

We never starved in our home, but we knew what it was to have almost no money, nothing extra and sometimes, as so many people during the Depression did, to go to bed feeling hungry. Sometimes bread and dripping, with a little pepper and salt, was all that was on the menu. From an early age, I was always on the lookout for anything that was buckshee – firewood, books and the odd turnip or carrot from the deep black soils of Marton growers.

My mother took in boarders and other people's washing. She was never very happy on wash-days – quite the reverse, in fact. I think it reminded her of how she was beholden to others in having to do this menial work. Looking back on it, if I'd been cheated of my father, she had been dealt a very rum hand. We used a copper and a bomb of Reckitt's Blue – sheer drudgery. We were at the bottom of the heap with prospects for improvement. The only comfort was that most ordinary people lived their lives by scrimping and saving. They had little to get by on, because these were the days before the Labour Government's social security.

Our villa had three bedrooms. My mother had one room, two rooms were let out to boarders and for many years I lived on the veranda, protected by a screen, a type of Hessian soaked in linseed oil that kept out the rain. I had a stretcher for a bed, three benzine boxes on top of each other as a dressing-table and a candle at night for reading. I was really quite comfortable.

There were plenty of blankets, although it got mighty cold in winter. I remember getting through a large volume of *And Quiet Flows the Don* by Mikhail Sholokhov, and loved reading of places far away. We'd often go to Marton Junction and watch the big steam locomotives come in and the shunters making up trains. I never lost my fascination for these black juggernauts, puffs of feathered steam rising to the sky and their sulphur-scented black smoke. If I thought of the places where the trains might be going, it would make me shiver: Taumarunui, Franklin, Auckland, Wellington.

There were other glimpses, too, of an even larger world. Marton had people from many parts. I can still smell the tang of the Jhing Yin family's place above their greengrocer's shop on the corner near the school. Dried vines and roots twisted in strange ways hung in festoons from the ceiling. An aroma of Oriental cooking, wind chimes tinkling harmoniously in the passage breeze and coloured posters of Chinese rural scenes.

My tiny world offered me other, unexpected views of a much larger life. I got to hear radio, which just a few people in Marton had before the 1930s. Later, I helped install household aerials. They were four or five metres high and stayed with guy wires. I got ten shillings a time. By then radio was becoming the rage. People who could afford it were buying sets, giving them pride of place in their best rooms and talking about 'programmes'. But in 1928 what drew us boys in was the glow of the green dials, the sound of foreign tongues on short wave, broken by the crackle and hiss of static. Contact with other lands. What a miracle! Garth and I used to visit a middle-aged chap, Jack Knight, who was very keen on radio. He had a shed behind his house and in May 1928, we went around there for the news of Lindbergh. We stood round his home-built *Popular Mechanics* equipment and heard of the aviator's triumphant arrival from Paris to New York in the *Spirit of St Louis*. I had a *Weekly News* picture of Lindbergh in his big-winged Ryan pinned to the wall of my bedroom for years after.

Fresh in our minds was the tragic flight of the two New Zealanders, in their Ryan, attempting to be the first to fly the Tasman, from Sydney. Everyone anywhere down the west of both islands got up to look out for them, on hill-tops and tankstands There was talk for weeks afterwards about where they had got to. Aeroplanes were a rarity; it was a novelty even to sight one in the sky – but this one never showed up.

For all of our financial struggles, I was lucky enough to have my first flight only about a year later. They had put up posters on the fences around the baths:

Take to the skies.
Fly a Moncoupe,
Piloted by Major Couper,
Distinguished WWI Royal Flying Corps Veteran.

Big-hearted Marge Cameron financed the excursion. Major Couper looked the part in leather coat and soft leather helmet, set off with a white silk scarf. The Monocoupe had a single rotary engine and was a high-winged monoplane – it carried the pilot and six passengers on a ten-minute flight that left me buzzing for weeks. I've never forgotten it, the rowdy take-off in a farmer's paddock, just out of Marton, the plane bucking on the uneven ground as the engine built up revs, and then the take-off, the propeller seeming to haul us over the macrocarpas as the magpies scattered. Once aloft we looked down from a greater and greater height on the Tutaenui Stream, the park and swimming baths, the railway station, Broadway and the steeple of St Stephens. Before we had even landed, I knew I wanted to fly again.

I got to see more of planes at the pictures at the Civic matinees, working for Lew, who made his own chocolate ice cream and other confectionery. Lew fitted out the sweet boy with a short white coat and starched collar and a tray strapped around the neck. It was packed with chocolate bars, and bags of assorted sweets – a shilling a bag. Trading began usually twenty minutes prior to screening, and resumed at half-time. A bloke courting a girl would always dig into his pocket for a treat at the pictures. The sweet boy usually got into the movies buckshee, which was good. Payment was one shilling for every pound of sales. After I had quit selling at the Civic Theatre, sometimes I would help Lew in the shop at rush hour. I saw many films. Charlie Chaplin, Fatty Arbuckle, Lew Costello, Greta Garbo and later, the cowboy films of Tom Mix, Gene Autry, Hopalong Cassidy. One of the great films from this time was the Australian production, *For the Term of his Natural Life.*

By then, with Woodbines at five cigarettes for four pence, I had begun to develop a taste for tobacco, a habit I maintained for fifty years. I also delivered *The Rangitikei Advocate.* I kept this run a short time only because it was over a loose metal road of Rangitikei river shingle, six or seven miles each way with twelve papers, for which I received six shillings a week. But the route was too tough on bike tyres. At the end of the run near the Bonny Glen, a dear old soul, a Mrs Bryant, would leave a jug of homemade lemonade and a couple of slices of cake on the veranda for the paperboy.

During the Depression, I had another paper run for a local newsagent-cum-tobacconist-men's hair salon. I delivered *The Wanganui Chronicle, The Dominion* and *The Auckland Star*. Saturdays were a double run as the weight of the Saturday supplements made the load too great. That meant a 5.00am start for seven shillings and sixpence a week. Most of my income I gave to my mother.

Alan 4

One of the great things about Koitiata was the space it afforded us to roam. It was a dreamland for parents and kids who shared the belief that children should be seen but not heard. Usually Barry and I headed out with mates from neighbouring baches. To the west the sea was contained only by Australia, 2000 km away, and the beaches were marked to the north and south by rivers that were almost too far to reach. Occasionally you might sight a ship far out at sea and the storms brought in evidence of another life, just over the horizon – empty Japanese whiskey bottles, *VAT 69,* and sealed glass-ball floats, encased in rope work and encrusted with sea life, that had broken free from their nets. Blown from sea-blue glass, these Japanese floats were a real prize, almost as valued as whale vertebrae and strung as trophies from the verandas of baches.

Nothing ever stayed the same here for long. This foreshore is so restless that from year to year great chunks of it would simply come and go in a flood – ships in the night. So the river mouth seldom remained in one place for long. No sooner would it seem to be established and within months dunes would spring up and build, sometimes to well over thirty feet high – even higher away from the beaches. They were soon covered in marram. Back from the beach, abandoned back oxbows of the river would fill, charged by the overflow in high flood. We called them swamps. In little time flaxes and sedges grew back, and fish and frogs and birds made good use of the edge, feeding on insects aplenty; in summer fat dragonflies pulsed overhead. Many of these creatures we chased for our collections.

For miles there were the dunes. Sometimes the bright orange-leafed pingao with its ropey roots would drape itself across the tops of the big dunes, holding them in place like rope on billowing canvas even as they continued to rise, until the river would flood mightily in a storm and break out, sometimes knocking over half a mile or more of dunes. Usually it was overnight. It was on these towering, sculptural dunes that we took great delight in the simple pleasures of skidding down. Occasionally we'd make a sled from a big piece of ply driftwood. Barry proved much more adept at tobogganing than I was – a real daredevil.

Even just leaping was fun. At maximum height the dune edges were steep from new wind-sculpting and we could jump from the top to maybe twelve feet below, bury our bare feet in the warm sand and ride the avalanche with the downward momentum until we came to a halt – and then ride it again after a new leap. The glide was deeply sensual, seeming to tingle through the whole body, as you felt the sand peeling away like a silk skin on the soles of your feet. As Barry said, 'It feels like someone just gave your feet a good tickle with a feather.'

We also walked right upriver as far as our legs would carry us, crossing farmland, clay cliffs and, on a hot day, diving dangerously nude into the water-holes where big eels nursed themselves in the sunlight. 'Have you seen their teeth? Man alive!'

One time we had paddled our canoes and then walked for miles upriver, when we saw two figures coming towards us across the mudflats in the heat shimmer. It was one of those days when the iron sand was so hot, if you walked over it barefoot, the soles of the feet got burnt. The pain was of the order Red Indians faced, of that I was certain. As the two figures drew closer we realized that the pair were boys about our age and that they were strangers, not of our village, but Maori. There was no one else for miles around and we were probably equally curious.

'Where are you going? You're on private property,' the one my age said. He was a solid build, and walked with a bit of a swagger. His younger, raggle-taggle mate followed through, 'Too right, you boys could be in serious trouble,' and then he giggled, looking at my hair. 'Ginger,' he said accusingly.

'You don't know what you are talking about – there aren't even any fences out here. Just wild cattle.'

'What do you mean, "wild cattle"? We've just come down here to check on the family herd.' He grinned conspiratorially at his mate.

I looked around – often cattle did roam through these places, but there were none in view. 'Anyway, what are you boys doing on our land?'

'Walking, what does it look like?'

'Well, you need to get permission, eh? This is private property.' He sniggered, with his hand over his mouth.

I decided they were kidding. 'Hey, it's hot – we're going for a swim.' I paused, not wanting rejection. 'You want to join us?'

'You go – we'll watch. Big eels in there, eh?' he giggled. 'Might bite your cock off – then you'd be like a girl.' He burst into laughter.

We went in, cautiously, and dried off quickly afterwards in the warmth and sun.

The older one was called Maurice. He often came down to the beach to fish with his family and occasionally he'd call by to see what we were up to – my parents liked his openness and he became a friend.

Over time, we realised that Maurice knew about this country. It was he who explained about nearby Ratana pa to us, and what it signified. 'Ratana, he healed my Nannie, she was blind. She saw again after twenty years.'

'How could he do that?' we wanted to know.

'There's this room up there, stuffed with crutches and wheelchairs that people have given away after Ratana healed them. He believed in everybody and they believed in him. He was great. My uncle says he wanted us – youz and us – all to be able to live together. He knew the future – knew about the bomb dropped on Japan long before it happened, eh?'

He added a little to our knowledge of the *Robina Dunlop*. Turning over a worm-eaten fragment of wood with a piece of copper attached to it by a nail on the beach one day, he said quietly, 'My great-grandparents came down to the beach to rescue them from the sea.'

Hector 4

It was a few weeks after the drowning that I returned to the beach with Davie McKinnon. I had borrowed some fishing tackle and we walked north to where there was supposed to be a good hole at high tide. I had never been up this way. Davie said he was happy to come along for some sea air. It's a strange thing, me fishing. Back home no self-respecting farmer would have anything to do with fish or even fisherfolk – nor they with us. We thought their food was beneath us and we made no bones about letting them know it. Terrible, the way the old country wove webs of intolerance at every turn. It was a way of life. Here, I've discovered I enjoy the taste of fish.

There was a strong wind blowing and I began to think that the wind was more of a presence here than ever it had been from the North Sea onto the Mearns. In their equinox it never seems to stop – it blows and then blows harder and buffets, it howls off the sea and hurtles in gusts down corridors it has made among the dunes. Sometimes it rips off the sides of the dunes, leaving them steep, with the roots of an orange plant sticking out from their sides. When it blows this strong it carries clouds of sand that sting the cheeks like needles and you have to close your eyes. The sea is grey and all chopped over in white – churning and tossing all the way out to the horizon. Gulls try to ride the wind and fight it, but they can get tossed about like bits of newspaper. There is something very bracing about it all and as I gaze at the turbulence I cannot help but think of the ships that came in under the weather too close to shore and got wrecked.

Davie said it wasn't worth our while being there, not for fishing, and we should go home. 'Oh come, Davie, let's take a look down on the beach,' I said.

'I'm going to follow the river. There's a bittern up there that I'd give anything to sight.'

'Well, never let it be said that I wasn't interested in birds. Even if it is blowy. Let's take a wee peep then.'

As we cut through the dunes beyond the river I spied a number of makeshift huts, where there were fires going and washing hung out to dry. A few Maori men and women and children were camped there. I did not wish to intrude, but I had to walk up the edge of the low valley formed by big, sprawling dunes, past their wee bothies.

I noticed, well above the breaker line, that there was a large, tidy creel boat hauled up and a net drying. The boat was in good order. They must have been fishing before it came up rough. Much to my surprise, someone hailed me, a stranger – surely? It was Billie, the odd Maori whom I had met beside the flooded river that memorable day. He stepped out towards me, a heavy man moving his legs in a fussy sort of strut. He still carried the plaid over his shoulders. How faded the tartan becomes in the fierce light of this land. As if the sun seeks to drain things of any foreign colour. He walked towards us and nodded towards an iron kettle hissing over the fire. 'Hello, boss, have some tea?' I told him I had come out here for some fishing, that I'd not realised how wild it was that day.

'Don't bother today, boss, the fishing's much better in three days – nothing doing today.'

'How is it you ken that?'

'Eh?'

'How do you ken – how it is that you know that the fishing will improve?'

'Maori fishing calendar – it tells us everything; it always works because it follows the moon. So we follow God's plan, boss.'

He blew his nose by closing one nostril at a time with his forefinger, the snot carried away on the wind.

'We come here every summer for fishing,' he said, nodding towards a dune that had been squared away with a shovel, creating a wind-sheltered area for a line, slung with fish and eels and some dead birds tied to it. I realised there were fires beneath the line for smoking the fish. 'So,' I thought, 'they have their smokies too.'

He took Davie and me to the far side of the dunes. Hauled out on the sand above the tide were two more large creel boats. There was a long sea-fishing net carefully draped over logs for drying.

'This was a good place for fishing. You have the river and the sea, always good. About 100 years ago a tribe allied to the great chief, Te Rauparaha, came this way. They had muskets. There were two battles. Many of our people died. Buried where they fell, back up the river.'

Then he looked at me, steadily. 'But you know about these things – you're a man with this knowing, I can tell.'

As we walked back to the bothies, I recognised the old man who was coming out of a hut but when he saw Billie and me he scowled and Billie quickly made his excuses. As we walked away Billie slipped a black stone with a sharp edge into my hand. 'Take this. This is from our old people. It's really a knife. There are many, many of them where we had our camps down here, but most of these tools have been buried by the sand. We used to trade for them across the sea in Nelson.' I pocketed the stone. My hand kept returning to it; it responded to my warmth. I kept the stone with me, even until now when I am ill.

Doug 4

Sometimes, just for fun, Garth and I would pelt rocks at the corrugated iron hut of Tom McDonald until he came flying out in singlet and cardigan to abuse us. We'd run away laughing hysterically. On a hot day near the Tutaenui Stream, we'd leave crawlies in the shoes of the tailor, Mr Beveridge, while he was swimming – a lovely old man with a fine sense of humour. We rode tandem bareback on horses, and fell off on gravel roads, leaving yards of skin behind. We would 'borrow' horses from the vacant paddock down the road, where they grazed while their riders took music lessons from the Badens. We had to ride them fast to get them back before the end of the lesson.

The gendarmes took a keen interest in blokes like Garth and me. 'I've got my eye on you boys,' McCarthy, the local bobby, a pale worried-looking man who never seemed to fit his uniform, would tell us. To him we were everywhere and always on the edge of trouble – lively boys not properly supervised, running wild round the place.

He accused me of putting tar on the ladies' seats in the public toilets. We were playing on our carts in Marton Park at the time. I knew who had done it. 'It wasn't me, true dinks, Constable McCarthy.' But I wasn't saying who, you didn't pimp on people. He also thought that Garth and I had stolen money from the Mission Box at St Peter's Church, where my mother cleaned. Again, although we were far from angels, we were not guilty, not on this count, although we must have looked it because we knew who had. We sang the Sunday School song, 'Hear the pennies dropping, listen while they fall, dropping, dropping, dropping, dropping, everyone for Jesus, he shall have them all.' But poor old Jesus did not have them all. Some of our pennies used to go into the Nestlé's penny dispenser outside the chemist. After the penny had fallen, a drawer slid open and a nicely wrapped chocolate bar was retrieved.

Sometimes Garth and I managed to stay out of trouble. We went calling around our neighbourhood on Guy Fawkes days. We took a guy in a cart, a rough body stuffed with sawdust and dressed in old clothes, with a hat and papier mâché mask. We woke folk early on the fifth of November and gathered a few pennies. We sang, 'Guy-Guy, stick him up high, leave him on a gate-post and there let him die.' Fireworks we bought from the Chinese fruiterers, the fruits neatly stacked with strange strings of dried things hanging above the oranges.

We knew Bin Hong, another of the locals. We delivered his produce, for a shilling a carton as well as a big carton of 'specs'. In the season Bin Hong was always asking us if we could find fungus for him – the earlobe native plants that grew on the side of lemonwoods and other native trees. 'You find, I give you half-crown – for one,' he told us. Sometimes we did, and we'd bike into the country too, to gather field mushrooms and sell them for a few shillings. We did alright.

Like all towns, Marton had its divisions. One was about religion, an attitude imported from the old country. My mother insisted that I never go out with Catholic girls. So of course, when I was older, I did. As kids we had rude rhymes for the Doolins about them being Catholic rats and Catholic dogs, that 'stink like frogs in their mothers' bathing togs'. Everyone said it. Kids love chanting out rhythms, especially so if they got on someone else's wick. It meant nothing. We usually had little to do with them, except on the rugby field, where I played at half-back.

But every once in a while the word would go out that there was a battle coming up with the Catholics and we would all troop off to Blainey's Hill, a sort of wasteland near an old quarry on the northern side of the town. Battle would commence, and battle it was. We used bows and arrows – tipped with nails, shanghais with small stones and a couple of Daisy air rifles. Adding to the atmosphere were the basket bombs, about two by four inches, in a basket case filled with gunpowder with a long wick-like fuse. You placed this inside an old benzine can, lit the fuse and threw the whole kit and caboodle high above the heads of the opposition. The roar was enough to rattle bones in the nearest cemetery, miles away. For some reason, no one was ever concussed. We would fight in earnest until one of us became really hurt, then a truce was called. One chap lost an eye in one of these incidents. But we did have no-go areas – you never kicked a man when he was down; in fact, once he was down, that was it, you left him alone. In those days it was a point of honour, practised the length and breadth of New Zealand.

When we stopped fighting a fire was lit. The older boys would dig out their packets of Wild Woodbines and light up. With wounds attended to, usually with saliva and a grubby handkerchief, we held a kind of feast, usually baked spuds cooked in the embers of the fire and we would be buddies – until next time.

The land around Marton was good and produced some wealthy farming types, most of whom knew how to wear their good fortune. I was about eight when I was greeted by a well-dressed woman who inquired, 'How is your mother, still begging, is she?' My widowed mother was quite proud; she worked hard cleaning the church as well as running her boarding-house. Later, she taught music. She didn't expect favours from anyone. She sometimes went out for the church on pastoral appeals. This woman's snobbery stung me with humiliation. I felt singled out and a smarting sense of injustice. On the way home, I kicked over a section of corrugated iron fence on Wellington Road. Someone saw me and for about two weeks I woke up feeling like a thundercloud, thinking that the police would be calling at our place looking for me. But I also began to notice that people like us had ways of dealing with people like her.

Charlie Marshall was one old character who showed me the way; a true pathfinder on a dark night was old Charlie. Some mornings, sleeping on the veranda, I would be awakened by him. He was the night-cart operator, so he rattled the four-gallon cans, exchanging a family's full one for an empty one. It was a comforting sound, that clanking of Charlie's on a sharp, frosty night.

Old Charlie used to get shickered and then go to the Salvation Army for a dry spell. The Sallies held a service in Broadway on shopping night. Above the quiet throb of the tuba and the warm notes of cornets echoing down Broadway you could hear Charlie's baritone proclaiming, 'I am no longer tempted by the demon booze, and am saved because I have found Jesus Christ.' The Sallies would follow him up with a selected item from their band designed to inspire conversion. Then a week or two later, he'd succumb again.

Charlie kept everyone in their place. The story went round about a snobby woman on the other side of town who was holding a bone china afternoon tea for her old biddy friends. For some reason, Charlie was doing his rounds at that time – maybe he'd had a night on the turps. It was a still summer's day. As he walked back down her front path, he turned and addressed the assembled ladies across a patch of prize dahlias through the open casement window: 'I've left a fresh can for you, Mrs Heggerty.'

There was a team of codgers in Marton like Charlie who kept the place on the straight and narrow more effectively than a host of Irish priests could ever have done. Mac Gibbons, Garth's old man, was another of the same school. He made his living from a milk delivery business. The entire family was involved. While they lived in town, they milked the cows on their dairy farm, within the county limits, and brought the milk to town by trap in galvanised tanks. Young Gibbons and one of his brothers or sisters would fill the billies from the tank by turning a brass spigot, then run into the houses and deliver a measure of milk to the customer's own container, left on the veranda. Should old bald-headed Mac take a dislike to a customer – and he was a man who made no bones about his contempt for snobs – Mac took his own special form of revenge, topping up the milk delivery with something warm of his own manufacture. Most people were very polite to him.

At the age of fourteen the pension that Mother received for me ceased. I quit school, having received six months' secondary education in the top year at primary school. I retained the morning paper round, and began a part-time job as message-boy and general dogsbody for Lewis & McLean, drapers in Broadway. McLean, who did not have a reputation for being over-generous, employed me full-time. For that I took his kids to school, and mowed the lawns at his house, as well as doing my deliveries. This and more was retrieved through 'extra postage' when dispatching parcels for out-of-town customers.

Before long I found myself at the Leckies. Andrew Leckie was a likeable Scot who deliberated before he made any judgment. He had a lovely lady wife, Jeanie, and three daughters of somewhat heavy build and curly dark hair. Mr Leckie originally worked for Stuarts, but became farm manager at Eccleston, just out of Marton. Here I had learnt to ride horses properly and care for them. Most of the cultivation of crops was done with a team of Clydesdales. I used to ride Andrew's hack and often tumbled from the saddle – no broken bones, but masses of bruises. Early in the 1930s Andrew moved to a farm of his own at Upper Tutaenui and it was here I acquired my first taste of farming as a rouse-about. I slept in a whare, some distance from the farmhouse proper but had my meals with the Leckies. Andrew brought me my first pair of long trousers, Palmer Knaps, strong, lasting work strides. And he was always telling me to eat all I could, as it was part of the deal. But it was only a few weeks before he had to let me go – the Depression meant that he simply could not afford to keep me, much as he might have wished to.

I still came back every Christmas for the harvest to work as a crowie on the stack, alongside Andrew, the stack builder. The crowie had to be reasonably strong, catching the sheaves of barley or wheat as they were tossed from a horse and cart.

He picked up the sheaf on his pitchfork, taking it full force – a bit of a test. I didn't drop many, because if you did, you put everyone out and the hands let you know about it for the rest of the day. Once you'd caught it, you presented the sheaf, butt towards the stacker, with its binding knot facing uppermost so he could take it.

I was paid 1s/3d an hour, some days working a ten-hour day. I would then cycle six to seven miles back home to Marton, completely knackered. But it was good money and great fun. When I think about it now, the best part was being accepted as a man by the rest of the team.

My mother was able to find me a job at a butcher's shop. His place on Broadway was lined with white and blue decorated tiles, with a concrete floor. I was to sweep up the sawdust at the end of the week and empty a clean sack over it each Monday. He showed me how to cut up the meat with cleavers on a large macrocarpa block. The deft blows and the saw cuts echoed round the tiled room, as if there were about six men working. The butcher's cheery voice boomed out over the crackle of brown wrapping paper, 'Och, it's bitter out there, Mrs Roberts, isn't it now? And that'll be just one and fourpence, thanking you kindly.' Mr Phillips the butcher offered me an apprenticeship, but I turned it down. After one week I came home, quite depressed – was this it, I wondered? 'Mother,' I told her, 'I can't stick it, I just cannot stomach the smell of raw meat.'

Alan 5

No matter what happened at home, there was always sunlight glinting on far-away distant hills, revealing the actions of how other people did things. There was the occasional visit from grandfather, the surviving one – my mother's father – granting us rare but precious times. He was not rich, not by any means, but he always came armed with gifts. A pair of clockwork Citroen racing cars, one blue, one red, chasing each other around a painted tin track, through a tunnel and over a hill, while overhead an aeroplane whirled on a wire. A fretwork set, a box of paints, a mechanical horse, a child's encyclopaedia. They were magical and from a far-away place. The nearest to it was the experience of Father Christmas's grotto in James Smith's, down in Wellington where he came from.

Granddad had eyebrows like a gorse hedge and a Gaelic gruffness and directness that protected the soul of a musician. We had no inkling of it for decades after his death, but when we finally got his war papers we found that he had been gassed three times and wounded twice on the Western Front. Neither my mother, nor any of her family, had had the faintest idea.

On his occasional visits he would tell stories about his homeland.

We would ask him for favourites: 'Tell us the one about gypsies.'

'Yes, gypsies they were, with their horses and carts, they were tinkers and pedlars – just like gypsies everywhere. They took the blame for whatever went wrong when they visited an area.

'Once, they came to our town. They stayed on the local domain. There was a girl who came to our house selling pearls. She was raggetty poor, with a yellow scarf over her head and bare feet – I do remember that. My father bought one for my mother.'

'Tell us the rest, Granddad.'

'Well, a long, long time ago, the doctors training at Edinburgh needed to have bodies to practise on. They would pay the gypsies to rob fresh bodies from new graves so that they could learn about surgery.

'They used to steal them from graveyards along the coast at night time. Sometimes the families would chase after them.'

He would take Barry and me to footie matches; we saw the 1956 Springboks play twice at Athletic Park in Wellington. It was cold and you had to get to the toilet before the game and then hold on, because you'd never get your place again. I was too big to sit on Granddad's shoulders, but Barry did. At the end, the insides of our mouths burnt by searing-hot pies, we sang with the crowd, the words printed in the programme, the South African traditional, 'Old Thorny Tree', and then our 'Now is the Hour', before reluctantly dispersing. We even had Springbok jokes; 'Danny Craven [the South African coach] went into a tobacconist's and asked for a packet of Craven A. The tobacconist took one look at him and said, "You don't want Craven A, Dr Craven, you want Players".' All Black winger Ron Jarden scored a famous try, dazzling but disallowed. I commemorated it in plaster of Paris packed wet into a commercial rubber mould and, when it dried, painted him in full stride in All Black jersey, shorts and boots, clutching the leather ball under his arm.

If Barry and I ever started bickering while he was on a visit, Granddad would provide instruction in boxing.

'Come on then, hit me in the midriff. Come on, hit as hard as you can,' he'd suddenly say, with his gentle burr.

'That's not a punch, put some oomph into it. Don't be afraid. If you don't get in first and hard, your opponent'll get on top of you.

'Right now, you can do better than that, don't be a namby-pamby. You'll be a man before you know it and you've got to be able to defend yourself.

'Come on, now, put up your fists and give it a real go. Oh, that's right, you're a southpaw, aren't you? You lead with your left. Okay, so that means left foot out in front – some of the best boxers have been southpaws. They can deliver a real surprise. But you need to strengthen your right.

'Keep moving your feet though; don't lock yourself to the floor – make your body weave – duck and dance. Hang on, you need to stand side on – more yet, more yet. You're much less of a target than if you are front on.

'Try to break through my defence. No, don't lower your guard while you do that, try to hit me hard.

'Come on, you'll never be able to defend yourself at this rate,' and he'd laugh.

I just didn't get it. I no more wished to hurt my grandfather than I did most other people. But it was clear from the lessons that the world out there was a place that a boy had to prepare for.

Once he took us to the boxing, for bantam to middle-weight amateur events staged at the Opera House. Sitting on its tippy upholstered seats we watched men in floppy silk shorts with bright sashes across their midriffs skipping around the floodlit ring trying to beat the daylights out of each other. Body hits were punctuated by a sharp out-rush of air dutifully amplified by the fine acoustics of the Opera House. 'Shhh-shhh-uh-shsh,' went the men as they pranced like foxies until the bell went for the end of a round. Each sat panting in his corner while his coach whispered to him, applying sponge and water. I wished I could hear what they said.

There were other sides to Grandfather, again which he never spoke of, perhaps because we were too young to inquire. When he first came to New Zealand he had surveyed forests on the West Coast for sawmillers. To live in bush camps in a lot of rain and cold required judgement, a canny understanding of our forest lands and of hard men. My mother remembers him being absent for long periods and of his returning home one evening with a beautiful bush orchid in flower that he asked my grandmother to save by planting it in a tree on the dark side of the house.

Best of all was when he took out his fiddle and with great feeling played the airs of his far-away home in Scotland, airs such as *Annie Laurie, My Love is like a red, red rose,* and *Comin' through the rye.* It brought forth an intimacy between the four of us, Mum, Barry and myself, that was unfamiliar to me. The violin sang as he pitched the bow, sometimes in sharp angles, across the catgut. It was a way in which a man might say things about himself that he could never say in words. Not then.

In the weekends my father, as did many men from that era and I suspect many before, went about his outdoor work whistling a lot, though not very tunefully. Whistling was about as close as that generation ever got to declaring themselves emotionally, and I now wonder whether it masked more than it revealed. Was it really a sign of cheerfulness? Or was it something you did with your mouth when you were emotionally preoccupied, when you didn't have a smoke in it? But when my grandfather, the violinist, played, you were taken to unspoken, uncharted parts of his life and which only his posthumous war record revealed: a sapper who served in Egypt, Ypres, the Somme and Passchendaele before he turned twenty-two.

When I hear live chamber music, of a romantic kind, it can still fill the air with the scent of his tobacco. One evening, it must have been fifteen years after his death, I came home late from work in Edinburgh. The landlady was out and as I warmed her prepared meal I put on Max Bruch's *Scottish Fantasia.* Without any awareness of its coming, like a thief in the night, grief from wells I did not recognise stole over me, possessing me. Music makes its own geometry, bisecting pinpoints of emotion previously unconnected in dark space, lighting them up with memory.

***

Most of the time, however, the gulf between the world of adults and the world of children seemed to be so vast that one had no idea of what it would take to span it. We were far too young to know that the most impenetrable opaqueness in the human mind may be completely cleared by an unconscious tweak on the most unlikely piece of thread – with unexpected deliverance opening like a silk parachute over calamity. In the same way, a word that had just been sitting unnoticed in the ether might get you there, a word so loaded with meaning, as you heard it for the very first time, it rang out like a gong in a hushed temple.

It was hardy, neglected Michael Collins, with black curly hair and a struggler's grin, who lived over the back of our place in a crumbling villa, who, first gave me such a word. Michael was a year or so older than me. We were playing in his yard, laid about with a great deal of what my father would call 'loot'. Corrugated iron, spouting, bits of spiked iron-railing fence, park benches – the stuff too good to ever take to the dump, kept for the day when a man could announce to his dubious wife, 'There we are, I told you – you never know when something's going to come in useful.' But in reality, nine parts of it was junk.

Amongst all this, Michael uncovered a rusty steel ladder of the type that used to be fitted to two-storeyed houses as a fire escape. He lifted it up, stood it on its hind legs and gazed knowingly up at its last rung. 'If I climbed up there,' he declared, 'I'd be in mid-air.'

The phrase was new to me. It was so inspiring of both vertigo and unlimited possibility I felt an immediate tingle in my insteps. I could barely contain myself. "Mid-air" – it was an idea as large as the universe itself, that took one's gaze to the traffic of cloud overhead and, beyond, to the deep blue mystery of sky. 'I'd be in mid-air – mid-air.' Cripes, I thought, or to use an adult term I'd just learnt, 'Struth'.

I was able to try out 'mid-air' a few days later on a staircase of wooden banana crates, stacked against a tall corrugated-iron fence about eight feet above a yard of nodding paspalum. That would get us close to mid-air. Surely? I wasn't quite sure. My friend Michael and I thought about it. We had tried tree climbing, but somehow, that didn't quite fit. Around at Richard Taylor's place, immediately behind the family grocery, there was this neat supply of banana boxes. We never quite could work out whether high on the stack was mid-air or not.

Richard's parents were always busy in the shop, so we were able to get on with things. On one occasion we'd decided to turn our banana-box airship into a mid-air barber's shop, with towels and scissors and Bay Rum, the ointment of manhood, borrowed from Richard's older brother's room. Our client was a tap dancer with hair that always flipped across his forehead, untidily, we thought, even though it was largely secured by lashings of Brilliantine. When he returned to his mother that evening, just days before he was about to appear in an important competition, my mother was a party to frantic phone calls.

'Oh, hello, Margaret, how are you?' That's my mother speaking.

'What, you don't mean to say? Oh, Margaret,' looking towards me as though I had just killed the cat, 'I am sorry, I didn't know a thing about this.'

'How much did they cut?'

'Oh, that's terrible. I'm so sorry. Terribly sorry. He's old enough to know better. I'll have to speak with him. I can assure you, Margaret,' she was glaring me down by now, 'it won't happen again.'

She tried not to show it, but I could sense a playfulness in the eyes that told me she was only holding up the adult end on this one because she was an adult. I got off lightly and the tap dancer made a full recovery, performing under cover of a beret.

One Saturday, when the boxes were still stacked up on the back fence, awaiting the pick-up lorry, we had a peep show from mid-air. Richard knew what was in store, but I had no idea. It was a summer's day and looking over the fence we could see tiny figures packed in a far-off grandstand. As we chatted and watched we could feel a faint drumming of the earth that grew louder, mounting in intensity the way a kettle drum builds up a roll for a march. Suddenly from out of nowhere the noise was thunderous as a group of brightly-coloured men, again in silks, standing up in the stirrups on their mounts, came hooping round the curve, the nags heaving and panting, the jockeys shouting, the earth trembling and chunks of turf flying off the pounding hooves in all directions. For us, just feet away, this was a stirring sight. A respectful distance behind the race, a buff-coloured Bedford ambulance brought up the rear.

About a minute after they'd passed there was a faraway collective roar that also grew in volume from the grandstand, and then suddenly stopped. It was like the sound from the swimming pool on a hot day, as I approached it most days in summer from a couple of blocks away. Except this wasn't continuous, like the noise from the pool with its spikes of whoops and yells and screams, this was a distant, slowly rising tumult of sound that at its very climax would suddenly stop.

In the late afternoon race as we watched, two racing horses collided and felled each other not far from where we were. They went down in a heap from which only one horse was able to emerge and stand, gingerly and riderless. The two riders slowly picked themselves up and the ambulance carried one jockey away. Shortly afterwards, a racing-green Morris sedan drove up and stopped behind the fallen horse. It was then we noticed that one of its legs was tucked unnaturally underneath its body. Two men got out of the Morris. One, a small fellow in a Homburg and a white coat, sucked on a cigarette. He examined the horse closely, the way my father, through his smoke, might look at a punctured bike tube. The other man helped him to move the animal's position, which seemed from its inertia and trembling, to be distressed – even we could tell that. He took another close look at the leg and went back to the car's trunk. Moving quickly, he pulled out something gleaming and thrilling – a rifle. He cocked it as he walked back to the horse. With the muzzle up at the animal's head, he fired. The horse jerked violently, kicked and died.

I wished I hadn't been watching, I really did. It was horrible – we had been privy to an execution. Blood from the wound poured thickly into the grass. A tractor with a digger came along to scoop out a hole under the long grass beside the fence, away from the track, but we didn't stay. We went back into the shop, where Richard's dad was hunched over a humming electric blade, slicing a ham in a muslin veil. Wafer slithers were falling in mounds onto a sheet of greaseproof paper. His mum was measuring dry goods into brown paper bags. She heard us out. Then she grabbed a scoop and a couple of cones and from the deep-freeze rolled us each a caramel ice cream, a double-header. It was hard to forget what had happened, though, and I didn't want to tell my mother – it was too awful.

Occasionally the adults' and children's worlds did merge voluntarily at some how-do-you-do of adults in which Barry and I might be present, the possibility of food having brought us inside. 'Looks like his father, doesn't he?' 'A chip off the old block, no doubt about it.' This I could never comprehend; I couldn't see any resemblance. But a grin was always called for at this instant. It was a brief moment of attention before inevitably chatter drifted back to the Cascade Bitter, the shandy and the potato chips. Then, while I was listening, I'd become aware of my father's laughter, maybe not malicious, but ill-timed, misplaced. He'd be quaking with suppressed mirth. Then I'd realise that he was looking at me. 'What is it?' I'd ask anxiously. 'What's so funny?'

'Just looking at those bloody great boats of yours, Alan. I'd never noticed how big-footed our son is.'

'Oh, Doug,' my mother would say. 'Leave the kid alone.'

'He's got a great grip on New Zealand,' some wag would put in. Jokes like these seemed to be in such short supply. I had noticed they were constantly dug out of the drawer for reuse and, like an old knife, never sharpened, never discarded.

'Doug, leave the poor kid alone, he's embarrassed enough for one day.' That's my mother speaking.

'I only take a seven and a half. I don't know where those plates of his come from.'

'Well, best if he doesn't take after his old man,' an uncle said, with a snigger.

'You never said a truer word,' my father would say grimly.

The trouble was that a kid could either be deferential, or he could be cheeky. I swung between the two, often having my father on, but mindful about the risks outside the home, as he would remind me.

'What about your stick-out ears?' I might venture, as a retort. 'No one's perfect.'.

'You mouth-almighty creature, show a bit of respect. That tongue of yours is going to get you into a lot of trouble. Just break it down, will you? Carry on like this and you'll end up on the scrap-heap. Learn some respect.'

A lot of the time, late childhood was like that. You were standing by a flooded river, waiting for the level to abate, so that you might find some way of getting across to a land of adulthood. You were always ready to cross, but when would you cross and what did you need to do it? It was the same for Barry. If he came in looking bedraggled, as often he did, he would be greeted by Dad's mirthful, 'Here's Harry from the Overflow. Man, you're a droopy-drawered looking thing.' Only, he took it all in his stride, did Barry, as if he knew that none of it meant anything.

Hector 5

My father had wanted me to be a flesher like him – someone to carry on the business. But I never liked it – not the killing of the beast, nor the dismembering of its parts and the removal of offal, its bone and flesh. Aye, I would accompany him to a roup gladly, I never minded the horses, cattle and sheep when they were on four legs – that was my life, after all. And I can still smell the straw and manure mixed with the smoke of the buyers leaning on the rail, watching the steamy rising of the breath and from the flanks of the animals when everyone came out for a sale. Luck sometimes favoured us; at displenishing sales and the like, we would often make good buys and, with the right pasturing, good profits. But we had our hard times too.

Slitting their throats, I never could do. It was men's work, the thing that men had to do, that was. And I hated it. There were some laddies that never seemed to mind. But my older brother, Sandy, whom I was closest to, he would put it off and put it off until the dogs were almost silly with meat hunger. He'd get more and more withdrawn – he'd never do it at the beginning of the day – and late afternoon he'd finally take out his knife with a deep sigh and sharpen it until he had an edge on it that could split a cigarette paper in two.

'Remember, laddie,' Sandy would always say, 'the sharper the blade, the more merciful the dispatch.' Then he'd move fast. He'd get the frightened, panting animal in the corner of the pen, flip it on its side and take the knife to its throat.

There was the awful spurt of blood as he'd force the knife through its vital cords. The animal would struggle, quiver, twitch and shake. Its eyes would go filmy – something went out in his eyes too – and he'd heft the body onto a bench to gut it, tearing out its insides, organs with the sheen of oil on them like coddled eggs, intestines that occasionally we kept for tripe and onions. He worked quickly, as if he hated it and needed to be finished as soon as possible.

The dogs'd be given the heart and bones to gnaw on, but most of the offal we buried. He'd take a cleaver to the neck and chest, skilfully tear the skin from the carcass the way a blotter comes away from a notepad and hang it by a hook in the back of the shed for a day to cure. Then he'd go to the house, get out of his bloody clothes and wash. Before he had his supper he'd toss back about three whiskys – usually he was not a drinking man.

All the way through he'd just mutter to himself, clacking his partial plate back and forth in his mouth saying, 'So there we are, so there we are,' as if speaking these words of consolation would undo what he felt was a crime against life. I noticed that of all of us, Sandy was the one who ate the smallest portions of meat. He preferred the mince – I think there was something less fleshy about its consistency and taste.

I was the youngest of nine and Sandy had already been working at my father's trade some years before me in Laurencekirk, a town that had been given its Royal decree to be a marketplace in 1780. This was before my father moved the family to settle on land near to Fettercairn, across the wide valley, to farm cattle.

As a large family, when it came to sleeping it was a top-and-tail affair, common enough in those days. But my father was a good trader and never saw us short of meat or bread. My mother always had a pot of claik steaming on the stove. Mother, she never really got away from the cooking. Ours was a good home. There was never cheek, no scoffing round the place – always plenty of cleating to be done. Bairns did as they were bid. On a Saturday night we younger ones were all scrubbed up in the tin bath ready for kirk on Sunday.

Mother was gifted with the second sight. Anything within the family she always knew, sometimes before it

98

happened. If it came to death in the family, she knew of the passing of aunts and uncles, some who lived away over in Edinburgh. She never needed to be stern with us because she knew always what was up, whether we told her or not. There was nae point in not speaking the truth. One day down the Luther in a hot summer, we bairns were fooling around. The water was always cool, but some of us got in. The other boys climbed up on the bank among the trees. They got silly and starting heaving sticks at us.

James Martin got a bit of branch in his eye and starting screaming. His eye was bleeding and we all got very scared. He had blood dripping down the front of his grey serge shirt. Some boys ran off home. The rest of us decided to take him straight up to Dr Kenna's, up near the close behind the kirk. The doctor said he would need to go to Montrose infirmary and he was taken over there in a taxi-trap. Hamish Buchan went with him and told us everything next day. 'He was propped up on pillows, covered in a thick blanket, with a bottle of sweeties beside him. His ma was terribly calm and pale sitting beside him. He wouldna tell what happened – they tried to make him, but he wouldna say.'

James later made a full recovery. But when I came home that night my mother met me at the kitchen door and straight off asked me if I was alright and what had happened to James' eye. She had known before I reached the house. I remember it because in my experience this was out of the ordinary, her knowing about someone outside the family. She would always ken when it was one of us in trouble, quick as a wink, but she seldom let on that she also had second sight for the plight of others. She made light of it, patted me on the head and gave me a drink of chocolate.

The work I most detested – and so did my brothers – was mucking out. We had to help with this from an early age. From the byres, the stables, the sties and the hen-houses there was much shovelling out to be done amid the reek of dung. It was so strong when the dung was fresh that it set your nose and lungs to protest. Of course that was just the start – we then had months of dunging on the fields and ribbing out, then drilling for turnip and potato. This was always a smelly task, but it was also hard and heavy work. We mixed it with lime from the kiln and spread it off the back of a sledge. Being late winter, it was always cold, often raining, and nothing we wore kept out the rain or the cold. By day's end we were sottled and frozen. All you could do was go at it with determined good cheer.

There was no way out of it. As I grew older I decided that I would be a ploughman. Ploughmen didn't dung and they didn't usually have to kill. My father said it was a good trade. 'You'll never be short of work,' he said. So I worked hard at my ploughing. I was fortunate to learn from old Ross, a hook-nosed, hardy runt of a man who had himself been a ploughman since the 1840s. He was a friend of my father's and had often worked our cropland with his two horses, both Aberdeen Clydesdales, standing about sixteen hands – big horses, good ploughing horses with plenty of power and stamina. He loved his horses – that was plain to see – he was tender with them.

'Always talk to your horses, Hector, never neglect them – they are your livelihood. It's only through them that you'll get on and get work – that and your skills.'

Out in the front paddock he showed me what he meant.

'It's a point of pride to make a good top on the furrow, Hector,' he began. 'As you plough you make as much soil available as you can on the ridges, so that when you sow your grain it falls in between your furrows.'

He called out to his horses. 'See, running behind you, you have that chain working off your swingletree, which runs in the bottom of that seam, between your furrows, so that you haven't a gap going right down. This is important, Hector. It means that your grain won't be lost and that chain pulling along behind makes a little bed for it.'

He stopped and went over to his furrow, turning the dirt over in his fingers.

'It falls down there, the seed, then you harrow your ridges across the way and level them off. That means your seed is covered to prevent the crows and ravens from picking it up.'

Ross taught me how use the wheel to regulate the depth. You loosened off the studs and pulled the wheel up to go deeper into the ground. If you wanted it shallower, you pulled it further down. The wheel also helped to stabilise and steady the plough.

Ross had learnt to use wooden ploughs and even wooden boards, but the smiddies in the Mearns had developed steel ploughs to deal with the heavy Mearn soils. Over time I made myself into a useful ploughman, good enough to be in demand. And I began to dream of having my own farm.

I do remember one occasion; it was a bleak November day after weeks of hail and sleet. Father had brought me in to help with the dunging. We were hard at it, dunging the north paddock, where there'd been a copse of trees that we'd taken out a year or two earlier. The rain was coming in icy from the east and there was a scattering of snow on the ground. I was driving the sledge quite fast when I spied a new mole-hole. The corner of the sledge caught on a tree root and the whole thing rose up and deposited most of the manure in a paddock that had already been dressed. Father was fair reeking:

'You ningcompoop, what in God's name do ye think you're doing? Is this the best that Ross can teach you?' He spluttered and muttered something about a beating.

'Father,' I replied quietly, 'if ye do try, I'm off. I never have to stay here. I'm helping you on your farm and I'll not take any more of this.'

'You'll do what I tell ye to do. You're my son.'

I paused. I'd seldom defied him before. 'Nae, Father. The train comes through Montrose twice a day and I can just buy my ticket and go to work at some other place. It can be far-off.'

He was beside himself. I thought he would explode. His face went red, and I detected a pulse in his eye. 'What do you mean? Look here, boy, a son's place is with his father. It's nae the son who decides these things.'

'But what about the others – what, two of them in Canada, James in Cape Town, John at the salmon cannery in California? No one said they weren't to go.'

'Exactly – we've let them go, like good parents. Let them choose and where does that leave us? Nine children we've brought to adulthood, your mother and I, and apart from Sandy, Jeannie and you, they've all flown the coop. Who's to look after us in our old age?'

But I was angry too and he could see it. No son had ever spoken to him like this before. Sandy was there, hanging onto his shovel, his eyes wide with his hat tipped back, watching in amazement, beside a heap of fence stones. Sandy shot me a grin afterwards, but he never said a thing about it and the snorl was never mentioned again.

I'd been considering going abroad, though, for some time now. It was a big step, to leave the place of your birth and the familiarity of your family and friends, but I was restless. Besides, there was only so much humbug a man could put up with. Everyone in the village, except for Mr Crombie the lawyer, who was said to be an atheist, was either Presbyterian or Church of England. For us, being Presbyterian was part of being Scots, of being independent from the Sassenachs. There were things about that kirk that I never liked, like the cutty-stool, upon which miscreants were seated while their misdeeds were hurled back upon them by the stern elders. It never mattered who was setting up there – and it was worse when it was an older person – I hated it and felt keenly the sense of humiliation it imposed. I'm certain most other folk did too.

My friend Andrew McKinley found himself there once. He had been caught blaspheming one night – he was in a close where a horse had thrown him as he hurried to get to a meeting at the manse. But one of the elders, who was also running late, came upon him and heard his language. He turned on him, all hoity-toity, telling him, 'Andrew

McKinley, if Satan himself is nae dancin' noo, laddie, I'm certain he will be by dawn.' A poe-faced, sanctimonious Presbyterian, God help us, there's nothing worse. I'd sooner face the devil himself than that. McKinley withstood the wrath at the cutty-stool. He said he never wanted to attend kirk again – he would nae say any other thing about it.

The kirk saw it as its business to deal with other matters – matters of adultery and so on – and, as happened with one of our number in the village, a child born out of wedlock, a terrible thing, mind you. And what a to-do there was. But plenty of people married once the woman was well and truly pregnant, no one murmured about that.

There was no work on the Sabbath, that was God's day. The whole of Scotland from John O'Groats to the Borders, was quiet as a mouse. The wharves were quiet too. They were rough men, those fishers, but no fisher would come in or put out to sea at Ferryden while there was still breath in the Sabbath. But so as not to miss out entirely, if you happened to be looking, you might see them, just after Sunday midnight, a line of wee lights headed out to sea. Scotland was strict, make no mistake, much stricter than England.

One night I noticed a glow in the kirk hall. I'd nothing better to do and slipped in to the back to see what was happening. A big moon-faced man in a suit, a blue ribbon pinned to a lapel, was speaking of the evils of alcohol. I didn't warm to him, but I was rooted to the spot. Most of the audience were women and young boys, setting there, the boys all a-figit, prodding one another and pinching and skylarking. He was a great preacher, this man; he had all the fire of John Knox. 'Drink,' he was a-thundering, 'is the devil's own handiwork, destroying homes and the lives of young children. It is drink that gnaws at the vitals of all that is precious in this land: thrift, constancy and faith.' He showed lantern slides. One of them was of a heap of liquor bottles piled up outside a hall after a ceilidh, not far from here, he said, airily – I certainly couldn't recognise the hall. 'Each bottle emptied represents a lost soul to God,' he told us. 'It may not happen on the first drink, or the second. But liquor transforms a man into something bestial, degrades him utterly. Its temporary comfort is a delusion that gives him a false idea of himself. Robbery, rape, fisticuffs and murder are its consequences. Drink is the ruination of family and of decency and self-respect.'

His hope of prohibition seemed a faint one, when we all knew that Scotland was a land with a public house on every corner and a distillery at every burn. Most men like their drop. At Laurencekirk they had a Young Men's Mutual Improvement Society. They wanted me to join, but it nae appealed. There was too much stinginess, too much blether about evil and moral improvement. It made good people so stern and frightened of what their neighbours thought; their fear sat like a ramgumshoch over the great spirit of Scotland. With all this humbug, I was getting more than acquainted with the idea of leaving.

The places where older members of my family had already emigrated in the New World, I never wanted to fetch up in. It just didn't appeal. I'd written to my cousins, the Carnegies from St Cyrus and Marykirk, from my ma's family. Some of them were out in Queensland. Ma's younger sister, Mary, had returned home from Australia, a right chatterbox, that one. She spoke of a big land, endless sunshine and plenty of chances. If I found it too hot – and many Scots moved on for the same reason – I could always go to New Zealand, just a few days' sailing away. Cousins returning for a visit to Scotland said the Hendersons, who'd run a mill near Montrose, were doing very well in the town of Marton. It was around here that a grand community of Scots had grown up – Hendersons, Campbells, Stirlings, Marshalls, Camerons, Stuarts, Grants. They were still clannish, some still spoke Gaelic and they conducted their services in the tongue. I didn't have the tongue, being a Lowlander, but still, it did a man's heart good to hear it. I could always find work there, they had said.

I think that being the youngest, you're the one who collects all the love that the family has. It's like the top of the cream can – all the good stuff is just there. Somehow you're freer – the love sets you free from the path of duty that the older ones take, even though you're the one who's given so much. In some ways, though, ye never know your parents the way the older ones do. There are too many relationships, too many faces – too much water under the bridge – before you appear belatedly in the family portrait. But the older ones have the advantage that they can head away to a new country, without so much as a backward glance, knowing younger members of the family are still at home.

There were few family photographs – they were an expensive luxury. But as a young child I would gaze for hours at what we had, perplexed at the possibility, the effrontery of it, of a family life before I came along.

As I look back, there were several particular events that led to my departure from Scotland. The first occurred when I was perhaps ten, although its effects on me were to endure. It was a misty morning that had brought news of a shipping accident in Montrose Harbour. Two boats had collided during the night, in bad weather, not far from the harbour mouth. One was a passenger ship bound for Antwerp and about a dozen men were drowned in the icy waters before the lifeboat could head out and rescue survivors. That afternoon, a carriage with her ladyship from up at the Big House had rattled past where we lads were digging at some ruins near Marykirk. When it had gone, I noticed a silver horn from the head of one of the decorative harnesses had come right away and was lying on the ground. I picked it up and took it home.

My father took one look and said I should return it immediately. 'It's never your property – it belongs up at the Laird's. You get it back to him without ado, double-quick-smart now, laddie.' I went back that evening to the big house into the pulices up a long drive through the trees. I went for the game-keeper's house in the kennels. Knowing his son, Andrew, I asked for him. He was pleased to see me. 'Ah, yes, that'd be from our stables. It's uncommonly good of you to return it. Would ye want to take a walk?' he said. 'It's nae quite dark yet and there are peacocks and, over the far corner, some Japanese deer that you might like to see. I'll be sure that this gets returned to her ladyship.'

We went across a lawn towards the peacocks. As we did, we had to pass a corner of the great house, three and four storeys tall, proud and grand as a castle. It was all lit up and there were beautifully dressed ladies and gentlemen chatting over their drinks in the lounge. It was like a scene in a painting. I looked into the empty dining room. Silverware glittered on the starched white tablecloths, light danced off mirrors and silver-mounted candles. Big paintings of hunting scenes in gilt frames hung from the walls. There were wine glasses and flowers set out on the tables and many settings of cutlery. As we passed, a dressed piper stepped into view, piping the ladies and gentlemen from the next room into dinner.

I remember thinking, 'There's been this terrible accident. Folks are dead, lying in their shrouds on the stone over at the morgue and they are just carrying on, as though it's nae happened.' It seemed they were people who stepped through life shielded from its horrors, never getting even their feet wet. Others did all their donkey work while they just enjoyed life, even when there was disaster in their midst. It was something I didn't understand.

You never could blame working lads for an accident like that. As I grew older I realised there were terrible goings-on for working people and I began to feel that it was the toffs were responsible for this. On a Saturday afternoon off I'd talk with the fishermen of Ferryden, at the port of Montrose, outside their bothies at the wharf as they cleaned their catches, their wives' washing flapping and cracking over the water in the westerly. They sold fresh, plump herring for a few pence, a smokie for an extra ha'penny.

Shortly after the SS *Chancellor* foundered and went down in the port it became a problem. But the port board would never do a thing about it. Its bones lay in the harbour, a hazard to any sizeable ship entering. I went calling on the Ferrydenners just after. 'They're puttin' the lives of sailors in real jeopardy, but they dinna care,' one of the old Ferrydenners told me, tossing the guts of a fish out into the tide. 'There is great unrest breedin' on the wharves and in the big mills of Glasgow, Dundee, Edinburgh and Aberdeen – and the powers that be will need to deal with it, not just sit on it and try to crush it with their overfed behinds.'

I had never before heard talk like that. But it made sense. This man was a scrawny individual, narrow-faced, prominent nose, with two fingers missing from his right hand; he wore a blue cloth cap and a heavy tweed coat. I'd never seen him before. Nor did I ever see him again. When he spoke he sounded as if he were angry and his accent was strange, as though he'd lived away from Scotland for a long while. He said he was a Worker of the World and that he believed in violent revolution.

'How will it turn out, do you think?' I asked him. 'You don't think the working people of Scotland will take part in revolution?'

'Have you read the newspapers? Those mining accidents tell of what's going on in Scotland. The Scots and English owners dinna care what happens to the men who go down the pits. The same in France. They rescued thirteen from the Courrieres mine, being trapped there in the dark and terror of it all for three weeks. It was an explosion. They'd eaten bark off the timber props and in the end they'd eaten from the bodies of some of their mates who'd died. Think of that! But men are injured and maimed every month down the mines simply because the owners don't give a tuppenny for the workers and their skins. Never let anyone tell you, laddie, that slavery's been abolished.

'All over the world ordinary working people are standing up for their dues and if we can stand together, we can make a change. The world – mark you,' and he almost stabbed my face with his finger, 'will be a very different place in a few years' time. The people will control it – America, Great Britain, France, Spain – you name it. Capitalism's just a fancy word for tyranny.'

I was full of this when I came home to dinner. My father didn't want to hear. 'This is none of our business,' he said, bringing the palm of his hand down on the table. 'We're farming people now. You keep away from the port, do you hear me? Those men are nothing but troublemakers, who wouldn't ever have known a day's work. There's too many agitators down there. Keep away, do you hear?'

I could see he was getting fussed and I realised that I'd gone too far in raising the matter. In the family his word was law; he wasn't used to debating a subject with his own sons. I began to wonder if that wasn't why he had lost so many of his family abroad. 'But, Father, you canna ignore this, it's part of a world-wide movement of workin' people.'

'My goodness, what on earth is happening to you?' He twisted his fork in his hand. 'Where do you get these ideas from, you're a man of the land? To think of a son of mine taking up these Godless creeds. What makes you think you know about the lives of these people? Most of them, if you gave them a proper income, would fritter it away on frivolous things and be no better off. People have their place and it's best if they know it, and not get ideas about themselves. We have a duty to the poor, but that doesn't mean we have to get caught up in their revolutionary antics. Now, that's enough. I have said my piece and that's an end to it. I want to no more of this claptrap.'

'Father, have you forgotten your Robbie Burns – Burns was no revolutionary. But people love him for the beauty of his words and because he is the poet of the common man. He's a humanitarian.

"See yonder poor, o'er laboured wight
…And see his lordly *fellow-worm*
The poor petition spurn,"

108

'Don't bring Burns into this,' he interrupted, 'I know my Burns – I introduced you to him. He is a man of a different cast. Poets must speak of these things, but it's not your job.' He was angry now.

'What we are talking about are organised spoilers, people who want to destroy society. Give them half a chance and they'll destroy everything that's been built.'

An article appeared in *The Review*, which the library held, saying Australians ate more per capita than any other people in the world, and actually did less work for it. It sounded from my cousins' letters from afar as though a man who wanted to work could get on well there – maybe even gets some land of his own. Aye, there were black-suited clerics frowning down from their pulpits like startled crows in Australia too, I had no doubt. But not too many of them. In the end, though, I plumped for New Zealand – better for its cooler climate.

As it turned out the harvest of 1905 was a particularly good one and everyone in the Mearns seemed to have a few extra coins in their pockets; not that the folk of Aberdeenshire and Kincardineshire would want to tell you that. But I noticed a few more were spending time propping up the bar at the Crown. The cartloads of tatties, of turnips and corn that came out of the fields that autumn were like no one had ever kent before. I kept a clipping: 'Not for so many years have we had such a favourable seed time.' That year my father did so well, he bought mother a new cooker. He talked of an inside water-closet, because getting out to the wee housie on a stiff winter's night was telling in their bones.

Although more money was coming into the country towns, I really couldn't see things changing. The more I thought about it, the more I couldn't see the rightness in what was happening. Some folks prospered, others continued to suffer. Just before I left, I read in the newspaper a sermon the Rev Michael Scott had given at Willy Mitchell's funeral, entitled 'Moral Nonentities and Spiritual Blanks'. This was a time when sermons were often carried by the dailies. I cut it out and kept it in my wallet. I liked the way he talked of well-to-do people who lived lives so self-interested, they never gave any thought to the lot of their fellow men. Did I really think it would be different in a new country? Yes, I did. So if I swithered about leaving, it was not for long.

But there's always guilt in emigrating. The songs of the old country haunt you all your life. For all the excitement of making a new start, I've nae heard a really good song about coming to a new country. If they exist they're never so memorable as those about leaving. Well, the sad songs are usually the best songs anyway. I believe that's why folk who came out a generation or so before me – when there was no going back, except for the wealthy few – why it was that they wanted so little of their traditions. They did keep what they called their Highland Games going, though I'd never seen the like of it in Scotland. For many of them, the ones who stayed away, there was too much sorrow in a backward glance.

I sailed for New Zealand on a chill autumn day in 1906 – I was a ploughman of twenty-five years of age when I finally answered the call. The hope in my heart was only a little shaded by the leave-taking of my kith and kin. I can see my folks at the station for the farewell. My ship sailed from Glasgow, for Southampton. My mother and father were in their 60s by then, my ma not tall, but a woman of bearing with those dark seeing eyes of hers, her still-dark hair in a bun. My father, tall for those days, a stern, decent man in his navy suit, watch-chain and boots. Sure, he could be contumacious and he'd given me a few hidings – with the razor strop. But nothing like the hidings he'd delivered to my older brothers. These were punishments, so they told me, that left them yelping, bruised for days under their kilts, even when they were pushing on to be young men with hair on their chins to shave.

I recalled one time the minister spoke from the pulpit on the importance of punishment in the family. I can remember my father turning his hands over in the pew and looking most uncomfortable when he spoke of this as a sacred duty. 'One that must be tempered with kindness and objectivity,' he'd said.

'Our Lord is merciful, our Lord is just. It is behoven on those of us with the sacred task of parenthood that when our children stray from the pathway of righteousness – that narrow pathway Christ spoke of so plainly – that we ourselves do not part from that path. When a child's behaviour demands a rebuke, be stern but never berate the child. When a child needs a taste of the switch, let the switch be wielded, not with anger, but with mercy. Never beat a child in anger. Just as the soft word turneth away wrath, so find the soft word in your own wrath before you rebuke the child.'

Although I felt a tenderness for my parents – don't mistake my meaning – I was impatient to seek a new life. I looked at the two of them, comforting each other on that chilly platform, hunched against the infernal cold. What did I know about them, these people who'd brought me into the world, brought me safely to be a man and were now, in old age, biding me goodbye, to fade into strangerhood, perhaps forever?

Mother I kent: wise, stern and compassionate, keeping a household going with its endless washing and drying in that Kincardineshire weather, a hoist above the cooker, she and the girls cleaning and cooking. Fingers to the bone. I nae think I ever saw her cry – except when my father would take down his fiddle and call up the songs of the old people. He knew hundreds of tunes for those long winter nights. She seldom rested, but my older sister, Jeannie, who never married, took the strain as mother became an older woman. It was they who scrubbed and cooked and cleaned in that kitchen.

For my father, it was work and duty mostly that kept him going. Although there was a gentleness in him, even a playfulness, that you could see in his eye when he got on the pipes or he danced at a ceilidh, he never let up on himself. So he never let up on us.

111

'Work is the soul o' man,' he'd quote as we closed the yard on cattle we had rounded up for the market at the end of a long day. Work was a virtue in itself, a tower in the landscape that threw its shadow over all of Kincardineshire, for all I knew maybe all of Scotland. Inside the head of the tower was a clock, its name was duty. My father never took his eyes off it – it was probably another of those inventions of religion, but it had become more powerful than faith itself. It never let him be at ease; it got him up at dawn and he rested little until his head touched the pillow at night. All most men in the district would want on their epitaph was, 'Here lies … he led a blameless life'. Free from accusation. They toiled and they paid their taxes for the poor, knowing that this would mean no beggars in their village. There had been, a generation before – registered by the shire and wearing a brass dog-tag. There were plenty of tinkers still on the roads, being a nuisance, but that was their choice and they never starved.

Doug 5

I was lucky, I think I've always been lucky – I've never had any money, but I've been lucky alright. I've made the most of my nine lives, and then some. In the midst of the Depression I landed a job at Marton Engineering. But soon I discovered why no one had wanted the job. Luck always has its price. The boss was Mac Lewis, a former blacksmith. He was a self-taught mechanical engineer and a clever bloke who could turn his hand to any automotive or engineering problem. I can see now, I was lacking in concentration – a real grasshopper – a fifteen-year-old who failed to use his god-given brains to their best advantage. Lewis used to tell me all the time, 'What's wrong with you, Roberts, is your head there simply to keep your big ears apart?'

He was a thin man, gaunt, with veins that stood out on his white arms, shoulders and legs and he was prone to chest ailments. He was at me from day one. 'Bugger and blast, you bloody…. you're nothing but a bloody idiot,' he swore at me, when I broke a screw housing. 'When God gave out brains, where the hell were you?' I'd never struck this before. The men I knew rarely swore at anyone, even themselves – even the rogues, given half a chance, you could usually get to like.

My pay was fifteen shillings a week, rising to twenty-two shillings in the second year. I got a shilling an hour for overtime. I supplied my overalls, did my own washing. There were no annual holidays, just six public holidays a year. No unions, no smoko breaks and no facilities for tea. The boss retired to his house at the rear of the workshops for a cuppa. The best his journeyman, Newman and I could do was a go-slow at those times. Otherwise it was full steam ahead all day, without a breather.

At the beginning of each day I barrowed in half a dozen loads of coal for the boiler – to keep water and fire up to it all day. Coal is heavy stuff to move, it was hard yakker. A small Tangee steam engine supplied the power to a line shaft, which in turn drove a lathe, drill press, milling machine and electric generator. We had a power hacksaw too. Hot water was drawn from the boiler into a kero tin. We washed with a piece of home-made soap and dried off on a sugar sack for a towel. It wasn't a place for airs and graces. Proper toilet paper was a rare luxury.

I swept the concrete floor of the workshop, served petrol at the hand-operated bowser, sometimes mending a puncture. I was so much at the beck and call of the boss and the journeyman, with a four-inch paint brush shoved up my rear end I could have painted the walls of the workshop as I went. This meant the boiler either had too much fire or insufficient water and so the safety valve frequently blew its head. Alternatively, too much water and a low fire produced a lack of power from the steam engine. It rumbled away in the workshop like your stomach did after an iffy meal and there were always complaints from the boss. Come to think of it, temperamentally the old Tangee was rather like the boss.

Lewis was a goat rider, a Freemason. He was also one of those guys who had to have a whipping boy. I could never win. Every morning, it would be the same. 'The fire in the boiler's too hot, bring it down,' or 'The fire's too low, bring it up. How many times do I bloody well have to tell you?' Then he'd summon a hoik from his throat, one of his green spittles, solid as a marble, projecting it right into a galvanised bucket where it would stick with a clunk to the sides before oozing to the bottom.

One time we needed to manoeuvre a large piece of equipment onto a truck. Instead of using the block and tackle, as we should have, we tried to load it by hand. The metal was still hot from our work on it and it was awkward, but we got it to a point of balance on the truck when the leading hand and I let it go. The boss was a bit slow. One of his hands caught between the load and the side of the truck and he squealed like a pig. He turned in fury on me. 'You bloody useless little prick, you did that deliberately. You wait till I get my hands on you.' The next day he turned up and moped about, bandaged hand in a sling. Every inquiry as to his health from customers was met by a grim accusation. 'That young bastard dropped a load on my hand.' Finally I summoned the courage to speak: 'Lewis, your luck was out yesterday, you were too slow to jump and you know it. Take your punishment like a man.' He scowled at me – I thought he'd sack me on the spot. But he didn't.

There wasn't even a bottle of antiseptic on the premises, and no first aid. If you cut yourself, to the tendon as I did on more than one occasion, he'd say, 'You'll be okay, just wrap a rag around it.' Fortunately, I had been a cadet in the Zambucks, so I had a smattering of first aid.

Once I had to climb inside the firebox of a traction engine to cut out six defective boiler tubes with a handful of saw blades and a bundle of cotton waste for a handle. The tubes were flared, tulip-shaped, at either end of their housings. Once the tulips were cut with a series of Vs, the tubes could be driven from the boiler. What would have been a twenty-minute job with oxyacetylene took me three days in there – it was cheaper to use me than hire equipment. This experience left me with a ringing in my ears for days. It was no use complaining. Jobs were hard to come by and a kid like me was one of thousands.

When a motor grader with a broken back came in for repair I had to cut a scarf either side of the cracked support. The journeyman applied an electric arc weld. I then attacked the scarf on the opposite side while the welding got underway. We used sacks to cut down the glare from the arc. But that night I woke with the feeling that handfuls of sand were being ground into my eyes. Bathing with cold water had no effect – I had arc eye, which blinded me for two days.

The worst day for this young apprentice was when an excavator bucket came in, its lip worn along the cutting edge. We forged a new lip using weld and hot-riveted it to the bucket. To do this, the apprentice (me) had to lie on his back with his head and shoulders in the bucket, holding the dolly to the head of the red hot rivet while the guy on top hammered the top side tight. What a racket! The noise felt as though it was going off inside my head. I was protected from heat by sacks, but soon hot scale from the rivets showered down, setting the sacks alight, smouldering flakes getting down my shirt. The other blokes thought it was a bit of a laugh: 'Look at Doug, doing a bit of burning off, are you, Doug? Get rid of those nasty warts.' 'What's wrong with you, got ants in your pants?' That kind of thing. They were jokes I failed to share – I carried those scars for years.

I spent nearly three years at Marton Engineering Works. I gained a smattering in the rudiments of blacksmithing, automotive and tractor repair work: valve grinding, brake relining – that sort of thing. But the day came when Mac Lewis said one day, 'Boy, work is drying up. You'd better find another job.' We had both had a gutsful. Lew was keen to see my shadow vanish forever from his doorway and I was ready to go. Happily, it was 1936, there was a new Labour Government and the world was emerging from the Depression. The following week I signed on at the local Ford franchise holder, where the atmosphere was great and the workshop training a far cry from that of my first full-time employment.

Alan 6

Roaming at Koitiata

To the south of the beach settlement at Koitiata lay the iron framed *Fusilier*. It had been caught in a big storm that drove her ashore back in the 1880s. Such are the furies of that coast, within a few decades her picked and plundered hull was lying broadside to the shore inside a line of sandhills well back up the beach. The coastline had advanced that far.

After talking about it for months, Maurice and I, two ten-year-olds with far too much energy, made the pilgrimage. It was a warm summer's day with the inevitable breeze coming off the sea. We took sandwiches, an energy pack in the form of a massive chunk of fruitcake from the previous Christmas, a can of baked beans and, since there was a surplus, a plastic bag of plums and some nectarines. It was not, as I recall, a fart-free journey. Carried like that, the fruit became a kind of puree. The beach sands were hard, the sand dunes hot and soft, and after several hours it seemed we would still have to walk for miles and miles. We crossed the Ohakea bombing range where the litter from what the jets did when they screamed and swooped, flexing like a hand on the wrist of the sky, was everywhere. Shrapnel and mortar cases lay in rucks of sand like traces of the broken seabirds' eggs we came across in the dunes.

At times, when the beach became too monotonous, we climbed back into the dunes. Maurice seemed to know things about the area that no one else knew. 'You know you get Sambar deer around here. They're really big, but shy and hard to hunt.' We looked for signs of them but instead came across a piece of nature's uncanny enchantment. Standing in the folds of the dunes amid low trees was a small lake of clear water, from which our noisy arrival discharged a family of fleeing ducks. Dragonflies hovered overhead, the lake encircled by verdant vegetation – Ngaio trees, flaxes, toetoe and rushers – and as I crouched down I saw the Golden Sand Sphinx caterpillar feeding on the convolvulus. It seemed a miracle that sand was holding water like that, but I was later to learn about dune lakes, this scenic gift in an apparently unrelenting sandscape. In the right conditions iron sand fuses into an impermeable bottom that holds water, as long as there is no disruption from earthquakes.

Further up the beach we came upon a fishermen's home-built, low-slung dune jalopy, an iron-framed, four-wheeler with a stripped down engine and two seats bolted on. No sign of a fisherman or a surfcasting rod, but footprints led over a high dune. We followed them and from the top looked down into waving marram and more lines of dunes. Not far below us there was a movement and among the marrams we could see two naked bodies, wrestling. There was a man on top of a woman. We could see his bald arse moving up and down on her while underneath she seemed to cry out in pain. The man's shoulders were matted in black hair, and while what he was doing seemed brutal and unnatural, her arms were wrapped around his shoulders in an embrace – there was something odd going on here. I was horrified. One of those adult words that you dared not ask about, that you often saw on the front page of *Truth*, came immediately to mind: 'Rape'. Maurice spoke urgently. 'Let's get out of here, we'll be in trouble if they see us.'

'But what about that lady, she needs help, doesn't she?'

He looked at me, his brown eyes filled with a mixture of contempt and pity. 'That lady, that's Mrs Jacobs from the corner, can't you tell by her red permed hair? Bloody hell – don't you know how babies are made? They're having a naughty.'

His words were a large key to a lock that I had dared not turn, had possibly even bolted against myself, that suddenly opened another door on the adult world – the secrets of the bedroom, babies, moonlight and roses. Almost all pop songs spoke of it. We were all in this together, no getting away from it. As we trudged over the sand dunes a song of the time ran through my head: 'and the same thing happens with the birds and the bees, as they flit among the flowers, as they nestle in the trees...' Everything made sense, but the coarseness of the scene we had witnessed was disturbing.

The distance to the wreck was almost too far for us. We ensured that most of our lunch was gone by 11 o'clock. We'd have to live off the fruit purée, warming and getting softer in a plastic bag, for survival. The ship's boiler stack, which we had presumed to be a mast (it had been both sail- and coal-powered) began to poke up on the distant curving horizon of beach. It was widely held that the stack had long been the target of RNZAF bombers from Ohakea air base. But so much had the shoreline changed in the previous seventy years that had this landmark not been standing, we would have missed the *Fusilier* entirely.

The ship's superstructure was of steel, a skeleton half-filled with sand. It remained a cage in which, another miracle of a seeming desert, bees had made a hive so huge we knew it was ancient – and guarded jealously.

That same summer Maurice also taught me I could fight in fury. The pheasants were squawking in the bracken, the lupins thick with dust, their pods swelling in the heat and exploding their shiny jet-black seeds. A group of us, hot and bothered, were moving around below the higher dunes, looking for frogs in a pond. Cattle grazed the tussocks and the rank grasses in the natural ponds, deep russet in colour. Occasionally we would disturb a cock pheasant that would rise out of the scrub in that strange, characteristic helicopter movement. We decided to climb to the top of the trig station to carve our names into its sides. Once up there Maurice and I had a disagreement about the Germans in World War One and whether they had got to the Pacific.

Maurice challenged me: 'Samoa? They were there because it was part of their empire.'

'The Germans never came into the Pacific – it was the Japanese here, they divided it up.'

'There were Germans out this way – I've seen the pictures.'

'What do you know about history?'

'What do YOU know, you ignorant prick,' pushing me.

'Don't push me, you bastard.'

'Who are you calling a bastard? Next thing you'll be calling me a black bastard.'

Suddenly, we both wanted to destroy each other. His arrogance infuriated me and mine him – it couldn't be left like this. With our hands on each other's throats, we went into a clinch, each trying to force the other to the ground. Down we both went, a pair of spitting tomcats, tumbling off the side of the mountainous dune through the lupins, locked like lovers in the embrace of hate, breathing in each other's breath, seeking to hurt, wanting to choke the life out of each other, rolling, rolling over and over, sky-side up then ground-side down, all the way to the bottom of the hill. The rolling took all the heat out of it all. By the time we both reached flat ground, we were somewhat abashed. Our anger had dissipated and we no longer wanted to hurt each other. Barry stood by, a silent witness to it all. 'What did you want to do that for?' Barry asked. 'I'm telling Mum.'

***

Very occasionally, the beach community did let its hair down. 'Parties' were rare, but at New Year it was allowed that you could 'have a bit of a do' with the beach community. For people not given to overt celebration, this was a powerful claim on their gifts of hospitality, which in those days seldom ran beyond salted peanuts and potato chips, with beer, Pimms and lemonade. After all, it was only a bach, wasn't it?

But as kids the evening was spent at the beach with a big bonfire. Around midnight we'd go back up to the bach where, not long after the radio pips and kisses all round, there came the call of the pipes and adults' laughter, distant at first and then drawing nearer along the dark, unlit street. Then a knock at the door. First-footers for Hogmanay! Jimmie and Marge Cameron, sometimes with friends and family in tow, would arrive.

The pipes seemed to do their work on my mother. On other occasions she always kept such matters strictly within the family, but now she would rush around kissing people and serving them tea and slabs of almond-armoured Christmas cake. 'You've got to have some – another slice is good luck for another month.' Dad would pour a few beers for the blokes. If the local tall dark man was available – a chap well over six feet was sometimes on hand – he was welcomed in first across the threshold according to the tradition. His name was McKinnon, Davie McKinnon. Occasionally old Bert would come and gift a piece of coal to the householder – a talisman certain to ensure warmth in winter, in our hemisphere still six months away, a rare gift from an old tight-arse.

Not far behind the tall man was the piper, another friend of Jimmie's. In preference to bagpipes, Jimmie would usually play his piano accordion, probably because playing the pipes would not have allowed him to be able to join in the singing of, *Ye Banks and Braes* and the mysterious but reassuring, *Auld Lang Syne*. Holding hands for this song was one of the few moments when the children – well past their bedtimes – were allowed into all of this. The next day, after providing such an open show of having fun, everyone returned to their ordinary lives as though nothing had happened.

The dark-haired man did call once at our place during the day with Jimmie. It seemed that he and Jimmie Cameron were great friends. By this time they must both have been into their 70s. If Jimmie was forthright and physical, this man was reflective but no less outspoken – in ways that were in that place and at that time quite distinctive. He was a reader who, when people almost never talked politics, made his presence felt by the strength of his observations.

Somehow the greatness of President John Kennedy came up in conversation. The visitor commented:

'Jack Kennedy is no friend of the United Kingdom's.'

'Oh, why is that?' someone asked.

'It's perfectly clear,' he said in a claret baritone shot with brogue that held the floor. 'Kennedy's dad, Joe Kennedy, is probably a Home Rule for Ireland man from the time of the Uprising, and his son treats the British in the same way. They do not trust the British, the Kennedys, neither do they humour them.'

Afterwards my mother described this man as 'someone comfortable within his skin – I gather, he's a Christian socialist.' She seemed to approve.

The conversation was soon left behind, but Mr McKinnon was not forgotten.

Hector 6

We all motored down to the beach this afternoon. Davie McKinnon, the Highlander whose company I always find agreeable, took us in his new motor. There are a number of gates one must open on the track to the beach. At Tunnel Hill are the remains of an old flax mill, whose workings Davie seemed to know something about. The flax trade along this coast was once highly developed. And the Turakina river, which moves up and down this coast, is as restless as the old North Esk, never satisfied, never finding its true home and rejecting old patterns. They have slunks here too, just as they were when I left Montrose – although Alex Beattie did write to tell me that it's all under better management there now and they're keeping the river in a single bed at its mouth.

Here the wind blows like I've never known before. Sometimes you can almost believe the gusts will take your head off. But the sea is always much warmer than ever it was along the North Sea, where a man overboard in winter is a man dead inside two minutes. The children enjoy the water here, playing in it for hours, even in autumn.

It's the absence of the human presence here that I find appealing – it's also what I find I miss most. Montrose was small, but it was substantial with its stonework, its close, its kirk. When I see the estuary and the dunes of Koitiata I am inclined to watch out for the knobbly spire of Montrose Kirk. I half expect to see, tucked on an imaginary cliff-line, the shape of ancient castle. But here, there is nothing like that. The only signs of people are the Maori middens – and you need someone like Billie to point those out to you. Often they are lost by the endless covering and uncovering of sand on this tireless shore. There's an emptiness, an absence of avenues and lanes of hedgerows and all that life that goes with them, like the squirrels, the crickets and the birdsong, and well-paved, well-trodden roads, some that the Romans built all that time ago. Here there are no foxes, no badgers and no moles, for which I'm glad.

I was delighted to see the bittern in the wild the other day and some of the birds here bear the same names as the birds at home, even though some are different. But thrushes, blackbirds, skylarks, yellowhammers and many of the finches have been introduced. We have some of the gulls. There's an absence, too, of prejudice. People nae care whether you're a Campbell or a MacDonald and the McGregors here are proud, but these ones have managed to shed the Rob Roy nonsense. Or so I had been led to believe – until the other day.

It was then I discovered that colour prejudice and clan nonsense are not entirely extinguished here. It came from a most unexpected quarter. One of the horses threw a shoe so I had to return at lunchtime to the stables. As I came round the side of the wool-shed, there was quite a babble of men's voices. Over in a corner of the yard behind some broken-down traps and lumber I could see a group of men standing in a circle, shouting. Some of them were shearers, visitors to the farm, and some of these were Maoris.

Inside the circle I came upon McGregor, thumping the daylights out of Billie, the funny Maori man. Since first meeting him down at the river that unforgettable day, when he hardly spoke, I've formed the view that Billie is strange, and indeed most talkative and more female than male in many ways. The men are always slinging off at him. He is not a fighting man, but here he was, trying to defend himself from a very angry McGregor, who was spitting tacks and punching with those hairy knuckles of his as hard as he could. No half measures for our McGregor.

'Don't you ever put on the McGregor tartan again, you bloody imposter,' he shouted. 'You've no right, d'ye hear, d'ye hear? No right, you're a coloured man. It's an insult to our people.'

'But Brucie,' Billie whimpered in his drawn-out words, 'we're half cous-zins.'

This seemed to inflame McGregor's temper even more. His brow was dark and his cheeks already ruddy. 'McGregor! You're nae bloody McGregor. You're a bloody Maori, born in a swamp. What my grandfather did in his spare time has nothing to do with me and my family – you're no part of our name. Stick to your own kind.'

Billie's style of fighting was to put his hands up over his face, his elbows over his chest, and try to fend off the worst of the attack. I noticed he had the makings of a good black eye, and his lip was split. There was blood on his face. Both men were panting, the one furious, the other frightened.

I knew Billie to be a pretty harmless kind of fellow – action was called for. Whatever he'd done, he was getting the worst of it, mostly because of McGregor's ill-temper. Some of the other men seemed uneasy and stepped in closer as they realised that McGregor wasn't going to stop until he had Billie laid out on the ground. I went across and seized McGregor's arm, a dangerous manoeuvre in such circumstances, I'm bound to say.

McGregor's fury turned on us both, but he was wrenching his arm from me, spitting his words. 'He's defiled my ancestors – what right does he have to put on the McGregor tartan? He's a bloody black cuckoo, that's what he is. It's high time he was put in his place and taught a lesson.' The crowd remained unconvinced. I stepped between them. 'Settle down, man,' I said to McGregor quietly. 'You're setting your prejudices against your better judgement.' His anger was now aimed at me, but his temper had almost run its course. Billie reeled away and McGregor, a little abashed, muttered about having warned him before.

McGregor has a reputation for bearing grudges. He'd not be alone in that as a Highlander, but I fear for Billie. Afterwards, I noticed there was a McGregor shawl, mud- and blood-splattered, lying on the grass. It must have been torn off Billie's shoulders. 'So what was that all about, then?' I asked one of the men.

Bruce McGregor and Billie, it turns out, actually do have the same grandfather. He was a man who married a chieftainess of these parts, had a number of children by her and when she died he took over all her lands. But then he married McGregor's grandmother, an Armstrong from the borders, and had another family. It seems the Maori part of the family got the thin end of the stick. But Billie's an odd one, when you think about it; he's a brown Scot, claiming his due heritage. Maori put even more store by their ancestors than do the Scots – half of Scotland seems to be descended from Robert the Bruce. So when you think about it why wouldn't a Maori want to claim his Scottish chiefs? But his problem is he's also a funny man, who likes to wear flowing, colourful clothing. The tartan shawl suits him well but the men think he's a nancy boy, an odious offence before God, that is sure, and I believe the real reason why McGregor got his dander up.

But I was still brooding next day over this, so I decided to have it out with McGregor. After all, I would have given him nearly ten years. 'What's it to you?' he wanted to know, his eyebrows knotted in anger again, but a wee bit uncomfortable now. 'The worst thing,' I told him, 'the worst thing to me is you're simply perpetuating clan in this country in all those terrible ways we thought we'd put behind us.'

'I'm not havin' any more of this nonsense. He's a coloured man and that's that. McGregors are not coloured people.'

I decided not to challenge that again.

'You know why I left Scotland? It was nae the dreich, I'd learnt to stand that – and there was plenty of work for me there and reasonable money too. It was all that humbug, Punch-faced Presbyterians settin' themselves up and tellin' everyone what to do, how to run their lives.

'It doesn't seem to matter what happens to Scotsmen. You can take them from the Highlands, you can take them from their homelands and you can turn them into New Zealanders –but what does it amount to if they're just bigots underneath?'

Then I must admit, I got a bit preachy myself.

'Judgement, McGregor, as you well know, is the sin that pinched Scotland for centuries, like a pair of boots that are too tight. It made most of our people into miserable wretches. Nae wonder the Sassenachs liked to laugh at our wretchedness.'

'What's this to do with anything?'

'Man, think about it. Judgement and law, they're like a thunderbolt. Judgement, it scorches the earth between two people.'

'What you are saying is none of your business, you have no to right interfere like this. Who in God's name do you think you are? You expect me to treat a native the same way as I would a fellow countryman?'

'Why not?' Now I had my dander up. 'Grudge-holdin's bad enough in friendship. In families it's the cack-handed substitute for love. Whether you like it or not, he's part of your family. Think about it, McGregor, what you're doing smears everything it touches with dung – especially your own tartan. Take it from me, it blights what should occur between a father and a son, leaving only bitterness. Believe me, it's the death of us all. Why start all this nonsense again in a new country?'

It was that night, or the night after, that Mr Stuart came over to my hut looking grave, with a newspaper under one arm.

'Have you seen this, Hector? The Germans have invaded Belgium on their way to France. They say we'll be in a war in no time.'

Doug 6

In 1938, the year before I joined up, I decided to lash out on dancing lessons. Mrs Fitzgerald had style. She looked Spanish, used perfume and lipstick, and sported long silky dresses and lots of jewellery. Her hair was cut in a bob. She knew her way round, knew the talk and the trends, Ginger Rogers, Nelson Eddie, Fred Astaire, she purred through the smoke from her cigarette holder. She even knew of Glen Miller just months after he formed his big band. Everything about her reminded her pupils that she was a woman. She'd select a record from its brown paper sleeve, place it on the turntable and release the brake. After a short introductory crackle on the speaker, away we would go. 'Ramona...' She'd step forward to take you in her arms as if you were the only boy in the world, as another song put it. 'Come on,' she'd say in an American sort of way, 'let's dance.' No one else talked like this. She held you with confidence, as if she understood men, knew them and knew how to enjoy them. She was mysterious. She smoked while dancing. If you were lucky, when you'd finished there'd be no ash down your back. But you didn't mind. You got the whole works with her – perfume, make-up, silk dresses and dance. It was as if she knew her own value, somehow, and played to it in ways that you rarely saw in a woman in those days. Not in small country towns. We didn't quite know where Mr Fitzgerald called home and she played to her mystery – there were rumours, a lot of women in the town hated her and were more than happy to put her pot on; we didn't see where it was she could have got her glad rags, no one knew where she spent her weekends, but she had been seen at nightspots in Wellington in the company of a racy jazz set. 'Come, young man,' she would say in a husky voice. 'Relax, loosen up, be tall – pretend you're Valentino. You have the makings of a very good dancer. You've a great sense of rhythm, but a woman wants firmness in a man – take the lead strongly. We don't want to be namby-pambied. Take the lead.' So I learnt to take the lead and learnt to dance quite well. Well enough to buy a pair of fancy dancing-pumps, shiny black and smooth leather soles with toe-and-heel plates.

When I came back from the war Fitzgerald's School of Dance, with its snazzy sign in gilt-edged red lettering at the foot of the stairs in Maxwell's Building, Broadway, was still there, but Mrs Fitz wasn't. She'd flown the coop with a former Mayor of the town, a married man. People said they were in a love nest in the hills above the Wellington Harbour.

I played at half-back for Marton Old Boys in junior rugby where I learnt to take physical knocks and developed a healthy taste for beer. I'm afraid not even the matriarch's reproachful stare from above the mantelpiece could rein me in on that one. Dances were held all over the district, usually with a five-piece band. A friend's father had a Plymouth and four or five of us would go to the Coconut Grove in Palmerston North, several halls in Wanganui or the Tutaenui Hall, Marton. They would also take the seats out of the Civic Hall; there were Hunt Club and Military Balls, complete with the presentation of debutantes. Run of the mill hops were held at the Druids' halls, where the suppers provided on the white-paper-covered trestle tables were massive. Some halls posted notices around the four walls, threatening instant eviction for anyone stomping and doing the heebie-jeebies. There was modern and old-time dancing, while cards were played by the oldies in the ante-rooms to the main hall.

That spring evening I had been helping out a Lew in his shop at the picture theatre and we adjourned to the Whitehart Hotel. Tubby Hancox told us there was a dance out at the Kakariki Pa. 'Doug, you work with cars all day – you can get a vehicle, how about we all go?' Not wanting to appear cowardly, foolishly I said, 'Okay. I can provide the vehicle.'

I knew there was a Graham Paige saloon parked outside the Marton Gentlemen's Club that our workshop had been attending to that day. The car belonged to a Scotsman, Davie McKinnon, a farmer and stock buyer, who lived about six miles out of town. I thought, 'Old Davie will have had a hard day behind the plough and will not be in to collect his car until tomorrow.'

So we drove the seven miles out to the dance at the pa where we had a great time and a fine supper. We picked up a couple of girls, one a Maori lass, and chauffeured them back to Marton. I drove the Graham Paige back to where it had been parked and placed the ignition key in its place under the driver's side mat. I couldn't decide whether to take the short cut through the swimming baths and the school, or head boldly up the Main Street. I opted for the latter, but coming round a blind corner ran straight into Brownie, the night-watchman.

'Morning, Brownie.'

'What sort of car is that you have just got out of?' he asked. 'Whose car is that? Belongs to Davie McKinnon, does it not? Davie knows that you have the car?'

I decided to come clean. There was no way out, but I didn't sleep well that night.

Next morning, on the mat before the boss, I got the telling off I deserved. 'Who do you think you are? You could easily go to court for this. Car conversion, it's called. How long a sentence are they giving for car conversion these days? Eh? They might put you away for eighteen months. What the hell did you think you were doing? What do you think this is doing to the reputation of the firm? You're a bloody ape and I have absolutely no sympathy for you.'

We went round to visit my mother, who did not deserve any of this. A good church-woman, she was humiliated and distressed. She clutched her cardigan and went pale. All she could say was, 'Oh, Doug, how could you? What would your poor father say? The disgrace of it. I can't believe my boy could do such a thing!'

130

Fortunately, soon after I was sent on a Territorials camp and when I returned the situation had improved somewhat. I learnt that Davie had been playing cards late at night at the club. On finding his car missing he phoned the workshop foreman who, to my astonishment, had just been informed by a lass we had picked up, a handsome Maori woman from Kakariki. She was a niece by marriage to the foreman who decided she needed to protect herself from trouble by spilling the beans.

They arranged a ride home for Davie. When his car was returned next day he carefully examined it. He then told the garage owner, 'If you take any punitive action against this fellow, I shall take all my business away from your firm, plus that of a number of other clients.'

Subsequently, I visited Davie McKinnon to make my humble apologies. He listened carefully. 'And thanks for letting me off so lightly,' I said.

'That's neither here nor there, laddie. Next time you want to borrow the car just ask me, but do not leave bloody combs and earrings on the seats, you will get a man hung.'

Over the years I would run into Davie once in a while. I was forever grateful that he saved my hide and kept me from taking the slippery slope that could have changed my life so completely. I always wondered, but never got to ask him how well he had known my father.

**

The older I got the more I loved machinery. Garth, though, was slightly different. He was apprenticed as a lineman, which was secure government work, and he seemed to thrive on it. He told me how on his first day the men tried to put one over him at smoko. One of them managed to drop part of a dog turd into his teacup without him knowing. As he got near the bottom its shape emerged, still recognisable for what it was. 'I didn't look up when I realised, but I could feel

131

their eyes were all upon me. I just kept on drinking as though nothing had happened.'

He was unfazed. 'I could hear one of the blokes snickering. When I'd finished, I just looked up at them, straight-faced, and said, "Bloody good cup of tea, I'd love another." He said that nothing like that ever happened to him again – he was one of them after that.'

One Sunday morning just before noon, Garth arrived at my home on his new motorbike – a Panther Sloper, named for the large powerful engine cylinder set at a thirty-degree angle that drives it. 'Come for a spin,' said Garth. Off we went in a cloud of dust and a clatter of small stones. At the end of the street we took a right and at then another right. We were about to run right once more into Wellington Road when suddenly, a large American car appeared in our path. It was a Graham Paige driven by Curly Charleston, mine host of the Marton Hotel. Curly and a cobber were taking it for a spin and fellow publican and the Graham Paige was taking up most of the road. It was, we heard later a test drive. Davie McKinnon had put this car up for sale.

As we raced towards it the car filled our entire vision. Garth laid the Panther over at an angle and we skimmed past the bonnet. I had time for one quick and anxious glance from my perch on the pillion. Through the windshield I could see two sets of eyes inside the car protruding as though on stalks. We leaned away from the driver's side mudguard with a bacon rasher to spare.

I was about to heave a sigh of relief when the foot rest of the Panther dug into the bitumen and we were flying, hell-bent for the gutter. This was long before the days of crash helmets, but we were both wearing old, heavy leather jackets. Garth left the saddle first and landed with the Panther on top of him, engine roaring. I flew through the air, across the footpath, and fair and square into a hedge that smelt of pine. Luckily I untangled myself rapidly. With unknown strength I pulled the screaming Panther off Garth. We stood the bike up, got back into the saddle and pillion and away we went – quite mad! I cannot recall any injuries, cuts or bruises. Someone was taking care of us. We certainly weren't taking care of ourselves.

Garth had a girlfriend over at Tauranga, and made plans to go and see her on Labour Weekend 1938. With war looming, little did we know it was the beginning of the end of our freedom. He hired a Ford Model A Roadster soft top. We left Marton late afternoon and made our way north, stopping at Taihape and then onwards to Waiouru, at that time just a desert outpost. The only signs of habitation were a couple of large farm homesteads. We began to navigate the Desert Road, which was not a road in those days, but a track through the tussock and mullock. It was barely visible, with ill-defined fords across the many streams. By this time darkness had fallen and there was little moon. The roadster had powerful headlights – without them we might have been in strife. We disturbed a couple of herds of wild horses which galloped off in clouds of dust – a great sight.

We finally came out of the rough desert tracks and made our way through Taupo and Rotorua. Dawn began to break as we approached Tauranga, arriving at the Old Masonic Hotel at about 5.30 am, only to sleep most of the morning. I remember carrying my case in one hand and a trusty .303 rifle through the hotel lobby and up the creaky, yellow-carpeted stairs with its sweeping polished banister, to our bedroom. No one questioned me. I'm not quite sure why I had brought it. Those were the days.

The next night while Garth was visiting his girlfriend, I went down to the noisy bar, smoke drifting up round the zinc-pressed ceiling. I got talking with a Maori woman in a backless floral cotton dress. She was about my age, her hair pulled back, and quite a lively sort, who soon told me she liked a drink, a cigarette and a good time. When I offered her a drink, she smiled and said, 'A gin'd be nice, thanks very much, Sunshine.'

She came from the East Coast, she said, and she'd come to Tauranga to work in a citrus orchard over the summer. 'We have a good time, there are lots of girls working there. We're outside in the sun every day and we have good parties. That's where I met my boyfriend, he'll be coming in quite soon.'

I decided not to hang about, discretion being the better part of valour and all that, so I went for a walk up and down the beachfront, then to bed to read a Zane Grey.

***

Garth and I would often join each other over a beer at one of Marton's locals, the White Hart. We would also drink sixpenny handles at the Club Hotel. At about 5.30 in the evening, half an hour before closing, there would be a whiff of cooked food from out the back. 'Here we are, lads, get stuck in to this.' Mine host Charlie Haddock would bring to the bar patrons plates of sardines on toast or hot baked potatoes with crusty skins. Charlie would always come around with second and sometimes third offers of more counter lunch. Garth and I never refused the offer.

There was a great deal of talk about war. A group of retired officers had come out in the papers attacking the government for its lack of readiness. They had created a big stink and everyone in the pub had an opinion. 'They need to enlist every man under forty,' said Charlie, a veteran from the trenches of the Somme. 'No, no,' piped up another veteran, 'we'd be better off out of it completely. Peter Fraser and some of those Labour men was conchies last time, this government won't be rushing into war. In my opinion, neither should we. Fat lot of good it did us last time.'

'We'll be in to do our share,' I told them. 'I'll be volunteering.'

At home on war leave after an absence of a couple of years, I called at the Club Hotel for a pint. Charlie extended a right royal welcome. After an exchange of pleasantries I asked Charlie, how things were with him. 'Well', said Charlie 'since you and your mate Garth left the town my spud bill has gone down fifteen pounds a month.'

Alan 7

If I'd been fishing down at the wharf, I'd be looking out for Dad when he came home that night. He might want to know how many I'd caught. He just might ask. It was that same feeling as the rugby, or like showing him your biceps as you entered puberty, pumping them up.

'Look, Dad, see my muscles.'

'Like knots in cotton, like knots in cotton,' he'd say, grinning.

I was left feeling that he hadn't quite given me what I was asking for. As we grew older, from early summer there were always the encounters at Koitiata with the flounder net. Barry and I were expected to take the deep end and drag. If you suddenly found yourself in deep water, it required great perseverance, and strength even, to pull both yourself and the net, tied to a manuka stick held upright and tugged with a belly in it, through the water, sometimes in a tide. Barry hated it.

'I don't like the fish, I hate floundering – why do I have to do it?'

'Because I told you to,' Dad would mutter. 'Just do as you're darn well told.'

'It's cold and we never get anything, it's stupid.'

If I took pleasure in their set-tos, it was because it took the pressure off me for a while. Barry was right, though, it was a huge effort pulling the net in deep water, then carefully arcing it into shore, bottom weights at the leading edge so that no flounder could be lost. Then watching for the tell-tale flapping as it came ashore – and usually seeing nothing.

'Bugger,' Dad would say. 'Bugger and blast. Where are the bloody fish?'

And we'd drag again, in the dark and cold, against the odds but not catching flounder. His optimism was wearing on us.

Yet as I grew older there were rare days when anything was possible between us, even when floundering. It happened we were down by the water on a scuddy spring Sunday afternoon at Koitiata. People whitebaiting, kids tossing sticks, dogs bounding from the bank – a bit cold for swimming, a gusting wind off the sea with slower-moving higher cloud, ferrying occasional dark shadows across the estuary. Inevitably, a skylark fixed somewhere overhead, seeming to pivot on its song.

Gradually the shadows unsettle, a mental wind intrudes on the outer edges of comprehension. You stare a little harder at those on the beach. A woman sitting on a towel reading, keeping one eye on her kids, an older couple beachcombing and a man sicking his German shepherd to 'fetch'. But their backs, could it be that their backs are slightly stiffened? Their heads, like those of the standing shorebirds, seem to crane often in the same direction. What is it that they see? No one dares to think the thought fully, to speak it out loud so that it fills the waiting cavity. Whatever happens, don't get it wrong. Don't make a scene, even if the realisation is starting to scream inside. 'Can't you see? Out there in the swollen river mouth, those two black heads that look like dogs. They are men and they are in trouble. THEY ARE DROWNING. Somebody do something.'

Someone is taking in water, maybe his last gasp, but whatever we do we mustn't be wrong – think of the humiliation in that. Take another look – they're there alright. Distressed – one of them going down again. We could wave to them, but surely they can make it in under their own steam? Just take your time. No – one of them has gone under again. Oh, no!

Finally, we register, Dad and me. It's all too clear what is happening – we can deny it no longer. We lay down our flounder net and look at each other: 'Let's go then, shall we?'

They're about 130 metres offshore. There is the occasional sandbar, but the water is quite deep and quite cool. There's no real danger for us.

As we swim towards the men it is plain that they are in trouble. There is an older guy, looking desperate, his face parchment and purple, and his son, who is desperately trying to help hold him up. The son holds a net that they have been dragging. I have medals for lifesaving training, so I take charge. 'I'll take the one who seems to be in real trouble. You get the other one.' The older guy is desperate, starting to thrash about, and as I approach I can smell the sickly sweet tang of liquor on his breath. I'm glad to see that he is not a big build – tall but thin, not a rugby drunk who might drown me. 'I'll get you,' I shout. 'Don't worry.'

As I approach he lunges at me. I break his hold with a textbook release that I can visualise on the relevant page of the Royal New Zealand Lifesaving Society's blue handbook. He comes back at me so, with great reluctance, I smack him firmly on the side of the face. He whimpers and I say again, 'Don't panic, I'll get you to shore.'

After subduing the guy, I pull him in. Dad brings the other one in, towing him on his back.

Out of the tussock a middle-aged woman appears in a billowing yellow and white summer frock and sandshoes, followed by another son. They are distraught, but they show great relief at the rescue. Then they ask, 'But where's Kevin?' 'We thought he was with you,' says the man I pulled in, shivering now with shock and cold. Someone produces a blanket and a whisky, which he downs greedily while the woman wails, tugging at her coat lapels, tears streaming down her face. 'No,' she cries, 'no, not Kevin. He swam out to help you about ten minutes ago.'

All eyes are on the broad, moving surface of the river, scuffed by the westerly, but to her question it is as placid and unyielding as the face of a sleeping child, its daytime sins just discovered. Someone rushes up to the store where they have a phone and much later the Marton police come racing out in their black Ford Zephyr, red turret-light and siren going, at top speed along the windy gravel road. They are stalled for a few minutes by McKenzie's cows plodding along for evening milking. The arrival of the ambulance gave everyone in the beach settlement the right to congregate and openly show an interest – suddenly there was a mob of people there.

And when the tide went out, at dusk, on the mud at the bottom of the river was a dark sprawled shape which the ambulance driver and his mate covered and collected on a stretcher.

For strong swimmers this place presents no great danger. Yet it was such a strange feeling, cooperating with my father in a crisis, a sense of triumph and togetherness. And an awkwardness that such things between us were so rare that it felt a little stilted. There was nothing much that could be said. A few days later, my mother, who only wanted my father and me to be friends, described the episode to someone who made the obvious response: 'How wonderful it must be for Alan to be grown up – what great mates the two of them will be now.' And of how, she told me with sorrow, that she really had no reply to make.

If it had been a long time since there had been such a feeling of achievement between us, the beach did offer one other opportunity. This time it was a fire in the dunes, mid summer, between the bombing range to the south and the beach settlement that was rapidly encroaching with the strong southerly wind blowing. Someone had had a brew-up about lunchtime. Everyone said afterwards, 'They should have used a thermette, everything's as dry as a stick. What did the silly buggers think they were doing?' The fire spread quickly across the bombing range and then advanced towards our dwellings.

The entire beach community turned out on the road with shovels, sacks and what water they could manage. A number of appliances from neighbouring towns arrived, suddenly there were firemen running their asbestos, unfolding hoses down by the lagoon, ready for pumping water. Everything that grew in the area, the marram, the lupins, pingao, dry flaxes and convolvulus, was ablaze by the time we got there. 'Go and get some sacks,' Dad yelled, 'there's some in the shed, soak them in the sink and bring them over in the wheelbarrow – as many as you can.'

When I returned with my load and some shovels, a line of men and boys were standing facing the flames and smoke, behind them charred marram roots – black and white porcupine quills across the endless dunes. As the fire was advancing in pockets across a number of fronts, the firemen directed us to beat out the new fires. They used what water they had, dragging extension hoses into the nearer baches' water-tanks for more. They ran the hoses down to the swamp and sucked it dry until they were taking in mud. Women produced baskets of scones and tea in thermoses to keep us going. Everyone was extremely hot, soot clinging to their arms and faces. Suddenly there was a flare-up right in front of a line of us. Something very dry just went whoof! and exploded into flame. I just stood there; all the puff had gone out of me, the heat almost scalding my cheeks and forehead. Then, a piercing whistle brought me to my senses. Someone dashed out of the smoke and grabbed me by the scruff of the neck, shouting with a strong accent, 'Get out o' here, laddie. Go on – scoot!' Even in the smoke there was no mistaking him – it was the upright figure of Jimmie Cameron.

Fire kept pressing closer and closer to the baches – it was only a couple of hundred yards away and the southerly showed little sign of abating. But eventually it did subside after a huge battle. I came back later and joined those who spent until dusk bludgeoning and stamping to death any sign of a flare-up. It was a night for a few beers. Dad brought old Jimmie back. But it was Jimmie who cuffed me behind the ears. 'You almost got carried away as a firefighter today, ginger,' he said. 'But we kept it at bay between us, now, didn't we?' Dad beamed but I just wished it'd been him who'd said it.

Hector 7

That Belgian morning the sky was pearly, cold, yet full of promise. But when you looked out at the land it was anything but – nothing but wasteland, wreckage and ruin, with the prospect of nothing but more to come. And nothing that any one of us could do anything about. Out in front of us was all pandemonium, the sound of the big German guns trying to take out our positions from the shelter at the edge of a bedraggled forest. With the barbed wire before us flattened by our bombardment, but still hardly a lesser barrier, we were instructed to advance. A straight-backed young lieutenant from Hokitika rose up a ladder from our trench brandishing a corded pistol and charged out in front of the New Zealanders – for it was with the New Zealanders that I'd decided to enlist.

As I watched him in his metal helmet with all his ammunition strapped on him jumping over the first line of what remained of the barbed wire, I caught it. They were firing artillery shells with terrible accuracy from about 700 yards back. You could just see the snouts thrusting back and forth on their carriages through the trees. They were lined up pointing towards us, smoke rising above them after each shell was fired. There was a terrible lot of noise as the shells landed and exploded, kicking up dirt enough to blind a man who got within thirty feet of them. An explosion felled one of the boys from Marton, Ross Carlaw, who was straggling at the rear. Carlaw was jolted, his arms flew up and he tumbled like a full bag of flour, as I remember, looking back out of the corner of my eye. Strange what one remembers in a tense situation. In an instant he was dead and in bloody pieces on the ground.

I hesitated for a moment, before moving forwards again, as something caught me in the right calf. Perhaps it was shrapnel from the same volley that took my friend. The pain bit into my leg and instantly took over my whole body. For a moment it was searing with heat, then numb, and then there was sense of blood flowing freely, sticky and with its smell of iron on my hand.

As I went down a wallop of emotion suddenly welled up. In my bowels I felt terror that I might die and fear that my eardrums might burst in the percussive booming all around. And relief, in the midst of the barrage, that I was still sensing and still alive; and dismay that Carlaw, such a card, had died. Odd that he of all people with his laughter and love of pranks should be taken from us in any action. Lying in deep mud with the added threat of a machinegun firing from much closer as more shells burst overhead, my thoughts roamed. Back to Carlaw's widowed mother in her tiny cottage next to the Haggity baker's shop where old Mr Carlaw had worked until he died of pleurisy. How might she take the death of her only son? I was visited then – the only way to describe it – by something most strange, an overwhelming sense of my mother. Thinking about it many times afterwards, I realise that it wasn't that I actually saw her, so much as I felt her there, in the midst of all that was going on.

She had passed away, living as a rather stern and somewhat lonely widow in her cottage in the Mearns, within days of the outbreak of war. She wouldn't have had an inkling of what was in store for us. Yet, here she was, a presence on the battlefield, calming and comforting. It's not a thing a man can talk about, certainly not these days.

Then, just before I blacked out, I had a vision that I would take to my grave. It was of two gunners, just young men, both of them manning a howitzer, which had just taken a heap of shrapnel from an exploding shell that could have been from the enemy or a malfunction of their own gun. They were part-naked, their flung-out limbs, like rag dolls', lay across the body of the war-horse that had hauled their piece into position. For all the world they looked like steeplechase riders, spilled from a fallen mount. It was bad enough conscripting men in war, but the dying horse, innocent and twitching on the ground, remained in my mind even more strongly than the men, who were actually dead. The sight of it just pierced my heart. Later, I would recall some lads from an ambulance corps carrying me on a stretcher towards the camp. But it was a vague memory from a delirium.

I was brought into a crowded ante-room, little more than a duck-boarded shelter, to the hospital. Judging by the distant crump of heavy artillery, I decided we must be about five miles from the front. All around me were broken, bleeding bodies. Someone was screaming. I recognised none of them and learnt afterwards that these were men from another regiment. Most of the casualties in my unit had been killed outright in the heavy fire. I was in some pain, but my time had not yet come, I realised.

The wound had torn open the calf muscle and I could see more of its stringy insides than I cared to. I was lucky that the bone was not damaged. I sensed the men around me. There was one with his arm blown away, another with a serious shrapnel wound to the chest. Others had been caught by the deadly machine-gun post we had all been warned about. They were all in great pain but the one with head and shoulder wounds was in so much torment he never let up his cries.

Others who could just walk were being 'played in' back to the medical station by a small military band. A grimy orderly, with a Cockney accent, who looked as though he hadn't slept for days, took down some details on a clipboard. 'You're a lucky devil,' said the orderly, looking at my calf. 'You'll 'ave to wait till we're through this lot, but we take out shrapnel pretty quick sharp. There's a pile of it out the back, enough to start another Krupps. It might take a few months for you to recover, Scottie, but so long as it isn't in too deep, you'll be apples.' He plunked a cup of tea, black with sugar, on an empty munitions case beside me.

I drifted off to sleep on a greatcoat spread on the duckboard, with my old bandages retied over a new dressing fixed by the orderly. There was still a lot of blood. When I awoke it was night. I was given a pannikin of diced potato heated on a paraffin stove by a fair-haired nurse from Liverpool. The ante-room was even more crowded. 'What's all this then?' I murmured.

'They're still coming in,' she told me. 'Black Watch. There've been dozens of them coming back from a raid and caught between mines and machineguns. They're still bringing them in. Some of the wounded are still out there, poor fellows.'

'Look,' I told her. 'This is just a flesh wound of mine; let me go.' She took a look at the wound and shook her head. 'You can't go back to the trenches with that – not here – you'll be dead within a few days.'

She called in a doctor between operations. A bluff Geordie, in a startlingly fresh white apron, took one look at me and said, 'I'll give you a medical certificate so you can get back to Blighty for some leave. See that you get fixed up there.'

I was taken some distance in a lorry to a hospital train from the casualty clearing station to Boulogne. One carriage had been shot away down its side by artillery fire. They had made repairs by boarding it up against the weather with matchwood – without any lining the wind came through and it was as cold as charity.

The train moved very slowly, as if the driver was uncertain about the safety of the line. It was reassuring that it carried Red Cross emblems clearly marked on the outside. I wasn't that badly shot – I felt like a deserter amongst a cargo of mutilated and distressed men lying on cots in splints and bandages.

Hollow-eyed nurses served a thin chicken broth to those who could take it twice a day and plenty of sweet tea from great urns. There were French guards, but no one ever came for tickets. No need, I mused – an unbecoming thought – most of us don't have a destination on this line.

During the night a padre came on board, a short fellow with a lot of teeth and a shock of oiled silver hair brushed back from his face. I only got to see him when he lit up, because there were no lights on the train. We shared some stale bread and cheese. After some talk I decided I liked him. I told him that what I'd seen in my short time in the trenches had changed my faith: 'How can He allow a war like this to happen to God-fearing folks? So many of those lads out there have died the most terrible and slow deaths, you just canna place it in any idea you've been taught. It won't fit.'

'This war is like no other,' he said. 'Our ability to build machines now is also our ability to destroy ourselves and our civilization. I can't see ordinary folk lining up to go to war like they did at the start of this one again, ever again. It will affect their church-going and all that, too; there are too many regimental flags in our churches, all over England. They won't stand for it. And, I tell you, I've always been a churchman.'

It was reassurance I was seeking, but his next words astonished me. 'Before the war I would have argued with you, fought with the devil for your soul, not let you sleep until we had you back on side,' he said wearily. 'The worst thing is that war puts one's faith to the test and goes on testing it – not until you begin to wonder, but long after you've stopped wondering.'

At that moment the train was passing across a long steel bridge; there must have been a river. The clickety-click changed to a clunkety-clank, as if we were crossing over a huge water-tank. Some of the sleeping men on the train stirred.

He continued: 'The worst I thought could happen was when they told us our son had died in a landing at Gallipoli. He was our only son, a shining son – he bled to death on the beach. My wife took the news badly – they put her in a sanatorium – she's still there. I don't know that she'll ever come out. He was planning to be a vicar. He was all we could have ever asked for in a son. We had a memorial service for him at home in Dorchester in December. There were 300 people there. I never imagined that he would die before me and I haven't got used to the idea that the family name will not continue.'

'It couldn't be worse than that,' I sympathised.

'There is worse. There's much worse, you know.'

'I've attended the shootings of men court-martialled for cowardice. Some of them New Zealanders, they were, like you. Young fellows, terrified out of their wits, most of them. You ask yourself, what are you doing in the midst of this, when a lad who wouldn't have gone to reform school for the same misdemeanour on civvie street, is curled up in the early morning on the lock-house floor like a baby crying for his mother. Just being made an example of is all it is, and they kill them for it.

'There was one who was defiant to the end – being a young drunk on guard duty was his crime – and refused a bandage for his eyes. Said he wanted to watch the bullets fly. "No prayer," he said. Nothing.

'They asked the Maoris to do it. Three of them, two with blanks up the spout, and him up against a dry stone wall in a bower of apple blossom and pomegranates. The officer turned away as he gave the order. It was nothing short of murder.

'You know what they put on their tombstones, these ones they say are disgraced? "Died of wounds" is what they say. Imagine what their families would think.

'It's them I think about. It occurred to me the day I was watching that young soldier die in the orchard. It's got nothing to do with the bombs or the rats, the bayonets or the machineguns and the dysentery. It's as though this war has nothing to do with the Germans. The whole thing is about punishment. It may not have started that way, but sometimes it seems like the older generation on both sides is punishing needlessly, endlessly, the flower of their youth. It's as though it's because they are young and beautiful. There's no love in us – all this talk about love of country, it's a form of hatred against our own kind. I've seen pigs eat their own, kill their young. How different are we? I no longer look on the flag the way I once did.'

Doug 7

When I was old enough, in the mid-'30s I joined the Territorials, the Marton Platoon of the Wellington West Coast Regiment. I was on Vickers machineguns – I loved it. We paraded twice monthly and learnt the rudiments of handling, stripping, firing and fixing the Vickers, some Sundays going to a range south of Koitiata to improve our skills with our trusty Lee Enfield .303s. As a sergeant, it was my squad who, in a guard-mounting competition, won a polished brass shell case from a First World War howitzer. I still have it in my possession – it serves as an umbrella stand on the porch.

But when World War Two broke out I felt a real heel – having this territorial background – that I did not join up with my mates in the regular army. My mother had gone away on holiday and before she left she said, 'I want you to promise to me faithfully that you will not join the army.'

'Mother, you don't understand, I have no choice – do you really believe that I will stay here in New Zealand while there is a war on?'

'I've already lost your father – this family doesn't need to lose another.'

She looked troubled and paused.

'If we don't fight this war, then none of us can have any certainty that we will be here,' I replied.

'Well, I don't want you to go.'

'I am sorry, but I will go – I can't stay anyway. I might as well volunteer, they will bring in conscription very soon.' She looked troubled. After some time she sighed deeply.

'What I want you to do, then, is promise me faithfully you won't join the army while I am at Kakahi. Promise me now.'

146

I couldn't defy her. As her only child, after all she had gone through, how could I do anything else? I obeyed her wishes to the letter. So instead of the Army, I joined the Air Force, as a flight mechanic. The Selection Board, on hearing of my experience on Vickers, Lewis and Brens, were keen to have me classified as an air gunner. 'Well,' I replied, having read *Yarns of Aircrews in WWI Flying Corps* and for once in my life using past experience to think about the future, 'I would prefer a career that lasted more than three and a half minutes.' Several of the Board looked a little taken aback. I surprised myself with my forthrightness, but I saw the chairman lick his indelible pencil and register my point. I have no doubt whatsoever that speaking out at that moment saved me from being an early casualty of the war.

It was my one argument when my mother came home. I confessed before she had closed the front door. 'What do you mean?' she cried, staring at me, fingering her cardigan. 'You've joined the Air Force? What do you think you're doing?' She burst into tears, slamming the door in a rage: 'Don't you think this family has suffered enough from war? How could you do this to your mother? After your promise. What an act of selfishness.'

Three months later, with my motor-trades apprenticeship served, I signed up as an aircraftsman second class, in the RNZAF. Garth joined the navy. He saw action very early on. He was aboard the light cruiser *Archilles* at the Battle of the River Plate when they forced the pride of the German fleet, the *Graf Spee*, to scuttle off the coast of Argentina. It was just before Christmas 1939. New Zealanders took a lot of pride in that. A framed reprint of the artist's impression of the battle was hanging in the boys' room for years.

Before I left for overseas I called on Garth's mother, a hypochondriac, always poking potions and lotions into poor old Garth, who was a bit of an asthmatic. Whenever I came, she would declare, 'Oh, Doug, how pale you look, I'm going to give you a good dose of Blue Flag.' Seeing me in uniform, she remarked, 'Doug, you poor boy, what a shame, off to war soon. I can see you lying in your coffin.' It was hardly a morale booster – just as well I'm not superstitious. Not in the least.

Alan 8

The bach Dad built was a simple structure, bolted to a
concrete slab that held the entire building down on the
levelled dune. We had a kitchen, with a wood-burning stove,
that opened into the living room and two bunkrooms. They
were almost in the image of the bunk houses of his youth. For
dressers we had the deep oblong rough-sawn wooden boxes
that carried two five-gallon cans of motor spirit, Caltex's
emblem emblazoned on the side: 'the Texaco Oil Company
of the USA'. Nailed together and laid on their sides, curtained
in front, they made a passable set of cupboards. They held an
odd assortment of old *Popular Mechanics* and *Champion*
magazines, among Dad's choices as a boy, and *National
Geographic*, *Saturday Evening Post* and *Life* magazines – all
cast-offs that others had given us. *The Weekly News* and
Reader's Digest were standard issue for most households. All
in all, you could read widely at Koitiata – in the early '60s I
read every detail of Adolph Eichman's famous trial from the
Saturday Evening Post.

For years there was no electricity. Cooking was on an
old stove hooked to a rock gas cylinder. Dad rigged a
wetback for hot water. In high summer it made the kitchen a
sweatshop. Nights were the best times. Dad primed and
pumped a Tilley lantern that, with a throaty throb, threw a
intimate pool of light into the room. Dad would coax it
endlessly with the pricker. Illumination meant we could read.
My parents liked to play cards at a fold-away kitchen table:
Eucre and 500, at which they became highly adept and
competitive with our neighbours.

My grandfather had taught us boys to play cards, but we
weren't invited to play in these neighbourhood games and we
knew not to ask. They were for adults.

Most evenings we kids roamed the sand-hill country, a world where adults only occasionally strayed. We still followed the river and back into the big dunes behind where the trig station was. Here the lupins were huge and old. In dry summer winds their seed-pods shook and rattled like castanets. Quail would burst out of cover and pheasants cackled away just out of reach.

On the beaches, we did no end of stalking. The river was not normally a large one, but on each outgoing tide, especially the springs when the wet shoals and strands were exposed to their inspection, a range of birds you never saw anywhere else was invariably on show. Bird-watching the terns, stilts, herons, dotterels and oystercatchers became part of what we did. We tracked lovers too, and, in endless games of cowboys and Indians, we seldom tired of creeping up. Barry did sometimes. 'Not that again,' he'd complain. 'I don't want to play this – can't we get the gramophone going?' And we roamed about together in a gang, Barry and me and a few others our age. On still summer nights when the moon dressed the river and mudflats in their very best, we'd go spearing flounders or eels. We ran wild for the sheer hell of it, we fished, got wet and cold, lit fires and mucked about in boats and raided other gangs. Mostly, we stayed out of trouble. Often it would be quite dark when we came in, our skins tight with sunburn and sea salt, and we'd just die in our bunks. Down here it didn't even seem to matter what time we got in.

Koitiata was a beach, however, that continued to strenuously ward off all but the faithful. Chances were there'd be driftwood all over the shoreline and the river's edge, or wind, or undertow or something else you didn't want, like mud from the last flood, about a foot deep until it dried as hard as pavers across the flats. Then through the summer it would crack into crazy paving, six inches thick. When it blew there was dry dust lifting in billows across the entire front beach. And there was the river to wade across, with its surprise holes and mild quicksand.

The beach's lack of style coincided with my father's utter contempt for pretentiousness. We all shared in it. Nothing delighted us more than to see visitors in flash cars drive down onto the seemingly dried mudflats – fine for prototype 'beach buggies' rigged up in blokes' garages – and become bogged down in a wet patch. It didn't stop us going in to rescue them, with shovels and sacks and impromptu fasces wedged beneath the buried wheels, but it certainly enhanced our own sense of moral superiority.

On the beach there was also the remote possibility of finding something inanimate that was really amazing. Everything that fetched up on that beach came in from the north, riding the long-shore drift across the Taranaki Bight. But more often than not the hours would pass and the rewards, sometimes in winter cold and wind, were rare.

In the course of his forays, Mr Whitaker came across a beauty. A rumour spread that a Maori canoe had turned up, high on the beach to the north. 'It would have washed out of the Whanganui River in a big flood, bet your bottom dollar.' Old Bert – it must have been on one of his good days— had told Mum that much. Barry and I raced off to find it.

Sure enough, when we got to the place, it was there alright, unadorned, definitely an old dug-out from a single totara, the blanket shroud of sand that for so long had enveloped it uncovered by winds. Seeing it lying there, in its simplicity and nakedness, left me enthralled. We'd seen pictures in Arthur Mees' *Encyclopaedia* of excavated burial sites of Viking kings. We were also shocked. Some firewood collector had taken a chainsaw to it. It was partially dismembered, a raw cut in a thing we knew should have been in a museum. At home Barry blurted out to Mum, 'Somebody's wrecked the canoe? It doesn't even belong to them.' He was really upset. Dad didn't understand his distress. 'Just a Maori canoe – plenty of those around. Dime a dozen. Cockies up the line use them for water troughs. What're you bleating about?'

It didn't take much to figure who had done the deed. It wasn't Bert, he didn't have a chainsaw. What a prick of a man that vandal was, what a hua. We soon found out. But no one would say that to his stony face; he was a Returned Man, and grumpier than Bert. No one would cross him. No one would say a damn thing. He got away with it, scot-free.

Sometimes, after a big tide or strong winds, a variety of shoes, always singles of course, would appear along the shore: men's lace-up and slip-on black dress shoes, women's smart stepping out shoes, some in bright red, sandals, also in leather, for all ages. Where these appeared from, we had no idea. But after a while, I thought I might know. Maybe these were shoes from that train disaster, back in the early '50s.

Ours was the nearest large town to the event; we had awakened early to our Christmas stockings at the end of the bed, always with the tang of an orange in the toe. Barry had opened all his presents and was playing with a Fun-Ho fire-engine he'd been given. I was still pulling the wrapping from a snazzy boxed toy car set from our grandfather, all clockwork and bright paint, when the bakelite phone in the hall clattered to life in the kitchen – such an impoliteness at that hour and of all things on Christmas Day, like a stranger having the cheek to knock on your front door rather than going round the back. The dizzy limit, Mum would say.

'Oh no,' I could hear my mother say. 'No, that's, that's terrible, Jeanette, oh no.' She started to cry. 'Not Gary, he was such a bright, intelligent boy. How many people did you say? –

'No, I can't believe it. More than 100?'

Then she caught sight of me down the hall ear-wigging. She turned away and spoke more softly, guardedly, and I couldn't follow her.

'Then they'll be days looking for them.'

There was a long pause while Jeannette spoke.

'Did he? He ran all that way with a lantern? Oh no! They *all* went into the drink?'

She came off the phone, still in her blue Vyella dressing gown, looking upset. She touched me, unusually, on the head. 'There's a train's come off a bridge up near the mountain,' she told Dad. 'It's gone into the Whangaehu River. Lots of passengers are lost.

'A bright young man, Gary Strachan, I taught him during the war, he's a cousin of Joan's, he was on board, going home from Collegiate for Christmas. The train was full. Many people are dead.'

Other calls came through during the day. The story emerged that Mount Ruapehu's Crater Lake had burst and got away into the river below, taking out the bridge. One man, realising that disaster was imminent, rushed to stop the overnight express with a lamp, but to no avail. With no warning, the train pulled the carriages into the river. The mountain, 100 miles away to the north, we knew well and several times as youngsters we went out into the backyard to watch it glow red-hot and spit fire into the night sky.

For years afterwards, you could not walk upon the beach south of the mouth of the Whangaehu River, at Koitiata, without thinking of a place away up the river a generation came to know as 'Tangiwai'.

Hector 8

After a perilous Channel crossing and another train ride I awoke in a noisy hospital ward in London. It was early morning and from the ground – what turned out to be several floors beneath me – I heard the rumble of a steam-crane and the thump of a pile driver. The ward was flooded in a warm half-light. Men were sleeping on cots all around me. Pigeons scuffled and warbled on a ledge outside. I could feel sharp pain in my leg, but curiously, I remember I was strangely elated because it told me I was still very much alive. The flash of a dream came to me and I realised that my mother had again been in my sleep. She kept saying, 'You need an operation, Hector.' I believed then that whatever happened I would get better and that I would return to New Zealand.

After a few weeks, they sent me to London General Hospital, on Wandsworth Common. The surgeon performed an exploratory operation and decided, 'No further intervention was required.' It was here, as I recovered in the sunshine, that I met Mr Herbert Guthrie-Smith. He had volunteered his services to work as a gardener in the grounds of the hospital. He was a gentleman, most generous, a well-educated Scot who had come out to farm in the North Island many years ago. 'I'm too old to serve, but there's plenty an able-bodied chappie can do here for men who are serving,' he said. 'It's the least I can do.' His wife and daughter were involved in the war effort too – helping to grow things, washing carrots and gathering sphagnum moss for dressings. They were a train ride away at Haslemere. I remember Mrs Guthrie-Smith sewing the sphagnum into muslin bags for dressings in their front room while I talked with Mr Guthrie-Smith.

As I grew stronger he would take me to see the beds of flowers that he had stocked – he was obviously a very hard worker, someone who loved every living thing of nature. We would talk about what grew in New Zealand. He was interested to inquire of the differences between the plants that would grow in the Rangitikei and what he could produce in the Hawkes Bay, which I have not visited.

'You can grow almost anything back there,' he said. 'I have had yams and sweet potatoes at Tutira, and all kinds of fruits – citrus will do well there and I've even had a banana tree thrive in a particularly warm spot.' He wanted to know, 'Have you ever been to Torquay? Have you seen the New Zealand cabbage trees that grow there – are they flourishing? Did you know that there was a time not so long ago when people in England thought that plants from New Zealand would never survive here – they actually believed that they were biologically inferior? Can you believe? The might of Empire.' We had a wee laugh about that.

He quizzed me about the flocks of birds that flew over the Rangitikei district at certain times of the year. He was particularly curious as to the direction they took, how big the flocks were and whether people were interested in shooting them. I told him of the time when I was ploughing, not far from Marton, when I heard the call of the dark bird and seen its shadowy form flitting through the trees. I described its call.

Herbert looked very grave. 'That's something to tell your grandchildren about, that's a bird we hope will survive, but it's one of those whose chances are very slim. Slim indeed.'

'So what was that bird?'

'Well, I wouldn't have picked it in that area. But I believe what you may have seen was a huia.'

He chatted about Scotland – did I still get up to the Mearns to see the family, he wanted to know? 'Such a wonderful estuary for birds there at Montrose, one of the finest places to see our wildfowl. Particularly pink-footed geese.'

'Ah, yes, that is one of the things about Scotland that I miss – I find myself still looking out for them in New Zealand.'

He told me, 'One of my great joys in returning to Scotland in the autumn is to see the skies still filled with those geese as they migrate north. It does my heart good – you've no idea. I've seen them gather at Montrose, where they farm the salmon. Since I came to New Zealand I've learnt to fear more and more for the birds that belong there. There's simply not enough of their forest retained – we destroyed far too much for farming and that is particularly a concern in the lowlands.' He'd made trips to remote parts of the country where shearwaters could still be found in great numbers. 'They congregate in their millions in the southern islands of New Zealand. The sound of them at dusk is like nothing that you've ever heard. Imagine every church bell in Scotland, England, Ireland and Wales ringing at the same time, and you begin to get the idea. The sky is blackened prematurely with the mass of birds returning from the sea.'

I told him, 'I've not much reason to return to Scotland now. I've just my older brother in Montrose – Sandy. The rest of us are all over the world, or were before war broke out – Canada, South Africa, Australia, New Zealand. My mother, God rest her, survived my father by several years until the outbreak of this war.' I felt a tug, a pulling away from my homeland. 'I'm glad in one respect only that she is gone, for she would be very fretful with sons bound up in all this. I'd not seen her in ten years. She had a weakness of the lungs and was poorly in that cold climate. I think with her gone, I shall not return to Scotland again. It's a hard place, its winters so long, the summers so short.'

As I got better and could move around more freely with a hickory stick Sandy had sent, I noticed there was a tall girl with a lovely smile who sold stamps in the post office at Bowes Park. She tied back her auburn hair with ribbons – she must have been in her mid-twenties. I still wrote to the Hendersons and one day when I was out on an errand, getting the correct postage, she summoned up the courage to say to me, 'I notice from the papers the influenza epidemic has travelled right round the world to New Zealand.' She had an East Londoner's accent.

'Ae,' I said, 'and ta'en a lot of them too, I hear.'

I took my change and tipped my hat.

Next time, collecting my disability pension, it was my turn:

'We're in for a wet day, by the look of it.'

'Oh well, it's not as if we don't need it – the parks are dry as a bone right now.'

''Tis overdue, I have no doubt of that.'

I watched her hands, moving deftly at the counter. Her fingers were slender and beautiful. Possibly she played an instrument. I found myself wishing very much to hold those pale hands. My heart was thumping like that pile driver at the hospital, but I decided to take the bull by the horns; I knew no other way. 'Pardon my asking, miss, but do you enjoy music?'

I think she was a little taken aback. She paused, speaking quite sharply. 'As a matter of fact we do have a piano at home. My sister and I play all the time.'

'Do you now? What do you like to play?'

She gave me a look, then, checking there was no other customer waiting, warmed to the idea. 'I love those Feldman editions. *Take Me Back to the Garden of Love*, *I Like Your Apron and Your Bonnet.*' Her eyes shone. 'Oh, and do so enjoy playing some of those pieces like *When You Come Home*, *Night of Stars and Night of Love.*' I noticed she blushed a little as she mentioned the last one.

'There's a Vaudeville on down the road at the Anglican church hall – the one with the porch at the front, you know? Do you think you'd like to come?' I asked.

'Oh,' she said, her voice faintly shrill. 'We haven't even been introduced. Come back tomorrow and I'll give you my answer.' But I could see that she was not displeased. Her name was Florence, a popular name of the time.

She came and we sat in a crowded hall while a parade of Tin Pan Alley songsters, including a real negro in a white jacket and white spats accompanied by piano and strings, went through their cheerful routine. It was not memorable, the seats were hard and what I recall was a group of highly painted performers in some burlesque about a fallen woman. It was bonnie, though, sitting next to her, sharing.

I was still in uniform, so I remained in London, my digs close to St Bartholomew's, where I was to continue taking treatment. As soon as I was fit, though, I wanted to get back to New Zealand. I longed for the outdoors and the feel of that familiar-yet-different landscape and the plough biting into the dark deep soils, the seagulls skirling behind. There was opportunity there and never a fear of going without, never that creeping cold of the Mearns that could freeze the joints together on your spine. Around the town back home at Turakina – just up the road from Koitiata – you could hear the pipes across the brae at evening, and in summer, if they didn't know you were listening, hear the villagers in their gardens calling and talking to one another in their Gaelic. It was a known fact that the ministers at the kirk at Turakina could only be installed if they were speakers of Gaelic. It had been a requirement for the job, but in recent years they've had to settle for less.

One night I was invited to supper with Mr Guthrie-Smith, whose wife was away visiting relatives. I was glad of the opportunity because I wanted his advice as an older man about women – well, about Florence. The war was coming to a close. As a young man I'd spent a lot of time on my own, working the land. There hadn't been a lot of chances for a man to get married. I told Mr Guthrie-Smith how attracted I was to Florence. 'But I admit there is something astray with me – it's as if there's this lever which I have thrown that has shut down something inside me. I am not in the fettle I was in

157

before I went away to the war.' I paused. 'To be true, I feel something inside me has died.'

I'll never forget what he said next. He stood up to say it: 'Look, man, you've just been through a war like we've never seen the likes of before. You were there. Hector, how do you think you survived? It wasn't by being a namby-pamby, was it? Any man who says they weren't afraid who fought on the Front is a liar. But they found ways to cope – most of them. They had to. They had no choice but to stay and fight, stay and die, put up with whatever came at them, long after they had stopped feeling anything.'

I must have seemed bothered by the turn in conversation, staring into the pink roses on my teacup. He said, 'Don't mind yourself, man; what you are suffering is not pleasant, but it is not unusual. I would never break a confidence. But most men from the trenches, in varying degrees, feel this way. I can give you that assurance drawn from my time here at the hospital. The question is, what happens to these men after all that? I know they don't forget the horror. It visits them night after night, hour after hour, in their dreams and their sleepless beds.

'Just remember, Hector, I've seen a lot of wounded men. I've seen what war has done as an outsider. The only feeling most of you have is anger after a few pints. It's not just your mates who've been stolen from you. It's your youth and your comfort. And it's even your faith. Men have never seen before what you have seen – not on such a terrible scale. You lads know what hell is. You've been there, day after day. You know what the worst is – and I am mindful of what happened to King Lear when he made a statement to that effect. But apart from doctors and nurses, no one who hasn't been there has the faintest idea of what you went through. More's the pity, you'll find out if you haven't already that they don't even want to know.'

He stood away from the table and paced the room before warming his hands at the fire. He told me my feelings were quite natural, that I wasn't to worry about my faith or my affections for Florence. 'As far as I can tell, and I'm only a farmer, a woman's love will be the best thing for you. You can't expect to be the same man who set off for the war. No one can. This war is over. They say it's the one to end all wars. Well, we'll see about that, but my advice, since you have asked for it, is take your life and get on with it.'

He told me something I didn't know. That he'd learnt that the casualties for some battalions at Passchendaele wiped out entire units – that included New Zealand units as well as British ones. The Scots, too, they took some terrible losses. 'Scotland is full of grieving mothers, widows and sweethearts,' I said, feeling great sadness. 'It's been that way for centuries.'

We went to the races, Florence and I. 'I've never been before,' she said. 'But it sounds like a lark.' She met me at the station in a wide-brimmed straw hat and a floral suit whose yellows brought out the warmth of her brown, brown eyes. We took the train, with lunch in her basket. We watched from cane tables and chairs set aside for Returned Men, on a platform erected in front of the Members' Stand, close to the track. Most were in uniform, some wounded. Everybody, all the men, smoked.

Behind us, toffs in beautiful clothes drank champagne and studied the horses through opera glasses.

We had little money to bet and had one small success, an extravagant half-crown on Go Lightly, a lovely filly that was paying fifteen shillings, five for a place. It was a fine March day and to see the horses stepping and strutting and turning on their stewards' leads, their scrubbed coats shining in the sunlight, keyed up for their events, did the heart good. Florence didn't know anything about horses so I was able to explain what to look for – strength in the chest, length in the leg, coordination and, most important, spirit. I told her about the horse I'd had as boy, Wee Donald, who won a prize for me at a derby in Montrose. This day, Go Lightly came in third, for a place, which was most satisfactory.

She thought the races a bit 'fast'. But I liked her even more for that. We had a good day until in the twelfth race, as I was crossing to the pavilion for some tea, there was an accident. One horse ran into another and collided heavily with a rail, and then never lifted its head again. A rider lay unconscious beside it. Before they came out to destroy the animal I suddenly felt extremely faint and the sensation, the last thing I wanted in the presence of Florence, gave me something of a panic attack. I made my way back to our seats, my head swimming, as they say. I was so embarrassed, I braced myself for the worst. But a force beyond my control took over and drained the blood from my head. So I tried to sit down and put my head between my knees.

When I came to I had a blanket over me and Florence was cradling my head in her lap. I wanted to get up straight away. 'No, you're staying right here. You've had a little turn.' What a fuss I'd caused. I flushed with embarrassment – what was wrong with me? All I knew was that the dead horse reminded me of the war. But, I must say, for all the loss of face, this moment brought us together.

On the train home we sat close to each other; I could feel her warmth beside me. I loved the way she seemed accepting of my unseemly behaviour. 'Oh, Hector, for heaven's sake, you're not a well man, please don't make apologies. There is nothing that calls for an apology. There are Returned Men all over England, trying to get back on their feet. Some of them, poor fellows, never will.' Since we were so close I even took her hand and told her I was intending to head back to New Zealand. She was surprised, but excited for me. So, after hesitating several times I took a breath so deep it could have made me giddy again and said, 'Would you think about marrying me, and come with me?' I even surprised myself by that. I wondered what else the war had changed in me and I was scared as I awaited her reply.

'You don't waste time, Hector, do you?' she said, a little edge to her voice, but then smiled. 'We've hardly met. You'll have to ask my father – what would I tell my family, they won't want to lose me?'

'Tell them we'll bring them out when we get settled. Then they can always be near.'

She laughed. 'You – you haven't even met them.' Then she said, tenderly, and more boldly, 'Hector, I would like us to meet again.' She hesitated. 'How can I say this? I would not like it if we were never to see each other again. I don't want you heading off to New Zealand before we become better acquainted.' And she laughed her merry, loveable laugh.

Doug 8

When war broke out again, Jimmie Cameron's fleet was confiscated by the Government for use by the armed forces. It was part of Labour's policy, to recruit capital as well as labour into the war effort. Too young to retire, but too old to enlist again, Jimmie took up all manner of odd-jobbing to put food on the table.

And in the season if the tides were right Jimmie was away whitebaiting at Koitiata, trying to entice a shoal into his net using mental telepathy. If the tides were wrong and all else failed he would head off down the beach six or seven miles to the mouth of the Rangitikei just for the joy of walking. He was a great fitness exponent; there wasn't an ounce of fat on him. The one time he went into hospital for a hernia the doctor complained that his hide was like leather – sewing him up afterwards was a real trial. He was one tough Highlander, but he was also one of the most generous of people you could meet. Should the occasion arise, Jimmie would give you the shirt off his back. Not long before I went away overseas with No. 9 squadron, I called on him. My grip, containing all of my personal gear, had gone missing on the train. 'No problem, I can set you up with a new razor,' said Jimmie.

'But,' I replied, 'razor blades are like hen's teeth – where are you going to find one of those?'

'I re-sharpen them on the inside of a whisky tumbler – here you are, take them. And speaking of whisky, I won't see you in a while.' He reached into the sideboard where a few wedding gifts gleamed with Silvo shine. 'Why don't you and I take a dram of Highland nectar? Glenmorangie's the job, made on the Tain, Aberdeenshire. Your father's favourite. He always said it ought to become the tipple of Scots and natives in New Zealand, because its name sounded like a true mix of Scottish and Maori.'

There was something I always wanted to ask Jimmie, himself an orphan. Was his interest in me on account of his knowing Hector all those years ago? Had Hector asked him to keep an eye on me? It wasn't a question I could bring myself to ask. Strange though it may seem, I never did.

The former centennial buildings at Rongotai, Wellington were converted to the main Air Force trade training wing. There were twelve rookie flight mechanics on our course. We had RAF instructors, good blokes who knew their graft. I soon saw how poor my apprenticeship had been. I duly passed out of the course and was posted to Taieri, Otago.

They gave us lectures and we studied engine manuals, dismantling and reassembling engines. We were even issued with a blunt file, a piece of quarter-inch mild steel plate, a worn hacksaw and a jigsaw pattern to work. The task was to file the steel to precision so that it would mate perfectly. We worked on a range of aircraft, including the two-seater Baffin trainers, Faerey-Gordons Hawker-Hinds, Tiger Moths and a number of oddball, ex-civilian aircraft, mostly of de Havilland origin.

Just before heading overseas, I carried out some major work on a Tiger Moth. The plane was test-flown by Harry Wigley, already a daredevil of repute, who invited me to take the seat in the front cockpit. Would I? Quickly strapped in, we were soon high in the wide blue yonder. Harry was a true test pilot. At about 3000 feet he began to put the plane through its paces. He shut off power, pushed the stick hard forward so that it began to spin and flutter in the sky like a large autumn leaf. From up there in an open cockpit, the world takes on a different complexion – the peggy squares of farm paddocks are quite unreal. At 500 feet he turned the engine back on and pushed the throttle to full power, taking sufficient height to execute a couple of double barrel rolls to port side, then to starboard. Wigley then drew another trick out of his box – pulling the stick hard towards his groin he went into a steep climb before pushing it forward to create enough momentum to perform a double loop. As we attained flight level, I put in my penny's worth, through the speaking tube, 'Most of the dust must be off the floors by now, Harry?'

'We had better make sure,' Harry called back.

In a flash the Tiger Moth was flying upside down, wings waggling. All that separated us from the earth 1500 ft underneath us was a seat belt. Of all the pilots I encountered throughout the war, and I flew with a number of them, this man was the ace of acrobatics

A few days later – it was July 1942 – the *USS Mackinac*, on a zig-zag course, carried us to New Caledonia, about forty men in the second half of the advance party. At night we bunked down on collapsible stretchers on the mess deck. But the second night we met with a violent storm; all the bunks hurled from one side of the ship to the other. We were sick as dogs, the lot of us. The turbulence passed and the next evening at sundown we sailed into Noumea Harbour, its skyline across the water dominated by a nickel smelter, its chimney flames and smoke rising high into the night sky.

Next morning the Americans laid on a number of heavy army trucks to transport us 180 miles north to the Plaine de Giacs to an airstrip not yet completed. My mate Frank Cassie and I were tail-end Charlies sitting in the baggage truck. We had travelled sixty to seventy miles when the convoy stopped at a small village where we noticed some French lassies. Cassie gave a whoop and evacuated the truck speedily over its high tailgate. But being bumble-footed at the best of times, his knee caught the tailgate as he fell and his nose came down on the sharp edge of the steel buffer, as the Americans called the bumper. He fell heavily to the ground and lay there. I followed him out and gingerly rolled him over. He was a sight for sore eyes – his nose was resting on his top lip. Our first casualty in the Pacific.

I dragged Cassie to a ditch where he immediately had a small chuck-up. He asked me to write to his mother. 'Shut up, Cassie,' I said. Grateful for my Zambuck training I placed the heel of my hand under the tip of his nose, gently easing it back into position. We called for a medical orderly and dispatched him to a US hospital where he received some excellent treatment. He recovered, carrying the horse-shoe shaped scar on the bridge of his nose for the rest of his days.

Our home for the next few months was no tropical paradise. The trees were stunted, and the place was crawling in mosquitoes and huge land crabs – some as large as dinner plates. The airstrip was under construction with bulldozers and motorscrapers. They covered the exposed light volcanic soil with Marsden matting. This was a clever invention – interlocking metallic decking that enabled really big planes to take off and land without getting bogged down in mud. But the whole place became a dust bowl, causing chronic sinus. A number of blokes had to be repatriated, some reluctantly, others with relieved grins.

Toilets were family affairs, ten-hole latrines. Your personal life disappeared. Gradually, though, we got some comforts. A forty-four-gallon drum over a fire provided hot water for a bath formed from another forty-four-gallon drum cut sideways. It was through this bath water that up to eighteen men would pass, leaving a thick paste of red volcanic dust around the rim.

A cock-up along the way meant that at first we ate nothing but our emergency rations – bully beef and biscuits. When the provisions arrived we could abandon our emergency rations. The line in food now was constant canned American chilli con carne and Spam, known widely as horse cock. There were no vegetables.

You are my Sunshine was one of the few 45 RPM records they had to play back at base over a loud-speaker. After a couple of days I would have been glad never to hear it again. On our third night we turned in early, smoked the last cigarette and awoke to find the entire Bell tent ablaze. Quick as a flash we rolled out of the side of the tent, dragging our gear with us. No burns, no loss of property. The camouflage on the tents had acted as an accelerant.

One tent mate was Dusty Mullins, a likeable rogue and an incurable kleptomaniac who had us believing he carried the marks of a number of bar-room brawls. In a short time Dusty had accumulated under his bunk everything a man in his position could possibly want: a complete carpenter's kit, a Smith & Wesson .38 calibre pistol and a large crate of Listerine. All this bravado was shortly to be put to the test.

Our RNZAF Hudson bombers were deployed on surveillance missions of Japanese navy movements, especially anti-submarine patrols. The Hudsons were an American plane derived from its civilian counterpart the Lockheed Electra. My war was spent keeping these wonderful aircraft in the air.

Being Kiwis, we befriended everybody, including a French subsistence farmer, Georges, his wife and two small sons, young Georges and Anton, who had a smallholding not far from the camp. I think these people were possibly of Bourbon peasant stock. Our friendship deepened after I was able to save the family cow that had swallowed a mango. I did it by jumping on its windpipe.

We also got to know the American army blokes quite well who were assigned to guard our squadron of Lockheed-Hudsons, parked off the strip in revetments. We grew to like these men and had several drinking sessions with them. In October they all headed off for Guadalcanal, a name that would soon become famous in the annals of the Pacific war, and which would be home for some of us for far too long. Sadly, some of our American friends did not get to use their return tickets.

Alan 9

It was Barry's love of music that brought both of us faster than anything to radio and, inadvertently, into the brash new world of rock music. He was family curator of a 1920s wind-up gramophone, which my parents had bought second hand, along with a large collection of old 78 records in paper sleeves or cardboard albums. They became part of bach life.

From an early age he'd bring out the device, fit a new needle to the head and hand-grind its spring. On wet days the bach was filled with the sounds of *The Student Prince's* drinking song, *The Electric Girl, Another Little Drink Wouldn't Do Us Any Harm, The Desert Song* and my father's favourite, *Ramona*. One September the wind-up mechanism wouldn't work. Upon investigation of the aperture where the handle folded back, a family of frightened field mice rushed out. They'd made their nest inside, mainly by raiding the bandages from the medicine chest, clogging up the mechanism that powered it. But all this belonged to another era.

From the mid-'50s music started to change, gradually at first. The new sound had little presence on daytime radio, but at night on our crystal sets the music diet was gradually transformed. Bill Halley was one of the first with his cheeky, *See You Later Alligator*, so different from its contemporary *How Much is that Doggie in the Window?* As different as *Blue Suede Shoes* was from Patti Page's *Tennessee Waltz* or songs like the Ames Brothers', *Naughty Lady of Shady Lane*. Now there were driving rhythms and lyrics explicitly about rebellion and desire, rather than polite longing. Decorum was suddenly out the window, and youth was gripped. Patsy Cline and Skeeter Davis's poignant country-and-westerns, the boundary-breaking Brook Benton and the Drifters, Connie Francis's haunting wistfulness, the amphetamine energy of the Everlys and Bobby Darin, and a little later Roy Orbison's poignant harmonics with his great vocal and narrative range and Sam Cooke's sheer talent and cheek. In the mid-'50s the '30s hit *In the Mood* was revived as a saxophonic rock music 45; it became a standard with the ability to drive us wild, any time, any place.

Transistors were just coming in, but we had crystal sets with help from Dad, who had built his own in the 1930s. We wouldn't have made them without him, although the circuitry was simple, connecting condenser, coil, resistor, crystal and terminals. By soldering these together and running a swaying wire from the house out to a tall pole, we could listen in to the debut of what became an era. Headsets comprised two hefty earpieces salvaged from old wind-up telephones, joined by solder to a strip of packing steel. Radio has never lost its magic.

Before going to sleep we'd read or on the right nights listen in bed to early hit parades pumping out their flossied words and African rhythms. There was something about the intimacy of those voices in your ear, the friendliness of the disc jockey – a new term – and, of course, the driving beat. As it danced down the wire off the aerial into your set and then through your headphones it seemed for the first time there was nothing between you and the world of adults. Ear-wigging had been legitimated.

An American test pilot called Chuck Yeager was suddenly famous. I remember Dad coming home and telling Mum in the kitchen before we read it in the papers, that Yeager had 'broken the sound barrier'. Now there was a phrase to remember, like 'mid-air' – 'the sound barrier' – what was that all about, but excitement? The intimacy we'd broken through to in radio was like that moment, that overhead clap of thunder the RAF Vulcan bombers made as those black darts barrel-rolled right overhead at the Ohakea air show, streaking our skies in a show of power. Rock 'n roll had to be a breaking of the sound barrier. For a curious child, there was a lot of valuable information in those songs, mainly to do with beating hearts, teen angels, proms and white sports coats, staying out late, holding, hoping, hopping, bobbing and rocking – a lot of that stuff that stuck with its melodies like spider-webs in your head. You could never get it out again.

***

There was also the brown suitcase. Some things from the adult world just kept inviting queries from Barry and me. It sat high on a shelf in the back shed, stuffed with memorabilia. A natural hoarder, Dad had brought its contents back from the islands and only he was allowed to open it. It was years later, reading his war notebooks, that I realised exactly where some of this loot had come from. A couple of times he'd gone with mates to actual battle sites between the Marines and the Banzai chargers up on Bloody Ridge, scavenging for souvenirs. But the places had already been plundered. There was nothing much left – rifles with their bolts removed, field guns that had been broken up and some wrecked artillery. Japanese whose bodies had been picked over, down to their gold fillings, by unsqueamish marines, lay decomposing where they had fallen.

The suitcase was privileged. We would no more open it than riffle through the paid bills, dating back to the beginning of their marriage, skewered on a wire spike – a kebab of respectability. His case offered a venture into his world, a place we were seldom invited into. But occasionally he'd ease it down from the shelf for us to comb through together, like a trousseau.

It was from a time when a man's own limited expectations of the world had opened up suddenly behind a great tear in the stretched canvas of his stage – tight with layers of familiar paint – to reveal new scenery. A time for him, yes, of boredom and longing and discomfort, but punctuated by sheer terror and occasionally horror. Yet also a time when life took on a greater purpose. When the possibilities he'd wished for in a small town – new places,

169

new people, new excitements – were suddenly there just through the tear, jostling at his elbow: a noisy crowd he hadn't reckoned on suddenly appearing where only moments before had been a quiet, regular watering hole.

Inside the case were webbing belts, military insignia and clips, shoulder flashes and unit designations, worked in felt and in brass. He had a short brace of live Japanese machinegun bullets still in their clip and a cut-throat razor that, folding out of a slit in its bakelite handle, challenged our notions of manhood. Looking at it with little imagination produced a chill in the base of the scrotum. There was a Zippo lighter, a leather moneybelt, a stainless steel pocket mirror, a water canteen, Perspex from the windshield of a pancaked Hudson bomber and aluminium pieces cut from bodies of other scavenged aircraft. He even had a brown bakelite hand grenade. Holding it in his palm, he assured us, 'No, this can't do any damage, it has been disarmed.' With Dad, we were never entirely convinced.

'This bit is off a Corsair, or maybe a flying boat that crashed on Manus,' he'd tell us, turning over a piece of metal. 'I took this from a Beaufort. This is a piece of wing of a Hudson bomber, good old No. 2080. I had just fitted extra fuel tanks to it when it crashed on Guadalcanal.'

As much as anything the suitcase represented the booty of a man who had had nothing at the beginning of the war but his dreams – and now had a lot of memories, some bad teeth and little more. He had gone off to the Pacific with practically all he owned in a rucksack and seen waste on a scale that only modern technology could create. 'Those Yanks,' he would mutter. 'No idea, absolutely no idea. Blowhards, so many of them. They had everything. Their PX stores were chocker with goods, they had movies, they brought in vast amounts of equipment wherever they went and they wasted stuff. It was enough to make you weep to see what they threw out – and what they lost through carelessness.

'The first sight that we saw when we arrived at Espiritu Santo was the wreck of a B17 Flying Fortress.'

Barry and I knew the aircraft from the Weet-bix card series – there were dozens to collect.

'It smashed into the jungle canopy and flattened everything.'

'How did it crash, Dad?'

'A team of US Air Corps ground crew got plastered on Christmas Eve and decided to fly home. The plane cleared the runway but failed to gain sufficient height. They were all wiped out when they hit the tree tops. Such a terrific waste,' he said, shaking his head.

Most of the time his salvaging ethic worked well for him and the other ground crew. Time after time they rose to the occasion. Often with limited spares they kept damaged aircraft flying, improvising as smithie, fitter and turner, and engine mechanic. He prided himself on keeping those aircraft flying safely. He knew when they were overdue, came to know that some would never return – some with aircrew that he knew well. Sometimes, however, his sympathy for salvage and his sense of liberty could skew his better judgment and land him, as he himself would say, using lingo from those allies about who he felt so ambivalent, 'in the cactus'.

Hector 9

It wasn't too long after we came to New Zealand, back to the familiar Rangitikei with Florence, who loved this countryside, that I realised my leg wasn't going to let up on me. If I did a hard day's work, the wound would become, at first, a nagging, dull ache that gradually increased in pain. Then after stopping, sometimes it was sharply painful. If I stood on it for too long the calf would swell. I started waking at night drenched in sweat and my sleep became choleric. The dream was always scenes from a war, now finished and 12,000 miles away, that I didn't ever think I'd bring with me. One night I saw units of tanks. They were a quite newfangled thing in the Great War and they advanced towards us, clanking over No Man's Land and driving through a stable of live horses, the animals toppled and tugging, heads nodding in their death throes, their teeth showing as if they were men in pain, theirs somehow worse than men's pain. Poor innocent creatures.

In this dream the noise of war was all about, the air filled with the cries of men and animals. When I looked aloft there were swarms of aeroplanes as these angels of death were pitted against each other, another contest in each army's struggle to defeat the other. This was man's genius for destruction. Mortars exploded all around, their fragments flying through the air. Men's bodies, mud-covered and strewn where they lay, rotting at the deep creases in the earth riven by the plough of war, deeper than any furrow. There were naked ones sprawled like still-born babes that had died in the act of birth, lifeless at the lip of the womb. To think of it – grown men, brought to this. The noise of machines and humans was one terrible, jaggled cry that stayed in my ears long after I had awakened.

172

I would open my eyes to Florence holding me in her arms, like a small child, with pity in her eyes. She would bring in a large enamel bowl of hot water and a white towel to the bedside table, bathe me and put on the kettle for a cup of tea. It felt unmanly, this treatment, and to begin with I sternly resisted her attentions. After a while I realised that surrender was the quickest route to peace. She was obstinate and wouldn't take 'no' for an answer. 'Hector, please settle down, won't you, and let me take care of you, dear. You've a wife now, remember, to watch out for you? You've been through a war, have you not?'

I had to tell her gruffly not to fuss, that I'd be just fine. But I began to know that something inside me wasn't right.

Our first-born was a son. He arrived on a crisp morning in late June. The doctors said it was a good birth and that his lungs were good. I remember seeing the frost on the ground when I rode into the hospital for news. We named him Doug, after an uncle of Florence's, and his second name Hector, after me. If we had been traditional, we would have followed the Scots way and, as first son, given him my first name. But neither Florence nor I liked our first names much. The laddie had a great constitution. He made me feel we were blessed, that we were putting the war behind us and making a new start.

With my savings and a soldier's loan we bought a two-bedroomed house in the village, with room in the yard for lots of chickens. The sound of their cheerful clucking in their boxes and their pecking in the garden filled me with a greater contentment than I had known since my days here before the war. But the shrapnel lay still buried like an awful secret.

***

I know that the pain is beginning to tell; in the mirror I look much older. Today we looked at a photograph taken when we were married. I was shocked by how youthful I looked only four years ago. The proof of my injury is written

173

on the lines in my face, the way I stand; there's nae getting away from it. I've lost condition. To think that after surviving the war and coming this far, getting a family together with Florence, it should come to this.

Sometimes I'm so out of sorts, it's hard to tell whether I'm bumping about hitting the furniture because I'm so ill, or because I'm melancholy. It is terrible to wake in the morning and have to ask yourself, 'How will I be today, can I get through it?' when you know the answer is that you have no strength and you'll nae be getting any more; it would be easy to stand accused of feeling sorry for yourself. I need to be more disciplined, for my own self-respect and the family's sake.

I'm sorely disappointed, that I know. But when I think of all those lads who died, younger than me so many of them, who never got to sire their children – many who were scarcely more than children themselves – there's no way I can complain. So many of them were never recovered from the mud. The bitterness is not in my heart; the bitterness comes from a foreign body that is making a claim on my vitality, just at that moment when it seemed the world was so sweet.

I awake from sleep so wet, Florence has to change the sheets in the night. The neighbours probably think that I'm incontinent – there's always washing on the line, especially now that we have the bairn here as well. On the lowboy beside the bed there are heaps of potions and lotions in bottles and tins.

I'm going to keep working. I cannot stand the idea of being a burden. I think a man who cannot feed his family is not a man at all. No matter how ill I become, that's not an idea that will ever change.

I told Henderson I'd be available for some ploughing over at Jackson's next week. At least it's not in the winter dreich of pastures of the Mearns that'd suck the warmth out as quick as wink at you. Lately, I have wondered if I can continue the work with the plough. A man has to be fit.

174

Tulloch, the leading hand, has admonished me lately for slowness. Plainly, a day's work for me is no longer what others can do. I try not to think of what I could do before the war when few could match me. I am distempered. The other day I felt so poorly, I stumbled and would have fallen over into the furrows had it not been for my grabbing the plough handle.

Henderson's been very good to me but he said the other day, 'Look, laddie, the last time ye came up here, it took a half day to do what ye used to do in a couple of hours. We might need to look at something else for you. I'll see if there's anything in the workroom.'

It was while working as a storeman, stacking sacks of grain for the mill, that I noticed Billie walk past the open doors. I called out to him, 'Hello, boss,' he replied. He came in in farming clothes and a hat, looking tidy. 'What you doing here?' he asked.

'I've not been feeling so good lately, so Mr H. has put me on light duties. Where's that tartan of yours, Billie?'

'Ah, boss, Mr McGregor, he give me another hiding. I got so mad, I picked up a baton and swiped him with it. Mr Henderson, he says, "No tartan here, Billie – otherwise, no work." I need the work.'

We all have our problems. There's the inscription in the Netherkirk at St Cyrus. 'As runs the glass, so man's life must pass.' Florence is upset. Florence realises that my efforts are not what they were and I believe she is beginning to suspect that I may be quite ill. The trouble is, I know all this is making me fretful and intolerant.

Slowly, I am having to give way to what ails me. My right leg sometimes swells and discolours and on those days I am not just fatigued from first waking, but I feel all day my brain is like the Har, but twice as thick as that fog of the Mearns. My body is no longer in step with my mind, even when the fogs lift occasionally. I know my senses aren't working properly. And I am not able to consider, or reflect. I am much less the man I was in spirit.

Today I had a fainting fit. I approached Mr Henderson and told him, 'I'm nae sure that I'm at all in fine fettle.' He looked concerned.

'What seems to be the trouble, laddie?'

'My work, Mr Henderson. I think I need to see the doctor. I think it may be the wound playing up.'

'Let's get you over to Dr Carter, right away. Don't tomfool around with this kind of sickness, laddie, I'm telling you.'

The doctor was a New Zealander, old enough to have seen active service. He came straight to the point. 'You've got the makings of paralysis in that leg. If we don't do something quick, you will lose the use of it. I'm putting you into care in Rotorua. They have some marvellous treatments for soldiers in the pools up there.'

I told him, 'Look, man, I've nae the money for even the fare and I'm nae again'.'

But eventually Florence persuaded me. She and the wee son saw me off from the Marton cab on the overnight train. It was a cool, starry night. Florence gave me a parcel of food she had prepared and some spare blankets. She was very brave. 'Just make sure that you get well,' she whispered on the platform, kissing me. I shook the boy's hand. From Marton Junction, with a changeover at Frankton Junction, it is a ten hour journey. The train was quite full, with several Returned Men in my carriage. You can tell. One of them was on crutches, his artificial leg jutting out into the corridor. I've not been on trains much out here. A train journey at night puts me in mind of the old country.

Doug 9

1942 New Caledonia

This is the life. We have this jeep, Dusty Mullins and I. We have driven it across the Plaine des Gaiacs, where we New Zealanders built our camp and completed an airstrip. Apart from the hardy Giac and its mate the Nnioli, there was little other vegetation around – that's how I remember the names.

We took a few days' leave in eastern New Caledonia where we found a dense tropical growth and plenty of tropical fruits. We even stayed at a pension, a sort of boarding-house, converted for the troops for Rest and Recreation. The powers-that-be later closed this establishment down because they suspected the people in charge were Vichy sympathizers. It was a great improvement on the WWI Bell tents we had been sleeping in, as was the food.

We kept away from the brothels over in Noumea; the Pink House was the main one. They didn't appeal greatly; the queues were too long and those painted women, well, we weren't quite that desperate. There were rumours that some of them weren't women! A few enterprising Kiwi blokes actually sold their places in the queues to over-amorous Yanks.

Beer was at a premium on New Caledonia; occasionally a man could score a bottle or two of Toohey's – the Australian beer. The local red wine at first sip gave the impression of tooth enamel remover. There was also an Ouzo tipple that tasted like liquorice, but after a few drinks proved to be a highly downable hooch.

We fell in with a group of Yanks who invited us to stay at their billet. The Sergeant was loading jeeps onto a freighter headed for the Russell Islands, north west of Guadalcanal, but he had a couple he'd held back for running about, that had missed the boat. 'Say, do you guys want this God-damned jeep? If you don't we'll have to run it over a cliff.' It didn't have a scratch on it. I glanced at the speedo – 500 miles. 'What a waste, we'd better take it,' I remember thinking.

But it was to prove more trouble than it was worth. Our American friends helped us paint over their insignia. Off we went. By day we rested the jeep in the scrub; by night we were on the move, touring the Noumea waterfront and the bays beyond, the warm tropical air blowing in our faces. We went shopping. One night we were drinking at the Beer Garden in the town centre, where ex-world heavyweight champion Gene Tunney was the Sergeant-at-Arms. Who should come up to us but one of our aircrew, Joe Bradbury. 'Your whole outfit is packing to move north – you guys had better get back to the Plains of Gaiac double-quick-smart.'

Since our outfit had no way of getting in touch – for we had yet to reach our destination – we decided to get up early next morning and head back north in the jeep. We had covered about fifty miles when a military police vehicle passed us heading south. I glanced in the rear-vision mirror. There was a great cloud of telltale dust. 'Blast! – he's seen us, he's made a U-turn.' Quick as a flash he was alongside us, forcing us to halt. He leapt from his jeep, Colt .45 drawn. He was a Red Cap, even younger than we were. Everything about him seemed very new. His uniform was fresh on and crisp, the white webbing and brass gleaming. It was cut in a way that the Americans liked, that showed it had been tailored. In this heat it was beginning to stick to his body. This was not flattering. He looked as though he would easily turn to flab. I could see that he was a scone-doer. But as I stared at the beads of sweat gathering along his top lip I found I was laughing to myself, 'How did we manage to get ourselves into this?' It was like a bad film: 'What pleasure it would be to fatten his lip.'

Above the noise of two engines running, dust clinging to the air, I could hear Jimmie Cameron laying down the law to me, after that time he heard about the Davie McKinnon incident: 'You're not a nipper any more, son, and you're gonna have to watch yourself very carefully. Ye have a knack of getting into trouble. For the love of your mother, just take charge of yourself, man, or you'll be the death of us all.' All the more reason to watch my step when I spoke to baby-face. He wasn't smiling and his finger was on the trigger. I glanced at Dusty – the man with the bruiser's reputation had gone white as a ghost, and his hands were shaking.

'What man's army are you guys in?' drawled baby-face above the noise of the two engines, his heavy Colt trained right on us. 'The RNZAF,' I told him. He didn't seem to understand. I said it again, pronouncing the 'zed' as a 'zee'. 'You follow me,' he announced, 'and don't try anything stupid.'

Over the ten miles to Military Police HQ I glanced at Dusty; he was still white. Soon we faced the Yank Provost Marshall, keen to learn how we had acquired one of his vehicles, and all the Cannon towels and footwear – legitimately obtained from a PX store in Noumea. He was convinced by our story and was on the point of letting us go, back to the place where we had been picked up, when he had a thought. He called up New Zealand Army HQ. I could hear the Kiwi accent crackling through the bakelite, 'Ah, so you have those blokes, do you? Thank you very much; we will relieve you of them as soon as possible.' The following day our adjutant, accompanied by a junior MO came south to escort us on our return to the Plaine des Gaiacs to face charges.

CO Don Grigg read us the Riot Act. 'What do you men think this outfit is – a chance to take a little South Sea jaunt? Lounging about taking an extended holiday, drinking beer and chasing bits of fluff? Is that all that military service means to you? There are good men up the line in the Pacific right now, dying in their droves. And you blokes! God-damn it, we might as well go back home now and let the Japs take over, for all that you care. Tooling around in American equipment living the life of Larry – who on earth do you think you are? You've had too much contact with the Americans already.'

He threw the book at us: failure to have the correct paperwork, failure to have a licence to drive, contrary to the good order and conduct of the RNZAF – we were imperfectly dressed, with blue overalls over our uniforms. 'I order you both to ten days' hard labour in the New Zealand Army Detention Barracks. March them away.' We found out afterwards that what he had done would never have stood up to a court martial.

'What are you doing here, Doug?' asked a guy in charge whom I had been at school with. 'Just ten days' porridge,' I confessed. I wouldn't be writing to my mother about this and begged that he keep my situation out of the Marton gossip. We were ushered to our quarters. A double-wire compound about twenty-five by fifteen yards, a tent fly over a wooden frame, four wooden slat beds with no mattresses, two blankets and one mosquito net per bed. The latrine was lacking in anything but the basics – an ammunition box upside down with a round hole cut in it placed over a long-drop. A tiny amount of paper, big enough for a postcard, nailed to a post. An issue of one gallon of water a day.

We marched to the chow line for meals, an armed sentry posted fore and aft, returning to the compound to eat. With water such a precious commodity, we let the ants and flies clean the plates. In actual fact, it wasn't a lot worse than our first camp here. Water shortages ran our lives.

Initially there were five of us in the Booby Hatch, stumping and clearing ground for tent sites. Two of us were habituals, the rest amateurs. The food actually was OK and with one of the guards being from home they were pretty friendly – they would share a smoke with you. The one-pip wonders who commanded them had told them, 'It's your job to make sure these men are kept working. If you don't you'll find yourselves in there with them.' So a man had to keep working. We lost a power of sweat in there, and we had to take salt tablets.

We were assigned to sandbagging around gun emplacements, even heavier work in the tropical sun. We also cut slit trenches in hard soil, sun-baked and packed down like concrete. But it didn't do me any harm; I knew I'd be fitter when I came out. My pals hadn't forgotten me. One of our kites dived low over the stockade every day – it must have been No. 9 Squadron poking the borax. How many men in detention got their own salute from aircraft? The worst thing was the sheer boredom at nights.

Mostly we played euchre until we slept. Three days into the sentence and Dusty was out with a rupture from lifting sandbags. I carried on until the end of my sentence, another five days. It was the full onset of the dengue season. The king hit came later when I was approached by an orderly room wallah: 'You owe the firm 16/6d.' – 'What the hell do you mean?'— 'You pay for your own meals when you are inside,' he said, with some vehemence. 'Well, I'll go to buggery, what miserable bastards.'

'Watch your tongue, soldier, or you'll be back inside.'

As I walked away I heard an unfamiliar voice. 'What did you do to upset them so badly?'

I turned. A very confident, fit-looking hombre, a New Zealander, was looking at me.

'What's it to you?'

'Take it easy, son, I'm not getting on your wick.'

His gaze was steady. I could see he wasn't taking the mickey. He looked as though he could raise a bit of Cain himself.

'Gidday, the name's Roberts.'

'Prentice. I'm a gun armourer – where do you fit in this place?'

'Aircraft engineer second class, probably about to be demoted.'

'What was your crime?'

I told him – he listened as we completed our meal.

'Christ, what a pack of jacks. I once went on the rantan after a long time in the bush. The demons put me in for the night till I sobered up. Care for a spot now?'

I was on for it – I immediately took a shine to him. He was about my height, and as I later learned, fit as a buck rat and wouldn't take strife from anyone. He seemed to have everybody's number, just quietly, but he was great company and liked a beer.

'How come you joined the air force?' he wanted to know.

'A long story. Promised my mother, a war widow, that I wouldn't join up to the army. How about you?'

'My father was a First World War man, told me about the army – all that square-bashing and balderdash. Polishing brass. I couldn't bear the thought. Most of my mates went into the army because they were good shots. I'm a deer-culler too, and handy enough with a three-o. But I thought I'd enlist in the Air Force. Might be a bit less bull-dust to handle.'

'Ever want to be a pilot?'

'Hell yes, since I was a kid. But I totally missed out on an education.'

'Me too,' and we both grinned.

Next day I was out. I was testing the bomb bay and cabin tanks in Hudson Bomber 2068 in readiness to inflict some well-aimed damage when we headed north. The target was anchored a short distance offshore and we dropped smoke bombs onto it. I had a great view of the island from the rear turret, that very spot the services recruitment board had in mind for me when I first fronted up to join up.

Just before we pulled out of New Caledonia for the New Hebrides, to be closer to the action, I was flown in a Douglas up to Tontouta airfield, near Noumea, to look at a damaged aircraft. Facilities here were poor. The thing about New Caledonia – Prentice, being a bushman, was the one who pointed this out – was that there was almost a complete lack of vermin – no deer, oppossum or snakes. But the place sure made up for it in mosquitoes – the largest I had ever seen.

I was given a tent with a wet mud floor to sleep in. There were more mosquitoes in there than flies round a corpse, but there is no malaria in New Caledonia. My one consolation was that while there I was able to make a trip to Noumea to stock up on cigars, gum and other necessities such as American beer.

Alan 10

I tried to figure it out. ANZAC services at school were full of those words of piety and gloom of, as dark as a funeral, the worst day of your life, full of preaching, just like church. But then there was all this celebration, so it seemed. Dad was always up at magpie fart, as he liked to call it, for the Dawn Parade on ANZAC Day and then off to the RSA for a few jugs. If it was cold, he had rum. Women never went, it was the men's day. A day when men got away with murder – women for once had no control over them.

It was a bit mysterious. Heroes came served up in strange ways. Most of the men I knew were fathers of my friends who were pretty remote figures. They were somewhere else, preoccupied, usually not interested in you. Mothers sometimes were. The men seemed restless, forbidding; sometimes their silences were even scary. You had to rely on women for a steer on how the world was. 'Mr Holt was so drunk – I heard Mum talking with Auntie Joan about the men on Anzac Day,' Barry told me earnestly one night as we were going to bed, his blue eyes expressive. 'Mrs Holt wouldn't let him back into the house. She locked him out.'

About a year later I got the good oil myself. I'd just come in from playing outside and was doing a quiet inspection of the baking tins. My mother was on the phone in the living room; her tone put me immediately on full reception:

'You don't mean to say? Did he?'

Silence while the person at the other end of the line spoke.

'And Mr Prosser fell over and knocked out one of his teeth. I heard from Elsie that happened.' More silence.

184

'Is that right? Oh, that's the dizzy limit. You mean to say that Judy locked him out, and told him not to come back?'

'Oh, not till tomorrow.'

Silence.

'Did she, is that right?'

'Well, I hear that Frank got locked out too. He was so under the monk that he damaged the front gate – couldn't work the lock, so he just pushed right through it.'

Then she responded. She said again, incredulously, 'Is that right? He didn't? Goodness gracious. Well I never!'

There were things you remembered as a child simply because they didn't make sense. I could never make these stories fit with the solemnity of those ANZAC services – the minister's prayers, the heads bowed, the quavering notes from a battered bugle playing *The Last Post*. What was it all about?

***

Small boys, very small, from age seven up, and burly unsmiling men dragging on fags, cardigans unbuttoned over Vyella tartan shirts, clipboard at hand. Queues of boys in their underwear waiting for the weigh-in on a couple of sets of scales, *Salter* stamped at the head of the flickering needle, under the grandstand at Spriggens Park. A roll-call for manhood.

'Name? Age? Stand up on the scales, sonny. No, stand right in the middle of it. You got any brains?'

The red needle teetered. Seventy-five pounds. 'Next.' In such ways a very young boy entered the portal to the great mystery of rugby, a ritual that in the '50s started early for them in the protein-rich towns, counties and boroughs all over the country. Weight, I learnt aged seven, was everything. I carried no surplus, but height and good bones gave me weight for my age.

The following Saturday, newly acquired second-hand footie-boots' sprigs clacking on the wooden duckboards –

laid to protect the frost-covered but familiar racecourse that encircled the inner playing fields — I discovered the needle had cast my fate. I was to be a forward – forever, as it turned out. A prop, sometimes hooker, the unusually sharp bones of my shoulders biting into the opposition's front-row flesh as we packed down before ruck collapse, buried in the smell of Bay Rum and fifteen boys on a dead man's chest.

Forwards were the heavers and grunters, procurers of the ball from the mêlée of copper-washed cotton jerseys and fresh laundered shorts. Snow-white laces worked in an excruciating lattice in the eyelets of the scrubbed black boots, polished to a shine each Saturday morning. The boots were for rucking, the shoulders for pushing, the ball to be got out for the glory of the backs who seemed, mysteriously, to understand what they had to do. For forwards, it was ritual preparation for a life of stoicism and servitude, preferably on a dairy farm, the clasping cups chugging away diurnally to drain the yield from the earth's goodness. The ball was always out there like the promise of riches, but seldom if ever reached. I never really understood what its possession amounted to.

Keeney-seeney, in which one boy stood out in the middle of the field and, facing the crowd, called for a runner that he tried to catch and bring down, thereby adding to the catchers, was physical too, but somehow more fun. Sometimes you'd have the shirt torn from off your back, you got dirty knees, the odd broken finger – it was great rough and tumble.

Year after year I pushed off for the game on the bicycle in search of something. As I came back round the side of the house, Dad would pause on his rake, panting slightly from the exertion of putting in a winter crop of lucerne or potatoes in the back garden. It would always be the same. 'Did you win?' – 'No,' I'd say with uneasy indifference. Then he'd say, 'Did you score any tries?' Later, after many, many 'no's', he'd say, 'Did you get stuck in?' Getting 'stuck in' was terribly important. It was hard to win when you played for Composite

D. Composite D and I had no future in rugby, not the slightest appreciation of the game, and yet I played for it season after season. Somehow, I thought I might find my way to him through the inexplicable tedium of all this. He never came to watch. Perhaps we knew that would have humiliated us both. It was, after all, the only game for New Zealanders.

'So how are you, son, scoring any tries?'

'No, Dad.'

'Well, what's the matter with you, can't you run fast enough?'

'I dunno. I'd like to get into harriers. I can run well enough.'

He grunted.

A few years later I got out of rugby and started with a local running club. I was taller than average, but slender, with, I discovered, great lung capacity. I was an ideal build for a long-distance runner. I found that with a small amount of training I could outrun most of my age group and that I actually enjoyed running.

I loved night training. Most people were tucked up at home in their lounges – by the early sixties you could see a strange blue glow emanating from the front room of almost every home, up and down the town. The glow was a sign of a massive migration from radio to the promised land of black and white television undertaken by an entire nation. The watchers were comfortable, I knew, but I was out there, my own hero, running in all weathers for some as yet unknown goal. The blue lights became a beacon for my own superiority. Not only was I out there running, but when I did get home, I'd be reading – Tolstoy, Dickens, Kipling, Buchan, Ion Idriess – anything I could get my hands on. Sometimes in winter on a frosty night, when mist gathered like moths around the street lights, the coldness in the lungs was sharp. For most of the year I would run for the sheer pleasure of my own vitality, a sense of being fully alive, almost out of my pale, freckled skin. Besides, there was the

187

prospect of a win in the school sports in the mile in March and in spring, the marathon.

I did do well in the mile, starting from behind and hungrily eating up the distance between me and the others as if it were a plate of steak and chips. Woofing it down, I knew the sweet taste of competition. We ran on grass tracks, burnt to the colour of creosote by summer, lines for lanes curved enticingly by the caretaker's white-wash at both ends of the field. I loved the power, the sense of acceleration, pounding around the final outside curve, closing on the boys who had the shorter, inside distance to run and then leaving them behind.

After a few years of placings I was regularly crossing the finish line for a win, Mr Cairncross thumping down the stopwatch button in his exaggerated arm gesture with the descending fist, finger on the button, brought up short at the end. The cheers of the crowd – those television watchers I ran past most nights – felt meant, deserved, my claim on life. It was recognition of who I was, without having to say a thing. The local paper's sports page did the rest: 'Roberts supreme in mile', 'Schoolboy mile talent wins again'. I cut and kept the clippings as a log against personal uncertainty.

Of course when Peter Snell broke the mile world record at Cook's Gardens in 1962 I was there in the delighted crowd, cheering him on to world fame. This was history, consciously made, dutifully and ecstatically reported. Snell ran a perfect race, made it seem effortless, and was a thoroughly unassuming, softly spoken man. Our perfect hero, in the Ed Hillary mould. I wasn't the same as him, but I took his quietness and determination as planks in an ill-formed campaign for my own advancement.

It was the endurance distances where I really came into my own. Mr Cummings had heard about Percy Curetty's techniques of training athletes in sand-country in Australia. Whenever I got the chance, I started to work out at Koitiata up in the dunes. One step forward, two back in the sliding sand, calves, lungs and heart screaming for a halt to it all. But with determination, I could gradually feel my body claiming greater strength and endurance. If there were long steep hills, which harriers always offered, then so much the better. 'You'll outrun those other boys,' Frank Cummings would tell me confidently as he slapped my legs and back with a heady wintergreen mix on a bench at the club-rooms before a Saturday event. 'You're built for this – if you take a grip on yourself, you can do anything.' Frank was always cheerful, and I'd never heard this stuff about believing in yourself before. If Frank hadn't been a Christian, it might have seemed almost arrogant, thinking of yourself like that, but it fed me, fed my drive. 'Drive' – now there was a word to savour, to think about when I got out there and just ran for the fact that I could. With hard training, on the day the energy came seemingly from nowhere.

I took Mr Cummings to mean that I ought not to worry too much about what the crowd thought, on the day of an event or any other time. So I got to love the cheers if they were there at the end of a big race, that swelled in volume the closer I got to the finish – just like that roar at the races. But I didn't care if they weren't. As I grew to relish the solitude offered by hours of training and people sensed that I didn't need them, my schoolmates left me alone. I wasn't a boy that others sought out.

The athletics won me more respect than I could ever win in the classroom, but instead of courting popularity, gradually I grew aloof. It would have seemed to classmates like superiority, a terrible attitude. As my ability to run for up to ten hours a week, eight of them in training, became a pattern, I realised that not only did I have few friends, but that I was unconcerned about it. My introversion grew, but I didn't care. Skinny guys with flinty blue eyes, ginger eyelashes and freckled faces were not in huge demand.

I didn't figure at school dances – didn't need to attend them, to try to mix with girls or buy in to the expectations of others. The music down the crystal set came to feed a dream world that could be fulfilled later. 'Don't you want to go to the school social?' my mother would ask, increasingly solicitous.

'No, Mum, I can't see the point.'

'Your father was such a good dancer. Wouldn't you like to learn?'

Dad would chip in, 'How do you think you'll find a mate if you don't go to dances?'

'I dunno. I'm quite happy the way I am. I'd sooner read a good book.'

'What a lot of baloney, everyone needs friends. A man needs to get to know women and find out how they tick. What's wrong with you?'

'Oh, leave him alone, Doug,' my mother chipped in. 'He'll make his own way. He'll do alright, just give him half a chance to grow up.'

'But dancing,' my father muttered to my mother. 'It's how we met. It's what people do – we had such a good time with it, it's what makes the world go round. What's wrong with that boy? Doesn't he like women?'

'Dad, I've got other things to do. Leave me alone.'

The great thing about all this running was that it got me out of the house and allowed me to think. The exercise cleared my head; I drove myself on physically, ignoring the hardship. Loving the solitude shaped my determination to cut my own track in life. I started to make plans. I decided that I wanted to travel and would stay at school another year after University Entrance. I would stay one more year because there was a harrier championship I wanted to secure and some study in accountancy would be helpful. Then I would find work down in Wellington as a shipping clerk, for the Port Line, on the Quay. 'That, my boy,' Dad's mate Garth who had served on *Archilles*, told me, 'is a great way to see the world.'

Hector 10

The Main Trunk Railway has only been open for ten years, not long before my arrival in this country. Just out of Marton we crossed the Turakina River, which today is just a bairn of a burn. Yet this was the same river I had seen in spate, carrying that Maori whare to its mouth all those years ago. I had been witness to so much more death since then. Why did we have to have a war? Next up, the railway crossed the Whangaehu, its acid waters brought up from deep in the earth, draining the volcano at the island's centre. No fish to be had here.

The track passed on the lofty Meccano viaducts over great entrenchments formed by the Rangitikei River. Though not as long as our magnificent Tay Bridge, they're probably higher, in really difficult country. You have to wonder at the enterprise of those who created them.

They slow the train down to cross these viaducts, the wheels giving out a hollow drum-like roll as we pass over them. Trains bring back memories. That sound took me back to the invalid train in France with the padre who had lost his faith. I wondered what it was that I believed now. I didn't really want to think about it. I couldn't speak of my doubts to Florence. She is a deeply religious woman and I have no wish to intrude upon her beliefs.

As we climbed higher into the volcanic country, it got colder. Nothing like as cold as Aberdeen in winter dreich. Now, the way my blood is, I feel it so much more. My bones are all aching, especially in my lower spine.

I dozed off and awoke to see the moon covering the land in its light. It was truly beautiful, as lovely as the Cairngorms, with the volcanoes in the distance at first, rising from the uplands. I overheard a laddie on the train telling his pal they've been planting Scottish heather up in the National Park, but sadly I nae saw sign of it.

At one stop I glanced across at the man with the artificial leg. He returned my gaze. 'Beautiful night for it,' he said, nodding towards the window. We introduced ourselves, shook hands and fell to talking. 'Harry Walker,' he said, putting out his hand. Harry fixed me with a squint; I suspect he may have lost a little sight in his accident and was probably lucky not to be blind.

As we drew closer the volcanoes were proud and naked in the moonlight, silent and marvellous – so much larger than I had imagined. Ruapehu was flying a pennant of cloud that curled back as a mantle in the clear night sky. As beautiful as Ben Nevis and so grand.

'Where is it you come from?' Harry asked.

'I'm a ploughman at Runneymede, out near a place, you've probably not heard of it, Turakina.'

'Maybe then you'd know the Stuarts who farm out that way?'

'Oh aye, I do – they're bonnie people.'

'So you must know those other Scotties that live out there?'

'Oh yes, Stewarts, Grants, the Camerons, Stirlings. Myself, I worked for Hendersons. It's a little Scotland, there's no getting away from it.

'I've been to a good ceilidih or two with those folk. I've even attended the kirk. It's so hard to find Gaelic spoken anywhere in this land, it fills your heart to hear the minister preaching his sermon in that sweet speech. The kirk is packed to overflowin' and the folk are fair canty about it, I can tell you. It does a man good to be there. It's a great wee kirk.'

'Do you have the Gaelic tongue yourself?'

'Nay, I'm from the Lowlands.' I paused. I didn't want to assume friendship too soon. I looked at him – he seemed all ears. 'A thousand years or more it is we've been out there on the Mearns, growing food. And since the Union we've got by very well selling our tatties from those soils.'

'Ah,' said Harry,' I love that country round to the north. Myself, I'm brought up English, in Surrey, but my mother came from an island out Lewis way. She gave me a great love of the Highlands and we visited her people when I was a boy.'

'So you have a feel of it, then? My father was a flesher and a dealer in stock, he made well of himself and later became a farmer.'

The train blew its whistle as it went through another small railway town, a straggle of wooden cottages with their backs to the train, their pitched roofs and metal water tanks glistening in the frost. Not a light showing anywhere.

I asked Harry if he knew much about the workings of these islands of New Zealand. 'If you think that Rotorua is a thermal area, you know there's a whole island of brimstone off the Bay of Plenty, don't you? They had a factory there producing bags of sulphur for the cockies? You might have seen the blue lettering on their bags. Right at the outbreak of war they had this terrible incident – you hear about that?'

He looked at me and I shook my head. He continued: 'I was working at a sawmill in Opotiki and some of the Maori workers there knew the skipper of the schooner. The first anyone knew there might be something wrong was when they pulled in with provisions for the workers and no one came out to meet them.

'There's no wharf. There was no possibility of landing without their assistance, so he had to turn around and go all the way back. He spoke with the boat's agents and returned some days later with a rowing boat. They could see that there had been an eruption and that the refractory and sleeping quarters had been wiped out by a lava flow. It was then that it dawned on them that all the men – about a dozen of them – had disappeared. In one fell swoop.

'A party of workmen was brought in to dig in the lava which was still warm. It was difficult work. You know, they didn't find a trace. The only thing that survived was the camp cat – they took him back to Opotiki.'

I wondered aloud whether something similar could ever happen 'on the North Island.'

Harry picked me up on it with a rare smile. 'If I may be so bold as to say so, what you just said is a giveaway that you are still a recent migrant here. You said "live on", which is what people from the distance say. When you are truly the inhabitants of an island, you live *in* it, just as English-speaking people everywhere, be it on islands or continents, live in a country.

'But even New Zealanders, looking from their country to, say, the Chatham Islands or White Island, will talk about people living "on" the island. It's something to do with relative size.'

The train chugged away through the night. I was anxious to get started at the hospital. Every whistle brought me closer to a cure. I couldn't wait to get on with the treatment. Harry was also going to Rotorua, where he was to receive his third lot of treatment. 'There has been a reduction in the pain in my stump. Most definitely,' he assured me.

We were met at Rotorua by a taxicab, pulled by a pair of bays. The driver was an Australian and he was accompanied by a young nurse, wrapped in a stole. It was cold and overcast. The wee town had a rotten-egg stench and there were large numbers of natives hanging about at the station, talking and smoking. The nurse wrapped us in blankets and they drove us to the hospital. The broad shouldered attendant who met us wanted to lift me into a Bath chair but I was having none of it.

This is a fine-looking establishment, in the style of a European alpine resort. The government has spared little in ensuring that every detail offers the best in accommodation. Each day hundreds of mostly well-to-do visiting tourists from all around the world came to take the waters. I heard French and Americans talking for the first time since I left Europe, usually chattering in the corridors. It was quite a place. The government had spared nothing in bringing it up to the highest standards and it seemed that their efforts were being rewarded.

I spent two weeks at the spa, my evenings at the sanatorium. Each morning we were taken to the warm Ward Baths where we were encouraged to swim. As a non-swimmer, I was content to use a wooden board to assist me in moving about in the water.

We were given an excellent breakfast back at the san, with its French doors opening out onto the lake. Then the spa therapy began. Under the direction of Dr Jergens and his team of masseurs and nurses I was lowered into hot pools and given treatments as good as all that Switzerland could offer. The Aix massage baths were first. The sulphur-vapour baths within the Blue Baths and the electric Bath chair were all part of my treatment.

The doctor had a fascination with electricity that I thought was a bit new-fangled. It was heartening, though, to feel the way my leg was activated when connected with mild electrical impulses. 'Just give 'em half a chance, you see, and those pins'll be running away on you again,' Mr Reddaway, the attendant said encouragingly. 'You'll be lucky to keep up with them.'

But it was the pools themselves within the specially constructed bath house which were really the cure. The favourite story, which everyone told me, was about a missionary priest, Mahoney, from the 1870s. Mahoney's arthritis had got so bad, the Maori he was serving carried him to one of their special places for a cure. They say he was so improved, when he got out, he was able to walk home. I couldn't help wondering whether it was one of those Catholic kind of cures.

I wanted to know how effective the treatment was. I wasn't sure about Dr Jergens' reply.

A quiet, nervy sort of man with sharp blue eyes under a balding forehead, he informed me, 'The heat will stimulate your blood, the sulphur will stimulate your lungs and the massage will help strengthen your vital organs, as well as your muscles. I want to see you walking again.'

'You're not the first one here with this problem,' he told me. 'We have had some degree of success with others – there's a young fellow, he was paralysed, who is now walking with the aid of crutches.

'Your treatment will include mudbaths, douche baths and bathing in the tonic mineral waters. For some people, there are real benefits. For others, the effects are not so marked. Few of our patients receive no benefit from the treatment. We'll be finding out what's best for you.'

The next day I was sitting in my towels in the steam room, drowsing, as we tended to do a lot in this place. I remember looking up one time while I was there. Above me there was an angel figure looking towards me in the steam. It wasn't until I heard the rattle and groaning of the elevator that I realised that I was regarding one of the marble figures put here to adorn the place. It was Psyche and Cupid, with Cupid in his chariot of doves. I was angered at such self-deception, such Roman-like thinking; I wonder what is happening to me. What would my father have said?

There is another statue here that really upset me, though. It was of a boy and his dog, found dead in an Italian church. I just couldn't get that out of my mind; it kept coming back to haunt me. I can tell you, it made me deeply sad. It's silly, what you think of when you are unwell, but I couldn't believe that they could have such statues around representing so much suffering.

A band would play in the rotunda on Sunday afternoons and if the sun was out, we would sit out on the lawn to listen. Myself, I prefer pipes and fiddle to the brass. I was wheeled out one sunny afternoon to view more sculpture in the gardens. One was for a hero of the South African war – an entire figure erected to the memory of one brave man. I found myself thinking that if this treatment doesn't work, what happened to me at the Somme won't be on any war memorial. I'm too late for that.

The best times were when we retreated to the cooling room. The men, their treatments over for the day, were able to smoke and talk. But we were comrades only in our suffering. We were convivial but little was shared in words. A few of us played euchre and two-up. Harry and I would pass the time of day. He knew a lot about New Zealand because he had worked all over. And I liked being able to share his knowledge. But the most that was said about the war was occasionally someone would mention a place, Messines, Ypres, Passchendaele, the Somme, perhaps, as if it were the name of a station on a sign that one had seen in a moment, flashing up at the window of a moving train journeying through a foreign country in the night. Then it would be gone.

Usually the name had stuck because that was where some terrible battle had been fought. If a man mentioned it, it was probably where he had been wounded. Some of the fellows were also very shy, and demoralised by war and by the way they had been treated. They had even less to say. A few others were shell-shocked. Even the better off ones of these lived in their own world. Conversation was not their game. One, a fit-looking man called Giles, spent a lot of the day in a wicker chair rocking back and forth like a pendulum. He was here officially because he had lost three fingers in an explosion and his hand needed therapy. But it was the minds of men like him they could not get to. For that reason, after three weeks there, I was glad to take the train back home and make way for another man, perhaps a more deserving case.

This time on the train I went to sleep, but I kept on waking from dreams. I want so much to live and it is a grand thing to be home. But I find everything here now very trying, the son particularly. He is lively and I find myself pushing him away and then regretting it. Somehow, when the pain is constant, the noise of a raucous child is the last thing you want. I remember my own father. He was so stern and remote: a switch of willow standing upright in a corner of the parlour. I had to beat my lad the other day for disobedience.

Three times I told him to go away and three times he came back in with some lizard in his hand while I was trying to rest. He whimpered for some while. I cannot control the pain and irritability. Then I thought, 'Is this how you want him to remember you when you are gone?' The guilt was like a dagger to my heart. The sins of the fathers are visited on the children, indeed. But knowing this doesn't change my habits, doesn't ease the pain. The knowledge of what I've done, it mocks the idea of the father I thought that I would be.

Doug 10

March 11

After eight months up the boo-aye we farewelled New Caledonia to follow our American mates further north to Espiritu Santo. We knew it would be warm where we were going. The journey was for a couple of hours but by the time we arrived at Buttons Airstrip we were frozen. So it seemed all the hotter as we stepped out of the plane and the tropical air hit us like a warm blanket. I don't know that I ever really got used to it.

Palacula Bay, Santo boasted a huge dry dock which lay offshore, towed out in sections from the United States. The camp was up a slight rise from the airstrip, a green strip bulldozed through the orange groves and palm trees. I went up to the cook-house and saw the wreckage of a plane there – a load of shickered Americans had crashed and killed themselves. I was pretty horrified at the time, but you soon became hardened – or so you thought.

Many of my mates had already gone up to the Canal – Cassie, Dusty, Harold and co. Prentice was there too. From what they told me, the Solomons sounded like a pretty grim sort of an outfit. I reckoned the rest of us would get better acquainted with Guadalcanal before long.

Santo was hellish hot and it rained every day. A lot of the time it just steamed. The jungle was dense and clammy; the trees were huge with many brightly coloured birds. The airmen's mess was back in the jungle and not the most inviting place, with mud all over the mess floor. For meals, if the Australian horsemeat was running short, we reverted to eating the Yanks' horse-cock.

Harold, who back home drove the local fire-tender, told me war was just like being a fireman. 'Most of the time you put up with sheer boredom – but there are bouts of extreme excitement.' What no one ever told us was how tedious war is a lot of the time. Home gradually took on a pleasurable glow – we longed for all the comforts we missed. We couldn't put all that out of our minds. And to think how glad we had been to leave it for adventure!

When the Japs weren't close and we had a bit of time off, we'd sit for hours on the beach under the shelter of a palm watching the huge man-eating coconut crabs moving up and down the sand. We bet durries on them, and lobbed the occasional grenade at them. Sometimes we'd spy a turtle on the beach that we'd lug up to the cook-house and get the cook to make soup out of it.

Flies were everywhere in the tropics; the exposed bodies of hot, sweating men were especially attractive to them. We had a lot of time to study flies. It didn't take long for us to discover that there was only one way to deal with them, whether one landed on you or on something else. Flies take off backwards. If you move quickly enough to hit one about an inch behind where you imagine it will take off, you kill it every time, sure as eggs are eggs.

There was also a bit of sorting out to do in a new camp. On my first day some big guy, who was probably drunk from a binge the night before, pushed into line a couple of blokes in front of me. I was prepared to deal with him, but as I figured out the best course of action, a familiar, clean-cut figure spoke out.

'So what's the rush?' he asked, standing steadily about two feet from the troublemaker. It was Prentice.

The other guy didn't respond.

I was narked by him too, so I said, angrily, 'Hey! Why've you got such a hurry on?'

The bloke squared his shoulders and strolled over. He was huge and I could smell liquor on his breath.

'Are you talking to me, pipsqueak?' He was head and shoulders above me, but I was keen to have a go. As I squared up to him Prentice just bowled right up to him. He grabbed the man by his shirt with both hands and pulled him towards him as he brought a knee up into his groin. The bloke had all the stuffing pushed out of him and Prentice shoved him to the ground. Prentice didn't even look back – he seemed to just dance back into line, not batting an eyelid. We sat together over breakfast. He didn't even mention it – started a conversation about the PX store.

After a few days we shifted from the hovel. We erected our new tents in a coconut grove. In this new possie we were further from the chow line, but away from the rank stink of the jungle and the large rats that lurked there in their hundreds. I was with a great bunch of guys, including Prentice.

We were able to catch up on washing at the pool – a large tree fallen across the stream had formed a natural washboard. We swam during lunch-hour in another pool nearby – crystal-clear semi-salt water. The quarter-master came bustling round with some new gear – the first new issue since we left New Zealand. I was more than pleased to be able to change into a fresh pair of shorts. The backside in the old ones was so frayed it had completely dropped out. The guys had started nicknaming me 'Teaser' as a result.

The camp had two good assets, though – good water and good hard butter. Food was now 100 percent better with vegetables and real meat. Unfortunately, I got dengue fever a few days after my arrival – I probably picked it up just before I quit New Caledonia. I had kidney pain, and aches all over – I doped myself with aspirin hourly. Fever in a hot climate is a strange sensation, and if I got on the turps, the next day felt like about fifteen hangovers all rolled into one. I was too crook even to make it to the sick-bay – I didn't have an appetite. It took a week or so to throw it off.

Prentice turned up one day, towards the end of the bout. He was holding a covered metal pan that was hot. He'd cooked up some cream chicken, served in a broth. And there was a glass of orange juice. 'Where the heck did you get this from?' I asked.

He grinned. 'The Americans. There's a cook I know who collects Jap mementos – it took a pair of pilot's boots to do the trick.'

When I improved we attended a concert together. There was a big band, Glenn Miller style, and a negress who sang along with them. She was attractive, in a sequined silver dress that fitted her. All the men had eyes just for her.

'What I wouldn't do for a woman,' Prentice said.

'It's been so long, I'm desperate enough to pay to hold hands with one,' I said.

'Come on, you don't mean that. I'd want a bit more than that for my money,' he said.

'I know what you're saying – once you've had a taste you just keep wanting it. In a way, being in the islands is a bit like being in gaol – the women are not to be had.'

When Prentice speaks to you, he looks you straight in the eye – there's no deception in him and he doesn't expect it in others. Dusty Mullins was singing his own praises the other day about some hunting he'd done in the Ureweras. Prentice was mending a shirt – I notice he's a neat sewer. When Dustie had finished describing the stag he'd shot, Prentice put down his needle and thread. Looking steadily at Dusty, he said, 'How many points did you say that stag had?'

'It was a thirteen-pointer.'

'Oh yeah,' said Prentice, 'and whereabouts in the Urewera was this?'

'Up the back of Maungapohatu, east about four miles.'

'What year was this?'

'It was Easter 1939 – I took the whole thing out on my back, why...?' he faltered, sensing Prentice's line of questioning might lead him into the cactus.

'You sure the local Maori would leave an animal that big for a stranger?'

'Too right I am.'

'You gutted it and carried out a thirteen-pointer in that country, with your rifle and pack?'

Miller nodded.

'I don't believe you.'

Dusty opened his mouth to say something else, then realized that he was now in deep water. He shrugged and said, 'You're the expert, maybe it was a smaller one.'

Prentice pulled out a cigarette from behind his ear – he didn't smoke more than about two a day, quite unusual – to give himself and Dusty a bit more time. He decided to light it and let the whole thing blow over. He didn't rub it in, but he clearly knew more than Dusty about deer and stalking them. It was no contest.

Dusty never spoke of hunting again. Funny thing was, Prentice never spoke of it either – not when Dusty was around.

Francis came out of the hospital after a bout of dengue. He has this theory that dengue makes you sterile. He's a bright boy, Francis. What a lot of bull! Prentice and I put him right.

The Yanks are so generous, but I could not believe how casual they were about life. One night seven of them were killed while watching a movie, *Star-Spangled Rhythm*. These chaps were sitting on an unexploded bomb when suddenly it went off – right in the middle of the movie. Lord, it gave me the shivers – I could have been one of them. The next day a Douglas dive bomber blew a tyre while taking off. It slewed off the runway, collected a salvage truck parked nearby and burst into flames. The pilot and gunner were both killed outright, as well as the poor salvage operator. The plane's motor got hurled about thirty feet across the runway. The same day I heard that one of our Hudsons crashed at Cactus, across the water from Guadalcanal, whilst the pilot was executing a ground loop. Who needed the Japs when we were able to do so much harm to ourselves?

Looking at the diary I kept back then – just a few short notes most days – I see it was only a day or so later we were awakened and told to make ready. Suddenly we were off, the whole No. 9 Squadron, headed north for Guadalcanal. We had heard so much about it already – this was the place where the Yanks and the Japs were engaged in almost continuous air-sea and land battles for 100 days until late last year. They said that the cost of holding the island was huge in men and munitions, and ships and planes. Those American marines showed what they were made of, not once but time and time again. The word was that if our side paid a price, the Japs lost more than 24,000 men, 15,000 of them killed in battle.

As we approached Guadalcanal we flew over San Cristobal, lying out in a calm sea, and then over Henderson Airfield. It appeared to have taken a fair dose of punishment with lots of headless and stripped palm trees. The port at Guadalcanal was a massive ship's graveyard – most of the wrecks on the bottom were from our side. The runway was steel-deck Marsden matting that made our plane rattle noisily as it landed and the engines were throttled back to a standstill. Guadalcanal. What a place.

Things were pretty rough to begin with. As we were putting up our tent a Fijian coast-watcher covered in blood walked through the camp. He had a rifle over his shoulder and from his right hand he was swinging the severed head of a Jap by his hair as he walked. What had we let ourselves in for?

On an all-night stretch of guard duty I managed to fire off a round from my rifle by mistake, putting it through the tin roof of the guard compound. 'Some mothers do have 'em,' was all the duty sergeant said. That was my lucky day, but it was my shout at the tent and the guys poked the borax the whole time. 'See the Japs coming did you, Doug?' – 'Fair go, what a showman: *One Man's War Against the Nippon Might*' eh? – 'Too many cowboy movies, squire, they warp your sense of judgment.' I didn't want to repeat that again – in fact I felt a bit of an idiot.

Alan 11

It wasn't long after our rescue at the beach that I came to know Rita. I was still at school, in my final year. There was a big group who often came from a marae somewhere up the valley to flounder and surf-cast at the beach. They had old cars, even by the standards of the 1960s. Mostly, the men did the fishing, whilst the women would get a fire going and make tea, and huddle chatting among themselves, their small kids playing, never far away.

I had been out in the surf in the kayak and was pushing it back on a little cart we had when I diverted across the flats to where I could hear a car in trouble. The starter was turning over, the engine roaring, but the car, an old Chevrolet, stayed where it was, stuck in the mud.

As I came nearer, I realised it was Maurice and his father. He was a big man in a navy T-shirt and jeans, trying to force the car out using the accelerator. He was getting riled. By spinning its wheels he was only digging it deeper into the mud. I didn't want to tell him what to do so I sang out, 'Hang on, I'll get some gear; we'll have you out in a jiffy.' Maori don't say thanks in so many words, but they never forget and he looked pleased when I came back.

Maurice and I dug down round the front of the back wheels, placing coal sacks and fence posts under them for traction. Then we embedded a corduroy pathway of stout branches. I noticed a young woman about my age was watching me. She was tall for a Maori with dark eyes, thick short black hair and long legs in very short shorts, folded over at the bottoms, most fetching. They called her Rita.

It took over half an hour to get that car out. Before climbing back in the car she strolled over.

Maurice finally introduced us as they were leaving. 'Eh, this is my cousin, Rita.'

'Hello,' I said. She was a stunner. There was a pause. I didn't want to show interest in her as a woman, certainly not in front of Maurice. I was lost for words.

'How far away do you live from here?' I inquired.

'Oh, we live out Marton way, in the country; on a small farm there.' Her eyes moved expressively as she spoke and I noticed how full and attractive her lower lip was.

A few weeks later they were back and I spotted Rita down by the river. She was in a sheer swimsuit, of the kind Jantzen used to sell in fabric that fitted like skin over the body. Mostly, they were worn for swimming contests, but they were ahead of the times when it came to frankness. Jantzen's ad was cheeky too: *Just wear a smile, and a Jantzen*, it used to say.

'Is that your kayak?' she enquired.

'Yep that's the one,' I told her.

'Can I come out in it some time with you?' she asked. I was staggered and impressed that she was so forward in front of her family. But I found myself shy, hesitant to let on.

A few weeks later we went swimming together on an ebbing tide. It was the first time I had entered the water with a girl that I fancied and I was excited by her, so aware of her body and her being near and the feeling of intimacy it brought. I was glad the water was so cold.

'So you know Maurice – how do you know my cousin?' She had forgotten our original meeting.

'Oh, I've known him down here for years. We still meet at the beach sometimes, have done since we were boys. We're mates.'

'He's got my gran's sense of humour.'

'Yeah, we get along well.'

'He's the eldest of his family, but it's my job to see he doesn't get a big fat head.'

'Aw, we're not all like that, you know. Some of us are quite modest.'

My dad wasn't too keen on the friendship with Rita. 'Just watch yourself with those Maoris,' he said once, 'and don't go getting yourself caught up with them.'

'You used to go to Kakariki for dances, you must have taken out Maori girls.' He didn't like my cheek.

'Don't give me lip, boy, or you'll get a good clip behind the ear.'

'You can't stand what I'm telling you, you just don't want to hear it.'

'For once in your life, you listen to what I'm telling you. Take my word for it, those Maori girls, you're better off away from them. It'll bring you nothing but trouble.'

New Year came around again and Jimmie Cameron brought his piano accordion and a small group of enthusiastic songsters, including his tall dark friend. They stayed for about half an hour around midnight and greeted the New Year. As they were leaving one of them, who may have been a little drunk, called out to me, 'Where's your Maori girlfriend? Why isn't she here tonight?'

Quickly my father countered, 'He doesn't have a girlfriend, let alone a Maori one. He's a bit of an oddity, this one. Doesn't even go to dances.'

There were a few guffaws, but they had other things on their minds. I didn't see Rita for some time. After I left school I had gone to Wellington to take the job in shipping, but I returned occasionally to Koitiata where, one day in summer, when the tide was high, we met again at the beach. I'd been going out with a few girls in Wellington, nothing very serious. But there she was with a dog on the river bank.

'Hello,' she said, confident as ever. She was a real looker, more than I remembered – slender and dark-eyed. 'How's Wellington?' she asked, tossing her head of tight curls. 'Have you got room to take me out in your canoe? I never get out in their boats. They always say, "No room for women – you stay on the shore." I'm a strong swimmer and I'd love to come on the sea.'

'Why not – there's room,' I replied, feigning a shrug but feeling quite heady.

I ventured my hand. 'We could go now. The tide's still coming in, so we'll need to be back in before it starts to go out again.

'I'll just go back to the bach for the spare life jacket.' I gathered up an old Hutchwilco, *recommended by the US coastguard*. When she put it on she looked really cute; her arms were slender and well-toned for a girl. As we headed out I was conscious of the breakers. 'We have to get the timing right between those couple of big waves.'

I waited for one to break and paddled like hell before the next one was upon us.

One wave crashed noisily behind us and another pursed its lips as it approached, but we cleared it before it broke. We got through the wild water into a safer place where a recurring pattern of waves that were still forming moved through the bow and body of the craft without upsetting it. We sat out on the bobbing sea and looked back to where we'd come from. Rita was enthralled, and it was great having her on board.

'It's pretty neat out here – I've always wanted to do this.' Sitting in front, she turned towards me. Her eyes were so alive and I found myself watching in delight at the way her mouth formed words as she spoke. 'I've always wanted to join the men out here,' she said. 'You can see right round the bay. Look, there's Taranaki, where my nanny's people come from – under that cloud.' I watched her straight shoulders rise as she drew an extra breath. 'We had her tangi last year. She passed away in September. We were all with her. She died at home. She was an old lady, born under the mountain only a few years after the invasion. That's where she died.'

I didn't want to let on that I knew nothing about what she spoke of.

I turned the kayak's bow towards the shore, working at my paddle.

'Where was this, exactly?'

'You know – Parihaka.'

'Oh,' I said.

I was wondering how to reply when she laughed, not unkindly nor contrived. Maori were different from us, but I didn't understand how she could laugh at something like my ignorance when the subject was so important to her. She leaned back against me, her head on my chest. Boy, that felt good. But I knew that there would be telescopes and binoculars ranged upon us from the baches – so many telltales with nothing better to do – so I turned the kayak back out to sea and stroked her hair with my back to them. After a while she began to stroke my knees, which came about to where her hands dropped. There was not much more that we could do without turning the kayak over. So, after a short but awkward kiss – with our backs saying 'don't watch' to the prying binoculars – we came back into shore. I hoped Mrs O'Hagan next door, who often conducted a sweep of the coast with her telescope, hadn't alerted my family.

'How long you here for?' Rita asked, always to the point, as we came ashore. She whistled for the dog to come, then turned and said, 'I've been thinking about you while you've been away.'

The next few days we spent together. In those times motorcycle helmets were not compulsory. After I picked her up on the Yamaha and we tore complicity up that winding valley road with the trees and telegraph poles egging us on heedlessly, the wind howling in our ears, pressing down on the flesh of our cheeks on the short straights. She sat in behind me, holding snug. We rode for miles, pushing the bike hard into the tight corners until we came to Laird's Reserve. Following a pathway leading into a tall forest of native trees we found a place where we could picnic privately. I brought a rug, as requested. She set her basket down, filled with 'kai', as she called it, producing a meal of tomatoes, lettuce and cheese and newly-made Maori bread. 'Come on, get stuck in,' she said, sawing into the loaf with a kitchen knife. I realised I didn't have much of an appetite, unusual for me.

She had brought a big thermos of tea and as we lay on the blue rug we drank from the screw-top mugs of the thermos.

Tentatively at first, we held each other, and kissed quite innocently. Her skin smelt of women's soap. I was aroused. The closeness, the scent of her, mixed with the smell of the rich forest soils added to a heady mix of desire. But I was not sure that I was ready for this. I had no plan, but perhaps I hadn't been able to admit fully to myself what I really wanted.

This became our favourite spot. We visited it on a number of occasions, becoming more and more daring through that summer. It was a wonder no one had yet spotted us.

Then one day, as we reached the trees by the road, a big Daimler came past, quite slowly. To my horror, at the wheel was the dark man of our Hogmanay, Jimmie's friend. I comforted myself with the thought that there was so much dust raised off the gravel road, he might not have seen me. But I had seen who he was.

To my surprise, I met him over on the beach a few weeks later while fossicking. Davie McKinnon. He must have been staying nearby. I had noticed his vehicle parked at Whitaker's the night before. They were probably playing cards. Now I dreaded what he might say.

'Good day to you,' he said, in his distinctive way, his eyes at work beneath the brim of his hat. 'And what have we here?' He nodded at a post I was dragging up the beach. 'Maire, if I'm not mistaken.'

'Dad needs some timber for a shed, so I thought I'd better bring this one up.'

'A good move – I don't see anyone else's markings on it, do you?' He smiled, with some warmth.

'Ah,' I assured him, 'I pulled this out of the tide, it's mine.'

His formality was helpful – because he appeared to have all he needed in himself, he did not seem like a man who required distance between himself and younger people. We walked back together towards the batches.

'I've noticed you are a motorcycle man – are you satisfied with the performance of these new Japanese machines? In my day we loved our Indians, the preferred mount of despatch riders.'

I let out the deep breath I had been holding – he had told me the worst, perhaps, and left me with room to manoeuvre. 'They are more reliable, on the whole, than other British and American bikes, I'm told, and I'm not so keen on fixing things. And they go really well. But my father always brought us up to admire the Indian.'

'Is that so? I do believe I still have an Indian in mint condition in my implement shed.' He paused, glancing to an area where the wind cut low hollows and hillocks in the sand, above the river's usual high-tide mark.

'Oh, would you have a minute? I've something to show you. I noticed it on my way over.'

I let the post drop and followed him for a few yards. The river had recently spread right over the isthmus that separated it from the sea, which meant the sand had been stiffened by an injection of new river mud and then cut by the wind. Just beyond this was softer sand and lying in a fold in shell grit and a few stones lay a dotterel's nest. Three eggs, brown-speckled and innocent, lay in the scrape. Standing just away from it, drooping its wing, the parent dotterel was loudly calling to lure us away from it.

'How long do they take to hatch?' I asked.

'About a month – four weeks, to be precise. They are a miracle, are they not?'

'People don't ever think of birds nesting in this way. It's beaut. Birds are what make this place special.'

'Wait until you get to know some of the rare plants here,' he said. 'So would you care to come out and see my Indian some time? A man like you, interested in ornithology and motorcycles is indeed a rarity in these parts and it'd be a pleasure to show you.'

I rode out to meet him, up the Turakina Valley. It was a balmy summer evening with sunset still an hour away. This was where Rita and I would come for our special outings. Thick cloud was gathering to the west as I rumbled over the cattle-stop. There was a stand of kahikatea at the road entrance. The house was a 1920's villa up on a bit of a rise. His front paddock was covered in weeds – this was a farmer who had other interests. The front door was open onto the veranda and as I knocked at the frame of the wooden screen across it, I could see him inside, reading under a standard lamp with a fringed shade. I could hear piano music, recorded – something classical, Chopin perhaps. He called out, 'Just let yourself in now, young man.'

I noticed he had a folding card-table set up for four, a cribbage board and cards stacked to one side. He introduced me to his wife, an elegant woman in a silk shawl, who sat on a settee on the other side of the room organising pictures into a photograph album, gluing them in with photo corners.

'What a great evening. Let's take a look at the Indian while it's still light.'

He stood up and gestured that we go out the back.

'I'll fetch you a cup of tea by and by,' Mrs McKinnon said, glancing up and there was no mistaking that she, too, was a Scot.

We passed through a connecting room with a heavy varnished table and chairs at its centre – every wall lined in shelves of books, floor to ceiling. I'd never seen so many together in a private home.

He watched my eyes widen. 'Ah, so you are a reader,' he murmured. I noticed one shelf was made up entirely of the *Journal of the Polynesian Society*, which I'd never seen before. I wanted to get back in there.

His Chief was in its own special hut, a lean-to against an implement shed that also held hay. The machine was immaculately restored, in army green. 'She's a five-horsepower twin. You're welcome to try to start her up, although it's been a while. We don't have time for you to ride her, not tonight, but another time. I'm sure you'd love to hear her engine doing its work.'

I stood, one foot on the footrest and flung my other leg over, settled into the sprung leather saddle, switched her on and kicked her over. The compression snorted and shrugged like some animal. I tried over and over and again, but I couldn't get her to fire. The v-engine was a lovely racy machine with its heavy mudguards and bicycle-style handlebars. But I had no patience with machinery that didn't work and he could see that.

'Oh, let's leave well alone,' he said. 'I'll need to take a look at the distributor. Let's have some tea and I can show you some things I have inside.'

'Mr McKinnon,' I replied, adopting his formality. 'I'd be glad to.'

'Come in, come in, my boy, sit you down.'

We sat in his library, while Mrs McKinnon brought us tea and ginger gems on a tray. It was evident that he had things that were on his mind. But he wasn't going to show his hand, not directly.

As we sat down I came out with the question that my father had been unable to ask him: 'How well, sir, did you know my grandfather?'

'Pretty well, pretty well – he was a Scot, after all, like myself.'

'So what was he like, did he ever speak of family?'

'In appearance he was not entirely unlike yourself – more like you than your father. He was a man whose company I am sure you would have enjoyed, as most certainly did I. I didn't learn much of his family, but he did talk about Kincardineshire and farming.'

I wanted to keep him going. 'What was the country like that he left? Do you know?'

'The thing is, lad, that there are many Scotlands. That's something I wanted to say straight off. The one I knew – and your grandfather knew – is not the Scotland of today. Besides, a man in the isles who speaks Gaelic and fishes for a living is quite different from the one who lives in the city of Edinburgh, or again, comes from your grandfather's country, which we Scots know as the Mearns. They speak another language there. The Doric tongue, recognisably Germanic in sound and root.'

He stepped over to his shelf of Polynesian journals, running a finger along the spines. Then he hesitated.

'You know, years ago I was involved in an archaeological dig down near the mouth of the Rangitikei, on the edge of a swamp. It was fascinating, learning how early Maori lived along these shores and how they provided for themselves. I think people are pretty much the same no matter where they are from. It's the differences that keep me interested.

'Anyone sensible knows that people the world over today are mostly of mixed blood, aren't they? Even the Scotties; good grief, man, I've got Pictish connections: there's the Scotia tribe, Viking, German, Angles and others besides. Blood's important, but blood's just a part of it.

'Your grandfather and I did talk of these things, I do remember. It was after an incident, a matter of race, involving a chap called McGregor.'

He glanced out the window. 'Come out here for a moment.'

We stepped onto another veranda. He pointed. 'Just look at that sunset.' The cloud was feathered, like a scarlet fleece and streaked higher up. 'Where would you see more glory? What I like to consider when I see that sight is, how does that make us here, seeing it, who we are and how does looking at it make us into certain kinds of people? – which I do believe it does.

'You know I am certain that a people's being over generations is touched by the colour of the prevailing sky here. It is edged by the beating of the sea, shaped by the turn of the hills, the slant of the light on the mountains, the way the burns run out through the land.

'And maybe a lot more? If you think about it, you get it with the sound of the wind, whether it moves through trees or over a plain, by the way the birds rise up in their patterning of the sky, or make their song; by the call of the wild – their wild. So many things we hardly notice.'

He then motioned me back inside.

'Sometimes, I wish I'd been a painter. You know, I believe it's what we do to the land, what we make of it, that determines the way it calls back to what I like to think of as our inscape. I have Gerard Manley Hopkins to thank for that word. He's as near as you can get to painting the land in words.'

He paused, stirring his tea – he was one of those men who liked it half cold. 'If you think about it, once a people get beyond mere survival, it's the land that turns the choices we make – to fell or furlough, plough or graze, cultivate or simply cherish for its own sake. It is that which affects us. Our ancestors must have been forest people. We Scots know that even when the English invaded, there were trees that they took down – huge trees – to build their castles. But how many Scots are forest people today? And does that knowing in their blood make them yearn for what once was? Can we know? Who can ever tell?'

He got up from his chair again. He liked to pace about as he talked. He took a last look at the sunset, now fading second by second. 'How different are my children just for being raised in this land and not Scotland?

'As villages go up, it's all in the curve of a wall, the throw of an arch – and the decisions, is it to be in timber or stone; thatch or slate? How we decide isn't only about what materials are available, or what may look right to us.

'If you take a railway line driven through a landscape, we all know that will mean a place is created where nothing much grows beneath the wheels. But what does a line of rail that runs through a town do over time to the inside of the minds of humans who live beside it?

'We know that if it affects just one human, that's not going to change a people. When it's just one, that's when you get eccentricity. Or madness. It's when it affects a whole group that you get a change in folk. So one day these people wake up and realise that they're not just from the same ancestor, but their thinking and how they see things is distinctive from their neighbours.'

He looked across at his wife through the French windows, still content with her albums, listening, rather than directly involved: 'You remember that poor Johnson lass, Jeannie?' She set her glue bottle down carefully and nodded – she'd heard this before.

'Memory is what holds us as individuals and peoples together. When people change – and they do, they can do, utterly – I've even seen people who've treated others really and consistently badly sometimes make themselves again. When that happens, the thing that reminds them of who they were is memory and that strange, niggling thing called conscience. Conscience is something we know a lot about in Scotland; you could say that since Calvin came to Edinburgh we pushed it far too far. But it's just a word for the way a folk bring up their young, is it not?'

He stood up, as though it were time for me to go, and took a step towards me, placing a hand on my shoulder. 'I did know your grandfather, we became good friends, even though he was my elder by some years.

'I know I've not spoken directly of him tonight, which is probably what you were wishing to hear. But I want you to know that we had some long discussions about these very matters, over a bottle of Glenmorangie. A long time ago, just before the Great War, when we both were wondering how living in a new country would affect our community. We were interested in the local Maori. Some of them were worse off then than they are today – poor as crofters and with many health problems. Which is where Ratana comes in.'

'Mr McKinnon, do you know about a place called Parihaka?'

He returned to his books. 'Here,' he said handing me a slender, red-bound one, 'you may borrow this if you promise to return it – Dick Scott did this, it's about Parihaka. Essential reading for those of us living all along this coast.'

I rode home out of the valley as the last light drained from the western skies, so excited that I had the bike wound up and almost spilled on gravel on a tight corner. I had plenty to think about. I'd never met anyone quite like him. When I searched inside myself, there was something there I wanted to hold on to – a feeling of being somehow understood.

Doug 11

December 1942 – April 1944

Soon after we arrived at Guadalcanal – a dot on the map that no one had never heard of before the war – I fitted a bomb bay to a Hudson and went up for a test. A figure in overalls ran up at the last minute and hopped through the hatch just before they shut it. 'Gotta sort out my geography of this place,' he muttered, tumbling into his seat moments before the pilot waved for take-off. It was Prentice. We had a good look from upstairs for over an hour.

There must have been a dozen or more islands in this grouping, thousands of acres in coconut plantations. There is a long stretch of water running the length of the Solomons between the chain of islands between Bougainville in the north and San Cristobal in the south. They call this the Slot.

We gradually pieced together a little more of recent events at Guadalcanal. We knew this was where the Americans decided they had to stop Japanese expansion into the Pacific, only a few months back. Battles here had become a do-or-die effort between the Japanese and the American forces. It was a close-run thing – if they'd lost, Australia and New Zealand would have been overrun and we would have all been slave labour for the Jap war effort. We'd heard about some of these battles; we knew from the papers that this had been one of those massive struggles involving ground forces, air and navy.

The pilot showed us where the marines had held out against tens of thousands of Imperial troops.

'They say it was touch and go,' Prentice shouted through his headset. 'Bloody grit and determination by those Yank marines, they were all that held Henderson Airfield – the Japs threw themselves into it, in wave after wave.'

Some of the Americans we served beside did not always display those qualities. They seemed to panic when they were in a corner and under fire. Often they showed no regard for human life – even the lives of their own men. You came to expect this from the Japs, but not from the Americans. You'd have thought they were like us.

I said to Prentice, 'Those Yanks speak the same language, they often look like us, they drink and fight like us and we know – all too well – that they like our women. But we are not the same as them.'

'One of life's mysteries,' muttered Prentice, who had a theory about it

'A lot of those soldiers who fought and held these islands were well trained. The Marines in particular who took on those big battles with the Japs have since returned home – they'd done their stuff. But most of these recruits around us now are new potatoes – not very well trained.'

Our camp was at Bloody Gulch, right below Bloody Ridge where General Vandegrift set up his command post. This was south of the airfield near the Lunga River. The worst thing about Guadalcanal was the stink of death. Nearly sixty years later I can still summon it up with little effort – all those years have not eradicated the sweet and sour smell of rotting jungle and decaying carcasses.

Prentice seemed to know how the war was going better than anyone else. With censorship keeping us lot in the dark, I couldn't figure out how he knew. One night, doing guard duty at about 9pm, I found him in with the radio operator. 'Huh,' I said, 'Now I know where you get all your dope from.'

We had our work cut out keeping these planes in the air. The Japs were playing for keeps. The first plane we lost was Hudson 2064, out on anti-submarine patrol when it disappeared over the Canal. Soon after, Hudson 2058, which

I had worked on only days before, fitting long-range fuel tanks, was damaged on the ground during a raid.

We seemed to be short of skilled staff and got few breaks. I would do anything for a break from the tedium and the heat, especially from midday into the afternoon. I got into the river whenever I could. An Aussie washing his clothes one morning was chased by a croc and had to run for his life in his birthday suit. Lucky to retain the family jewels. This created quite a bit of mirth round the camp. His mates reckoned he'd been rejected by the critter on account of the pox. The Lunga was fairly swift-flowing. As a rule crocs like still water, but they still managed to catch an eighteen-footer there. A Yank had dived in and broken his neck. It was so hot, I just had to go on taking the risk.

A whole day off was unusual in the life of an erk – it was the one time when we could make our own plans. One morning Prentice and I moseyed down to the beach for a swim. We then jumped on a string of rubbish barges that were headed out of the harbour to empty out their loads into the ocean. We visited a couple of Liberty ships and stayed aboard the *Doug V. Daniel* for a dinner – roast chicken and apple pie. They lived well, those Americans. To top off a good day, when we got back to base they broke out an issue of free beer.

On another one of our rare days off I made a tour of our tent line and part of the combat area with Prentice and Harold Francis. I saw many signs of warfare that were pretty grim. This was where the US Marines dug in to defend the island from the waves of charges from the Japs, backed by Bettys from above and heavy naval armoury in the Slot. Our guys took some punishment.

Every so often we would come upon a field of death – you could smell it coming. Dead Japs were initially given bulldozer burials, thousands of them, but the stench hung on like nobody's business. The Yanks told us they gave up bulldozer burials after they were caught by so many booby-trapped bodies – like a hand grenade set to go off under the armpit of a corpse. They also gave up taking Jap prisoners after so many of them attacked their captors with whatever they had left – knives, forks, bayonets. The rules of combat were entirely different with these people – there was no pussy-footing. Without the Yanks in this war effort we would now be up the creek without a paddle.

At one point in our tour, emerging from a thicket on the edge of a small plain covered in tall tiger grass, we came across the remains of a huge Jap underground dug-out which the Yanks were said to have dynamited, killing maybe 800 men. It was a terrible mess, and the smell was putrid. We trekked on through the jungle, getting lost at one stage, then retracing our steps.

Cassie, Harold, Ralph and I were in the same tent. The tents and surroundings were pretty rough. It was hard to believe then, as it is now, but I saw Cassie out several times with a home-made net chasing tropical butterflies. In the middle of a war he was making a collection of them – it takes all sorts, I guess.

Apart from the smell, we were plagued at the Knoll by giant rats forever pestering our tents at night. No wonder most of the natives took to the hills. In our tent we set a bait on a see-saw over a bucket of water. In the middle of the night there'd be a splash and then it was the next guy's turn to deal with the offender with a bayonet blow on the head and reset the trap.

That was the least of our worries. We quickly got into the routine of tumbling out of bed into a nearby fox-hole for Red Alert, listening for the tell-tale throb of the unsynchronised Jap aircraft engines, soon followed by the swishing sound of earth-bound bombs. Best of all was to see a bandit caught in the beams of searchlights and the Lockheed Lightning Night Fighter readying for the kill.

I adopted Prentice's habit and stood by the Radio Shack at opportune times and listened in to the instructions issued by Radar Control to the searchlight crew and the Night Fighter. 'Two degrees port, straighten up, now hold it steady, you're right on target, give it a short squirt right up the arse. Bingo! Over and out.' A direct hit produced instant flames and the enemy craft was soon a flying inferno headed for the sea off Lunga Point.

For the air crew, flying anti-submarine patrols for hours just fifty feet above the water in glaring bright sunlight was hard, boring work. Every so often, though, it paid a dividend. Flight Sergeant Franks and his crew spotted a large Jap sub off the coast of Vella Lavella. Its conning tower was open and three Japs were standing in it. Before the sub could dive, the aircraft attacked with depth charges, scoring direct hits. They followed up with a couple of 250lb bombs. Soon the water was covered in oil. But it was not claimed as a kill, because we didn't know for sure. There is a lot of uncertainty in war. On April 2, 1943, our squadron took its official first kill here with a Hudson downing a Jap float-plane.

Alan 12

In late summer I went out to see Mr McKinnon again, returning his book.

'So how are you, my boy? Was it a good read?'

'I'm so glad I read it. Thank you, Mr McKinnon.'

'An instructive work, no doubt about that. I trust you found it so? William Fox comes out of it with no credit at all. You know of his old homestead, don't you – it's not so far from here – Westhoe?'

He gave me a glance. He was one of those people who can read you even though they appear to be absorbed in their own talking. 'Come inside, won't you?'

Taking my elbow he ushered me into the library.

'What was it,' I wanted to know, putting the book on the table, 'about those settlers that let them treat the Maori so badly? And they thought of themselves as civilised – and Christian too.'

He almost dismissed that query, saying, 'Whenever I hear the word "Empire", I wait for the next word that goes with it – you can guess what it is? "Conquest..." Look at what those pious Pilgrims did to America's Indians. A complete disgrace.

'The more you read, the more the story is the same. Te Whiti and Tohu represented a strain of peace-making in a warrior race – that's what makes Parihaka so distinctive. You could see it, if you wished, as another part of what we discussed last time. You know, about what makes a people who they are.'

He looked at me. 'I'm pleased that you're asking the questions.' He paused, took a deep breath and smiled, the sunburnt creases around the sides of his eyes closing up like folds in a concertina. He had thought about our last meeting.

He stepped across to a shelf of books, running a finger down the spine of one of them.

'Remember what I was saying the other night? I think the greatest contribution to the distinctiveness of a people may arise from what folks do to each other. The idea that stern parenting, say, breeds a different kind of child from gentle parenting. We all know that – that over time, speaking softly with a lilt becomes part of a people, so that after years of it, everyone speaks that way. It's possible this means they also think it – the patterns have become that way and the language becomes recognisable as a language, or a dialect, maybe.

'There is always contrariness of course, the ones who remind us that rules about folk are as easily broken as they are made – like the softly-spoken person who can still mete out misery to his children. Or behave in an ungenerous way just because they've known hardship and – wonderful old word – covetousness.'

'I'm not sure that I follow you.' I asked him: 'Let me think … Are you saying things like poverty etch themselves into ways of thinking? A bit like the way salt eats into metal on a beach – in the same way with people and their being – and this can stay for generations?'

He hesitated. 'You give me pause here, Alan. Not because I know nothing about metals. I think I take your point. Everyone likes to say the Scots are miserable. And I've found that to be true in certain people, in certain parts of the country. Tight, some of us are, tight as a lid on a cream churn. In Aberdeen when I was a boy visiting, those shopkeepers, they'd not give you a stale butty – not even if you were dying of starvation at their keyhole. But I've found there are miserable people everywhere and given half a chance the Scots are as generous as any. The poor more so than the rich, of course, it will ever be that way.'

'Well, where did that idea of meanness come from if it's not true?'

'But maybe the English made that up about us to justify their own cruelty and the way they reduced us to beggary. I really don't know.'

Keeping up with him was hard work. I paused and asked, 'But there are some ways that we, ah, fit ourselves to, aren't there, just because of the way humans conform?'

'Maybe, maybe it's not that simple,' he thought. 'The thing that matters is belief – and it is belief that makes us what we are. Something from inside ourselves, worked on by the tides of generations, that points like terns on a strand in an estuary, that lifts our noses – strikes an attitude as we say, in how we see and what we see, and equally important, what we choose to disregard.

'Oh, that disregarding must be a whole story in itself. Over time, collectively, in ways we do not yet know, we as a people get to be affected by these things and they make us who we are.

'I'd love to know, if they like to sing and to share their songs, does that quicken the music within their children? Does their jigging make their great-grandchildren better dancers? Their fiddling make their grandchildren more musical? Their poaching, even, does that make them better burglars?

'I'm interested in how a proud fighting people like the Maoris find it in themselves to take another pathway. Maybe it was always there, in those people of Parihaka.'

Listening to him talk I felt how little I knew, but was also flattered to be able to share his thoughts. As we walked out to the bike he turned to me.

'My boy, I do think that when you are able, you need to visit the places your people came from. You'd find it helpful. It's only then that you can begin to know where, or perhaps how is a better word – how you truly belong.'

***

It was still summer and I took my annual leave at Koitiata. It was now Rita who became the reason for visiting, more than any other.

One day after our picnic up the river valley I said to her, 'Why don't we walk across the paddocks to the river?'

'Okay,' she smiled. I took her hand and we ran.

The river's north bank here was high, about thirty feet above the river, at the edge of a large flat area. We descended through big trees and ran across freshly piled sand from the last fresh down the bank to the water. The piercing warning cry of a kingfisher sounded across the valley. As I looked for it a flash of gun metal glanced off its darting back. By now the sun was high and the day was hot. To my astonishment, Rita pulled her shirt over her head, undid her jeans, removed her underwear and moving from her hips with a commanding grace strode quickly towards the water. Then, with the river up to her neck, she turned her head toward me, giving an impression that she had resumed her modesty. 'Come in, Alan,' she called, 'it's quite deep here.' And she began to swim across to a hole in an easy freestyle, with short, neat strokes.

She was so free. I undressed more deliberately, but was drawn towards her as if by a powerful current. The image of her nakedness was overwhelming. In a moment I was holding her, kissing her and she kissing back, so intently that, without supporting arm movements, we both went down beneath the surface, spluttering and laughing as we came back for air. The current pulled more strongly, insistent, irresistible and yet wanted, yes, as if a long, long wait was at last over. We moved quickly: the kiss, a deeper kiss, the press of her breasts on my chest, then the urgency of old longing, of overpowering, animal necessity and excitement. As we wrestled ourselves up onto the soft aggregate of sand and mud on the bank, desire became desperation, as strong as the need for another breath – our hearts thumping – that brought us completely together.

She grasped me firmly; it was how I had always imagined it, but better, this closeness, mouth-on-mouth, skin-on-skin. I had brought no protection. I had wanted but hadn't expected this and I had to make sure that I didn't make her pregnant. I had to get the timing right. Beyond all the physical sensations, this felt too like the most wonderful act of piracy – that we had stolen something precious from the sideboard of polished respectability and claimed it for ourselves. Then, as our breath quietened, the kingfisher called again, from further away, just round the river bend. I felt reckless, unchained.

'Isn't this neat? Aren't you so neat?' she smiled, languid now, lying back under the trees on my outstretched arm, her wide eyes watching the gathering cumulus-rack stacking from the west. 'Don't you just want to do it again?' I told her it was my first time. She showed no surprise, then kissed me.

As often it can on hot mid-summer afternoons, it started to rain, a gentle splash here and there at first, single big drops pitting the sand, then quite heavily, drawing forth a rich smell of earth and manure from the parched fields. We gathered ourselves up, dressed and stood to run. I glanced down and there in the yielding mud, not quite dry, lay the imprint of our union – the impression of her entire body with my weight on it hollowed out as if in a soft bed – her head, her shoulders, the curve of her back, a pressed print of her buttocks, and then of flurried legs and heels, the ghost of our love-making. Mud in our hair, we made for the reserve, taking shelter beneath a stand of kahikatea until the cloud-burst rumbled away to the east. The air had chilled slightly and everything felt washed.

Doug 12

When we did guard duty at night the Radio Shack operators often switched to Tokyo Rose for a bit of entertainment. 'Hi guys, how's tricks?' she purred, a sentimental hit from the '30s playing in the background. 'You'll remember this catchy little number? The first time you heard it you were probably strolling down the boulevard, arm-in-arm with your sweetheart in those peaceful days before the war. Days of wine and roses. Now, all your buddies back home will be having a great time with your sweethearts, while my favourites, the wandering boneheads of the Pacific, sweat it out in the jungle. You men in New Zealand, do not bother to finish those runways at Ohakea and Whenuapai. Take a well-earned break. Very soon we will be down there to pour the remaining concrete, and make good use of both airfields. You cannot win against the might of Japan – we are irresistible.' We all got a good laugh out of that.

With the Japs all around us pressing for advantage, we also witnessed how tragically our own rules could work against us. A Liberator bomber had returned to Henderson after a night of heavy operations decidedly the worse for wear and some of its landing gear had been shot away. We think the rear-gunner may have been killed in battle.

The Japs were so close, there was a daily IFF (identify friend or foe) radio code that had to be sent before the control tower would give permission for a plane to land. But the IFF had been shot out. The crew talked with control, identified themselves in ways that only they could have done, and they pleaded for a waiver. But they weren't allowed to land. They even signalled their codes with the Aldis lamp, making several approaches. But their number was up. As far as the base command was concerned, they had failed to follow correct procedure – even though everyone on the ground could see it was one of theirs. The command was given. On the aircraft's next pass over the field the Americans turned their anti-aircraft guns on the plane and it became immediately a fireball, the charred bodies of the crew entombed in the crumpled metal that burned on the runway. They told us that it could have been hijacked by the Japs, that they couldn't be too cautious. I wondered what on earth they told their families.

A mate of mine attached to the American radar unit at Cactus swears the Americans in that outfit were completely loco. In fact the senior officers finally took those guys' guns off them. Whenever there was an argument, Colts would be drawn – sometimes with tragic consequences.

Rumours continued about dangers still lurking in the jungle. They said there was an unknown terror, known as the Strangler. They claimed he had already taken seven victims. It's all baloney, but I kept a sharpened bayonet under my pillow – there was still the odd Jap wandering round in the jungle.

The mail came only irregularly but it was welcome when it did. Food parcels arrived from the Mater, as well as the shared ones from the Red Cross. Good old Mater, she always wrote. Sometimes her sultana cakes were spoilt by their passage through the tropics, but we didn't waste much. There was a real shortage of reading material, but a Yank lent me Ernest Hemingway's *A Farewell to Arms*, not a bad read at all. There was so much rain, we had to keep the tent in good order and keep the trench around it very clear.

Close at hand to our camp was a marine cemetery and a few abandoned Jap vehicles, including a caterpillar tractor, probably a gun-hauler, with a diesel – a Mercedes-Benz air-cooled job. The Japs must have thrown everything they had at this island.

There were large buzzards flying about, a flock of red parrots, and a horned toad sat near the tent. Sometimes at sunset you could see large flocks of birds flying north. I found myself wondering how far south they had come from – silly really, but could they possibly have come from New Zealand? Prentice didn't seem to think so. 'Not those ones, Doug, Not much Kiwi in those.' He shook his head.

Prentice seemed to be better than most of us at fossicking what he needed from the Americans. He had perfected the art of bludging, among New Zealanders, even, he was King of bludgers.

He'd start by offering an American a cigarette and would finish up with an armful of PX supplies – they were generous, but with Prentice, the whole deal was handled with a patter that they couldn't resist. They almost begged to give him stuff. We all got into it – one of my first deals was a trade of a cut-throat razor for a squadron insignia. I used it for quite a while but gave up the practice when I realised I got a thrill from not cutting myself. It was all a bit dicey.

One afternoon we returned to our tent and Prentice had prepared a three-course meal, plus entrée. He turned on crab meat, turtle soup and home-made damper that he'd wrapped in the leaves of a big tree and cooked slowly in the embers of a fire. He'd bribed his way into the kitchen and roasted a chicken that he'd swapped with an American cook for a prized Jap pocket compass taken from a fallen son of the Nippon Empire. We got peach pie for desert and some American ice cream. The meal was a pearler.

As we wolfed it down we arranged for four of us with a day's leave on our hands and nothing better to do to go walkabout. The idea was to follow the evacuation route the Japs took to Cape Esperance, after their defeat at Henderson Airfield. It had been only a few months earlier. Numbers of enemy left behind were picked up by Jap ships and relocated to other islands like Bougainville.

We set out early along the Tenaru River, then followed an offshoot of a dry riverbed overgrown with jungle, tracking steeply back into the hills. As the sun rose higher the atmosphere was tropical in the extreme, and the insects turned out in their thousands. You couldn't help but admire the tenacity of the Japs – even though we hated them. They had struggled up this steep stony creek under full marching orders carrying their kit, and all the paraphernalia of assault. Some of them hauled on ropes attached to wheeled field-guns.

About two hours up the creek we came to an area shaped into an amphitheatre, where the Nip advance had awaited the arrival of their forces from their troop carriers. The banks of the valley had been terraced and two-man bivvies had been set up at two-metre intervals. The entire area was sown with landmines, saucer-shaped, lying shallow in the ground and then exposed by heavy rains. We gave them a wide berth. American patrols had made a thorough sweep of the area and most items of interest had been lifted.

It was late in the day when we set out on our return. We were suffering from dehydration and were very tired, so when we reached the river again, we lay in it for half an hour to regain strength. We finished up discarding all but a few items. I souvenired a clip of Japanese rifle bullets.

At my suggestion, Prentice and I also went to Gold Ridge, where at the start of the war Aussies were still mining. It was impossible to get to the actual mine, in the side of a ravine, because the prospectors had blasted away the bridge. At Kone Field, a bomber and night fighter strip, I saw an abandoned amphibious tank and also a Jap steamroller. Tojo's son was buried on a hill about four miles from here. His grave was converted into a urinal and his face stopped a large percentage of the flow.

We took Atabrine tablets for malaria. There was no quinine available because the Japs had taken over all sources, so we used something based, strangely enough, on a German preparation. After a while it made the skin turn yellow. We also got very skinny in the tropics – although the food on Guadalcanal was excellent, with fresh meat flown in and the water none better.

Alan 13

Mr McKinnon led me into the library. Looking at him, I realised immediately that there was no point in trying to hoodwink him. I was foolish to have not considered that before deciding to come out to visit. It became, suddenly, a little like a summons to a headmaster's study, except that he wasn't about to tell me off – rather I was about to tell him something I'd much rather not.

'So here we are. You're looking peaky, Alan, that's not just summer's sunburn fading, is it?'

I didn't hesitate. 'Well, I have to confess I got myself into a bit of strife.'

'What seems to be the trouble? The Maoris always say it is either women or land.' He smiled. He'd given me an in.

'What would it be for you?'

I must have hesitated. 'Come on now, nothing is too terrible to speak, I can assure you.'

'I have been stupid – I have gone too far with a girl, and got her into trouble.'

'I see, I see,' he said, looking pensive. 'Alan, do you think you love her, then?'

'I, I, um, well, I really like her, but no, I don't think so.'

'Very well. So are you clear as to your responsibilities?'

'I am going to have to pay for the child's upbringing. I'll do that, on my honour.'

'Of course. May I ask, would this girl be a, a, local girl?'

I took his meaning. 'She is a Maori.'

I nodded, knowing that he knew.

He fell silent for a moment.

'Have you told your parents?'

'No.'

He paused. 'You should do that. You also need to decide whether you will play the role of father with this child as he grows up. My hunch is that this is a decision you need to consider most carefully. If you do, I warn you, it is a lifetime commitment. On the other hand, you may choose not to now – and I emphasise that this is your decision – in which case you need to exercise that role as a father more fully as he leaves childhood. That is a must – something I cannot emphasise sufficiently.'

I fell silent – I was still digesting the embarrassment that I had unburdened myself to him. I felt vulnerable and checked his face, but it showed nothing but acceptance, concern even.

Again he was silent. Then he said, 'You know, I think it would reflect well on you were you to go out to her people, to a formal meeting. Face them all. Yes, right now, that's the best thing you could possibly do.'

'I'll think about it,' I said hesitantly.

'If you want my advice, don't think, just do it. Everyone will feel much better, including yourself, once you have done this. The Maori will respect you for it, and it will discharge some of the burden that you are carrying.'

He then decided to shift direction.

'It's a long time ago since we spoke, your grandfather and I – he's been dead almost as long as your father has been alive. But as I understand it, your grandfather's home was near to Laurencekirk. I'd warrant that your father's not visited these places?'

He hesitated again, before he again almost set on me with his gaze. Suddenly I realised for the first time that his eyebrows were as thick as hedgerows. 'Laddie, when you are able, and this may be a few years away yet, I want you to spend a little time looking at the places of your granddaddy on the East Coast – Laurencekirk, Montrose, St Cyrus – go up to Stonehaven too, when you have the chance, it's a pretty wee port. Take a peek in the smaller villages of the Mearns. You'll not be disappointed in any of it, even if it isn't in the brochures. In fact, that part of Scotland remains untainted by the nonsense of all those 19th century romantics.'

'I won't be disappointed? Why do you say that, Mr McKinnon? I don't understand.'

'It's hard to explain, especially to someone on this side of the world. But we are still such recent arrivals in this land – we think once we have a roof over our heads, that this is our country.

'One thing I have learnt – it takes time to be here. We are keen to shed what we have left behind, but sometimes we lose sight of what it is that keeps us human. My generation, we know the past, or at least the old country and, much as we enjoy our new land, we don't really belong yet. We put in the oak trees, sometimes in the warm ashes of old native forests – some of us even allow a few kahikatea or totara to survive. We think we belong. In my humble opinion, your generation know neither your past nor your future. Perhaps that *is* the future, I really don't know.

'But I am certain that for you, to visit the places of your forebears, and get to know the feel of their history, that cannot but make a difference for you and your life here.'

He had already lifted my spirits a little but I said, 'From where I stand I still can't really see what difference it could make – but I accept what you say. And I am interested in travel – or at least I was until this happened.'

'Well, plenty wiser than me have said it already – there's no substitute for experience – but you can start by reading.' He took down another book, and opened it. 'You see, son, to take an example, Montrose was a centre for the Presbyterian Covenantor insurrection that took place against the Crown, until the Duke of Montrose changed sides. I believe that you will still find Grahams – for that's who he was – who live in the vicinity.

'Then there's another piece of history, almost another story. When the Old Pretender marched on Scotland, he had ships waiting at Montrose, because at that time it was a Jacobite stronghold.

'Now Covenantor and Jacobite may be words that you've not heard before, but they are a part of what your grandfather's family would have lived with. So in a way they're a part of you – and what is unknown but important in your past can become a kind of deficit of your own humanity. It is something that you can begin to remedy by travelling thoughtfully.'

He handed me the book, shook my hand and said, 'Believe me, once encountered these places will do you a power of good. The best of luck now with those Maoris.'

Again, I found myself walking out to the bike thinking that life was not so bad after all.

Doug 13

Prentice

In May and June 1943 Condition Red became almost a nightly thing. Unpleasant and scary though it was for us at times, we realised that it was the Japs who were taking far more punishment in the sky than our side. When the battles were on you could think of nothing else. When you were working on the aircraft there was little else but the job in hand, even if the heat was a distraction. But when I put pen to paper, or wondered when the next mail was coming in, thoughts turned to home. The more I thought about it the longer it seemed that we had been away. We missed the familiar things – the scent of sweet peas in summer, beer in a pub, meat pies and roast dinners with potatoes, pumpkin and gravy. But as Jimmic Cameron would say, 'No point in moaning, laddie, there's always someone worse off than yourself.'

He was dead right, of course. We had five Aussies who came into the camp who had spent the previous nineteen months on Bougainville coast-watching, always on the jump dodging 15,000 Nippons. If the Japs had caught them they'd have put them to the sword – if they were lucky. Those men had a really tough job. No regular supplies, sometimes short of tobacco, down with fever and no medical support to look after them – though we heard the natives carried out some doctoring when duty called. But really they had no entertainment of any sort, no mail – those boys did a real war effort. In spite of all their discomforts – these Aussies appeared to be in the best of shape.

The chaps in the tent were great company, but we only used the tent for drinking and sleeping. The biggest problem here was the foot-rot, which ate the skin off your feet. We had all sorts of cures. Often you'd see one of the chaps stand on one leg and scratch inside his toes with the nail of the other one, like a dog with fleas.

On 5 May 1943 our aircraft made a mass raid on Munda Point, New Georgia. Fifteen Kitty Hawks strafed the beaches, silencing a number of gun positions. One torpedo fighter bomber was lost, another returned minus his tail unit, making a safe landing. Our planes were out again that afternoon with fighter escort. We expected reprisals from the Japs. The powers-that-be gave us a buckshee issue of cigarettes, shaving cream and matches – we were definitely getting very short of soap. I had a bet with Harold, I remember, for a quid, that I'd get home by Christmas.

The Jap reprisal came about a week later. There were plenty of them and a fair-sized dogfight took place about sixteen miles out at sea. We saw one Corsair pilot bail out and another was reputed to have parachuted somewhere over Lunga Point. The Yanks shot up one of our Kitty Hawks in error, another took a walloping from a Zero, riddled with cannon and machinegun fire. But the pilot was uninjured. One Zero downed, a probable.

At the same time a massive sea-battle continued between the Jap and American navies. Another of these do-or-die efforts, but those of us on the island had little intelligence to hand. Every so often a damaged American aircraft of a make we had never seen before turned up on our runways. These craft put me in mind of strange sea-birds you find occasionally after a big storm on the shoreline at home. It was odd to think that all this was going on probably quite close by and all we knew about it was what we saw in the way of these battered planes. Or the rubbish we heard from Tokyo Rose.

Quite often, usually at night, we received word that we were in 'Condition Red' – usually brought on by the imminent arrival of Tojo's high-flying bombers. Thanks to the early warnings from the coast-watchers, we usually caught a few of the first over in the beams of our searchlights.

Next instant, hell was apopping as their eggs began to fall. As a rule we were very smartly into Harold's fox-hole, which commenced to sway a little if we had a near-miss. Often I counted ten or twelve explosions on the ground.

Some nights, in a period of eight hours, we could have four Condition Red alerts. One night in May about twenty bombs were dropped. Three Jap bombers were downed by Yank night fighters. We witnessed one kill when the Boggie was caught in the lights. He was at approximately 3500 feet when the night fighter swooped on him, firing cannon shell, tracer and incendiaries. Two of the raiders burst into flames and immediately began to fall, making a great spectacle as they crashed to the ground in an inferno. One lasting vision was of a lone port wing, torn from the fuselage of a third plane that came down, the light catching its tumbling surfaces. We cheered from the sidelines, tucked in our fox holes.

It didn't go all our way. Fifteen Yanks were killed in this raid, with sixty-odd casualties. A big fire was started in an ammunition dump and the No. 2 runway fighter strip was hit plumb centre. Fortresses and Liberators were still able to take off to blast Jap bases to the north.

On June 16 Condition Red sounded about 2pm. Shortly afterwards radar reported seventy-five bandits on their way here – bombers and dive-bombers. As soon as they arrived ground gun positions threw up everything they had. The air was filled with bursting ack ack shells and the sound of pursuit ships dog-fighting the Japs, shrapnel and bullets flying in all directions. Our aircraft were soon aloft, rapidly juggling with the enemy to gain the upper hand so as to be able to strike at the jugular. From our vantage point we witnessed at least six kites in flames and parts making their way earthwards. Tojo's dive-bombers were active above Tulagi, coming down in screaming dives and dropping their payloads on our ships. A Yankee destroyer in the harbour caught fire, which they managed to extinguish. A large landing barge stopped a direct hit and had to be beached.

The noise overhead was unbelievable, with the high revving sound of the engines of the bombers coming in vertically on their respective targets, continual gunfire and bombs exploding. Zeros strafed the ridge where our camp was situated, as well as the beaches and other parts nearby. As I watched I sensed a high-pitched whine above the noise of battle and puffs of earth kicked up by something which appeared along my line of vision. Suddenly, in the bat of an eyelid, above us was a Kitty Hawk tight on the tail of a Zeke (Zero). The Kiwi's guns were raising the 'dust puffs' along the runway. I dived under a ten-tonne truck.

I found Prentice under it already. 'That was close,' was all he said, drawing on a ciggie, cool as a cumber.

'Do you remember the film, *Hell's Angels*,' I shouted.

'Too bloody right,' Prentice said.

'I saw it at the Civic – that First World War aerial combat had nothing on this.'

There was further noise of mid-air explosions, planes enveloped in flames spiralling back to earth. When we looked out we could see the pilots and crew who survived the destruction of their planes hanging in their parachutes, canopies billowing.

'Look at that poor devil,' Prentice shouted as an unopened chute formed a white scar against the night sky.

It seemed our pilots had acquitted themselves extremely well – even the Kitty Hawks joined with the Corsairs and P38 Lightnings for victory rolls over the field. I counted nine of these performances. One Grumman Wildcat crashed and burnt on landing. But we appear to have suffered no other injuries.

Scores to hand were a night's total of sixty-seven Jap planes downed – maybe too good to be true. Operations reported that 104 Jap planes came in. The coast-watcher said that only thirty headed back home. Some of these, too, failed to make it to base. Just north of Guadalcanal, our Russell Island-based craft caught more Japs, short of fuel and ammunition, bringing down the Allies' biggest bag of the day. Two days later Prentice reckoned the final total was of eighty-six Jap aircraft destroyed with a loss of two of ours – we were told that both pilots were OK.

The next night, according to a diary note, I watched *One Night in Lisbon*. After, with a few New Zealand beers saved, we celebrated. When the beer ran out Prentice asked, 'What happened to the brew that Shag Wright put down?' Shag immediately replied, 'Aw that, it went sour.' One of the team took off for Shag's tent. He returned staggering under the load of a large wooden ammunition box — 'Gone sour, eh? What a load of baloney, share and share alike, Shag.' Without further ado we put his drop to the test and, following a few trial sips, favourable judgement was passed. That was the end of his brew. Shag kept up a bleat that we had deprived him of a Japanese motorbike and sidecar, a trade he had planned with an American in exchange for the prune wine. 'Mingey bugger,' was all the sympathy he got from us.

Alan 14

I was working at the Port Line, looking out across the Waterloo Quay office at rows of grey loading cranes behind a huge, piked Victorian fence that ran the length of its windy quays. Quite often, in the course of my work, I went aboard ships that had berthed there with place names on their sterns from all around the world: Antwerp, Cape Town, Hong Kong, Bombay, Marseilles, Liverpool, Valpariso. The names made me almost silly with excitement, to use an expression of my father's. I loved all that my position offered – I liked meeting matelots from other countries, with the prospects of work abroad. I even considered entering the merchant navy.

Rita's parents were told the news and then, hardest of all, I knew I had to explain to my parents. I worried and worried about it. In the end I decided not to tell them just yet.

I kept mulling it over for a week, eating poorly and taking little interest in anything. I wasn't ready to be a father, I wasn't even ready to be a lover. I was resentful and couldn't see myself fitting into that Maori world. Whichever way I turned, I was caught in a web of my own making. She and I met at the Ben Nevis one evening, where a few drinkers and pool players had that unabashed curiosity of rural pubs. We sat at a far table. She looked beautiful in a violet blouse and short skirt, her pregnancy hardly showing.

I bought a couple of drinks.

At first she was angry. 'You bastard, you're just going to leave me to it. You wait till my family get to hear about this.' Then she burst into tears.

I tried to comfort her, but she was having none of that, no embracing. I was self-conscious because I knew those bar-flies were watching – it would have been bad enough without them. This meeting was not a good idea.

'Leave me alone. We made a mistake, meeting like this. I need to be with my family.'

'Look, we must try to talk. It'd be wrong to marry for this reason – it's not a good enough one to commit to marriage. I'm sorry … what else can I say?'

'I wish I'd never met you. You're leaving me all on my own? I thought you were a better man than that – what kind of morals have you got?'

Hell! I had little to say to that. What could I say? And as she argued, I liked myself less, but I hardly liked her more. 'How am I going to manage?' she wept. 'What about me, I'm supposed to become a nurse. You have ruined my life, but not yours – you get off Scott-free, you're just a bastard, Alan. You'll be off getting some other poor girl in the family way before long.'

'That's a bit rich, come on now, Rita.'

To give her her due, although she didn't follow my logic, somewhat reluctantly and after a lot of tears she came to accept it.

'If that's how you see it, then there's no point in us getting married. I've seen that kind of thing end in misery and disaster with some of my cousins.'

'I would like to come to your marae and tell them about my decision – I think that would be the right thing to do.' It wasn't quite as Mr McKinnon had suggested I do it; time was marching on and the new life was growing. But she nodded and her eyes told me I had done something right in suggesting it.

In October, aged nineteen, I became the father of a son, Rangi. One thing remained certain to me – I wouldn't marry Rita; I was clear on that much. We were simply too young, too inexperienced. I was still strongly attracted to her, although the biological jolt of the baby had meant the idea of physical love with any woman had, for the moment, lost much of its appeal. Having signalled my intention to them, shortly after the child was born I was summoned on a particular day to the meeting house by the family, her people, as she called them, to explain myself.

***

It was a Saturday – I was told to be there at 1pm. This was early spring, a boisterous westerly rustling the pampas grasses busily beside the meeting house. When I arrived I noticed a number of old cars and trucks pulled up in the paddock beside the house. As I switched off the bike engine I was met by Rita carrying the child in a shawl. He was tiny and shiny-brown and I was unsure about wanting to hold him. 'Come inside,' she said, pecking my cheek as I took in her familiar, still attractive smell. 'They're all waiting.' I had never been inside the place, in fact had never been in a meeting house before. All the shoes, freezing workers' gumboots and army-issue boots were off at the door, so I took mine off. Inside was a blur of brown faces; thankfully, there was no ceremony that I might have been expected to respond to.

Nor were there any smiles. Some heavy looking henchmen from a gang in one corner were smouldering at me behind their dark glasses. 'Cousins' – she had told me about them. On the walls were photographs of the ancestors, but to my surprise, there was almost no carving in the small house. It was crowded; there were perhaps thirty people in the room, about half of them women with a few small kids, all related to Rita. 'Sit on the right hand side, boy,' someone had muttered. I tried to figure where the attacks would come from.

The discussion began with prayers in Maori. Their talking went on for an hour and a half and whether in Maori or Pakeha, it seemed it was mostly aimed at me. I found myself staring across the room at the wall of framed pictures of Victorian forebears. There was a couple in one frame. It struck me that it was somewhat unusual because he was Maori and she was Pakeha. Both were confident and handsome. She was well dressed, her long dark hair pulled back from her face in ribbons, and she carried herself with dignity. Her unyielding gaze stared out from the portrait at me. There was something about her – some of the features in her strong face, and her stance, that were Rita's.

As people talked in Maori in long speeches in an ever-warming, stuffy room, my mind wandered off. The photograph got me thinking about the old European ladies like her who had lived around us, attended church and for whom, as the good Scout in my teenage years, I might be expected to run errands and mow lawns. Some were 'the old maids' of the neighbourhood who had lost their men in World War One. Like the others, obedient to the parental command to look after them until they died, they found themselves eventually alone and over-ripe, clinging to a ropy vine, living out solitary lives in declining villas – a brass plate on the front doorstep.

They gave away little of themselves. You might hear them at work in late winter or early spring with secateurs, dead-heading the hydrangeas behind privet hedges, some even pushing a poorly-set reel mower through long grass. They were figures glimpsed through their old sash and spindle gates. Occasionally they'd come out. Often dressed up in hats, gloves and veils, they'd arrive at church for communion, courteous, aloof, a few of the favoured in their genteel British cars: big Rileys, Sunbeams and Wolseleys. One or two simply walked. They were adults and therefore commanding of respect, and silently they 'set the tone' for entire streets, their presence far greater than they might have imagined. Yet as the latches on their gates closed with a click behind them, it seemed to signify a closing in of their lives.

Here I was, now beyond that pale, sitting among a group of Maoris and getting my comeuppance for breaking every rule in the book. The shame of it, the shame of knowing, was bad enough but the shame of their all knowing, that was something I could hardly even bear to think about.

Rita's father got up. He was in old blue dungarees, his stomach bulging under a maroon rugby jersey.

'Tihei mauri ora
Tuia te rangi e tu nei
Tuia te papa e hora nei.'

He continued this way in Maori for ten minutes.

As he came to the end of his oration, for the first time he nodded at me in a neutral way. I knew he was a railway worker, and a man who loved a party and had trialled for the Maori All Blacks. He spoke quietly now in English in a dignified baritone: 'You have no respect for our people, no respect for the sacredness of the female, you are a typical Pakeha – just use our women, one of them Kiwis who eats, roots, shoots and leaves. My people have seen your kind for 150 years. Nothing changes. Next thing you'll be back here, sniffing round for what's left of our land. You take a look out the matapihi in the back of this house – what do you see, boy? An over-grown paddock and over the river, a sand dune that's spreading wider and wider with every passing year.'

My mind drifted out the window and back to the meeting. Rita's Dad was still talking. 'But we are Maoris, boy, and we are here to listen to what you have to say for yourself. I can tell you now that you had better make it good. A hundred years ago my ancestors would have killed a man for less. What have you got to say for yourself?'

I stood up; my left leg had pins and needles. The room was hot and except for a couple of people asleep on mattresses, everyone was looking at me. I had no experience of speaking in public. Nothing in life had prepared me for this. Despite the anger in the room, when I stood up I was surprised at the sense that the walls, the ancestors glinting at me behind their glass and the people assembled, seemed almost supportive. I was sure of one thing – I didn't want to sound as though I was making excuses.

'I see all your ancestors up there,' I began slowly. I felt that I was easing myself out towards the edge of a long plank over a ravine. I could hear a voice in my head, maybe my father's, saying, 'Take it easy.'

I began falteringly, 'I-I don't know where to begin – I feel there is a lot to say but … let me say, I want to say … I am proud to be Rangi's parent, but I am ashamed that it has happened in this way.'

My mind went blank, I wanted to sit down. An old lady in the corner was snoring softly and a blow-fly, snagged on a spider's web on an inside window, buzzed the sound of very early summer. There was a slight commotion as a late-comer arrived. It was Maurice, who nodded towards me.

I began by greeting them, in English. It was hard to know what they thought; those dozing on the mattresses were also unnerving.

Then I looked to the wall and saw the ancestral portraits again.

'These are your ancestors and you know who they are, and I know a little of how special they are to you. But may I say that my ancestors were people, just like yours. They made mistakes, I am sure. But something other than Rangi has brought us all here today together.'

They were all listening. Maurice's eyes gave me his complete support. I really didn't know what I would say next. I tried to focus away from the scowls of the young men in the corner. I thought of the Parihaka book that Mr McKinnon had recommended. It had moved me like few other books. 'Yes, you people had lands taken away from you by the Pakeha, I acknowledge that. It was wrong, it was violent. Rita has told me about some of your own losses.' What on earth was I saying. What right did I have to say anything except 'sorry' for my own actions?

I heard my voice, almost as if it were someone else's. 'But isn't it true that you have Pakeha ancestors too? I see them on these walls? So I place myself at the mercy of you all.'

I expressed my remorse for the shame and dishonour that I had brought upon Rita and her people. I made a promise to

246

support her and the child. 'You had better, man,' growled one of the brotherhood in the corner of the room before a young woman angrily shut him up. I was a bit unnerved. 'Look. I'm sorry, truly sorry – it's not something we expected,' I said tamely.

'You should have thought about that before you got her up the duff,' shouted a long-jawed fellow in a stiff Hong Kong jacket sitting not far from me. He was elbowed into silence by the man next to him.

'You need to do the decent thing, boy, she needs more than your support,' fumed someone else.

I didn't know what to say and their taunts left me more confused. 'I've only just left school a year or so. I don't know enough, I don't earn enough to be married.'

There was a pause. A woman spoke. I'd not heard her before, she was poised. 'You're saying you're not going to marry our Rita, is that right?'

There was a longer silence. Again I heard the fly in the corner, in its dying throes. 'That's right – yes.

'I want to say that I am sorry for what has happened. Deeply sorry. I think that's all that I can say. I can only ask for, and not expect, your forgiveness.'

Again I hesitated. 'What I did was not out of disrespect for your daughter, or your people. It was the opposite – we are very fond of each other and what we did may not have been right, but it was an act of love.'

An inner voice kept telling me that I needed to connect with them, to meet them in their own world. I looked again towards Maurice. His expression was calm and deliberate. He held up his hand, palm towards me. There was something inside it. It was a piece of old burnished copper. Suddenly, I was flooded with inspiration, memory and gratitude to my friend. I knew what I could do.

Quickly I gathered in my mind the story I had been told, years ago, by my grandmother, my father's mother, when our family first began going to the beach at Koitiata. It was the story of the meeting house on the flooded river. So I began, telling them how my grandfather had come to the mouth for the first time and had encountered the people on horseback. And of how he had witnessed the sudden death of one of their number. As I spoke they grew interested, then attentive. All the sleepers were now awake and listening. Without realising it, I had reached across to their side of the meeting house and for a moment become joined with them. I am not a person to 'gild the lily' as my mother would say, so as soon as I was able I brought the story to a conclusion.

'My grandfather was deeply upset at this death and apparently he felt the need to show comfort to these people. But as my grandmother put it, he was newly arrived in this land and did not understand the ways of its people. He walked away feeling miserable. In fact, thinking about it, at that moment, he might easily have turned around and gone back to Scotland. But he did confide years later in my grandmother, which is how I know this story. We still have a stone that one of your people gave my grandfather. It is always in a special place in our home.'

I stopped and sat down on a mattress.

It was as if I had broken a dam. Several men were on their feet the moment I was finished. Rita's uncle took the floor. He was the elder brother. A stocky, broad-faced man in a brown pinstripe suit and orange tie, gesturing energetically. His eyes flashed, his free hand moved and he thumped his stick on the floor. 'That house, those people – our ancestors!' he cried. 'You know about this, you know because your tupuna was there with our people. This is in the time before our prophet Ratana, from up on the hill there – before anyone here was born. No one can tell how the ways of God work – but his ways are mysterious. This story tells us again of the proverb that we are always facing the past as we face the future.

'Ratana, he told us that we could be one people. We have our covenant from 1840. Today you have reminded us of that. We are always one people, but we must honour one another. Boy, you sure did wrong, but you have also shown

248

us who you are. It is hard for us to forgive you.' He suddenly looked stern. 'And that will not happen today – not overnight – but you have taken the first steps that will allow us to begin to forgive you. That is, provided you look after this moko of ours.'

Rita's people had no dining room; they put up marquees for a tangi or when at Christmas and New Year the family would all come home. But the day was still warm enough, so we filed outside for a cup of tea and sandwiches served from trestles under a flowering tagastasi. One of the brotherhood, a meaty fellow in vinyl, jostled me as we filed out. 'Smart bastard,' he whispered. It was perhaps a fellow Rita had told me about that had always had the eye for her, but she had never liked him. I was still keen to leave as soon as possible; guilt had left me with nowhere to go, and the child in Rita's arms who might in another time have been a source of joy was a constant reproach. When he began to cry for a feed, my instinct was to bolt.

As I looked at him, only a few months old, he seemed very brown, with his mother's flawless skin. It seemed evident even then that he was always going to be Maori, to identify with Maori. No one had said anything, but it was clear to me where he would belong. Wrapped in a bright knitted shawl, he lay still, his hair black and clumpy, sticking to the sides of his head. When his eyes opened, his presence seemed so Maori, I could see nothing of myself in him. Nothing. A Maori baby, that was mine, who belonged to me as much as to her. But who would never be attached to me.

How could this be? One single act of passion bringing forth life into the arms of a family I barely knew. I couldn't grasp it. This was crazy. I was irrelevant. I was not of them – once again, I just wanted to get away as far as possible.

Rita's mother came up to me with the teapot. 'Another one, dear?' In fine Maori tradition, the brew was stewed, the milk already added to the pot, steeped in tannin. 'I'm fine, thanks, Mrs Rawhiti.' She put the pot down and returned to me. She was tall for a Maori woman, deep-bosomed, in a buttoned-up red cardigan and a dark skirt and nylons. Behind her glasses her features were striking and you could see where Rita got her looks from. I liked her warmth. 'You know, boy,' she said in her deep voice, speaking softly, 'there is something I am going to add to your story. My father was a Pakeha, and I want you to know this, because my people would never tell you.

'The meeting house that your grandfather saw headed out to sea – our people did not follow the ways of the old ones when they built it. They were already poor; they had lost nearly all their land and they were on the beach at the time of a shipwreck. It was in the 1800s, just after the wars, I think. They were in the rescue, everyone was saved – and the seas were heavy at the time. Some of our people put themselves to a lot of trouble. They were good and kind and true believers in Jesus Christ. Everyone tried to save the ship – they ran a line out from the shore, but on that coast it was impossible and the wreck began to break up.

'So in return for our trouble we were given the salvage rights – the ship was no use to anyone else now it had begun to break up. It would have floated away in bits, with a bit left buried in the sand. Our people had a bullock wagon and they had the job of stripping the wreck down for its timber and valuables, then getting all that across the river and bringing in the bullocks for the journey to the marae. It was tough. They were able to sell some timber to farmers in the district for wool-sheds and so on.

'But the great thing it seemed at that time was that they were able to build a new meeting house from it. That is the same house that your grandfather found floating down the river. They should never have made a house out of the bones of a wreck – it was bound to come back on them. But these were hard times for them and they were almost landless.

'Some of that ship stayed stuck on the beach, didn't it? Even in recent years pieces have turned up on our coast. Usually they just appear in the sand. You can tell because what remains is from the bottom of it, which was sheathed in copper.'

'Ah,' was all I said, nodding, and she could tell that I too had seen these pieces from a shipwreck. 'The name of that ship,' she said, 'was *Robina Dunlop*.

'Now, I heard what you said in the meeting house. I want you to look me in the eye and promise me that you will always provide for your son. You may not welcome him now, but one day you will.'

Her look was stern. It was not a request that I could decline, or even wanted to.

'But of course, I have given my word.'

'Yes, but life changes, people forget – and there are always demands for money.'

'Mrs Rawhiti, I give you my word, Scout's honour.'

She held out her hand and we shook on it, solemnly.

I decided that I would not tell my parents – this was a burden they could do without and I would shoulder it myself, alone. Personal stuff like that was not what they would want to hear and they were happy that I had picked up the job with Port Line in Wellington. If I needed to speak with anyone there was always Mr McKinnon. But it was not long before, on a business trip to the nearby village of Ratana, that my father got wind of a grandson. One of the McGregors who ran the store told him about it. Next time I was home I caught it. 'Alan, is this true what we hear – surely not?' Seeing my face my mother continued, fighting back.

'This is not the way you were brought up. How could you? You've dragged us all through the mud. Alan, how could you do this to us?' she shouted, bursting into tears.

My father was furious. I'd never seen him so mad. 'What do you think you're doing? Bloody idiot. How did you manage to land yourself in this crap? Never could show respect, could you – always knew better. What have we done to deserve this, for crying out loud?'

I looked at the mantelpiece. I wanted to wind the clock back, wishing the event into non-existence.

'All that healthy exercise, Alan,' this was my mother speaking, 'healthy body, healthy mind.'

'Mum!' I protested.

My father was watching, waiting for signs of contrition before he erupted and punched something.

'Well, he was probably meeting her for a bit on the side when he did all that running.'

'Doug, don't be crude, please,' my mother said.

'It only happened once – give me a chance.'

'Well, Alan, what do you propose to do about this child? You do realise, don't you, you are a father now yourself? And we will be grandparents – something we were looking forward to when the time was right. It's sad it's turned out this way.'

She was trying to take some of the steam out of my father.

'Control,' he said, looking at me, though it was meant for himself. He looked hot and bothered, on the point of blowing. At that moment we hated each other. My mother stepped in front of him. 'What's done is done, don't make it any worse, Doug.'

'You bloody great lummox. You've made your bed – now you can damn well lie in it. You're old enough and ugly enough to look after yourself.' Later, when my mother wasn't around, he had another go. He whispered, 'I warned you to keep away from those darned Maoris. Playing with fire – things like that always go haywire. What a bloody disgrace. What on earth made you do a thing like that? I can't understand it.

'There are New Zealanders fighting the commos in Vietnam at the moment. Maybe you should go and join them. Make a man out of you.'

Instead of driving home, I decided to first to head in towards Koitiata, only a few miles away. When I reached the village it was late afternoon. There were few people about. By then they had their own volunteer fire brigade and a roller door was up in the shed that housed the fire-tender, parked half outside. A couple of old blokes were leaning on it, chatting. They lifted their hands as I drove past. The wind was dropping away, with the promise of a still evening.

I stopped the car, noting that the river was at low ebb. I slipped into a pair of shorts and waded across, setting a brace of standing birds into flight. On the muddy bed a few baby flounder scurried away, raising miniature 'vapour trails' of mud from the bottom. Over on the beach the waves were some distance from the high-tide mark, but there was sufficient salt left in the air for a mild haze.

I had walked northwards for maybe a mile when I saw a figure away ahead of me, a shape moving amongst the driftwood. As I drew a little closer, it became evident that this was a man of average height and erect bearing, probably in a suit and a grey felt hat of the sort that today only very old men wore. Mind you, at Koitiata such garb was hardly unusual.

I found myself gaining on him, quite rapidly. He wasn't carrying anything, so he wasn't a fisherman or a gatherer of wood. I imagined us passing the time of day when I caught him up.

One hundred and fifty yards off he raised his arm and reached out to something with the flat of his hand and moved behind a huge white, bark-less willow trunk, its bare limbs splayed – a nude with shaved legs – sprawling across the beach. Then I couldn't see anything of him. When I reached that point I took a few frustrating minutes looking for him. There was nowhere he could have gone, but there was no sign of him. When I looked for footprints, however, the ground where he had stood had been trampled by a horse. But the prints didn't go anywhere. I could find no trail. It was as if he was never there.

At that point I decided to turn back to the car. As I returned along the beach, I decided that some day, before too long, I needed to make a visit to Scotland. I could get there with the help of a small legacy my mother's late father had left me.

Doug 14

24 July, 1943

It was four months to the day since we first landed at the Canal. Prentice, Cassie and I were tramping around the back of Bloody Knoll when we spotted a Jap asleep in the grass. As we approached he awoke and took to his heels, leaving behind a diary which was passed to Intelligence. We chased him for a while, but when the disturbed birds of the forest had quietened down and we couldn't find him, hiding in the bush, we pulled back – too dicey for words. There was still a need to move round with care.

Now that military pressure was beginning to ease a little, the place suddenly swarmed with brass-hats, fish-heads, and bludgers. There we were, doing four patrols a day with a technical staff of just eighty on the strip, working on up to 240 planes 'to keep 'em flying'. You needed a bundle of engineers, electricians, armourers and fitters to keep each aircraft aloft, so we were going like blue-arsed flies.

If it hadn't been for the order coming in that this was now a malaria-controlled area, we erks would have been on our way back to New Zealand. All the officers of this squadron had had trips home. My twenty-fifth birthday came and went – Bombhead Prentice shouted me a bottle of American ale. We'd learnt that a lot had been made in the New Zealand newspapers of all the personnel who have had twelve months or more of tropical service and haven't been able to get home.

Every so often we lost aircraft and with them some good men. Snow Lambert was a former flying instructor at Taieri and a fine bloke. One night I cranked and warmed Snow's Hudson engines ready for take-off. As he was about to taxi he asked me if I had a torch, so I lent him a new one of mine. He and his crew went out on a special flare-dropping mission over a harbour in southern Bougainville. Their task was to illuminate any shipping for an attack by American torpedo bombers. Snow's crew did a great job, but then suddenly disappeared from the view of his American air comrades. They assumed Snow's crowd were shot up by a Jap night fighter. We might never know for sure what happened.

After a repair job on the standard mainframe I took a test flight on Hudson 2090. We brought her down after the first circuit because she was flying left wing low. I had to make a minor adjustment. We got her onto the runway again, headed towards Tulagi and then on to Esperance, coming down in a steep dive with the front guns firing. I tested the turret and beam guns, which gave a good performance. Hudsons are usually armed with 0.50-inch machineguns, fitted with reflector sights, much more stable than the old ring-and-ball sights. Every time I sat in the turret I thought of the recruitment board and their plans for me. We took the plane low along the coast, revealing the beached and rusting hulks of ships that had been driven aground during combat in what proved to be a great naval battle of World War Two. All told, about fifty warships lay on what has become known as Iron-Bottom Bay – Japanese and American, plus the Australian cruiser *Canberra*.

On a day off, Prentice and I left before dawn on a trip aboard a lugger to Tulagi, out in the middle of The Slot. I had arranged it through a friend of a friend. We went a distance of about twenty miles, mostly in darkness. Two Higgins barges were in tow; one broke away, holding us up for an hour.

On Tulagi we met up with an Aussie bloke in charge of native labour who made us lunch. It was the best meal in weeks – canned chicken. He showed us over The Rock, about five miles long and a couple of hundred feet wide, one of the prettiest spots I've seen in this area. The residential commissioner's house had been a palatial mansion in its day, with terraced gardens and tennis courts. It showed little sign of damage.

On our return Tokyo Radio was claiming to have shot down an RNZAF Hudson Bomber from one of their destroyers, which I presume was 2021, Captain Lambert's craft.

Some weeks after, Trevor Blainey returned to New Zealand. He was the sole survivor of Flight Lieutenant Lambert's crew in the Hudson 2021 on July 24. While on X-ray patrol flying up The Slot to a point north-west of Vella Lavella and then south-west to the Treasury Islands their craft was jumped by eight Zeros out of the sun. The fight lasted twenty minutes, and two Jap planes met their end, but the others took the Hudson, sending her into the sea in flames.

Lambert made a perfect landing. All the crew got out safely. But the dirty Japs swooped down and strafed them while they were in the water, killing the entire crew except for Trevor, who was left for dead. He'd already been wounded in the arm and sprayed with shrapnel in the forehead by cannon shell bursting on the turret's armour plating. After the bandits departed he swam two miles to a small island off Vella Lavella where he found Jap rations and a small lifeboat. Later he rowed to the mainland where he was cared for by a coast-watcher. This guy operated on his wound with a razor blade and a bottle of brandy for anaesthetic. These coast watchers never fail to amaze me. Blainey was finally picked up by an American PT boat and returned to Guadalcanal.

I thought I was handling the stress of war quite well until one night in September 1943, about one in the morning, I gave the boys quite a scare. I was having this dream in which a wombat or some such animal was gnawing away at my throat. I leapt from the bunk and shot through the mosquito net with a blood-curdling yell. Everyone woke up, thinking that the Japs had landed. Much to my surprise the guys didn't say very much. But I must be getting the tat-ta's. What a give-away! A few more exhibitions like this and home will be the caper for me, in a strait jacket.

One night in September 1943 as the sirens screamed we tumbled from our cots and staggered up the ridge behind the camp for a better view. Two bandits were caught in the spotlights. 'It's OK,' said one of the blokes, 'they're ours.' In the next instant we heard the familiar express-train-in-the-tunnel sound and six or eight of us ran and dived for the small entrance to a large fox-hole. Only just! As the last bloke clambered over a fallen comrade, face down, specs in the dirt, the 250-pounder hit, blowing with such force that it raised the coconut log roof on the dug-out up about six inches before it fell back down again. As the roof lifted, I noticed at the far end of Henderson Field the glow of an old-fashioned kerosene Hurricane lamp on low flame. At the moment of blast I saw it give a feeble flutter and die.

After the All Clear we made our exit to discover we had no casualties, but the surrounding jungle was ablaze. The fire was short-lived. Returning to the scene the next day we made the comforting discovery that the Japs were getting short of iron – the bomb was made up of old pipes, couplings and socket fittings – lethal enough, though.

A few days later, about 4.30am, the Japs again paid us a visit, dropping eighteen bombs on Henderson Field and a further batch on Kone. One bomb on Henderson Field scored a direct hit on an SBD, burning it to the ground. All we saw afterwards was the charred remains of an engine. Other eggs finished up nearby, but no one was injured. As it turned out, this was the beginning of the end.

But the Japs still got in under our radar to drop their sticks. They came in one night over No. 2 airstrip, where most of their bombs fell harmlessly into the Lunga. One set a gas tanker on fire and one fell into A camp where two Yanks were killed. To our delight the Night Fighter then blew the Jap to pieces. Later they paid us another visit and managed to set a Mitchell B-25 on fire.

One stick of bombs landed over on Fighter Squad One, wrecking an F4U Corsair. It demolished a tent, killing two Yanks and wounding a third. Another Boggie was brought down by our Night Fighter as he was clearing Esperance. The Japs were reported to be dropping parachutes with wires attached to try and fool the radar. The All Clear sounded – it was 4am. We were scheduled to get our machines off the ground at 5am, so we were short of sleep. Next night I saw Cary Grant in *Lucky*, a fine show.

Bombhead Prentice had made it back to New Zealand. As ever a great source of information, he wrote to say that the Venturas were grounded because of faulty welding in the shock-absorbing legs and would be out of service for some weeks until new parts were available. Not sure how it made it through the censors. This was certain to delay our relief even longer. The Liberty ship *JV Francis* was anchored off Red Beach, bringing up Fighter Maintenance Unit 4 and the New Zealand Army.

By early October Henderson Field looked pretty bare and desolate with the Liberators moved to west of Guadalcanal and a lot of the Torpedo fighter-bombers and SBDs to Munda. All that we had left near the runway were Catalinas, Douglases, some Lightnings and a few of our Hudsons, and a Ventura or two.

But the war was still not quite over. The guys at Munda were raided by fifty Jap dive-bombers but afterwards the New Zealand fighter squadron were all accounted for. As we began to watch *Tales of Manhattan* at the canteen we were rudely interrupted about 8.30pm by Tojo, who dropped two lots of parachute flares, then ripped into a ship of about 9,000 tons, presumably a Liberty ship, lying off Red Beach. Their torpedo set it ablaze and it sank after being turned out to sea. A lot of ack ack went up. The Yanks managed to wing one of their own Liberators – a bad show.

We heard that when the Venturas finally arrived we would move to Buttons, Santo, where they would reshuffle our squadron and the squadron already operating Hudsons in that area. With luck in his favour a man might be in New Zealand earlier than he expected.

Alan 15

I had little reason to stay in New Zealand. I felt shamed and removed from my family and I had no wish to return to the marae. They had been pretty gracious, Rita's people, but I felt an outsider, an intruder – which I was. I kept turning over and over in my mind how foolish I had been to get myself into the cactus. I breathed a sigh of relief as the ship pulled away from Wellington Harbour, Glasgow-bound.

Looking back on it, of course, I can see now that I had simply resorted to the remedy of my school days – when things got uncomfortable, I simply put distance between myself and the problem.

In Edinburgh I found digs, as my harrier mates called it, in a Georgian-style tenement on the university side of the town overlooking sports fields. My landlady, a Mrs Fergusson, lived upstairs. She was a cheery widow, an Edinburgh native, always turned out in twin sets and immaculately made-up, who cooked, cleaned and washed for me. She was a stickler, but also very kind, although disappointed to discover that, while I had good references, I wasn't a weekly church-goer.

The first thing I did was join a harrier club, University, because it was handy. There were all sorts in it, some clever, confident types, a few academics and a lot of chaps who were quiet and happy to run because that was what we did best. Some of them, like me, were running away from themselves. They were a hardy lot. Sometimes the temperatures we ran in mid-winter were sub-zero, and wet, so there were great incentives to get back to the locker room showers, out of the cold and wet. But it was always good to see some Scottish countryside, often through a descending veil of grey sleet.

Sometimes we'd get together for a few beers after a race and I went to the pictures with one or two of them. But outside of work, I kept to myself and my running. Mrs Fergusson insisted on me being on time for meals. 'It's all I ask, Alan, that's not too much now, is it? I know you'll want to get out and meet with your chums, but just let me know if you're not coming in for tea.' Discovering that fish and chips, such a treat in New Zealand, in Scotland were something you wouldn't feed the cat with, I readily complied.

I could never think of her as having had a living husband. It was a time before I had recognised grief's pain, or had even fully registered real regret – callow is the word, isn't it? This was when innocence was stretched across my being like a latex mask, a prophylactic against hurt. Mrs F. loved to have a chat over tea in her impeccable drawing room, with its gold-framed mirrors, grand chinz leaf-patterned settees and nests of French polished tables. Her husband had been a chartered accountant. His picture was mounted in a wooden frame in a corner of the room, in uniform. Here he looked no more than thirty, upright in the uniform of an officer.

'Miles served with distinction in the Great War,' she told me. 'Unfortunately, what with his wounds and then the TB, he passed away well before his three-score and ten.' They had a son, based somewhere in the Bahamas, whom I never met but who wrote to her every week – she allowed me the stamps, which were unfailingly exotic.

The shipping office stood in King's Road. Five storeys high, it was, after the walk up the hill, always a snug place from the cold. Marble steps led to a colonnaded ante-room displaying in oils a century of Port Line ships and mustachioed Port Line magnates. Between the old attendant-driven lift with its concertina folding doors and the entrance sat a tiny receptionist, a heavily made-up ancient on a high seat. This was Maggie, who smoked, knitted and operated the manual plugs on the company telephone exchange behind a polished wooden counter. She knew everybody and you soon learnt how important it was to stay in her good books. Upstairs was a mess of desks separated by opaque and frosted

260

glass partitions, each one screening a seated eccentric, most of whom seemed to have worked for the company since the end of the Great War.

My boss, Mr Craig, was a pleasant enough family man of about fifty, who made me welcome by introducing me to the staff as 'our man from the colonies'. He enjoyed a joke. Mr Craig told me I would be working mainly on shipping to the Far East, which included New Zealand, mostly on inventory and maintenance planning. This I did diligently for three years, keeping my head down. Staff communicated between floors by way of Lamson vacuum tubes which wheezed and squeezed their capsules all over the building. Boilers in the basement warmed the building through another set of pipes and radiators. In the breaks we all got to share tea and shortbread under the ornate ceiling of the cafeteria.

In spite of the weather, I enjoyed training in the town around Edinburgh, the elite streets and apartments of the New Town and up and down the Liffey past the ruddy tenements to its mouth. History, being mostly cast in stone here, was much more obvious everywhere than in New Zealand. I found myself, for the first time as an adult, visiting museums and exhibitions to find out more.

Nearby was Greyfriars church, at Grassmarket in the city. Greyfriars is a sort of mausoleum to hundreds of Protestant martyrs who were executed for their beliefs there. You could still smell the horror of it in the churchyard, men killing each other for their ideas. Covenanters, the persecuted were called.

Although Mr McKinnon had alerted me to them, I couldn't comprehend how it was that religion had been fired with such sectarian fervour in Scotland. I bought a book about it to try to understand, but it was Victorian, written with such vehemence and recrimination that its arcane sneers and jibes made it impossible to follow. Were the mysterious battles between Catholics and Proddies of my father's boyhood and even the Guy Fawkes of my own, a pale shadow of these bloody divisions, cast in non-sectarian New Zealand?

Every month I sent off a money order for the child from the post office, stamped indelibly with the Queen's head. It was never acknowledged. As the spring-loaded stamp was forced down on the inscribed order I always thought of him, but I couldn't allow the thought for long. I hoped he was healthy and well looked after. When I next saw him, things would be very different.

Doug 15

Everyone is out there in the heat, craning their necks. There's a Jap fighter plane, a Zero, moving extremely fast across the Pacific sky. It comes towards us like a bat out of hell, towards Henderson Field, sunlight splintering off its Perspex windows. Suddenly it fills the entire sky – kamakazi. The noise of the engines at full revs as it dives towards us is like the screaming of rivets going off inside your head in a bucket. Our engineers, working just in their baggy khaki shorts outside the hangar, scatter like rabbits. Their hands and arms streaked with black engine oil, some of them still carry a spanner, or wrench, as they run. I have an impression of Jack Carruthers just before the explosion – he is a man in full flight diving like a half-back into a heap of aircraft tyres. Everyone is taking cover. There's a terrible wallop as the plane plants its nose in the roof of the hangar. Then the whole caboodle, plane and hangar, goes up in a great whoosh of flame. A couple of men caught running from the hangar are burning from head to foot. We forget ourselves and throw them in a big open tank of water.

That diary passage became a dream that I had for years after the war. It woke me sweating, like I did in the tropics, but this nightmare was back in quiet New Zealand, in a suburb – thousands of miles from Guadalcanal. The streetlight showed though the pink glass of the bedroom fanlight. The boys were fast asleep, my false teeth – replacing teeth I lost through poor diet in the war – stand in a glass on the bedside table. Beside me Janet, bless her, would be shaking me: 'It's alright love, wake up, it's just a nightmare. Doug, you're just having a nightmare. Wake up!'

I'd come to, shivering.

'Now, you just hold still – I'm going to make you a nice cup of Bournevita.'

***

The weather was now showing signs of becoming a lot hotter. Italy had thrown in the towel with an unconditional surrender, which should cast a new light on the European situation. They made a beer issue of DB lager – a surprise as we had figured that the rations had already run out. No one complained.

Twenty-five Liberators and fifty SBD's pounded Ballale Strip today. The first four BMU Venturas touched down on Henderson Field with more expected. Reports to hand indicated a short stay for us at Espiritu Santo merely for the fitting of long-range tanks to our craft and to await transport to New Zealand.

We left Guadalcanal by DC3 at 7am and arrived at Espiritu Santo at 11.10am. It rained cats and dogs on our departure, so all the gear got damp and to top it all off the SWB forgot to order early breakfasts. I managed to sleep in a bunk most of the way, despite the cold. I arrived hungry and bad-tempered.

Espiritu Santo seems such a farce – 1500 men approximately on this rock with work for no more than 300, from all appearances. The fighters did advanced operational training and our Hudsons just seemed to go up spasmodically for all the world as if the place was a flying club. These 4 RD jokers have been away from New Zealand barely four months and yet are moaning about the crook deal being handed to them. What a laugh.

In December 1943 we left Santo, after preparing our planes for the return home. We were the last of that lot to leave, in a DC3 (Dakota), reaching home on Christmas Eve 1943. After 18 months in the wop-wops, we were skinny, yellow with Atabrine and just a little troppo. Most of us were also minus quite a few teeth than before we set out.

Alan 16

Ben Nevis was sprawled out in the late summer sun, a great sleeping cat, the last bits of snow and ice glistening like spittle on its fur. As I looked at it I had a sense of someone's presence in close proximity. There was nothing that I could see, nothing to hear, it was entirely felt and somehow, don't ask me how, I knew emphatically that it was my grandfather. I was also aware that he was looking at me and smiling. It was most strange – I've never felt anything quite like it, but whatever it was, it left me with a feeling of unusually deep contentment.

As this sensation faded away I noticed something else, a short man in a navy-blue wind-breaker, striding along the road. As he approached it, he stopped and lowered his head before the Black Watch memorial. His black hair was greying and receding untidily – he may have been in his sixties. I didn't want to intrude, but after a minute or so he raised his head and looked directly at me, into me. There was no hostility in the dark eyes, just unblinking candour.

'What a wicked loss of life,' he offered to me, as I stood beside him. 'You know, don't you, that in the trenches their heavy kilts never dried, that was a real killer.'

I paused, thinking. 'Scots shedding their blood in England's wars,' I said, returning his directness. 'Isn't that what you've been doing for a long while?'

He wanted to know where I came from, then what my family name was. His face was weathered and he used his huge hands as he talked. He was moving on again in a day or so, he said, and would be parking his caravan near the sea at Oban. When I gave my family name, he told me it was near where my ancestors hailed from.

I couldn't be certain that he was correct, but it was thrilling to think that there was a place in the world where your name was located by a place – in New Zealand it was something associated really only with Maori.

'Where is it you're headed now?' he wanted to know.

'I've decided to stay at the camp down the road,' I told him. 'I've got a tent that keeps pretty dry, even in Scotland. So I'll be there tonight.'

'You'll be chilly,' he said, looking at the sky. 'But that's where my caravan is – the only one with a green Bedford lorry hooked up to it, 1959 model. Just look out for that. And don't tell me you don't drink whisky.'

Later in the day, sure enough, there he was. 'Come away in,' he called to my knock. He introduced his wife, Sheila, who was knitting from red skeins of wool beside a kerosene heater. Pearl earrings set in her grey hair, she smiled back a welcome, a little more reserved than her husband. She had a tooth missing, and stood up almost immediately to set about making tea.

Her figure was bulky – wrapped up against the cold. 'Did he invite you for a whisky?' she asked. 'Fergus here hasn't taken a drop for five years now, have you Gus?'

Off the grog but with its tide marks written in his cheery, bruiser's face, Fergus allowed himself a wry smile. 'I've still a half-bottle of Grants in the back cupboard, a test of my strength – the visitor' – he'd forgotten my name – 'would be more than welcome to a taste.'

He poured me a tipple, offering it neat without the usual palaver about water. Fergus was a wanderer whose family had been displaced since Culloden. 'Not that we dinna haeve any land,' he said, as we settled in for what he called a crack, 'but after what The Butcher did on the Moor, and in those bloody days that followed, my people were driven to the hills, or put on the boats and exiled – America, Canada – after Culloden Moor. You're lucky you are of Lowland stock. Your people had their struggles, no doubt about that. Those people of yours from Montrose, they would have been tangled up in the Covenantor wars, without a doubt.

'But the question of whose side are you on … that got so complicated in the Highlands; most of the time there was intermarriage. It was maybe a little more cut and dried in the Lowlands. The killing was never less vicious, and wherever there are folks, there is always treachery, but there it was maybe less complicated – but only by comparison.'

He told me he was a Stuart. 'Of course, you will find there are Stuarts all over Scotland. Do you know about the Red Fox?'

'A little, we learnt about his murder at school. I seem to remember there was a Danny Kaye film we saw as small kids.'

'I tell you what, if you're headed for Oban, I could take you there.'

He told me of a narrow glen, where the highland forest grew along its floor with a path to a waterfall. He said that Colin Campbell, the Red Fox, had drunk the water from here before he was caught and killed by the Stuarts. 'The water from the fall ran clean, but not clear – a rusty brown. It nae was a suspension but a solid,' he said. He shrugged. 'Och, just the boggy soil – you know what peat is. That's peat water – what they make the best whisky from.'

He said that there were English toffs who would come to a place like this and drink, but they'd take water from anywhere. No discrimination whatsoever.

His words kept on coming. He was a scrap-metal merchant who still roamed the country. 'My people used to be called tinkies. But this night I'm a-sitting with my wife, quite content to be here, and talking with yourself.

'I've long lamented the desertion of the crofts, the passin' of the Caledonian pine, the introduction of American trees like the Douglas fir, growing so close, ye canna walk between them. I didna mind when there was room for walkin' – but now there's none of that, and them squeezin' out our heather and all.

'Scotland's a bonnie place, but it's a-changin'. It's not good for our people and it'll nae be good for anyone in the end.'

'He loves nothing more than a chat,' smiled Sheila, as she put the teas on the table, covered in gold embroidered cloth. The teapot was swaddled in a bright cosy.

Her warning left me excited, expectant. Yet there was sorrow in his talk. He was saddened by the way the Highland hospitality was being ruined by people 'out for their split'. He mourned 'the passin' of the good folk you could just drop in on without knockin'.

'I grieve,' he said, loading three sugars in his tea with deliberation, as if each one was a thought, 'I grieve for the disappearance of the displaced, the wanderin' salt of the earth clansmen. Even in beggary they clung to the worn family plaid and to their harsh pride.'

'So your people have always been discriminated against then?'

'The lords and lairds, strange to say, that class of people were always polite and respectful if they were buying a pearl, say, from one of us. But the ordinary people are always affeared of us. They have never spoken kindly to us.

'From their bairnes – mainly – you'd get:

'"Tinkie, tinkie, tarry bags

'"Go to the well and wash your rags."

'The old people, whether they be travellin' people or not, simply had more time, more space for the important things.

'You know, they had the time to tell the stories of their people and there were folk who had the time to listen to it. Highlanders became great storytellers. That had much to do with the long winters with ice and snow on the ground and all around them for months and their long nights of small peat fires that bound them into their crofts and into each other's lives in the telling – until eventually it became something original and part of their character – the way smoke gets into a woolly pullover.'

I told him how there was still room to move and breathe in New Zealand. And how easy it was to fit into Scotland as a New Zealander.

'So I hear, so I hear,' he nodded. 'And the fit works the other way, even better,' he confirmed. 'Scots have no trouble whatsoever being accepted over there. I have several pals who were in the merchant marine who settled in New Zealand, they love it. But me, I'll always be here, I can never tell whether it is the people, the countryside or both makes me love this place.'

It had been a long day. I wanted to stay talking, but I was tired and needed to think over what he had said. 'I'm off now. Will you be here tomorrow, I'd love to talk some more with you?'

'I tell you what, my friend, we need to walk. Walkin's always good for talkin'. There's a trail off the road that leads into the mountains along from here. I used to go in there for salmon, but I've not taken one of those for a while now. If you come here tomorrow, we will need to drive for a distance and then we can walk for an hour or two.'

Outside, the sky dripped with stars – as he had warned, it would be a clear, cold night under the thin fabric of the tent.

Doug 16

Back at Ohakea, the RNZAF airbase, we continued to keep Air Force kites in the sky. I took part in a flight engineers' course, mainly aerial gunnery, with many hours aloft in the turret of the Hudsons, flying at targets along that familiar Tasman coast where I had fished so often as a boy. We fired at a drogue, a sausage-like tube towed by a stooge aircraft. The wreck of the old Fusilier was a frequent target. It was an odd feeling, letting off long belts of ammunition from twin-mounted 303s in the gunnery tower, trained on the old wreck.

I told Garth about it, who was home on leave from the navy. We met up, both in uniform, in The Club in Marton. 'Bloody hell,' he grinned as he slapped my back. 'Let me buy you a drink, you skinny bastard, what've they been doing to you?'

'Aw, we live mainly out of the Yanks' rubbish bins up in the Tropics,' I kidded, noticing that the boy who'd enlisted in 1939 looked like a man – he'd seen a lot of war, although he said little about that. He had a slightly pinched look; he spoke mainly of ports he'd been to, women he'd met. At one stage the barman dropped a bottle of scotch he was fitting to a metal sling for pouring. It fell heavily to the floor and as it crashed I noticed poor Garth jumped about three feet off the ground. Neither of us said anything.

'So how's your mum?' he wanted to know.

'She's fine – she's glad to have her only child back.'

'You always were a spoilt little bugger, weren't you?'

'Come on, Garth, who was it got left five hundred quid by his giddy aunt?'

'What do mean? Do you need a loan?'

'For God's sake, no! Have another beer – there's still a war on.'

'So you are going back?' he wanted to know.

Like most of the troops, I was keen to get on with life. But it was quite obvious that getting rid of the Japs from the Pacific was going to take a lot more effort. I wanted Garth to meet Prentice, but he'd gone back north. If I'd realised what a return to active service would mean with new mates, not my old ones, I might not have been so keen to go.

We were moved to a posting at Air Base Ardmore, working on the chunky F4Us, the Corsairs. These were originally a seven-ton torpedo fighter bomber, single-seater with a massive twin-row, eighteen-cylinder Pratt & Whitney engine. I recall that it produced a mighty 1400 HP. They were fitted with a supercharger that the pilot could call on once for about three seconds – to get him out of trouble. If he did, the engine had to be dismantled and examined for signs of metal fatigue and stress. These brutes may have been great fighter planes, but for mechanics they had a few unlovable features.

The designers had built in a cartridge start. This was of cordite, similar to that for a shotgun cartridge, placed in the breach. When the engine was turned to a position of compression, the mechanic signalled 'thumbs up'. This was the pilot's cue to press the starter button. The engine would cough and fart, squirting raw petrol from the carburettor and causing a minor fire. The mechanic, standing at the ready between the under-carriage legs, had to put it out. After this curtain-raiser, the engine's fourteen cylinders would all be firing in harmony, the plane trembling with power, straining at the wheel brakes, ready to roll.

Ardmore was an advanced training centre for rookie pilots, not long out of their elementary training. One pilot had a rush of blood to the head. He took his Corsair to a great height, pushed the stick full forward and headed earthward at a speed later estimated to be 800mph. He pulled the plane out of the dive without taking his hand off the throttle. Looking at it afterwards, the thrust on the wings was so great it rippled the metal across the surface. We engineers were the lucky ones who got to sort it all out and fitted the new wings.

I did volunteer for another stint among the swaying palms. Little did I realise that the second time it would drag like a wet week. We went through a short commando course at Swanson where we lived rough for a while, with emergency rations and sleeping out in the open. This was early 1945 – a pity we hadn't had it before going overseas the first time.

Before I left I called on Jimmie Cameron, with a carton of Camels for him. He insisted on shouting a double whisky. He drove me down to Koitiata for a few days where we went fishing and played cards. For me, as much as I loved my old mother, this was my homecoming and Jimmie, on reflection, treated me as a second son.

On April 25 1945, after a good break from war, we returned to the Pacific. We rose early that morning, and took off from Whenuapai at 7am in a C47. We had a smooth flight, reaching Jacquinot Bay, on the south coast of New Britain, at 3pm GMT. Although they didn't tell us, there was talk enough even in the newspapers to figure out where the war was and roughly where we might be deployed. I met some mates who had a liberal ration of chilled beer – the only stipulation was that it must be drunk in the compound. We made short work of it.

We were shipped across to Santo where we worked on bomber reconnaissance and did some rifle training, with time for swims and films in the evenings. On May 7 we received a press signal that the war in Europe was virtually over. It was still to be confirmed.

In early May we heard the official announcement of an unconditional surrender of Germany. Hitler was apparently dead – he'd topped himself. Two down, one to go – but the fighting was still in our neck of the woods. A short thanksgiving service was held outside under the palms and we were given the rest of the day off. We played volleyball in the heat. I'd also been playing a little baseball with the

Yanks. One of them, Horace Marsocci, had been teaching me to fire a Browning pistol from the hip. One or two of the chaps were great, but most of this crowd really got under my skin – Day-old Dangerous types who wanted to run the whole show.

After a short spell we were shipped via Guadalcanal and Green Island to Los Negros, a dot in the ocean just half a degree off the Equator in the Admiralty Isles and actually north of New Guinea. The Americans had taken the Admiralties from the Japs early in 1944. Up here it was even hotter than Guadalcanal.

We had just one raid by the Japs during our time in Los Negros. Tojo despatched a lone float-plane that dropped a single bomb on a floating dock, causing minor damage. It was quite a contrast to the eighty raids in six months we had on Guadalcanal. This time, though, it was not as stimulating and I wonder whether those ties I had formed with the guys in the Squadrons in my earlier years of the war were something I'd experience ever again.

On the day of our arrival at Los Negros a group of American servicemen near camp were hard at work, stripped to the waist, toiling in the hot sun unearthing the caskets of comrades who had fallen in battle some months previously. The caskets would be shipped back to the States. It was hard, unpleasant work. They did body recovery all over the Pacific and boy, that was a job for a face mask. This was also a sign of who was now in charge in the Pacific – that the Japs were on the run.

We still lived under canvas, with wooden floors located just half a metre above sea level – this time there were only four of us to a tent. We fixed our own water supply and I used a stove we'd brought from Cactus to boil the washing. It was our task to service the Corsair F4Us. By 11am the temperature hit forty degrees. You could fry eggs on the upper skins of the wings, no exaggeration. We'd often go out onto the harbour in small sail boats to cool off and then start work again about 2.30, finishing at 5.30pm, by which time temperatures had dropped.

Seadler Harbour was a body of water formed by Manus Island and a half-leg of coral jutting out into the sea. This was where the American Pacific fleet was moored prior to what became the final assault on Okinawa, with a clear victory for the American Pacific fleet. We sailed on the harbour in the yacht *Hokonui* – one of the guys had won it in a raffle. Occasionally there'd be a big wind that would almost upend our boat – then we could sail from the middle of the harbour back to the port in half the time. It was almost as good as being on a motorbike. By talking with visiting crew out there on the water you could pick up all sorts of gen about shipping movements.

There was a large floating dock near our camp where damaged ships were under repair. We had the occasional boxing tournament between us and the ship repair guys on this dock – two minute rounds and the contests were pretty even. I saw a demonstration bout between an American Negro and a naval boxing champ – the sailor couldn't get near the Negro, who moved like a panther on his feet.

A big C47 missed the strip one night and went straight into the bay, leaving no trace of wreckage. The Jap air force continued to attack. In May we had five Red Alerts, sometimes interrupting our movie shows. They hadn't given up yet.

On June 22 I turned twenty-seven! My mates who had managed to get home were marrying and having kids. It was about time I settled down and started taking life seriously. But how could I when I didn't feel any different from when I turned eighteen? Surely my mentality had improved with age?

We had more than our share of rain – sometimes ten inches fell and flooded the hangars. We kept hearing how the war wouldn't last much longer. The government announced that it would pay us £3.15s for every month overseas. I'd served twenty months abroad, so it would make a useful sum towards buying a home.

On August 15 everything came to complete a halt and at 10am the news came through that the war was over – Japan had completely thrown in the towel. We were all packed with our kits ready to fly to Borneo when the A-bombs were dropped on Hiroshima and Nagasaki – with the Japanese surrender immediately following. I was grateful they did. They gave us the rest of the day and the next day off and some free beer – they even put on a bit of a smoke concert. We knew that we must be home by Christmas.

Top Brass began calling for volunteers for garrison duty in Japan.

'Are you putting your name down for the trip, Doug?' asked a mate.

'Not bloody likely.'

'Get away with you, where the heck is your spirit of adventure?'

Even I was surprised at how quickly my answer came back. 'Long dead.'

Don't get me wrong, I was glad the war was over and grateful to be still intact. But even in an outfit as casual as the Royal New Zealand Air Force, you got sick of others ordering you around, of being at the mercy of brass-hats and redcaps who didn't seem to know the difference between up and down. It was no place for a grown man.

Alan 17

Next morning Fergus turned up and we went well out in the country, some miles from the last village. He pulled over by a tarn and pointed to a gravelled foot trail beside a stream. After half an hour we found ourselves in a narrowing valley where sheep browsed among rocks and moss. A lively burn cut a charming meander across a meadow. The sun was out but weak, for it was the end of summer. 'I was brought here as a young man,' he said. 'My uncle was a pearl fisher in the Conon River – he loved this place and had taken a few salmon out of it. There's no rhyme or reason to its specialness – there are so many beauties in Scotland. Some of them stay with you and some you don't remember. All I can say is, it's just something about the look of the place that I've always liked.'

He searched around him as though he might find an explanation.

'Our people don't forget much,' he said. 'I think it's because we've decided for ourselves what it is that is important. We don't change much, we stay with what we believe is true. We don't let other folks decide that for us, which is why the people of Scotland, well, so many ordinary folk, have so little time for us. As I was tellin' you last night they're affeared of our free lives – just like they feared wolves until they'd shot out the last one.'

He gestured to a sharp crag in the distance that jutted out from the highest peak, giving it a Gaelic name: 'I never forget its shape, the way it stands to the sky, I can always bring it up in my mind.' He paused again – looking skyward his attention drawn to a delta of geese moving across the sky.

'A lot of Scots left their country, never understanding what it was they'd left behind. They roamed the earth, but our people were content to roam Scotland.

'Us travellin' people like to be as we are, we nae want to be stuck. We were forced from our lands, it is true, but our people discovered a long time ago they could belong to this land in a better way when they didn't own it. There's nothing like a shut gate at the end of a tidy path to begin to close your mind.'

'But people like to feel secure, don't they?'

'Of course; it's ownership, or rather the insistence on lording it over property – that's where people go wrong – everyone wants to be a laird these days. And then there's people who think they own their children.'

He paused again, and again his eyes searched the skies: 'But we all struggle with that one.'

He stepped down the mossy bank to the stream, the current braiding the water around his leather boots. He stooped and took water to his mouth in his cupped hands. Then he reached again and seemed to mutter something to the water before letting it trickle through his fingers.

'So much of all this is held by a people in their stories. Stories...' He hesitated and looked hard at me. 'When civilisations get to the stage where their people no longer tell each other their stories, how do they know who they are? Where do they belong? I believe that's a thing to worry about, truly, I do.'

'What's that? I don't quite follow.'

'Well, the stories that bind people together – they are not being told any more. There's history. But people no longer seem to know who they are. I am sure they did once. My grandparents had certainties that I envy in them now.'

He paused before looking into me: 'Do you have your stories in New Zealand? What is it that actually brings you to Scotland? Why are you here travellin' on your own?'

'Well, this was the country of both my grandfathers.'

'I understand that, but you know that is not my question. You are a young man. Why are you not with your own people, with your own crowd?'

'Just exploring, as you do.'

'"As you do?" Explorin' what? What is it you hope to find, laddie?'

He saw in my eyes the fear that he was on to me and quickly waved it away with his huge hands. But his words stayed with me, filling the space of an unanswered question.

'Well, let me suggest – not why you are here, that's really none of my business – but what it is you are after. I think you are here because you believe that there may be clues that will help you come to terms with the young man that left the country of his birth. That's why I've been talking with you – it's why I've wanted to spend time with you. I think your next move, laddie, is Kincardineshire.'

We returned the way we had come. I had plenty to think about.

At the end of the harrier season, I took the train to Aberdeen, staying on Constitution Street, just off the Square, at a spartan boarding house. There were a lot of oilmen in the town and accommodation was hard to find. I took a hire car and drove back down the east coast.

My first contact was by telephone with the librarian at Laurencekirk, who probably ran the entire town with good-humoured efficiency. When I told her I believed I had a grandfather from the town, she repeated, 'Roberts', and I could picture her licking the top of her pencil. 'Roberts, another one of those big families, right here, wasn't it? I believe you had a great uncle, Sandy, who survived until quite recently – well, until the late '50s, wasn't it? He was a figure round town when I was a youngster. Sandy, I think, was the only one who didn't go abroad. He lived to a good age.

'I tell you what, I'll put my thinking cap on and see if I can help you.

'Oh, and you might call at Stonehaven library, if you want to look the family up.'

I made progress at the Stonehaven Library using Kincardineshire records. The Roberts were all at Laurencekirk in 1881, including the newly-born Hector. By the following census they had a small farm-holding on the road between St Cyrus and Fettercairn.

Here I found a landscape with woods of mature oak, old stone-walls and bridges and winding lanes edged by trees. Mills were almost always in a state of abandon. The names were old Pictish, some starting with 'Pit' with Pict-carved stones harking back to the seventh century, depicting hunting and animals, with angels surmounted by Celtic crosses. Others, like Drumtochty, Auchenblae and Fettercairn haunted both ear and eye with their beauty.

Near St Cyrus is a row of mature trees and beyond a beautiful view of the North Sea, pewter today, across the green of the descending downs. A flight of geese passed overhead, heading northwards, the leaders sliding back and forth in their formation and calling one another. I headed inland.

I found a public telephone box and reached Mrs Carick, the librarian. She had a name for me, a Bruce Farquar, of Stonehaven, where I had just been. 'He's getting on a bit, but he keeps himself busy as a gardener for the shire,' she said. 'He knew Sandy, your granddad's brother, and he will help you. If you were free, he'll meet you at noon, when he finishes, on the path to Dunnottar Castle, above Stonehaven; you'll easily find it.'

'This is wonderful, thank you,' I told her.

'Her voice became mildly playful: 'Are you a royalist?' she asked.

'Not particularly, why?'

'Bruce wants you to meet his cousin. He used to be a gamekeeper; he'll want to tell you all about it. You'll find Bruce is no royalist – good luck, then.'

Dunnottar Castle, at the cliff edge near Stonehaven, looked ruin enough for the whole of Scottish fighting history to have passed through it – which proved almost to be the case. I set out along the cliff path towards it, but there were signs posted that it was unsafe. A thick-set, mane-haired man with a leonine head – broad-browed and strong-necked – was planting daffodil bulbs near The Black Hill. This was Bruce Farquar.

'You really don't mind not goin' down that path, Alan, do you?' he offered as he shook my hand. 'It's quite dangerous. I've plenty to tell you. Some of the most memorable history is about a lot of killin' and mayhem – and this place is full of it, and wanton cruelty besides.

'So leave the path for now, Alan,' Bruce said. 'Besides, has it not occurred to you yet that, like many things, old castles are always best seen at a distance? Can I interest you in Roman camps?' he smiled. 'Redykes is up on the far hill overlooking the bay. They always brought their fleet with the army.'

'Bruce, I think I've got my work cut out trying to understand the last 500 years in Scotland. Can we leave the Romans for another day? What is this castle, how do you pronounce it, Donnator?'

'Du-na- the emphasis is on the first syllable. It'd be a pleasure.

'Oliver Cromwell is a good place to start. It was from the Black Hill over here that the Cromwell shelled the castle with heavy artillery, in the hope of seizing the Scottish crown. He had this real set on Royalty, he planned to exterminate it. He had already destroyed the British crown. But the Scots foiled him – they smuggled the coronation crown out under a maid's petticoats then down the coast. Grainger, the local minister, hid it until more peaceful times at nearby Kinneff Church. You can still worship at Kinneff, well worth a visit.'

Out on the sea on an icy wind a single sailboat was making parallel to the coast toward the castle. From up on the rocky path the pitted cliffs were steep with their teeth exposed, the path's edge falling into a flat sea far below, gulls skirling and puffins sweeping the bay in flocks. Above the path Farquar pointed out Whin Bush, which seemed like impenetrable gorse, and beyond that an incomplete Grecian-style monument to the heroic fallen. 'Unfinished,' murmured the unassuming gardener, his eyes holding mine, 'like their lives.'

Bruce recommended a visit to St Cyrus, a village just down the road that time has divided in two. It was a warm day for September. On the cliff top sits the village of today, its stone church tower rising proud from the intensely tilled fields beside it, the tidiness of the stone-walled cemetery a sign of an active community. The new church has been here, in the 'Parish of Mearns coastal', since the early 18th century.

I took the path down to the sea and followed the stones exposed in the sand country through the browning bracken, the jangling pods of broom, the briars and the last of the season's wild flowers, to the turn of the cliffs.

Along the way were the salmon fishers' bothies, shuttered and hunkered in dune slacks, as the Scots call the sand valleys, drying poles staked out for the nets they would use in summer. Rabbits bolted from the lupins. Startled pheasants rose up with their cry like the cackle of an intercom. It was so familiar, the differences mostly subtle, rarely ample. It could have been the dune country I knew so well. In season this was an extraordinary place of poppies, buttercups, ladies bedflower, harebells, Scotch lovage, sea michaelmas daisy and sea meadow-grass. So special to the North Esk. Through it all, there was marram – but it was rooted in a red, volcanic sand.

Living off the vegetation is a rich supply of bugs, moths and butterflies. In turn, they host spring and summer explosions of small birds, like buntings and finches, pipits and warblers.

Looking skyward, buzzards and tangles of crows spilt from the relict cliffs – there was something reassuring about these buttresses and the way they held the space between land

and sea. After a while I noticed what had to be peregrine falcons nesting up high – nothing else could fly that fast. On the shoreline gulls and oystercatchers skirtled about.

Unexpectedly I came to the graveyard of the Nether Kirk, a high-walled, ample cemetery, reached by a stile, beside it the sunken ruin of a roofless church choked by old trees. Under the weight of years, even Christian duty hadn't been enough – perhaps only secular hankerings for a glimpse of the romantic past was what protected these remnants. Possibly the fishers kept it going, back when there was always enough fish for a living community. But the old church had lapsed nearly 300 years ago when they rebuilt at the top of the cliff.

Long after, people continued to be buried here, their names chiselled on still-upright, but fading granite; there was even a family tomb and something called a Watchers' House.

A small salt marsh at Kirkside was the South Esk's most recently abandoned river channel, protected from the sea by the main line of dunes. The North Esk emptied into the North Sea. It seemed stable, but when I returned to the top of the cliff with questions, an old man was sitting on a bench with his daughter.

A frail old man, Mr Petre, whose fingers when they met my hand were curled by arthritis, remembered when the Esk was forever shifting about, leaving slunks – backwater lagoons – along the beach. 'It was once called Ecclesgreig,' he tells me. 'Ecclesgreig, son, is a name buried in Pictish and Celtic antiquity.'

I asked him why the 'watchers' house'?

His voice was thin, but he smiled and asked if I had read Robert Louis Stevenson. 'Of course,' I said.

'The answer is that on dark nights there were figures in frock coats shipping their muffled oars, who came as shadows here. They had business with shovels, breaking into the freshly piled soil to exhume newly buried bodies. A fragrant corpse delivered up for dissection fetched seven pounds – a huge sum in those days. This was part of the illegal traffic in human flesh.

'But the bodies were of good Scots stock; they were not your usual gypsies and there is no man can say otherwise. They did useful work, and lived hard lives, they deserved to be left in peace.' He shuddered a little as he spoke.

'What do you mean?'

He screwed up his eyes. 'Well, I'll tell you. All that cleverness in Edinburgh, we produced the finest doctors in the world for over a hundred years, but have you any idea how it was they got the drop on the rest of the educated world? You just wouldn't read about it – and in a country where everyone went to kirk on a Sunday.

'These doctors, they paid ceathairneaches, the canterans, to kill ordinary folk in lonely places, the kind who wouldn't be missed for a long time if they were taken. Guess who they were? The tinkies – them travellin' people. There are a couple of famous trials you can still read about – it all came out. Some men hanged for it, but not the doctors.'

It seemed more shocking than the cruelties inflicted at Dunnottar Castle. I asked, 'So the watchers' house was for the benefit of families who needed to stay until the corpse's value had diminished sufficiently to protect its, what, its sanctity and the grave robbers had moved on?'

'That's just how it was.'

Mr Petre was about eighty. It occurred to me that he was born when my grandfather was a young man in these parts. I was grateful to have met him.

'In the 18th century salmon fishers attempted to realign the lower course of the river,' he told me. 'This was an effort to win the rights to net salmon from the river – by then they were packing them in ice for shipping to the lucrative market in London.'

The next day I went on to Marykirk, a short drive through the tilled landscape of the Mearns. The village's actual church, Marykirk was a high-walled, light-filled prism dominating a small rise in the Mearns above the North Esk river. In the early morning the big trees that border the graveyard were filled with bird song. There was a breath of early frost among the graves, those nearest the kirk dominated by our old family name. A beautiful morning in a beautiful place – I felt in no hurry to leave and, indeed, returned several times just to be at Marykirk.

I took a short path down to the river, streaming under the stone and steel railway arch at Marykirk which may be as old as the 150-year-old railway itself. Here the river flowed quite slowly, flattish with a few small rapids. Some riparian trees gave it a Gainsborough look, a medium-sized river moving in an old land, flattened by time, bitten-down bull-rushes at its verge. Along the lower field was a row of village houses overlooking a small flood-plain of shaved maize and some hay, cut and rounded up into bales; the kirk riding the river terrace behind. It was here my grandfather's parents were wed.

It was my last day in the region. I decided to take one final look at the old family property, the holding. When I reached it, the late afternoon skies were clear, a light wind shaking the oak leaves. But for reasons I couldn't locate, immediately upon arrival I was afflicted with a deep gloom that I couldn't shake off. Surely it wasn't because my stay had come to an end – it was too strong for that?

I borrowed the key to the church and crunched up the gravel drive to turn the stout lock in the heavily timbered door. Inside, embroidered on a framed psalter, was the name of each minister who had served here with his term of office, dating right back to the Reformation. Just room enough left for a couple more names. It was as if there never had been anything in the Mearns but Protestantism – Presbyterian and Episcopalian.

I thought of how in New Zealand, old churches desiccate over a generation or so from the inside, slowly losing the sap of their congregations until either they fall over in a high wind, or they are taken up by more ardent, more conservative faiths. Sometimes they are deconsecrated, a word dangerously close to 'desecrated', for re-use as an artist's studio. But here one could only imagine the fury and prejudice, the politics and war, that could choke out most of an entire belief system with its cathedrals and churches after hundreds of years of domination of the entire country.

I sat in a pew that, like the one at Marykirk, flooded with morning light through expansive clear lead-framed windows, spilling off honey-coloured wood. It was all that was needed in a church. Alone in its body, I felt its stillness. Unconstrained by anything from my past except a vague sense of continuity, I felt could fill myself with whatever my mind chose. The old tinker's words about the importance of visiting these places, and the wisdom of Mr Kinloch who sent me here, came back to me. I thought of the Black Watch memorial, of the dead warriors of Scotland, of two grandfathers on the Western Front and of how war and death across a span of half a century could in this place still speak to a young man who knew nothing of either. And for the first time it came to me that my father had, beyond the age of six never had a father. Then, from nowhere, an unbearable pain, far stronger than guilt, struck – what of my own son?

Doug 18

Before we could leave Manus, we had work to do, re-fitting engines to the Corsairs. Some of them were close to the limits of their hours for safe operation and they all had to fly home. But before the parts arrived we still had time on our hands.

We were granted seven days' leave and a group of us embarked on a long trip. We decided to borrow the Yacht Club's rescue cutter, powered by a big Gardiner marine diesel. We built wooden decks fore and aft, adding steel hoops to carry tent-flies for shelter. It looked like a Yangtze riverboat. We scrounged provisions, tanked up with clean water, and took a chart and compass to head out into the unknown, seven souls in all. It became a sort of celebration of the end of the war for a few restless Kiwis who really just wanted to get home.

The seas were tranquil to begin with, which was probably just as well. With the aid of a map we made Elephant Harbour, some distance from Manus. After navigating through more small islands, admiring huge turtles swimming in the clear sea, we tied up at Hogg Harbour. The missionary couple there had neat gardens and well-painted buildings – a bit of a change from what we had become accustomed to. We were given an excellent lunch, served by two shy teenaged kanaka lassies who came forward when their mistress gave a tinkle on her silver hand-bell. I still remember the sweet taste of Ladies' Fingers Fried Bananas.

There were many uninhabited islands, some only a few acres in size. We made landfall on an island recently inhabited by Japs. We tried using their bivouacs but were soon chased back to the boat by fleas. We drew alongside a tidy jetty with a Lever Brothers sign – a palm-oil plantation. On the wharf was a native wearing ragged shorts, a Sydney tram-conductor's cap and, around his neck, a length of lavatory chain. 'We go ashore?' I inquired.

'No, you no go ashore!' he shouted. I produced a couple of packs of twenty Old Gold cigarettes. He beamed.

'You go ashore now.'

He had a few buddies. One had lost an arm just below the elbow, which he told us had been amputated by a Japanese captain. He wore a small woven cord cap covering the still quite fresh wound. Stumpy was offering us a rather crude carving of a man with a monstrous erection. 'How much?'

'Twenty dollar.'

Several days later, still heading north, we hit a submerged reef. We were smartly over the sides and soon had the craft sailing in better water. 'Wait,' called one of the crew. 'I've left my sandshoes on the reef.'

'Don't go back,' shouted the lookout. Looking into the clear water, we could see them – quite menacing: weaving, diving and doing stall-turns – four black eight-foot sharks. We gave our craft full throttle but soon realised that all was not well with the boat, which was thumping and jumping about. The propeller had been damaged – we made for the next island for repairs. But a storm was brewing.

We put down four anchors and we rocked all night until dawn. We couldn't get the stern of the boat out of the water, so we had to work from an inflatable. One man lay in a prone position in the rubber boat, holding a piece of timber behind the blade. Another, wielding a hammer, struck the wooden dolly. A third kept close watch the whole time for sharks. After a great deal of difficulty, the blades were beaten to a reasonable pitch, give or take two or three degrees.

We were then able to sail further over the top side of the equator, heading generally for the Philippines, until we suddenly woke up to the fact that our week's leave had expired. I seem to have a knack of doing this while taking military leave. So much for the benefits of detention in New Caledonia. There was work to be done on those Corsairs. We headed back as fast as possible and three days later sailed through the ditch between Manus and Los Negros.

The next morning we were on the mat, facing a dressing down from our CO. We had figured that we would not be missed, but the boss had already organised an air search. It felt somehow familiar.

With the arrival of the replacement engines from the United States we worked for another month on the Corsairs. Then I farewelled my mates to await the *Wahine*. We sailed to Bougainville, a large island, quite steep and covered in jungle. A large volcano kept firing rocks into the air, spewing molten lava over the crater's mouth. The earth trembled, making earth waves on the ground. I waited a week on Bougainville at Torokina Air Base, mostly with Cassie and a few old mates in big surf on its black sand beaches. It was a good time. They told me that the previous year the Japanese, acting on poor intelligence, had lost about 8,500 men here in a single battle to 320 Americans killed.

I had a two-berth cabin to myself with no porthole. The heat was so intense; the only way I could sleep was by going on deck, where I remained until two hours out from New Zealand.

I went home to visit my mother for a week or so. 'What have they done to you – you're all skin and bone,' she cried. 'I'll have to feed you up.' She did too – shepherd's pie, roast lamb and beef, lots of puddings and cakes – seed cake, louise cake, caramel crunch. When after ten days I told her I had to leave, she was most unhappy.

I took the train from Marton to Wellington, all the more enjoyable because Garth and a navy mate of his joined me and we went on the ran-tan. We put away, from memory, a dozen beers between us. Full-sized bottles – we were thirsty boys. Garth had been repatriated after an escape from a German POW camp through Yugoslavia. He wasn't the kind of guy you could keep inside.

At Paekakariki we felt we couldn't go past the old pub. As the train drew into the station, but before it stopped, I jumped – too soon. I found myself turning somersaults, coming to rest on the edge of the platform as the train stopped, receiving a playful nudge in the derrière from the battery box slung beneath a carriage. It was a close thing – another couple of feet and it'd have all been over.

I picked myself up smartly and walked off as if I had intended the performance all along. I was wearing woollen gloves and I'd torn the palms out of them – fortunately the trou were still intact. Another of my nine lives wiped from the slate.

Upon my discharge, I received another king-hit. My name was drawn with some others for fatigues. The task was to clean out a troop-ship that had carried home Air Force personnel and their wives from the UK. I was seething at the outrage of this, after all that time overseas, when up at Anderson Park was a camp full of Johnny-come-latelies, five-minute wonders the lot of them. But I decided there was no sense in getting the pricker at this stage.

On board the ship was an utter disgrace, like a brothel. We spent two weeks knee-deep in rubbish throughout the living areas. My protest was to not lift a finger while I was there. Now, with my time with the Air Force over, I must confess, I missed the company of the men.

It's funny what stays in your mind, though. Here we were, home permanently and still reasonably young in years, like all Returned chaps, keen to put the war behind us and get on with life. And all I remember after getting out of that ship was meeting up with my old schoolmate and partner in crime, Garth.

We stayed at his sister's flat on The Terrace, which had been used by an American serviceman. He had left behind a large tin trunk. On opening it we found a number of American tropical uniforms and, wrapped in a white skivvy, a human skull. Skulls had been a pretty common sight on Guadalcanal. Some of the Yanks liked to have a Jap skull attached to the bonnet of their jeep. Garth, who, being a navy man, may have seen fewer skulls than I had, announced that he wanted nothing to do with it.

'Here, you take the bloody thing – get rid of it. I'll be back when you have.' Garth was a bit like that. It wasn't a thing you could put out with the rubbish. My thoughts turned to Marge Cameron and her séances.

I must admit that on receiving my gift, Marge was not quite her usual unruffled self. She thanked me, a little coolly I thought, and declared that Zippo, as we had come to know him, would be introduced at her séance group's next meeting. However, when some months later I asked, 'How was the meeting with Zippo then, how did it go?' Marge's reply was almost curt. 'I gave it a decent burial.' I dared not inquire further. It seemed Zippo had put an early finish to the séance. In such strange ways did one man's war come to an end.

Alan 19

'I've worked it out. I believe your grandpapa from the Mearns was one of those soldiers whose lives were unfinished, was he not? But he died later, not in the field?' Bruce said.

'You're right – did his brother Sandy tell you this?'

'That he did. He was a great chappie was old Sandy, a kind man. What was he to you now – he was your great-uncle, right? He taught me a lot about gardening did Sandy, he loved growing things. He had visits from his brothers and sisters who went to live in different parts of the world. I'm uncertain whether your grandfather ever visited.'

'Was Sandy married?'

'No, he never did. There were always unmarried men about in his time, it wasn't unusual – women too. Everyone had aunts and uncles who had no children of their own. It took Sandy a long time for the grief to pass after his brother's death. I think that they were very close. I seem to recall that he used to write to your grandfather, to Hector, very regularly.'

His news left me disappointed. It meant that I had no living family on this side that I could pursue. But there were still things to know and Bruce was anxious to share. He was a talker alright.

'Anyway, you've your car here somewhere? We can grab a bite and then I can give you the tour of the district, if you like. There's someone I'd like you to meet.'

We bought sandwiches and took the road from Stonehaven to Montrose. A patchwork of grazed and heavily-cropped hills with quilted contours so like the country my grandfather had ploughed in New Zealand rolled up and down slowly towards the sea, except this was to a hard rock shoreline, a lighthouse coast.

'Coutts Bank, Montrose,' Bruce was saying, 'was founded on slavery and tobacco. That's what made this port prosperous.'

The landforms are gentle and shaped by long pastoral use – and by stands of old trees, gorse, rock walls and narrow curving roadways. From Aberdeen, south down that coast, gnarly old seaports are tucked in along a castellated coast, at night their cuddies chinks of light winking at the night sea. The late evening skies glimmer on clouds that stretch forever with a pink afterglow.

Clochnahill, four miles from Stonehaven heading for Montrose, is where Robbie Burns' grandfather had his farm. 'The bard's father left the family at nineteen years of age,' Bruce mused. It was a remote claim on past glory. Once again, it came easily, the idea that all along this emigrant coast is a place of remembering. But these associations can be vague, like a man with too many pints in him: 'Didn't Burns' coach stop near here at one time?' asks a cheery drinker at a wee cuddie of a pub in Johnshaven.

The town of Montrose rears up unexpectedly, stone buildings on a sandy island bound by the North and South Esk Rivers. It is reached by a couple of staggering old stone bridges. The church steeple towers over rock-hewn buildings that seem too burdensome and too presumptuously close to the sea. Yet within a bold distance of the shore and just a few feet above it is a town of cobbles, closes, greening headstones and spike-railed, tree-lined parks with grand stone edifices to the memory of great men of Scotland and this district.

It seemed that the entire town, on a shore of ebbing humanity, had been in an almost continuous state of farewell for several centuries. It had learnt to live off the gestures of its departed sons. It is as if the hollows left behind by the departed were filled by marble shapes and other remembrances to commemorate their achievements in enterprise, letters and, always, in war.

'Montrose is a town that has outlived its great expectations,' I said.

Bruce agreed. 'Now it seems to be preparing to farewell itself.'

He seemed to be quoting from someone. 'The town of Montrose is a reminder of impermanence even in the midst of granite's certainties.'

'Emigration means so much loss from the mother country.' I wanted to make a contribution to his thoughts – though I'd never thought about it before. 'But there is always this pride associated with achievement in far-off lands.'

Bruce was eloquent, almost indignant, on the subject: 'You're telling me? You are saying that to me, boy? "Will ye no come back again?" is the lament of the Stuarts for Prince Charlie, but there is also pity there, the self-pity of the bereaved – an entire nation – who are separated not by death, but by migration – "better loved ye canna be" is the sharp truth of loss. It's our bloody national anthem.'

We stopped the car and walked along Montrose's seaport, Ferryden. 'Once its tonnages were greater than Aberdeen's, can you imagine?' Bruce asked. The port entrance is marked by a lighthouse at the end of a long, green finger connecting it to the land. There were still Ferrydenners living in bothies below the wharf, catching a bit of salty sun, flying their washing in the westerly. An exuberant old woman in a blue dress recited an old chant that went around about Ferrydenners, who used drums for toilets: "You cain tell a Ferrydenner by the ring on "'is boom",' she chortled, like a naughty schoolgirl, as she darted away.

Bruce took me around the estuary to meet his cousin Gordon, the gamekeeper retired from his hereditary position to his laird, the Earl of Esk.

'So you're still alive, you old devil,' Bruce greeted Gordon, as we arrived at his spare, tidy flat.

'I'll outlive you, my laddie – it's all the salmon and game food I've eaten, thanks to my laird – they tell us now its all healthy living. We never knew at the time. I think I'm the luckiest man alive.'

'Ah,' Bruce laughed, 'still taking food from the hungry and the poor, are we? Living with the toffs in the lap of luxury, exceeding our entitlement?'

'Get off with you, you, you Red wrecker – you'll be telling me next you don't believe in God any more.'

'You know I don't,' Bruce replied, expressionless.

Gordon was a kilted royalist. He must have been in his eighties, rangy yet still with an air of boyish mischief. He hinted with pride that his father, though a gamekeeper like himself, was almost certainly conceived by Royalty on the wrong side of the blanket. 'Gamekeeping was an occupation by which he could stay close to his origins, be amongst his own kind,' Bruce muttered afterwards. 'But without exceeding his station. Bloody royals and their Morganic offspring. Who needs them?'

Gordon had one thing in common with Bruce – they both spoke as though from a book and seemed to incite each other to such speech. You could tell Gordon had said some things many times before, proudly declaring he had never owned a pair of trousers, preferring the kilt: 'As worn by James Graham, one of the greatest of the Covenanters and Duke of Montrose. The kilt gives me freedom of movement and if a gentleman has difficulty bringing a salmon in, I just wade out and get it. The kilt floats up around me and soon dries again.'

As a gillie, it was his task to 'bring in the bags for the gentlemen, fourteen bags of salmon – bars of silver', he called them. 'In the season the gentlemen also hunted,' he said. 'There was grouse, snipe, partridge, woodcock, duck, hares, rabbits, quail and deer.' He loved his dogs. He delighted in telling too of how, 'I lived at the kennels, caring for the Labradors, the all-rounder hunting dog. The setters would find a bird for the advancing line of gentlemen, and waiting, would point nose to tail, until the flushers got to it.'

'While the Ferrydenners got by on a few pennyth a week,' snorted Bruce.

It was hard to see how ordinary men like my grandfather fitted into this world, with its staircases of privilege, and what exactly might have prompted his leaving. But I was beginning to see the attraction of the Koitiata coast, an evocative, rather than an entirely familiar shore, in a new land.

Gordon broke in on my thoughts. 'You know that it was hunters like the Earl who kept this considerable estuary – with its salt lands, its rushes and reeds, and fertile tidal mudflats – until it was gifted to the Scottish National Trust. Thanks to the generosity of the Earl, it is now preserved as a wildlife reserve – a place without guns.

'I'm glad about that,' he said, 'but I'm glad too that I lived to hunt, I wouldn't have missed any of that. We'd shoot everything that was there. Wild geese, eiders and mallard. The west wind was the best. And on a stormy night when we'd shoot the birds coming in off the basin and the retrievers went in to haul them back. There was a lot of plucking for the kitchens to do.

'Right now, early October till November, is the time when thousands and thousands of pink-footed geese come in to roost at Montrose. They're on their flight from Greenland to parts further south. They fly in great arrowheads of extended family groups, you can hear them honking.'

Bruce interrupted, wanting to show me there were plenty of places where Romans, far from their Mediterranean home, camped. Remains of Roman walls, erected to help trap salt for the table from the tide, still stand in the inner estuary. 'The whole area was so important for salmon,' he said, 'that there were ice-packing houses of Montrose, built for the heady trading days when ice was trapped and stored there in winter for summer use and salmon were sent by the ton to London.'

But salmon was Gordon's territory and he took back the conversation. He wanted to talk about how salmon spawned in winter, their kelts moved down the river and died, providing a source of food for gulls, crows and even otter.

'Seals, too put their noses in here to feed on them. The salmon are the basis of life here.'

'And what about other fishing?'

'Flounder, eels, lamprey and sea trout are all taken, and sometimes they get grey mullet in summer.'

I found myself glancing in a two-way mirror, between the New Zealand and Scottish coasts that expatriate Hector surely must have gazed into. Now I was working it back from Scotland. If he thought of Montrose as he walked Koitiata's wind dunes, he would have contemplated the absences of the West Coast, its voids of human culture, filled by a restless and turbulent nature. As I think of it now, years later, the differences in the landscapes created another form of exile. My being represents a part of that loss, marked in the New Zealand ledger, but several generations later, on the migrant shore.

At Koitiata in his day there were birds, plenty of them and varied, but scarcely a village in sight, not a steeple, not even a lighthouse. Just the odd rough bach, an occasional circle of burnt stones, a broken skull in an open dune, perhaps, the occasional 'pa' upriver and those constant artefacts of vicariousness, the shipwrecks.

***

Acting on impulse, I decided that I should phone home. In those days it was impossibly expensive. I worked out the cost of a three-minute call, got the correct coins from the bar of the local and dialled, knowing it was a Saturday morning their time. My mother answered.

'Is that you Alan?' she said, shouting as they did on toll calls. 'Thank goodness you've called. I'm afraid I have some bad news for you.'

'What's that?'

'Well, prepare yourself – it's serious I'm afraid. Your son, he got sick and has died. The notice was in yesterday's paper.

'Had we known he was ill, we would have done something – let you know sooner. I am sorry, Alan. The funeral will be in three days.'

Suddenly I felt very weary and the fog of gloom I'd sensed at the old property became a tent of darkness. At that point I decided it was time to return home, by plane.

Alan 20

'We've you been?' I came through the gate, the toitoi rustling beside the tin fence like stiff petticoats. I was immediately spied by Rita and her sisters, all clad in black. She looked older and tired, her face drawn and pale, but still beautiful. To my astonishment, all but one of them hugged, hongi'd and kissed me. Rita, her eye sockets blackened with grief, whispered, 'I'm glad you came back,' and her tears flowed freely. Then Rita's mother came up to me. Her greeting was cold, hostile, so different from last time. 'So, the father's here at last.'

The brotherhood were standing nearby, watching the effect of their menace behind their sunglasses: *Cool Hand Luke*, I thought. One of them sneered, in a baritone whisper, 'Nice shoes – don't leave them outside the house. Might not be there when you get back.' Another, a huge figure in black with a crude blue tattoo in one corner of his face, jostled me as he came in under the carved lintel of the house. Rita's father saw it. 'What kind of Maori do you think you are, doing that to a guest?' He was shaking, white-faced. 'Get out of my way, you bloody mongrel.'

The accused shot back, 'How can you forgive this bastard for what he's done to us?'

'Done to us, my bloody arse. He's whanau now, whether you like it or not. Plenty of young Maori fathers have done far worse. Who the hell are you to judge... anyone. You've dipped your wick all over the place. Go on, get out, scram – beat it. And take your no-good mates with you I don't want to see you here again. Get out of here.'

I wasn't ready for what happened next. I went across to the son. The sweet smell of steamed veges drifted across the marae from the kitchen at the back. He was lying in an open coffin on the paepae, his aunties and gran on the veranda, in

298

their black dresses, green leaves in their hands, waving his spirit on. A woman sat beside his head, a relative, watching out for him. I looked at the small face, its eyes shut. He was like a little old man, his life now taken from him by a virus. I thought of the last time, the only time, I had seen him, heavy-lidded in his mother's arms. I thought of the two meetings here, either side of the rupture of the intervening years, and of how I had cut myself from him. If he were alive he would still have no idea of who I was, an incidental in the score of his short life. I was at one of those God-confounding moments where thought becomes a shipwreck that must be swiftly abandoned for something else.

In the next moment I was taken over by an emotional wave that had started somewhere far out at sea. The feeling was layered with another, straight out of raw childhood, a terror of the humiliation that would follow my uncontrollable disclosure of myself, in full public view. But it was as though I was not in charge of myself. One moment my body and knees tensed to absorb the impact, the next it was all on – I was sobbing, eyes running, mouth blubbing, chest heaving. I hadn't cried in years – the last thing that a man ever did. But somehow here in this place where, I dimly knew, feelings were customarily vented and released through the power of ritual and landscape, it was not just acceptable, it was the place to do it. Rita came and put her arms around me – affectionate, sisterly. I was streaming tears, wetting our cheeks and necks. I realised that she was crying too. It was hopeless to fight and for some time we just held each other.

After a while her new man came over, handsome, watchful, but calm and smiling. 'Gidday, Arthur's the name.' He carefully held out his hand. He was snappy in a black leather jacket, and flared sports trousers. 'He must have been the boy's father-figure,' I thought.

The coffin was carried to the white, battoned church resting at the end of a row of missionary oaks.

As I stood in the church, I felt more than a stranger – a man who had put distance between himself and the people whom fate seemed to have chosen for him. As the singing began the Maori voices vibrated in the seasoned timbers as though the entire church was an old cello. There was no getting away from it, this was a poignant lament. Its tune, now familiar, still haunts me years later:

Nga whai ra I taurima	By what means now my dear friend
Te marae I waho ngei	Will the sanctity of our marae be upheld
Nga te tika, ma te pono	It will be as it has always been
Me te aroha e.	Shall be with me all the days I have left.

I remember little of the service. An inexhaustible grief seemed to engulf my core, it was so overwhelming, I could barely stand.

The waiata had worked its old magic, and I was left facing myself, in all my denial, perhaps for the first time. I thought of nothing but the child, of my years away that had kept me from knowing my own son, and of my feelings of dislocation and my search elsewhere for acceptance and love.

Around me the gathering filtered out behind the small coffin in a staged procession. Then all was silent. Just creaking of the match-lined church in a growling westerly – like a ship at sea.

***

When the food was served afterwards I found I had no appetite. I was hardly in a fit state to drive, but I decided that the best thing was to take the thirty-odd kilometres back to my parents.

My mother answered the door. 'Oh hello, Alan, we thought we might see you today. This is so sad for the family. And yourself – are you well?'

'The family', as if there was no other connection. I made no comment. My father greeted me with gentle concern. 'How are you, son?'

300

I looked at them, for the first time seeing their vulnerabilities, seeing them as people rather than as parents – the changes were in me, rather than them. So he was no longer an authority figure. He'd carried much in his life that I had neither known nor noticed, nor had to experience – there was so much I now had to consider. Seeing him as he was in this light revealed all those bits that were missing that might have been there, if he'd had half a chance. There were the bits that didn't fit, that made him rebellious and stroppy, that he'd had to wear anyway – like his long-dead father, his living through the Depression and the strange mix of neglect and care that he'd grown up on. He'd made little of the effects of this on himself, but I had needed to know.

There had never been much talk. Conversation was a ragged little rug on a highly waxed floor, around which we lurched as if – in a child's game – to stray off its edges would plunge us into a chasm.

'We are sorry that it has turned out this way,' one of them said. I was too raw to field the offer, leaving it to bounce into the far corners of the room, well off the rug. My mother picked it up. 'It's very sad. But once he got sick with that illness – sometimes these things are meant to be, aren't they, and it's not for us to judge.'

I still made no reply.

'We'd like to see you more, since you've come back.'

That was walking on the rug's edge. The next statement would be: 'Why didn't you write?'

It was time for me to speak. 'I, I was far too young to be a father. What happened, what I did, shouldn't have happened. And I should never have gone away. I was very immature – I behaved badly. Now it's all done, and I can tell you, from the bottom of my heart, what I learnt today at the marae, at the service, it's too late to undo.'

My father stepped forward, toward me and looked me in the eye. 'Take it easy on yourself, it could have happened to anyone. It's been a long time. We have missed you, son.' He had never said anything like that before.

301

Overwhelmed and pleading tiredness, I went to my old room. I lay on the chenille bedspread, turned back to expose the pillow, and fell into a deep sleep. It was dark when I awoke; it was evening, with my mother calling me softly to dinner. We never spoke of these matters again.

Coda

'How are you, son?'

My father retained his robust, ring-crushing handshake. Later in life he may have even put more effort in. His greetings are a ritual, a ritual with vigour, a way of denying, with laughter, old age.

'How are your eyes, Dad?'

'Getting better everyday,' he says cheerfully, after another operation to relieve pressure on them for glaucoma – this one requiring a deep incision into the side of the eye. He can't show any sign of weakness. Advanced age is no excuse for self-indulgence. So, he undertakes the operation fully conscious, recording it in detail on an old typewriter. It's part of some writing he's been doing about his life and the war. His pecked-out typescript on the eye operation carries a user's warning posted at the top: 'Not for the faint-hearted' and, 'No complaints, and I've still got my licence'. It is one of a series of operations beginning in his forties that took bits from him, though never involving his heart or other vital organs or cancer. Unsuccessful surgery on his declining hearing left him quite deaf.

'Each day the sun rising is still a gift,' he grins. 'I am still mobile, I can still drive if I have to. I can grow most things in the garden, as long as I keep the water up to it. Just look at my beans, zucchinis, lettuce and sweet corn in a warm summer. I've got my potatoes in – got to have those. Pumpkins, the Crowns are good keepers, and acid-free tomatoes in autumn. I always keep the seed for next season. And brassicas most of the year. Plenty of leafy stuff over the winter. There's a retired guy who delivers manure on his trailer down here – I always keep heaps of that up to the garden, compost, with a bale of hay to break it down and a little seaweed.

'And I still have a trellis full of sweet peas as a keepsake, it reminds me of my mother.'

Even when it is grey and cold, he says, 'Look at the view out that window,' facing out towards the beach. 'It's paradise, just paradise. What more could I want?'

In his late life my father has come to a time where his tides have found a point of balance in departures and arrivals, where loss and gain can meet – he has become the stillness in the vortex. He and my mother took the risk to be away from hospital and security to live for as long as they could at Koitiata, where he first came when he was about six with Jimmie and Marge Cameron. For more than eighty years he has loved this place. The westerly still howls in here, building and then breaking down dunes defeated by the flood, in an endless tussle. The river mouth still hauls itself for miles up and down the coast, as if it never can decide – an equivocation upon which the wildfowl flourish.

The wind, the blowing sand and the moving river are the guardians of this coast against almost all commercial encroachment and it is only true believers choose to live here, still in simple dwellings. Wherever the nomad river ventures it still reserves its backwaters and old oxbows. The waving flags of the tall edge plants, the peroxide-headed toitoi and the red-tipped spears of nodding flax, the bull-rush, as well as the dauntless juncus and the sedges thrive here and the fish spawn and wildfowl proliferate, migrate and return.

The old crew of birds is here still at it, sandpipers chipping at the water's edge, the dotterels and oystercatchers – fewer now than when I was young – scurrying away from their nests with diversionary tactics, the circling harriers yellow as the sun catches their bellies, and the terns and pied stilts. There are new arrivals too, like the smaller shovellers among other, more common native ducks, and now the amazingly productive black swans, from the distance like burnt stumps on the water and, joy – other newcomers, the leggy, silky spoonbills roosting here in pairs. Nature eternal:

dynamic, restless and, given half a chance, highly productive, casting itself about on a long shore, a gaining shore.

'When you can't go fishing, you can still watch the birds coming and going. You can watch the sun rise and set. You can see Kapiti and the South Island on a clear day, and right up to Egmont, and across to Ruapehu,' he says, picking up his worn binoculars with the broken strap from the window-seat. 'We've got everything we could want here. We live like millionaires – the best view in the world and we can scramble round with the arse out of our pants.

'There's no hardship,' he protests, if I suggest moving. 'Stan, the grocer, does a run out from here with his truck every Friday. There're enough customers to make it worth his while and we can get milk and papers by special arrangement with rural delivery.

'I'd keep hens still, except that eggs are so cheap, it's hardly worth the trouble.

'When I do go, then so be it. In a few years' time no one will remember me, except for my family – that's how it is. If there's some sort of emergency, I have good neighbours and a medic-alarm. There's nothing to be afraid of. We've all got to go.

'Strange things happen as you get really old though. The other night I could have sworn my father was in the room, in his hat and coat, standing over by the dresser, as I was going to sleep. I must be going a bit la-la. As he disappeared I swear I saw him climb on a horse.'

'Was it scary?' I asked him.

'Of course not, it's all in the mind, all in the mind, son. Anyone tells you any different, it's a load of baloney.'

The bach may bear the clutter of a lifetime, but an old life well lived can, in the midst of this, still be uncluttered. Some of the imposed order is hard: friends he knew all his life have all gone, and so too many other folk much younger than him. He's been to more than his fair share of funerals. Every month there are several to attend in town, if he can get a ride. That's just how it is, he says. Although his memory is

305

long and sharp, it does not weigh him down; in fact, surprisingly little does.

There is none of the grief of the old shore, nor the forgetting of the new shore. There is no forgetting, only memory on a long reach called into view without pain or a sense of loss. Old photographs matter. 'I found this photograph the other day – it's me and Prentice standing in front of a Hudson when we were at Henderson. Would you like a copy of it?' He also keeps the black Maori stone on the mantelpiece, just as his mother did, beside the Wee Donald trophy.

The mere fact of old age is no guarantee of this, but aging as he has shown me becomes a life in which there is no longer regret, only wonder at the whole nine yards of it, its highs and dregs, then and now, that sit as lightly on his mind as the tui out in the garden rocking perilously on the end of a honeyed flax pod.

As he dissolves towards his essential self he knows what he is letting go of. If you push him, he will admit that, 'With no father, without money and no education – that gives you a sense of being hard done by, you feel inferior to others. It takes a long time to get over that. Far too long.' But he would rather not talk in any way that might sound like complaint.

'When you are young you worry over what people think about you, all the time. But in the end, it doesn't matter – there is so much baloney in the world, why would you worry about the opinions of others – about anything? It's simply not worth it and it's of no account.'

After persuasion he agreed that he would pay to have a man come in to split his firewood for the wood-burner, an admission that there were risks in hefting a sharp axe on hard timbers at his age. He kept to that agreement, but still hauls the firewood up from the beach on a small cart with bicycle wheels and keeps his chainsaw sharpened for a little action. He tells everyone that this coming season he will be out after the whitebait, but it is physical, just getting the nets to a possie and lifting all day. He grins as he says it.

Almost thirty years behind him, it seems that there is much ground for me to cover before I reach such a point of becoming, where, with his delight in the simplicity of the moment, the inessentials are planed away from the grain of being. Despite this I find now, to my amazement, and perhaps his, that there is little separation; his pared-down humanity offers a transparency in which a son can apprehend himself, born to a different time and with different interests, yet so similar in outlook and humour. There's no getting away from it – 'coming, ready or not' as we used to cry in the children's game of hide-and-seek. I'm no replica, but in so many ways his being now is a reminder not so much of where it is that I have come from but where I might be headed.

Some of the patterning goes deep – there are marks on my body that I can recall seeing on his when he was my age. It's mostly about how we hold emotional energy. 'Where did you get an idea like that from?' he would say if I told him.

The knowledge that he now has grandsons who love him is a kind of coming home, a profound reminder about being connected to the continuous human stream. Their living abroad, one in Scotland, possibly strengthens the ties between the two of us.

Occasionally, though, the placid surface of his life is disturbed. Quite recently the last mate from his youth, Prentice, gifted, irascible free spirit that he was, died while whitebaiting on a river further to the south. They had always kept in touch. He was a widower, he had a dickey heart and he went missing one wet October morning that was too cold for anyone to be out in. Dad was heart-broken. I phoned him. 'Dad, I'm so sorry,' and as I said it, something sympathetic in my voice immediately brought him to unaccustomed tears. He was embarrassed at his response. The moment was familiar, but how? Then I realized, not long before my own son's sympathy had brought out the same thing in me, in similar circumstances and over the phone.

Having a father you can love and who loves you is quite extraordinary and a double blessing, in that for so long neither of us considered it possible. There is the great freedom that comes from it, a sense that one can get on with the business of being fully oneself, without the weight in the attic of what might or should have been. This knowledge leads to the passageway that has shown me that to know him, and something of my grandfather, is to begin to know myself. Again, such little separation; even looking at photographs of myself in certain moods comes as a shock of recognition of the familiar other. To honour one's father is to come to know how fully, as you age yourself, and as he evolves gradually into the spare humanity that can come with great age – down to his still-resilient but un-redundant self – of how a generation is scarcely separation at all. And yet it is also everything. And two generations, well, the beginning of a long time, but maybe not. In living apparently as individuals, often we lose sight of the ways that genes, those faithful carriers of mysterious old memory, are also the presenters of destiny, picture cards face-up, with each of us still having to make the choices for every hand that's dealt.

References

Eric Bergerud, *Touched with Fire: The Land War in the South Pacific*, Penguin, New York, 1996

Shari A. Cohen, 'Second Sight and Family History: pedigree and segregation analysis',

Shari A. Cohen, Journal of Scientific Exploration, Vol. 13, No. 3, pp.351-72, 1999

Alexander Fenton (ed.) *At Brechin with Stirks, a farm cash book from Buskhead, Glenesk, Angus 1885-1898*, Canongate Academic, Edinburgh, 1994

Robert Leckie, *Challenge for the Pacific – Guadalcanal the turning point of the War*, Hodder and Stoughton, 1966

E.P. Marren (ed.), 'The Natural History of St Cyrus', Natural Conservancy Council, 1976

Charles A. Mollyson, 'The Parish of Fordoun', Aberdeen, MDCCCXCIII

Timothy Neat, *The Summer Walkers, travelling people and pearl-fishers in the highlands of Scotland*, Canongate Books, Edinburgh, 1996

Mowbray Pearson (ed.) *Fitting the Flakes: the diary of J. Badenach a Stonehaven farmer 1789-1797*, Aberdeen University Press &National Museums of Scotland, Edinburgh, 1992

Bruce Sandison, The Sporting Gentleman's Gentleman, London, 1986
J.W. H. Trail, "The Wild Flowers of St Cyrus', reprint, The Transactions and Proceedings of the Botanical Society

Oral histories September 1999, Scotland
Ned Coates (gamekeeper),
Alan Thomson (Heavy Horse Centre),
Beryl Finlay, (Ferrydenner),
John Anderson, (early 20th century Scotland)

Thanks also to
The Institute of Scottish Studies, University of Edinburgh
The Kings College Library, University of Aberdeen

Other:
Philip Young, war journals 1943-44, Phil Young memoires [unpublished]

Robert Burns, extract, from Man was made to mourne, *Poems of Robert Burns*, Laurence Brander (ed.) OUP. London, 1950 p.93

Notes RNZAF No.9 squadron movements 1942-5

July 14 1942 left NZ

18 Jul arr Noumea, USS Macanac

11 Mar 1943 to New Hebrides, by DC transport

21 Apr 1943 to Solomons, Guadalcanal by PBO

640 miles from Henderson Field to Santo

25 Oct 1943 to Espiritu Santo by DC 3

23 Dec left Santo for NZ

Returned Manus, Los Negros Apr 1945

NZ Oct 1945